DEAD WITNESS

a novel

Joylene Nowell Butler

DEAD WITNESS

Copyrighted © 2008 Joylene Nowell Butler

All rights reserved. No part of this book may be reproduced, copied or used in any form or manner whatsoever without written permission, except in the case of brief quotation in reviews and critical articles.

For information, email www.Lulu.com

FIRST EDITION

Cover designed by Lulu
http://www.Lulu.com

This is the work of fiction. Names, characters, places, and incidents either are the product of the author's imagination or are used fictitiously. Any resemblance to actual persons, living or dead, events, or locales is entirely coincidental.

ISBN: 978-1-4357-3249-0

Manufactured in the United States of America

To order additional copies of this book, contact:

Http://www.lulu.com/content/2294973

www.amazon.com

Published by Lulu.com

ACKNOWLEDGMENTS

I am eternally grateful to my family for their patience during the writing of this novel. Their support & encouragement cast a strong light during many dark moments. Thanks to my dear husband Ralph Butler & my dear friend Judi Geib. I couldn't have written this without them.

Numerous writers/critiques aided in the development of DEAD WITNESS. Deepest gratitude to my good friend, author Keith Pyeatt who went above & beyond in helping me whip this book into shape. Special thanks to Dave Swinford's online writer's list Novels-L & to J R Langford's online writer's group Novelpro. Great thanks to authors Bridget Moran, Chris Hoare, Art Tirrell, Alan Jackson, & Mark Albert. Much appreciation to Dave Watt, Dave Shields, Pat Brown, Doug Osborne, Jan Holloway and JoAnn Yolanda Hernandez.

I would also like to thank members of the Prince George RCMP Detachment for providing insight into the daily workings of the police force. Thanks to Attorney Chris Hansen for supplying pertinent information on extradition laws between Canada & the United States.

A special acknowledgement to my brother Gregory Nowell for sharing his expertise on handguns & investigative procedures, & for being the catalyst for DEAD WITNESS.

A big thanks to Vietnam Vet Rick Hill for taking me on an imaginary tour of the day in the life of a grunt In-Country. The comments from Sandra Melanson, Bob Zumwalt, and Meg Westley were invaluable in fine-tuning the opening; thanks guys. Also, I owe a special thank you to my neighbour and friend Margaret Clark for her many hours of proof-reading, plus her unwavering support; and to Bernice McKeown for forcing me to dig deeper. To my family & friends who contributed in a variety of ways, thank you.

Finally, a debt of gratitude to my parents Charlie & Gabrielle Nowell. When I was certain I'd fail, they kept on believing.

Bev Walisser

In memory of Jack & Jody

CHAPTER 1

Camera in hand, Valerie McCormick stepped from the bus into intense daylight. She put on her sunglasses and crossed the grass to the edge of the hill. Seattle's skyline loomed in the distance like a giant sandcastle. Closer in, waves rocked elegant yachts, sailboats, and cruisers docked at brown scribbled wharves, jutting along the waterfront. Fifty feet below her, a chain linked fence enclosed acres of quiet warehouses, buildings, and small sheds in both directions. Just inside the gate was the marina office.

Glancing over her shoulder to the air-conditioned bus disappearing into traffic, Valerie took off her wind-breaker, zipped up the pocket with her wallet in it, and tied the jacket around her waist. The driver had warned that if she missed the bus at the stop across the street at ten to three, fifteen minutes from now, she'd have to wait an hour for the next one. No problem. She'd find the boat, snap several photographs--there was only one on this roll of film of her standing in front of the hotel--and be back at the bus stop in plenty of time.

Valerie slid sideways down the hill on the soles of her running shoes, walked through the gate, and stepped inside the marina office. The only person present, the man behind the counter, wore heavy green coveralls. Was he nuts?

He took a handkerchief from his pocket and wiped the sweat from his neck and forehead. "You're the Canadian wanting to buy the 35' Bayliner?"

"Oh, no. It's way too expensive for our tastes. We own a very small logging company. I'm just here to take some photographs for one of my husband's clients."

He frowned. "You came all the way to Seattle to do that?"

Valerie laughed. "No. I won the trip. I'm just taking time out--" Noting his disinterest, she stopped trying to explain, pulled the clipping Ed had given her from her pants pocket, and recited the item number.

The man flipped through his ledger. "It's berthed at Pier 7."

"And that would be ...?"

He pointed in the opposite direction from her bus stop.

"How far is that exactly?"

"Halfway to the end. About 400 yards."

Valerie's whole body slouched. "That's ... lovely," she said, wishing she'd brought her hat. "Perfect day for a stroll."

The man refrained from agreeing. "This heat wave is freaky. Look, Labour Day weekend's not 'til tomorrow, business is dead, so I'm closing up early. This gate will be locked, but when you get to the end, you'll see a small pathway leading up to the street. Where are you parked?"

"I took the bus."

"Well, you'll have to follow the street back to here because the next bus stop's quite a walk."

"That's fine."

She followed him outside. He locked the door to his office and pointed to the north end of the marina where it disappeared around a bend. "You can't miss the pier," he said over his shoulder. Valerie looked toward Pier 7. Because she was a serious runner without an ounce of fat anywhere, she was sure she could make it there and back in fifteen minutes, easy.

The first building she passed had a 'Back from Holidays Labor Day Weekend' sign on the door. Valerie stepped over discarded oil cans and trampled cardboard boxes. She thought of jogging past the next building, but the sun's heat left her feeling sluggish. In central B.C., the temperature had barely reached 27 degrees Celsius all summer. This was quite the contrast.

The air smelled of diesel, sea salt, and lavender, a nauseous mixture. She passed two empty buildings, the street above no longer visible. Clutching her camera, its strap around her wrist, she looked at the long line of warehouses and felt like somebody had taken a spoon and scooped out her insides. It was that hot. And she'd dressed for cool, rainy weather. She wet her dry lips and wiped the sweat from her forehead. Squawking seagulls circled the sky above. Somewhere, a tugboat blasted its horn, while the hum of traffic seemed to drift further away.

Focus, she told herself. Focus on getting this over with so she'd be back in time for her bus. The splash of a jumping fish made her glance at the water, then up at the chain linked fence stretching across the base of the hill.

An open dumpster was positioned against the side of a building just ahead to her right. She batted at the circling flies and tossed the crumpled clipping into it as she passed. Her toe nudged a scrap of wood lying in front of her; she kicked it and followed its path as it twirled a few feet away. The whacking sound disrupted the stillness.

The length of one large warehouse ahead, a man in dark clothes appeared, then disappeared behind a small hut skirted with castaway motors and fishing boat parts. He'd tell her how much further to Pier 7. She pushed her sunglasses to the bridge of her nose and jogged toward where the man had disappeared.

Men's voices. She slowed to a walk.

Loud voices. She glanced along the row of vacant buildings and saw no detour. At the hut, she hesitated. Sweat trickled down her back.

Shouting.

This wasn't how she'd pictured her afternoon.

More voices. Louder still. And angry.

A long, narrow building, beyond the small shed, blocked her view. Valerie inched past a rusty engine leaning against the hut and peeked around the corner. Two men in black tee shirts and black pants stood at the stern of the sleek cabin cruiser docked at the wharf. Three more men stood on the pier: One young, one old, one dangerously attractive. Facing her, she could see he was perfect, in fact. Except, why was he wearing a long, tan raincoat? Maybe she wasn't the only unprepared foreigner.

No way would she interrupt their business.

Two of them walked away. Mr. Perfect, the handsome Latino in the tan raincoat, smiled after them. His sensuous, slightly accented voice broke the silence. "Gentlemen, please. It has been my experience that even in times of indecision, a solution exists." His arms spread wide as if to embrace them.

The two men stopped and turned back.

Still smiling, the Latino reached inside his raincoat and pulled out a gun.

Valerie gawked at him. She heard a pop.

The older man fell backward onto the wharf.

Pop. The young man's head exploded.

The man in the tan raincoat leaned down and fired a third bullet in the older man's head. The body twitched, then lay still.

Valerie's stomach lunged to her throat. She looked at the bodies, at the blood, at the man in the raincoat. Without looking about, he climbed aboard the cruiser.

The two men in black walked down the gangway carrying buckets. Valerie couldn't move. She couldn't blink. She stared with such focus, her eyes burned. She watched them tie something to the men's ankles. Watched as they rolled the bodies into the water and splashed the bucket contents across the wharf. Watched as they returned to the cruiser. One man disappeared under the fly bridge. The other climbed to the helm.

She inched backward, holding her breath. Her foot dislodged an empty oil can; her leg barely touched the motor--CRASH!

She jerked forward. The camera dropped to the ground.

The man at the helm turned. He yelled something in Spanish and pointed down at her.

MOVE NOW!

The man from the helm slid down the ladder from the bridge, vaulted over the side of the cruiser, and landed with a thump on the wharf.

Her feet, obeying, scrambled backward; the toes of her running shoes dug into the grimy blacktop, and with a burst of adrenaline her body accelerated.

She heard a pop and felt a bullet zing past her head.

She ran, ran as hard as she could, passing the next vacant building, cornering left. Open water. A dead end!

Valerie spun around. Raced back to the warehouse. Footsteps pounded on the asphalt behind her, rapidly gaining ground, closer. Closer.

She ducked around the building. Spotted a broken two by four lying next to her. Grabbed it. Listened, gauging his steps. Heard his panting. And swung!

Before he hit the ground--she was gone, racing toward the next building, dodging behind another, crossing the yard.

She reached the path leading up to the highway. Gained the crest of the hill. Her legs throbbed; her lungs blazed. She dared a backward glance, heard him yelling, and saw him reach the last corner.

Another pop and a bullet whistled past her head.

She ran into the middle of the four-lane highway and waved frantically. "Stop!"

Two cars swerved around her, horns blaring.

The third screeched to a halt. She ran to the passenger side; the door was locked. She tugged at the door handle and gasped for air. "There's a man after me," she stammered. "Please!"

The middle-aged driver stared at her. She glanced back toward the hill. Then at the driver. Her eyes pleaded. He stomped on the gas and sped away; her fingers grazed the paint on his car. She felt the panic rising in her chest, swung around, and ran toward the skyscrapers of Seattle. She couldn't see the bus stop, couldn't risk running all the way back to find it. Traffic zoomed by. She zigzagged into the oncoming lane. Tires squealed.

A taxi pulled over. "Better jump in," he laughed. "Before you get yourself killed."

"Thank you, God," Valerie whispered and climbed into the back. "Please hurry."

"Where to?"

The words *police station* stuck in her throat. Did she have a choice? "Uh--Downtown. Please."

The taxi rolled forward, waiting for an opening to join the traffic. She twisted around, peered out the back window, and saw her pursuer reach the sidewalk at the top of the hill. She couldn't see his gun.

He slumped forward and pressed his hands to his bent knees, his chest heaved. He scanned every direction until his eyes locked on her cab. Her heart leapt. A semi trailer moved between them.

The taxi darted in behind a car. The driver glanced over his shoulder at her. "You okay?"

Valerie trembled, thought of undoing the wind-breaker around her waist, but couldn't exert the effort. "Sure," she said slouching in her seat, while images of the two dead men flashed before her. She nudged their images aside and folded her hands together on her lap. Then gagged.

Her camera!

CHAPTER 2

From the stern of his yacht, Miguel DeOlmos looked first at the calm waters of Puget Sound and then the city surrounding his boat. His soldier, Lope Ramirez had served him diligently for many years. For that Miguel had shown his gratitude. Lope's only child, Rosa, living in San José del Cabo, had been well taken care of. After her graduation from high school last spring, Miguel had arranged a position for her at one of his hotels on the Sea of Cortez.

And what had he asked for in return?

Loyalty.

For several days, Lope had been acting suspicious: sullen and distracted; going so far as to argue with Reynaldo in Miguel's presence. And now Lope's inability to see the woman before she witnessed the disposing of the greedy gringos threatened everything Miguel had worked for. If the family empire fell, Miguel would accept his fate, but what would become of his *hermanito* Vicente? Although a grown man, Vicente would never survive on his own; his mind was that of a child's.

Miguel relaxed his clenched jaw, his tight fists, freeing himself of his anger. With his emotions now in check, he faced Lope. "Contact Sanchez and tell him to send the seaplane. Then prepare the boat. When we are airborne, instruct the captain to continue through the locks. Someone will pick him up."

"*Si, patrón. ¿Y la mujer?*"

The sun's brutal intensity was of no consequence, and Miguel did not blink. The soldier standing before him had become a threat, and Miguel could barely tolerate his presence. After all these years, did Lope not understand that family meant everything to him? "I will take care of the woman. Contact Sanchez."

"*Si, patrón*, but allow me to assure you the woman was not in the area when we arrived. I searched the grounds. There was no one."

Miguel lowered his head but kept his glare on Lope.

"I will contact General Sanchez over the secured line." Lope turned and rushed to the radio communication center.

Miguel was sitting on the white leather bench, his eyes half-closed, his arms crossed, his mind saddened, when Lope returned. "Well?" he asked.

"General Sanchez has given the pilot the coordinates. He will meet us in ten minutes. As soon as you are safely aboard, the captain will take the boat through the locks. When he reaches open sea, he will sink the boat and escape on the dingy. The Coast Guard will find nothing."

Miguel raised his eyes. "You have been with me how long?"

Lope stood rigid, as if to ward off the blow. The flesh under his eyes paled. "Since 1990, *patrón*. Six years."

"They have been good years?"

"*Si, patrón*," he said in a quiet, strained voice. "They have been good years."

"You made a mistake today. You said the area was clear."

The Adam's apple in Lope's neck clawed for freedom. "Give me any order and I will obey without question. I will not fail you again," he said.

"Any order?"

Lope swallowed hard and wet his lips again. He stood at attention; his gaze fixed on the land behind Miguel. "*Si, patrón.*"

"*Está bien.*" Miguel saw the relief on Lope's face. "I do have one order." He unfolded his arms, his right hand gripping his gun. He pointed the 9mm at Lope's head, ignored the horror on his face, and said, "Die." Then he squeezed the trigger.

* * *

Seattle's skyscrapers jutted higher above the horizon. In the backseat of the taxi, Valerie hugged her arms close and despite the day's warmth, trembled. She fought tears. Not from fear. She grieved for the two men killed. Their lives were over. They were dead. Dead. And she saw it happen. Strangers who should have meant nothing to her. Men who were probably drug dealers or thieves.

Husband?

Fathers?

Sons?

"Are you okay, ma'am?" the cab driver asked, looking at her through his rear-view mirror.

Valerie blinked. "Yes."

He glanced over his shoulders at her oil-stained pants, her unkempt ponytail, then faced forward.

"I was jogging," she said to his reflection in the mirror.

The driver's forehead knotted.

Valerie swept long strands of hair off her shoulder. Her stomach did flips in time with the pulse ramming in her head. Sadness overwhelmed her. What she was about to do would change her life forever. This she knew instinctively.

To calm herself she thought of her precious daughters. Megan the oldest, eighteen and ready for college, was eager to test her wings. Christine was ten months Megan's junior. Her sole interest at the moment was clothes, and she had recently amazed Valerie with the announcement she wanted to be a model, this after proclaiming she was going to be a litigation lawyer. Twelve-year-old Brandi had announced at the Prince George Airport Friday night, "I'm going invent arcade games, Ma. They'll call me *KAE*, The 'Kewl Arcade Engineer.'

God, how she loved them. So much so that her heart hurt.

The driver pulled up to a brick building and turned off his meter.

Valerie handed him a twenty. "Thanks again." She slipped out, rushed into the precinct, and almost tripped when a hand reached out and grabbed her.

"Whoa. Can I help you?" an officer said.

"I need to report a crime."

"There." He pointed to the long counter across from the entrance.

Valerie hurried past the civilian behind the desk and stopped in front of the closest officer. She fumbled with her wind-breaker and put it on.

"Yeah," the policeman asked, his head bowed. His nametag read: Sgt. Jackson.

"I need to report a murder, but you should contact the Coast Guard first because the killer has a boat and is probably heading through the locks, and if you call them right away--"

"Slow down, slow down." He laid his clipboard aside and looked at her. "You okay?"

She shook her head. "No, I'm not. I saw men murdered, shot dead, then thrown in the lake. They were--"

"Slower, miss. Start at the beginning."

"There's no time for that. If you don't contact the coast guard, the shooter will get away."

"Hold on. I can't help unless I have the whole story, so let's start at the beginning, and see what we have."

"But you don't understand."

"Ma'am, I'm busy. Unless you can tell me what happened, there's not much I can do."

Valerie steadied her breathing. "A man shot and killed two men on a wharf--I'm not exactly sure where. Near a marina. The porter at my hotel knows the address. The shooter's on his cabin cruiser heading through the locks. He could be in the Sound by now. You have to contact the coast guard. Please. The men on the boat saw me. They know I saw them. I dropped my camera. There's a picture of me standing in front of my hotel. Please, you must call the coast guard."

A strange expression crossed over his face, and Valerie, a long distance from home, trembled.

"Detective," the sergeant called to a suited gentleman standing at a pop machine across the room. "This young lady would like to give a statement."

Valerie felt the flush on her cheeks. Why did everyone keep referring to her as *young*? She was the mother of teenagers. "You don't understand."

"I understand," the sergeant replied, his voice deeper. "I understand you need to talk to a detective. When he verifies your story, I'll contact the coast guard. If it's like you say, there's no rush. It takes a long time to get through the locks."

She had an argument on her lips, but one look at his wrinkled mouth stifled it. "It'll be too late," she said, her voice barely audible.

CHAPTER 3

Valerie looked around her hotel room and shivered. As soon as she'd returned, she'd put on a second pair of socks and a thick pullover. But the trembling continued.

She pulled a blanket off the bed and curled up in a chair next to the window with the electric heater underneath. The policewoman, sent back with her, sat on the end of the bed, and watched a Jim Carrey movie. Her gruff moments of laughter added to Valerie's despair. During each commercial, she'd give Valerie a reassuring smile.

Valerie wrapped the blanket tighter.

The sun had long since set, and in its wake, a full moon rose in a cloudless sky. Valerie leaned her elbow on the windowsill and looked at the city lights, neon signs flashing promises of the most delicious steak and lobster dinners, the best computer sales, the friendliest car salesmen. Traffic streaked down I-5 and Madison, and a cruise ship left the harbour, lit up like a Christmas tree. She slumped back.

An untouched plate of Vietnamese noodles and greens sat on the dresser next to the bed. The officer's empty plate beside it. Had either of the two victims liked Asian cuisine? Valerie tried to imagine them eating, but dead was the only way she saw them. Blood, exploding through the air while the man in the raincoat smiled.

Her eyes blurred. At that precise moment, she imagined the victims' families hysterical with shock. Desperate to believe it was all a bad dream. Just as she had the night her parents had died. Only now there were visions to go along with their deaths, visions that she'd never allowed herself to imagine before tonight. The sidewalk covered in blood. Her mum and dad falling to the ground. Did they think of her and Aidan and worry about leaving them? Did they suffer? Had there been some comfort in knowing they were dying together?

Valerie wiped the tears from her face. Her sympathies went out to the wives, mothers, and family of the two dead men. She sent them silent condolences and told them she understood their grief.

What she couldn't say was that the repercussions of today would diminish every happy moment of their lives from here on. Just as her parents' deaths had changed everything for her. Not just the births of Megan, Christine, and Brandi, but also every celebration, birthday, and holiday since. And she sensed it had been the same for Aidan.

Their parents had died twenty-three years ago. And yet it felt like yesterday ....

May 1, 1973. And Valerie, fourteen, had snapped at her mother, and was ordered to her room. Before leaving for their dinner reservation, her father appeared at the door for his usual goodnight kiss, and she'd pretended she was sleeping. Still, his kiss lightened upon her cheek, while her mother whispered at the door, "How can she seem so content in sleep but so miserable when awake?"

"Honey, she's a teenager. They're supposed to be miserable."

She should have said goodnight. She should have apologized to both of them for being such a snot. *I'll do it in the morning* had been her last conscious thought.

The next morning, she didn't get the chance. At two a.m., five Mounties, three of whom Valerie knew because they were friends of her dad's, and some lady from Victim's Services appeared at her front door. One of them said, "Let's go inside."

"Why?"

"We'll talk about it inside."

The door opened wide. They filed into the front foyer. And somebody said her parents were dead.

She laughed. "Yeah, right." They couldn't be dead--

Valerie shook her head to dispel the memories. Nothing good ever came from thinking about that night.

A loud knock on the door brought the officer to her feet. Valerie blinked, then caught her breath as the policewoman stepped away from the bed, unclipped the safety catch on her holster, and took a position next to the door. Valerie's heart seemed to pump three times faster than it should.

"Yes?" the policewoman answered.

"Officer Andrea Broadhurst?"

"Yes."

"FBI."

She checked through the peephole and unlocked the dead bolt. A small man in a black suit entered the room, displaying his ID. He bent his head toward the officer, whispered something, and she stepped out of the room. Thirty-five or younger, he had brown hair, cut short, and swept in waves from his forehead. His skin was clear like a little boy's. His suit was immaculate with a perfect crease down the front of his trousers. His black leather shoes shone.

"Mrs. McCormick?" His brown eyes showed little emotion. His outstretched hand held the identification wallet. The name underneath his photograph read: BAILEY, PETER. Special Agent. "Could you come with me, please?"

"Where?"

"We've secured a suite on the top floor. It'll be safer if you relocate. Someone will gather your things and bring them upstairs for you."

He stood patiently, surveying the room. Valerie glanced toward the open door of the bathroom and wished she'd put away her lingerie hanging from the curtain rod.

"The coast guard didn't find him?" she asked.

"Not yet."

She looked through the window to the high-rise two streets over. She tossed the blanket to the bed, switched off the television, and followed the nattily dressed little man through the door.

A police officer waited inside the elevator. They got off on the twentieth floor. The quiet hallway smelled like carpet shampoo. Glaring lights lit their path, and she moved with the three men, conscious of the hand guiding her. They stopped at room 2011. Agent Bailey tugged at his perfectly starched shirt cuffs and knocked twice. The door opened, and Valerie looked into the face of her father. Only this wasn't her father. It couldn't be. Her dad was dead.

This man's hair was gray, thin, short, and untameable. His dark suit was worn at the elbows. The skin below his wide cheekbones was shadowed by white and black stubble. Without having to ask, Valerie knew he was in charge. The deep crevices around his hazel eyes showed wisdom as well as age.

"Come in, Mrs. McCormick. I'm Assistant Special Agent in Charge Vamozzi. Please have a seat." He indicated the chair a few feet from the breakfast table.

Special Agent Bailey sat down at the table where files were strewn across its top. The only other person in the room was a young woman reclining on the sofa. Judging by the gray suit and white blouse, Valerie guessed her to be FBI. When she glanced at Valerie and sat up self-consciously, there was something familiar in her eyes. Compassion? Regret? She was in her mid-thirties, pretty in an exotic way with black piercing eyes and black hair. The dark circles under her eyes made her skin look chalky. She smiled, but her eyes said something else.

Valerie, unable to unwrap her arms from across her chest, approached the young woman. "My daughter will be at the Prince George Airport. I haven't time--"

"It's been taken care of," ASAC Vamozzi said. "Please sit down."

"We contacted your husband and told him the situation," the woman said, laying her hands in her lap. "I'm Special Agent CT Kalamai."

"Who spoke to my husband?" Valerie asked.

"I did." Bailey organized some papers into files.

Valerie stood her ground. "What did he say?"

Bailey straightened his shirt cuffs and studied the file in front of him. Valerie's stomach muscles tightened. She almost snapped at him to answer her when Vamozzi again gestured toward the sofa chair. "Please sit down, Mrs. McCormick."

She walked over to the sofa chair and sat down. Agent Bailey took the armchair across from her. Vamozzi joined Kalamai on the couch next to him.

Three against one?

Vamozzi took a cigarette package from his inside pocket and offered her one. Valerie shook her head.

"We need to ask you a few questions. We know you've given your statement to the police, but it's important--"

"My father, brother, and uncle were policemen. I understand how these things work."

"Provincial, City, or RCMP?" Vamozzi asked.

"Mounties."

All three of them gave her an indecipherable look.

"What?" she asked.

"Then you understand you're in a volatile situation?" Vamozzi said.

The blood rushed to her brain. She knew what he was thinking. "Not necessarily. I'm a foreigner."

"They saw you, Mrs. McCormick."

"That doesn't mean they know who I am."

"Your statement is on record. Access to your file requires a simple signature."

"Not until the case is closed."

"Members of the court, police officers, clerks, to name a few, have access to your file."

Valerie thought of her camera and the photograph of her standing in front of this hotel. "Why are you trying to frighten me?" She rose to her feet. "I can't stay here."

"Please sit down, Mrs. McCormick." Vamozzi's voice sounded tense. "There are questions we need to ask."

At that particular moment, he resembled her father even more. Valerie sat down.

"You're from Canada, why are you here?"

"There was a contest," she said, unable to stop wringing her hands.

"What contest?"

Valerie took a deep breath and entwined her fingers together. "Last May my girls entered a Mother's Day contest."

"And?"

"Their paragraph was picked as the winner, and the prize was a 2-day stay in Jasper, Vancouver, or Seattle to be chosen before the end of the year. I chose Seattle."

"Why?"

Here it comes, Valerie thought. She'd tell them about Ed hoping to persuade a potential client, and they'd look at her like she was a criminal. The thought of telling them made her so embarrassed she felt like crawling under her chair.

Vamozzi squinted at her. "Are you hiding something, Mrs. McCormick?"

Great, not only did he resemble her father, he was psychic. "I decided on Seattle because … uh." She could lie. No, she thought, sitting up straight. "We have a client. He mentioned he'd seen a Bayliner advertised for sale in a Seattle trade magazine. He has several blocks of timber he wants contracted out, the land cleared, including stumpage fees. Ed asked me to take photographs for him."

"So he'd look favourably at hiring your husband's company?"

"Yes."

"Why didn't your client come down and take a look at the boat himself?"

"Too busy, I guess." She glanced at Bailey and Kalamai. Kalamai studied the carpet at her feet while Bailey picked fuzz off his pants. "What difference does it make?"

Vamozzi ignored the question. "How long were you wandering around before you heard voices?"

"A few minutes." Valerie remembered something her brother had once told her. A good investigator spent a few moments asking irrelevant questions. If only to put his witness at ease or at least get a sense of whom he was dealing with.

"What was the name of the boat?" Vamozzi asked.

"I couldn't see the transom from my angle."

"Any numbers on the side?"

"I didn't see any."

"Would you recognize the boat if you saw it again?"

"Yes."

"Did you see any others?"

"No."

"You saw no one other than the five men?"

"That's correct."

"You know for certain none of the buildings were occupied?"

"How could I know that?"

"Then someone could have seen you walking past?"

"I suppose. Yes."

"Did you hear any noise from any of those buildings?"

"At the police station, no other witnesses stepped ... forward." Valerie clamped her mouth shut. She understood what he was getting at. She was their only witness, she was Canadian, and that meant if they didn't find another witness--

"You reached the crest of the hill and glanced back. Could you see the cruiser?"

"No. I didn't see the cabin cruiser. Or the man in the raincoat. Or the wharf. Only the man following me."

Vamozzi didn't blink. "Did you recognize any of them?"

"I'm Canadian. How could I possibly--"

"Okay, from the beginning," he said, frowning at her.

"I don't understand."

"Tell me *exactly* what you saw."

She pushed the air from her lungs. "Can we do this later? I'm so tired." And openly irritated, which wasn't like her.

Vamozzi took another long drag of his cigarette; his eyes fixed on hers. Bailey massaged the knuckles of his right hand and tugged at his starched cuffs. Kalamai looked vacant.

Valerie repeated what she'd already told him. "I arrived by plane yesterday, late morning."

"You got off the bus, then what?"

Then what? She remembered standing at the top and witnessing how the lake captured the sun, turning the water into glittering blue gems. A sudden gust of hot air whistled through a maple tree. The leaves transformed into a myriad of crystals before settling into green stillness again, a sight that would have captivated her eldest daughter. Megan loved trees. She would have--

"Mrs. McCormick?" Vamozzi said. "What did you see?"

Valerie closed her eyes. In the distance, steel and concrete skyscrapers had towered over the background of a dark green ocean. Closer still, a neighbourhood full of houses of all shapes and sizes, lawns still plush and green, and short plump trees, a living contrast against the glassy-gray Space Needle. In the west, a tugboat towed a cruise ship into port and a sleek white cabin cruiser ... moved slowly ... from the narrow channel leading from the lake, and headed toward shore.

"The cabin cruiser arrived." She opened her eyes. "As I was descending the hill. I didn't think much of it then. I didn't realize ...."

"Please continue," Vamozzi said, glancing at her statement. "You were heading toward Pier 7."

"I heard arguing. I looked around the corner and saw two men walking away. A man stood near the cruiser."

"Any distinct characteristics?"

"The younger man was tall, over six feet. His hair was medium-brown. He wore a blue suit, red tie. The other man was older, shorter, balding, dressed in a dark blue suit. His shoulders drooped, and I remember his neck was thick. More so than normal."

Vamozzi's face turned gray. "I meant the shooter, Mrs. McCormick."

"He might have been in his late forties," Valerie said, feeling the flush to her cheeks. "He was dressed in an expensive tan overcoat, tan alligator boots. He was maybe five-ten, coffee-dark, Latino."

Repulsed by her first impression, she rubbed her eyes. She was too ashamed to admit what she had really thought, that the man from the cabin cruiser was attractive. His hair matched the colour of midnight, thick and well groomed. Warm and enticing, his face and his smile could easily grace the cover of Forbes magazine. Everything about him implied money, prestige, and power.

"Their meeting on a dock in the middle of nowhere seemed normal."

Unsure whether that was a question, Valerie said, "At first I thought the man in the raincoat was a broker, and then I assumed they were friends."

"You alleged they were arguing."

"Friends do that sometimes."

"You thought they were friends because ...?"

"He kept smiling at them. But more than that, he seemed relaxed. Their arguing didn't seem to bother him."

"Did you change your mind before or after ...?"

"Before."

"Why?"

"The older man turned and I saw his face." Without moving her head, Kalamai's eyes locked on her. Valerie took another deep breath and continued. "He looked worried. It was as if he understood what was going to happen and could do nothing to stop it."

Valerie rubbed her forehead. She had seen the fear in the older man's face and only now recognized it as such. He knew he was a dead man. A tear stung her eye. She blinked several times and looked at the three FBI agents. Their faces were drawn. Bailey squeezed Kalamai's hand.

"What happened next?" Vamozzi asked.

"You knew those men?" Now she understood what she had seen in Agent Kalamai's face. "They were FBI agents."

"Yes. What happened next?"

Valerie glanced at Kalamai. That was what she'd seen in her eyes. Grief. Perhaps the younger man was her boyfriend or possibly the older man was her mentor.

These people were grieving.

"I'm so sorry." An image of the man in the raincoat flashed through her mind. His right hand glided through the air like a Tai Chi Master. His graceful tanned hand floated out into a wide circle, and with the smooth cadence of a dancer, reached back inside his raincoat, pulled out a gun....

Valerie swallowed hard. "It happened fast. The man in the raincoat shot the older man then the younger one. Then he climbed aboard the boat. The other two men, his companions, were already coming ashore carrying buckets. They tied something to the ankles of .... They rolled their bodies into the water then grabbed pails and splashed the contents across the ... wood." One man had kicked at a glob of blood as if removing mere dirt.

She lowered her head and tugged at the cuffs of her sweater. She saw Vamozzi shift his weight, but neither Bailey nor Kalamai appeared to be breathing.

"He never stopped smiling," Vamozzi said.

Again, she wasn't certain if his remark was a question. "He smiled the whole time."

Valerie closed her eyes tight and tried to erase the memory. But no amount of concentration would destroy it; the memory was like an insect crawling around in her brain.

"You saw him smile, then you saw him ... shoot the two agents?"

Valerie squeezed her eyes tighter. "Yes."

"Will you testify?"

The question didn't surprise her. They were bound to ask eventually. "Testify?" she replied in a weak voice.

"You witnessed a double homicide--for Christ's sake!"

"Saul," Kalamai said glancing at Vamozzi.

Vamozzi rubbed a hand through his hair, his expression softening. "Will you testify?"

Valerie wrung her hands, then tucked them between her knees. Vamozzi waited. So did Bailey and Kalamai. "I need to call my family."

No one spoke.

She glanced across at Vamozzi. Confused, trapped, angry, she felt like yelling: I LIED. I DIDN'T SEE ANYTHING. I MADE THE WHOLE THING UP until she looked directly at his face. The face that looked too familiar.

"Actually, I need to discuss this with my brother. There are mitigating circumstances." Valerie couldn't think of any mitigating circumstances.

"Mrs. McCormick, I know what I'm asking you to do. But you made a decision when you went to the police. It's too late to change your mind."

Valerie struggled to her feet. "Agent Vamozzi, you know that's not true. I'm Canadian. You can't force me to testify. You can't keep me from leaving either. I want to go home. I can't think here."

She stood in the middle of the room and pressed her palms against her temples. If only her brother Aidan were there with her. A private investigator, he'd know what questions to ask, none of which she could think of.

"I want to go home," she blurted, disturbed that despite being thirty-eight, she could so easily feel fourteen again. "You're confusing me with all these questions. I can't think."

A hand touched her arm. "We'll make arrangements," Agent Kalamai said. "It's okay, you don't have to make a decision now." Her dark piercing eyes looked sincere and incredibly sad. "Somebody will bring your suitcase in to you in a few minutes."

Valerie nodded and hurried to the bedroom.

Thirty minutes after lying down, she heard a light tap on the bedroom door.

"You'll be leaving soon," Kalamai called.

Valerie rose from the bed. She zipped up her suitcase and braided her hair. Seattle's night sounds beckoned, and she approached the window. Fourteen floors higher, she could now see clear across the harbour. The Space Needle appeared smaller, and the traffic below was a streak of light burning down the black pavement. Life goes on, just like the night her parents died.

She felt the pain again, and relinquishing an old wound, pushed the memory of her parents from her mind and entered the sitting room. Vamozzi, Kalamai, and Bailey sat on the sofa. A stranger sat in the chair across from them. It didn't matter. Even if the room filled with investigators, she was still going home.

The man rose. "Hello. I'm Paul Rostov from the US Attorney's Office."

He didn't extend his hand, and Valerie was grateful. She didn't want to touch these people; witnessing their grief was hard enough. She sat in the second sofa chair and understood that she wouldn't be going home just yet.

Mr. Rostov went across the room to the kitchenette and refilled his coffee cup. An attractive man in his late thirties, dressed informally in a black and white wool sweater with gray trousers, he looked as if he'd just left his home. In contrast to the dark suits, he looked relaxed, as if his visit was sociable. She watched him tug at the material above his knees before he sat down. He rested his arm along the back of the chair and smiled at her.

Apprehensive, Valerie gnawed on her lip. Again, she tried to imagine what her brother would say. Aidan was more than just another investigator. He understood things before they happened. And what about Ed? His face flashed through her mind, the heat in her own face escalating. If he weren't so preoccupied with their dying business, he would have come with her. It wasn't as if the few trees they could harvest were going anywhere. Yes, and it wasn't as if he had to pay for the damn trip.

"Mrs. McCormick?" Rostov spoke in a voice that suited the face, smooth and charming. "Normally I wouldn't be questioning you this soon, but since you'll be leaving the country shortly, I need to talk to you first. The State of Washington, not the US Justice Department, will prosecute this case since the murders took place here. My job is to determine whether we have enough evidence for an indictment, and if we can prosecute."

"As I explained to Agent Vamozzi, most of the men in my family were police officers" She'd felt brave when she'd been at the precinct and had pointed to photos of the two men from the boat; she didn't feel so brave now.

Rostov nodded, and Valerie, controlled by the apathy in his face, squirmed in her seat. "I'm aware of that." He continued as if she hadn't spoken a word. "I'm sure you feel as if you've been dealt a dead man's hand, but Assistant Special Agent Vamozzi was unable to enlighten you because he didn't have the authority. That's why I'm here."

She didn't like him. Why? Pretentious, ambitious, were the quickest words that came to mind.

He settled back on the sofa as if his presence was welcomed. He sipped his coffee, wiped at the brim, and smiled back at her. Was his last statement more for Vamozzi's benefit than for hers? His smile was like the icing on a burnt cake.

"Several months ago," Rostov said, "the United States Government set up a task force to investigate the activities of a cartel in South America. It was later discovered there were links between this cartel and executives in Miami, New York, and Toronto. The two men you picked from the precinct's computer are known members of this cartel. They specialize in the organized distribution of illegal drugs into the United States and Canada. The FBI believes their employer is the man you saw murder the two FBI agents.

"We've yet to find anyone outside the cartel who will identify him. The only photographs available are those taken in 1956 when he was ten. With today's technology, we can guess at what he looks like now, but that's exactly what we'd be doing: Guessing.

"In the past, he may have had plastic surgery. We do know he's powerful and shrewd. The FBI has been hunting this man for a very long time, Mrs. McCormick. With you as our Ace-in-the-hole, we may now have a strong case against him."

"Do you know where he is?"

Rostov stole a glance at Vamozzi. The look between the two men disturbed her. It was as if having a secret gave Rostov some power over her.

Vamozzi continued to look at him when Rostov turned back to her and said, "No."

"You're not going to arrest him tomorrow?" she asked.

"I won't retire until we get him. And we will get him," Special Agent

Vamozzi answered.

Valerie glared over at him and back to Rostov. What did they think? She was stupid? "How do you plan on arresting him if you don't know what he looks like?" She rushed on as if their response might frighten her further. "Maybe I'm just a bookkeeper, a small town housewife, but I'm not a total imbecile. You think the perpetrator of that crime is the head of a drug cartel in South America. But you've never seen him. No one has ever seen him. Now you're going to go out and arrest a man no one has ever seen. Then you want me to come back and point at him in a court of law?

"What about those two men with him? They're American, right? I picked them out of the police computer; you must know who they are. Wouldn't it be easier to arrest those two and have them identify him? Couldn't you give them immunity in exchange for their testimony?"

Everyone stared at her.

"Okay, so I don't understand what it takes to police a country this size. But you have to agree, what's been said here today doesn't make any sense. You're not telling me everything; granted you may think your reasons justify that. But don't expect me to answer without ...." My brother's counsel, she stopped herself from saying.

She leaned forward, hugged her arms, and looked at the floor. "You don't have to explain to me how dangerous he is; I saw what he did." She raised her head and looked at Rostov. "Sir, you can say whatever you like, but you're not going to rush me into making a decision that not only affects me, but my family."

A memory crossed her mind, and her temper flared. "Besides, it's not my fault he got away. I warned the police. I told them to contact the coast guard. If they'd listened, you'd have your killer now."

Rostov no longer smiled. In fact, he didn't look very happy. "Mrs. McCormick, must I remind you you're a witness to a double murder? Measures can be taken to guarantee your testimony."

"You can't force me to testify if you have no one under arrest. I came forward under good faith."

"Do you also realize if you attempt to enter this country again, for any reason, you'll be arrested for obstruction of justice?"

"Fine, threaten me. I'm still going home."

Vamozzi looked at her with a long face. "They have your photograph, Mrs. McCormick. That places you in a dangerous position."

"I feel it, Agent Vamozzi. I feel it in this room despite all of you here with me. I need to go home. If you won't let me go, then I want to speak with someone from the Canadian Consulate."

"That won't be necessary," he answered.

The men rose. Valerie forced herself to stand. She shook Rostov's hand. His lips pursed. She could see there was something more he wanted to say. He stood for a moment then excused himself and left. Valerie almost fell backward onto the couch; she was so very tired.

She steadied herself and wrapped her sweater tighter. "Agent Vamozzi, what now?"

"We'll escort you to the airport." He studied her.

Valerie would have given anything to know what he was thinking. She suspected he didn't like her. His men were dead, and his only witness didn't know what to do. "You haven't told me their names."

"I didn't think it mattered ... to you."

That hurt. Still, Valerie kept her head high. "Tell me anyway."

"Charlie Onston and Gregory Vanderhal," Vamozzi replied then turned and faced the window.

"We have to leave now, Mrs. McCormick. Or you'll miss your plane," Bailey said.

* * *

Miguel DeOlmos took the cognac from his valet, swirled it twice, and took a sip. He slipped off his loafers and leaned back against the couch in his stateroom. The air-conditioner hummed through the floor vents. Outside, the soft lights on the yacht's foredeck blended with the moonlight reflected across the wet deck. The air held a comforting aroma of Cuban cigars and cayenne. Miguel closed his eyes, inhaled, and then heard the cellular phone ringing.

The valet crossed the room, listened for a moment, and handed the phone to Miguel.

"Yes," Miguel said.

"Her name is Valerie McCormick. She registered at the hotel for two days then disappeared late this evening."

"Her destination?"

"The Feds are all over this case. It's a miracle I found her camera before they did. You realize those men you killed were FBI ...? You still there?"

"Find the woman." His voice as gentle as the waves rocking his yacht.

"I'll try, but--"

"Sergeant Jackson, forgive me for not inquiring about your son? I understand he attends Yale and resides in an old and prestigious fraternity." Miguel took a drag from his favourite Cuban cigar. The silence on the other end was gratifying. "Find her," he said, as firmly as a father might speak to his son.

"I'll try, but--"

Miguel clicked off his secure scrambled cellular phone.

CHAPTER 4

Special Agent in Charge of the DeOlmos Investigations in Florida, Mike 'Candyman' Canaday parked his car on the street in front of the tiny stucco house with its red tiled roof and tall palm trees. An outside light shone on the flower bordered driveway and pebbled sidewalk leading to the front door. There was only one car in the double carport.

Canaday's gut churned. He avoided looking at the clergyman who sat quietly beside him. Good thing the man wasn't in any hurry to move. Canaday's legs seemed frozen.

Yeah, he hated this part of his job.

His job? It was getting harder and harder to remember why he'd joined the Bureau.

Two tours in Nam, and he'd decided the only thing left for him was to hunt bad guys. He'd been damn tired of losing people he cared about. Like Sergio. The first to tag him, *Candyman*.

Candyman, the nickname that stuck like the bits of blood and fragments and stink of Vietnam. "Hey, GI, you got candy?"

Candyman, always a pocketful of candy for the kids with the almond eyes.

Candyman, the Special Agent at a crime scene. Always searching his pocket for a piece of candy, something to do with his hands, something to suck on while his stomach felt as if it would empty its contents right there in front of everybody. While his subordinates, who never knew what he was thinking, kept their distance, afraid to speak.

Candyman?

Tonight he wasn't delivering no fuckin' candies.

"You ready, Agent Canaday?"

He glanced at the clergyman and eased his hand toward the door handle. "I suppose so, padre."

They walked down the short driveway, across the pebbled sidewalk, and stepped up to the front door. One inconceivable thought flashed through Canaday's mind. Special Agent Charlie Onston, a brother-in-arms, one of the few men Canaday could call friend was dead, and Canaday had to tell Charlie's wife. He swallowed the candy in his mouth and tapped his knuckle on the door.

* * *

Summoned to Washington, unnecessarily as far as Special Agent Canaday was concerned, he sat across from the Deputy Director of the FBI in silence. He waited as Leonard Tomlin read the Key West file; a file Canaday had prepared then spent three sleepless nights studying. He waited, while examining the surrounding artefacts outlining Tomlin's long career, a career winding to a close. The photographs and plaques were as old and as memorable as Tomlin's expression.

In the past year, Tomlin's cheeks had hollowed, and his eyes sunk into their sockets. Another man might mistake the empty stare for indifference, but not Canaday. Forty years in law enforcement had reduced Tomlin to this. Forty years of watching the influx of crime spread had ruined his health and nearly finished him off. Canaday leaned forward, studied his boss, and wondered if he was looking at himself in another twenty years.

Tomlin closed the file. "I spoke to Agent Kalamai after the Vanderhal's funeral. She requested clearance for the field."

"It's been a month. Vamozzi needs her in Seattle."

"She took Vanderhal's death badly. Were they ...?"

"No," Canaday lied.

Tomlin flicked at the pages on his desk. "Did I tell you I lost my partner in '69?"

"Yes, sir." He didn't want to hear another *hero's death* story. He was sick of them.

"It took a long time to get over his death." Tomlin shook his head. "Have a cigarette, Canaday. If you like."

Canaday thought about the wrapped candies in his pocket and his cigarettes back in his rental. Neither one seemed appropriate for the moment. "It's all right, sir."

Tomlin's fingers stretched out and tapped on the sheaf of paper. "I'm retiring next year. It would be nice to go out with this settled."

Canaday nodded, his mind drifting. Away from Tomlin and his small talk. Away from the sterilized confines of this office. He thought of his friend Charlie Onston. He thought of Charlie's wife. The look on Linda's face when he showed up at their vacation home in Miami. She knew without having to hear the words. "Charlie?" she whispered. He nodded and watched as grief shrouded not just her face, but also her entire body.

Linda lost her husband, lover, and best friend, yet at the gravesite services, she'd walked through a crowd of Brass to tell him that the years he and Charlie were partners had been Charlie's best with the Bureau.

It had meant everything to hear that.

Canaday, Vamozzi, and Charlie had been their own kind of hell-raisers in those early days. Every conviction was a notch on their belts. They'd go without sleep, without food, without a woman until the bad guy was behind bars or on a slab. One more scumbag off the street. One step closer to making the world a better place.

Until the day they looked around and saw the same thing. Nothing had changed. Each scumbag had been replaced by a dozen more.

Canaday looked across at Tomlin, who seemed to be waiting. "I'll do what I can, sir," was all he could think to say.

"I know you will. I also know it would have been more convenient to fax me this report. However, you deserved to hear this in person. You're being temporarily reassigned to Seattle. Fredericton will take over as SAC for you in Florida."

Canaday straightened up. This was good news. The idea of handing this case over to someone else had sat like rotten eggs at the pit of his stomach.

"Your report says DeOlmos didn't know Agents Vanderhal and Onston were FBI. Do you believe that?"

"Ward says the word is they died because they wanted more guns for the same price."

Tomlin shook his head in disgust. "Any last minute progress with your two undercover agents?"

"No. After six months, Kyle Ward is no closer to meeting Miguel DeOlmos. Agent Angela Parker is still working directly under Miguel's younger brother Vincent. As it says in my report, sir. Parker informed Seattle that DeOlmos was enroute, but she's never actually seen him. She did verify the two men seen by Mrs. McCormick, Reynaldo Martinez and Lope Ramirez normally answer to Miguel's top general, Sanchez."

"Then our real hope lies with this McCormick woman?"

"Yes sir."

Tomlin opened the Seattle file and pulled out a photograph. "She's a pretty little thing."

Canaday leaned forward and glanced at the picture of Valerie McCormick. Tomlin's assessment was right. She was the girl next door. Curiosity had him wondering if she still felt safe after what she'd witnessed.

"You believe it was DeOlmos she saw?" Tomlin asked.

"Yes."

"The Canadians have her under constant surveillance?"

"Yes."

"I understand the RCMP isn't passing along anything other than the basics? What have you got so far?"

"They live a relatively quiet existence. They have three girls, a small logging business. Testifying is going to change her life. She may not realize that, but her brother, a retired cop knows what testifying against a man like DeOlmos will mean. That's also in my report, sir."

"She's the only one who's ever seen DeOlmos?"

"Her statement proves she'd be a good witness. But it's been a month, and she's had time to think." Canaday shifted forward and thought of his two undercover agents and the scumbag Gordon, one of the cartel's soldiers, who was in protective custody in New York. "We have Jerry Gordon."

"That's another reason why I asked you here, Mike."

Canaday's fingernail snagged on a small tear in the arm of the leather chair; he resisted ripping it bigger. Tomlin seldom called him by his first name. Whenever he did, it meant bad news.

"I want surveillance at the border tightened."

"That was done three weeks ago, sir."

"And the coast guard?"

"Done," Canaday said. *Why are you wasting my time.*

"This could go on for years if DeOlmos gets across the border."

Canaday stopped himself from sneering. Who's to say DeOlmos wasn't already back in Canada, his country of birth. "Yes sir, the last extradition with Alberta took seven years."

Tomlin avoided his eyes. Canaday squinted at him until confusion turned to discernment. He knew why he was there. "Gordon is dead?"

"His body was found minutes before I called you." He handed Canaday a report. "It's all in there. Take it with you to Seattle. I want to know the minute you hear from Ward or Parker."

Canaday's finger tugged at the snag.

"Gordon escaped protective custody and was on his own for three days. His death is unfortunate," Tomlin said. "But all the more reason to convince Mrs. McCormick to testify. I'll talk to Ottawa; you contact E-Division in Vancouver. Make certain they understand how serious we are. If DeOlmos can locate Gordon in three days, as soon as they discover she's

Joylene Nowell Butler

Canadian, she's dead. Michael, I'm counting on you. Make them understand ... she has to testify. And we're the only ones who can protect her."

CHAPTER 5

The loan manager for the Bank of Northern Canada in the highlands of Prince George, placed his manicured fingertips onto the loan application, rotated the papers, and slid them across his desktop toward Ed. The sun glared through the office window and reflected off his bifocals, making it look as if miniaturized duplicates of his desk items were tattooed on the bags under his eyes. He smiled a salesman's smile and handed Ed his own personal gold pen.

Why shouldn't he smile? At twelve percent, she'd smile too.

"Please press hard, Mr. McCormick, so your signature will be legible on all six copies."

Ed scribbled his name and handed the forms back. "The first payment isn't due for 30 days?"

"Mrs. McCormick needs to sign." The loan manager pushed the papers toward her.

"My wife isn't part owner of the company. For tax purposes, she's listed only as an employee."

Valerie pulled the pen from Ed's grasp.

"I realize that Mr. McCormick, but she is part owner of your home, and we are using it as collateral. The first payment is due the end of November. I hope that's clear. It's important you understand this."

"Yeah, I understand," Ed said.

Valerie scanned the fine print. A third mortgage on their home would bring the monthly payment over double the current amount. And that was fine as long as they met their obligation. Ed had assured her if that changed, they'd go back in and have the mortgage reduced to a more manageable amount.

"Hurry up, Val."

"I'm reading."

"What for? We've gone over how you can't make money without spending some. This is expansion, for pity's sake. Just sign. I've worked it out already. Besides, the day is rushing by, and I've got work to do."

"What would you like to know, Mrs. McCormick? It's my job to make certain you understand." The loan manager rested his elbows on the arms

Joylene Nowell Butler

of his leather chair, steepled his fingers together, and smiled.

Ed's face settled into a frown, and he slumped back in the chair.

Valerie ignored him. There were questions she needed answers to; and she wasn't signing anything until she got them. "If we miss a payment?"

"There's a Skip clause written in. Essentially, that means if you can't make a payment, it's applied to the end of the scheduled final payment date."

"What if we miss a second payment?"

"We foreclose. But I assure you that any such action is not beneficial to this financial institute, and every effort will be made to assist you in fulfilling your contract."

Spoken like a true banker. "What if something should happen to Ed?"

"Come on, Val. Nothing's going to happen." Ed fidgeted in his seat; the keys in his jeans jacket jiggled.

"Actually, Mr. McCormick, that is a valid concern. If you look at the bottom, you'll see the insurance premiums are substantial. In the event of your accidental death or disability, there is an Election of Coverage clause. The loan would be paid in full. Of course, because her name is on the mortgage, the same holds true if something should happen to Mrs. McCormick."

"Are you satisfied, Val? Now can you sign?"

She looked at the desk phone and felt a sudden desire to drop it on Ed's head. The pen dangled in her hand. She looked back at the loan manager and his annoying smile.

"What's the penalty if we need to rewrite before the anniversary date?" she asked.

"Three months."

Three months! Ed had better be right: You had to spend money to make it.

A credible assumption as long as the forest industry stabilized.

The loan manager checked all copies and flashed another salesman's smile. "Your copy will be in the mail, and the funds should be in your account no later than Tuesday." He rose and extended his hand to Ed.

Ed stood and, towering over the manager, shook his hand.

"It's been a pleasure, Mr. McCormick. If we can assist you in any future ventures, please call."

Not if she could help it.

Valerie shook the loan manager's hand and followed Ed through the door into the main area of the bank.

"Wait in the van. I have to check the safety deposit box," Ed said, heading for the counter.

Valerie walked across the room and pushed at the heavy glass doors. Outside, the air, fresh and clean, was finally free of summer's pesky insects. She stood at the edge of the sidewalk and enjoyed the cool breeze from the west. A beautiful October day, the huge silver birch trees poised along the outer edge of the mall's parking lot exhibited a procession of oranges, yellows, and fading greens set against a brilliant blue sky. East, lay a wide ditch and beyond that the double lane highway.

A logging truck slowed toward the intersection and squealed to a stop; black exhaust fumes bellowed from its stack. The load was some of the finest spruce and jack pine Valerie had ever seen. The straight logs were forty feet long and from twenty to forty inches at their bases. She estimated the value of the load to be between four and five thousand dollars. To ensure a profit, McCormick Contractors would have to pull out the equivalent at least three times a week. The block line they were working on had as much dead wood as it had live. The prospects weren't good. Years of abuse and pilfering had stripped the land, and now it was rendering its own form of revenge.

Could they compete against the international companies?

Would they lose their home?

Her shoulders slumped. She bowed her head and felt horrendous regret; doubting Ed's ability was as good as admitting failure. He understood the industry. Since she'd known him, he'd made wise business decisions. Okay, so times were tough. Instead of whining, she'd do whatever she could to help him. She owed it to their girls.

"Why aren't you waiting in the van? It's no wonder you get too many colds. You're supposed to be a grown up. Remember?"

She turned to see Ed exiting the bank. Why did he persist in speaking to her as if she was the poster girl for blonde jokes?

He tucked a folded white envelope into the back pocket of his jeans, then crossed the parking lot with heavy steps and headed toward their van parked in the first stall thirty feet away.

Without rushing, Valerie walked to the passenger side and climbed in. "Shall we pick up lunch for everybody at the drive-thru?"

Ed stuck the key in the ignition. "We're up to our necks in debt, Val. We can't afford diddley-squat, let alone lunch."

She fastened her seatbelt while numbness traveled from her heart upward. She wasn't even hungry. So why the need to speak without thinking?

Because the silence between them was becoming unbearable.

"You're right. I'll prepare something when we get home."

The engine roared to life, and Ed's face turned from indifference to glum.

This moment was reminiscent of so many other moments, arguments that started small, then quickly got out of hand. Was the key to working out their problems to start within herself? Nipping the sharp words before they escaped her mouth? Saying something encouraging instead of cutting deep?

"Don't worry, this recession can't last forever," she said in a flat voice. "We'll make it. We'll cut back on stuff around the house. Takeouts, dinner parties, designer jeans for the girls--"

"That should have been done before now. Ah, hell …."

"What…?"

Ed pulled himself out of whatever trance he'd been in, glanced at her, then shifted into first. "I'm sorry. I'll think of something."

"You don't really need me at the office full time. I'll find a job."

The tires squealed and the van shot out of the parking lot. Ed shifted into second gear and headed north toward their home. He hollered over the engine's noise. "I'm doing the best I can, but you're going to land a job and save the family. Thanks for your vote of confidence." He glanced sideways at her, gave her *the look*, then slammed the stick shift into third. "Val, your wages wouldn't cover the GST tax payments."

"That's not true. Forestry pay their employees well, and they're always looking for reliable tree planters." She felt like banging her head against the window. Tree planting didn't start again until next spring.

Ed kept his focus on the road, apparently unaware of her mistake.

"Maybe they need bookkeepers at the mill," she said, with more enthusiasm.

Ed rolled his eyes at her and looked back to the road. "You don't listen. I told you last week they laid off thirty management staff."

"I'm trying to help. Stop acting like I'm your enemy." She took a deep breath, determined not to argue. "I'll ask Aidan to keep his ears open. He knows a lot of people."

"Yeah, right. Ask your brother. The famous private eye will know where there's a great paying job that'll lift us out of this damn recession. Of course, ask Aidan."

"That's unfair. He always tries to be there for us."

"You mean he's always made sure I look like a failure in front of my family."

She opened her mouth to say something but took another deep breath instead. Arguing would prove nothing; it never did. Besides, they'd be home soon. Arguing in front of the girls was forbidden. It was a promise neither of them had ever broken.

"Aidan's a thorn in my side," Ed added. "And always has been."

But the girls weren't there, and Valerie couldn't let that go. "Shut up about my brother. I owe him, and so do you."

Ed kept his eyes forward and had the good sense not to say anything else.

They reached the four way stop sign at Austin and Kelly Road. Valerie felt a cold breeze sweep past her and folded her arms across her chest. They turned north onto Kelly Road. White knuckled, Ed clutched the steering wheel and concentrated on the road. His silence was neither comforting nor reassuring.

The night she returned from Seattle, he'd been everything she needed. Compassionate. Understanding. But too soon, his loving eyes turned blank, as if looking at her was like looking through the windshield of their van.

What had it been: One good night's sleep before he asked if she'd taken a picture of the boat? Flabbergasted, she'd said, "No." And he'd said, "That's okay. I think we got the contract."

Four more days before they'd find out if he was right. Meanwhile she couldn't help wondering what would have happened if he'd gone with her to Seattle?

Nothing consoling came to mind, and Valerie thought of Rostov. Had he carried out his threat? Was there a warrant for her arrest? It had been a month, and she'd heard nothing. Probably Rostov had found those two men she'd picked out of the computer, and they'd agreed to testify.

Ed turned west on Chief Lake Road. The scene changed from a crowded residential area of quarter acre lots, to ten and twenty acre lots. The houses, from ranch-style to tutor were set back from the road on large landscaped yards with shrubs, hedges, white fences, and tree lined boundaries. She wondered how many trees had been harvested to make way for these over priced homes. And then it occurred to her why she was depressed. They were stuck in the middle of a *Catch 22* scenario. The forest industry was hurting. Which meant there were fewer trees. Fewer jobs. Building was at a stand-still. People were leaving the area.

How could McCormick Contractors possibly survive?

Ed turned into their long gravel driveway. Bethum spotted them and bounced across the leaf covered yard to meet them. His long bushy tail swept leaves aside. Brandi dropped her rake and waved. Ed parked in front of the garage and was out of the van before Valerie touched her doorknob. She watched him head toward the house, then opened her door and climbed out.

While she took a moment to scratch Bethum's ear, Brandi, full of her usual antics, threw the back of her hand to her forehead, imitated a faint, and fell backward into a large pile of leaves. Valerie grinned and rolled her eyes. Brandi jumped up, crossed the lawn, and ran circles around her. Bethum barked. His tail, wagging ferociously, smacked Valerie behind her knee, almost knocking her to the ground.

She laughed. "Goodness, stop--Both of you. You're making me dizzy."

"Ma, could you drive me to the store?"

"Money to burn?" Valerie walked toward the back door.

Brandi closed in fast. "I made a bet with Christine. She lost and I've got a Toonie." She pulled the two dollar coin from her pocket and showed her mother.

"I knew it, I'm raising a hustler." She opened the back door and let Brandi go first. "What was the bet?"

"You know that cop car--"

"Police car."

"Right. Police car. Anyways, you know that police car what goes--"

"That goes."

"Ah, Ma."

Valerie took off her coat and hung it on the hook above the shoe rack in their mudroom. She smiled at Christine, standing beside her father at the kitchen counter, then turned back to Brandi. "I'm sorry, go on."

"Anyway, that po--lice car I seen go by our house all the time, I bet prissy Chrissy it'd go by around 10:30 this morning and again around 1:30 this afternoon. Well, I was right, and she had to pay me." She pulled the coin from her pocket and waved it under Christine's nose.

"You are such a--"

"Christine." Valerie gave her daughter a weary look. She took the coffee Ed offered and leaned back against the counter. He picked up his mug and walked out of the room. As usual, he was too preoccupied to enjoy the pleasure of such wonderful and different daughters.

Valerie grinned at her youngest. "Why don't you put that money in the bank, and next time your sister accepts another bet, you can both go to town and buy me something special. Considering I've asked on numerous occasions, Christine, that you not encourage this sort of thing."

"I wasn't, but she kept bugging me."

"Yes, I'm sure she did. But that's my point. You're seventeen, now. It's time you stopped being influenced by a twelve-year-old. Do me a favour and don't bet again. Actually, that's an order," she said, putting on her serious face. "Understood? I mean both of you."

"Sure, Ma," Brandi said, distracted by something outside the kitchen window.

"Yes, Mother." Christine glanced at Valerie's empty arms. "Did you get my skin cleanser?"

Valerie pulled a small paper bag out of her pocket.

"Ma?" Brandi faced the kitchen window and looked out at the front yard.

Before Valerie could answer, Christine grabbed the bag out of her hand, and kissed her cheek. "Mother, you're a lifesaver."

"Mum!" Brandi repeated.

Valerie nodded at Christine, aware of the change in Brandi's voice. "What is it, Peanuts?"

"Two cop cars are here." Brandi looked back at her with an expression Valerie seldom saw in her baby's face. Panic. "Nobody died, right?"

CHAPTER 6

Valerie maneuvered past Christine in time to see a RCMP cruiser with two Mounties park in front of her house. A gray Buick stopped short of the rear bumper. "Christine, get your father." She turned to see Brandi staring wide eyed up at her. "Please go and clean your bedroom and don't come down until it's finished."

"But Ma?" Brandi pointed toward the window. "Uncle Aidan's here."

Valerie looked over her shoulder and saw Aidan's car come to a stop behind the Buick. What the heck.

"Brandi--go to your room."

"But Ma--I didn't do nothing."

"Go."

Brandi pouted for a second then about-faced and marched out of the room.

Valerie listened to Ed's footsteps in the foyer. The front door opened, and she heard muffled voices. She glanced up and saw Megan standing in the kitchen doorway, her emerald green eyes filled with adult concern.

"They're asking for you, Mum." Megan stepped closer. "I think it's about Seattle."

The day after arriving home, she had told Megan a condensed version of what happened. Next year Megan would attend the Northern University of BC. She had to know what kind of world was out there.

...blood exploded out the back of the younger man's head....

"You okay, Mum?"

Valerie blinked. The buzzing in her ears stopped. "Where's Uncle Aidan?"

"He's talking to the cop outside."

"Let me know when he comes inside."

"Hi?" Aidan said, appearing next to Megan.

Valerie couldn't seem to move from her spot at the window. "What's going on?" she whispered.

"I got a head's up from a buddy of mine that these guys had flown in. Thought you might like some company."

Valerie nodded. Though Aidan wasn't a lawyer, and no longer a cop, and he didn't represent the government, he still knew a hell of a lot more about the ramifications of being a witness for the Americans than she ever would.

"I'll be in my room if you need me," Megan said and left.

Aidan stepped inside the kitchen and lowered his voice, "It'll be okay, sis. Come and see what they want. Then we'll talk."

Valerie wiped her palms down the side of her slacks and went into the living room. Ed, his face set in a deep frown, stood next to the fireplace, making no conversation with the men seated before him. Her unexpected guests stood when she entered and remained silent until Assistant Special Agent Vamozzi spoke. He reintroduced himself and State's Attorney Paul Rostov.

Valerie introduced her brother and her husband.

Once again, Vamozzi's voice claimed her attention and her trust. "We're here to ask for your assistance."

"Agent Vamozzi," she stuttered. "Can I get you gentlemen something to drink? Tea? Coffee?" She was stalling, and she wasn't sure why.

"This isn't a tea party, Val" Ed snapped. "Just tell them what we've already decided."

Valerie sat down on the wing chair behind her and glared at Ed. "What do you mean: We decided?" she said, her tone icy. "We didn't discuss anything. Remember?"

Ed turned aside and leaned his elbow on the mantel. Aidan sat down in the chair across from Vamozzi and Rostov and smiled cordially.

Valerie's hands shook.

The awkward silence seemed too much for Rostov. "Tea's not necessary. We won't be here that long."

"What Mr. Rostov is trying to say is we're sorry to have bothered you at your home, Mrs. McCormick, Mr. McCormick," Vamozzi said.

"Yes, of course," Rostov said, relaxing his shoulders. "There wasn't time to call first. I apologize. "

Valerie nodded unsure what to add to that. It took a moment to realize Vamozzi was staring at the Robert Bateman painting on the wall behind her.

"How are you, Mr. Vamozzi?" she asked.

He blinked and looked at her. "Fine. And you?"

"Okay." The acid in her stomach burned.

"Can we get on with this," Ed said, agitated.

Rostov looked relieved to comply. "Mrs. McCormick?" He pulled five photographs from his briefcase and handed them to her. "Which one of these men shot the agents in Seattle?"

She took the prints from him while trying to steady her hands. It wasn't until she examined the third photograph that she remembered his smile. From a distance, she hadn't noticed the hard black eyes. They didn't light up like the rest of his face. Up close, his cold expression made her tremble. She held up the photo. This was real; it hadn't been a bad dream.

"Mrs. McCormick?"

"This one." She stretched out her arm and passed the print to her brother.

"You saw this man execute two FBI agents?"

Valerie's throat trembled. "Yes."

Rostov leaned forward. "Will you testify?"

"Who is this guy?" Aidan interrupted. He handed the photograph to Ed.

"Miguel DeOlmos," Rostov said, his eyes on Valerie. "He was picked up five days ago by fluke. His driver was stopped because the Limo's signal light was burned out. We had DeOlmos in a holding cell pending a preliminary hearing."

"On what charges?" Aidan asked.

Rostov cleared his throat. "That isn't relevant--"

"Miguel DeOlmos was indicted for the murders of five Customs officials in Florida. The FBI there had flimsy evidence and no eyewitness."

"Why didn't you tell me this while I was in Seattle?" Valerie asked.

"I didn't have the authority. I still don't." Vamozzi glanced at Rostov. "We're here because we need your help. You're our only hope."

"Is there more to this case than you're saying?" Aidan asked Rostov.

"I'm not at liberty--"

"Agent Vamozzi?" Aidan said.

Vamozzi was studying the Robert Bateman painting above the mantel. A majestic golden eagle, its eyes targeting an unknown prey, its wings spread open in a downward thrust, seemed to elicit a disturbed reaction. Valerie wondered what Vamozzi saw. The freedom or the hunt?

Vamozzi frowned. "Nothing spoken here will leave this room?"

Ed rolled his eyes. Aidan nodded.

Vamozzi continued. "Mrs. McCormick, the two agents you saw murdered, on a tip from an informer, set up a meet with what they assumed was an arms dealer. They didn't know he was Miguel DeOlmos."

"You're kidding," Aidan said.

"It happens," Vamozzi answered with sadness in his voice that tugged at Valerie's heart strings. "Several months earlier, two undercover agents had infiltrated DeOlmos's Cartel. One of them was able to report that a large shipment of cocaine was on the way to Miami on a freighter returning from Cartagena, Colombia. Miami agents, along with DEA, waited in Miami, but the freighter never showed.

"Unaware of our investigation, five Custom officials seized the boat at Key West. They were all killed.

"Jeremy Gordon, one of DeOlmos's men, was caught. The rest escaped."

"DeOlmos gets around. How do you know it was him in Key West?" Aidan asked.

"Gordon agreed to testify."

"Why do you need Val?" Ed asked.

Rostov shot Vamozzi a disgusted look and shook his head. Vamozzi continued. "Gordon is dead."

"Where?" Aidan asked.

"New York."

"Do you understand, Val, why I've always said we should mind our own business?" Ed glared at his unwanted guests. "You people are trying to cover up your mistakes. I'd like to remind you this isn't the States, this is my house, and you have no authority here."

"For heaven's sake, Ed." Valerie felt the heat rush to her cheeks. Why couldn't he just shut up?

"Ed has a point." Aidan faced Vamozzi. "You weren't successful at protecting your last witness."

"He declined our offer."

"Arrest the other two from the cabin cruiser," Valerie said. "Maybe they'll testify against him?"

"They've disappeared."

"Where is DeOlmos?" Aidan asked.

"Early this morning he was arrested--"

"In New York?" Aidan added.

"Yes."

"For conspiracy of murdering your eyewitness. What was his name ... Gordon?"

"When the detectives identified themselves, DeOlmos held out his hands and looked bored. He knows we don't have a case. He thinks the legal system is a joke. They can only hold him for 24 hours. If we don't come up with new evidence quickly, your government will step in."

Aidan glared at him. "Why would our government--"

"He was born in Toronto."

The silence seemed unnatural. Valerie looked at her brother. He glared at Vamozzi with his mouth clamped shut. "Does Washington State have the death penalty?" she asked Rostov.

"Yes."

"Which means if he gets back to Canada, you'll be fighting extradition laws for the next five years," Aidan said.

"I'm not a gambler." Rostov sighed. "But I'd bet even longer."

Aidan leaned forward in his chair. "Why are you telling us this? I wouldn't think it's FBI policy to share such elaborate information."

"It isn't," Vamozzi answered. "The truth is, Mr. Roth, we're desperate. And that really is the truth."

"At least you know what this Mr. DeOlmos looks like." The glances she got back frightened her; nothing was solved by knowing DeOlmos's identity. "I need time to discuss this with my family," Valerie added.

"What's to discuss?" Ed snorted.

She looked at Agent Vamozzi and was instantly trapped by the compassion in his eyes. For that brief moment, it felt as if they were the only two people in the room.

"Please believe me; we'll do everything in our power to protect you and your family."

She wanted to believe him. But in effect, he was telling her if she testified her family would need protection. Protection. Valerie remembered Christine and Brandi's bet. The police had been driving by her house for the past few days. Did that mean they were already under some type of protection? If she testified, would they park outside her door? Would they drive the girls to and from school? What about the weekends? Would they escort Christine to dances? Would they join Megan in the Prince George Public Library twice during the week and on Saturdays? Valerie grasped her hands together to hide their shaking. How could she put her children through that? An image of her father sprang to mind.

Go away, dad.

"As long as you understand," Rostov said. "Legally, you don't have to testify. However, without your testimony, he'll walk. Who knows how many more people he'll kill."

Rostov signalled to Vamozzi then stood. He grabbed a business card from his pocket, scribbled something on the back, and handed it to her.

"We'll be at the Prince George Airport until six tonight. This is a secured number where you can reach me, but no later than six. After that, you can call me at home. Like I said before, Mrs. McCormick, by nine o'clock tomorrow morning Miguel DeOlmos will be back on the streets."

Valerie took his card and looked out the front window. A strong breeze whipped through the front yard and scattered the leaves Brandi had raked earlier. Crisp, orange, deadness, rolled, skipped, and twirled, an inflated sense of their own free will.

CHAPTER 7

Valerie leaned over the bathroom sink, closed her eyes, and splashed water on her face, then imagined the water evaporating as it carried away her heat. She splashed again, afraid to look up. This was the decisive moment. She should have been prepared, but she wasn't. She had wanted to pretend, but pretending was the same as lying.

She'd known instantly, after witnessing their deaths, that her life would never be the same again.

Why hadn't she accepted that?

Because Ed made it easy for her to ignore it all? "We'll forget it happened," he had said.

No. It wasn't his fault. She knew better.

She raised her head and patted her face dry, avoiding her image in the mirror. She couldn't look. She'd either see a stupid woman or discover she wasn't even strong enough to cast a reflection.

A decision?

What choice did she have? How could she risk her daughters' lives by doing the right thing?

But now how could she ensure their safety and retain a clear conscience?

Valerie left the bathroom and went downstairs to the kitchen. She took a seat opposite her husband sitting alone at the kitchen table. "Where are Aidan and the girls?"

"Aidan's outside talking to the Mounties. The girls are upstairs. I told them we had to talk, and I'd call them when we're finished."

"Call them now."

Ed shook his head. With all the will she could summon, Valerie stared at him until he rolled his eyes, stood, and went to the bottom of the stairs.

"Have you decided?" Aidan asked, coming in through the back door. He took a seat opposite her.

"I need to talk to my girls."

"Little sis, I--"

She reached across the table for his hand. "Do you think Vamozzi looks like Dad?"

Aidan gave her a sad smile. "I was wondering if you'd noticed."

Brandi rushed into the room and flung her arms around his neck. "Hi, Uncle Aidan."

"Hi, Peanuts, how you doing?"

"My room's clean," she said, rolling her eyes at her mother. "How come there's still a cop--police car in our driveway?"

Ed took his seat at the kitchen table and motioned for his girls to sit down. "We'll explain in a minute. First, your mother has something to say."

Everyone looked at Valerie.

"Megan, pass me the teapot, please." She swept the hair off Brandi's face. "I saw a crime committed when I was in Seattle. Those men who were here earlier want me to go to the United States and tell a jury what I saw."

"Cool," Brandi said. "Did some dude blow somebody away?"

Aidan coughed then grabbed his mug and took a few quick sips.

"Yes, Peanuts," Valerie said.

"Mother, are you serious?" Christine asked.

"Very."

Megan filled her mother's teacup. "Are you going?"

"That's what I want to talk about. I need you to understand that things may change around here. Even if I don't testify, what I saw could put us all at risk."

Brandi burst out, "Was there blood and guts all over the ...?" She stopped, silenced by the look Valerie gave her. "I think you gotta. I think the bad guy's gotta go to the slammer, so he don't hurt nobody else."

Valerie cringed over Brandi's poor grammar.

"Peanuts? Have you been watching reruns of those Humphrey Bogart movies again?" Aidan laughed.

"Uncle Aidan, you shouldn't laugh 'cause you could learn a whole bunch from him. Even for an old guy, he's pretty tough."

"Hmm," he replied, attempting a serious tone.

"Does he always get the bad guy?" Valerie asked.

"Yep, he does, Ma. Bad guys always get caught cause good guys like you tell the truth."

Good guys like her? Valerie blinked back a tear. Brandi's innocence and the world as she saw it never seemed more precious. She turned to Christine.

Christine tried not to bite the fingernail she had propped in her mouth.

Ed made the decision for her and pulled her hand away.

"You haven't made up your mind, have you?" She folded her hands in her lap. "Mother, I know you've always told us we have to look out for one another. But, does that mean people in the United States?"

"It means everyone."

"Sometimes on TV the witness gets threatened. Sometimes they even get hurt. Could that happen to you?"

"There's that chance, honey. But I can't let that influence my decision. You girls are what matter to me."

"Exactly my point," Ed snapped. "We don't know what that man's capable of."

"You mean he could hurt one of us?" Christine said, her voice panicky. "Geez, I don't know."

"Mum," Megan said. "Whatever you decide to do, I know it'll be the right decision. I have faith in you."

"Me, too," Brandi said.

"Yes, Mother. Whatever you decide," Christine said.

Valerie loved her daughters so much. She looked at Aidan. "You're awful quiet."

"I was thinking men like that eventually make a mistake and get caught. You're not responsible if he hurts someone else. Who's to say he hasn't already."

"All the more reason why he should be put away," Valerie said.

"You've made up your mind," Ed said. "I thought this was a family decision?"

"If you'd seen what I saw. The way he pulled out his gun and with no hesitation--"

"Val! Let's spare the kids the details, huh!"

"Dad, it's all right, we're not babies," Megan said.

"Ed, I can't live with myself if I don't do this. If he gets away with it this time, I'll always wonder who else he's killed."

"For God's sake, we live in Prince George. You'll never see him again. We'll never hear anything. Damn. I knew I shouldn't have allowed you to go on that trip."

"I don't recall asking for permission."

She tipped her head querulously while an unfamiliar sensation wrapped itself around her stomach and flamed up through her solar plexus. She took a quick sip of tea and studied him. What she saw dulled her reaction. Deep planed edges outlined a rugged face. Green eyes, overshadowed by thick frowning eyebrows, blinked rapidly. Valerie's face muscles relaxed; Ed was frightened for her; he didn't mean to sound like a macho jerk.

"I'm sorry you don't understand. But I'm going to testify."

"Aidan. She's your sister. You talk to her. She never listens to me. I'm just the one who pays the bills around here."

"Oh Dad." Megan lowered her eyes.

Aidan leaned his head in his hand. "I know what I'd do. But that's me, not my kid sister. The night you called, I was never so scared in my life. It was everything I could do to stop myself from flying down to Seattle. I feel the same as you do, Ed." A resigning sigh escaped him, and he looked at her. "If you decide to go, I think Ed and I should go with you. But I have to tell you, little sis, I hope you decide not to."

He stretched out his arm and cupped his hand over hers. "Even if he's convicted, there's no guarantee he'll face the death penalty. DeOlmos could serve only a few years. Political influence and million dollar lawyers make parole easy. Guys like that get revenge. I'm afraid for you. Men like him are willing to do anything."

"What if I don't testify?" She pulled her hand away. "And he decides I'm still a liability?"

"We always said it would be fun to live in the wilderness."

Aidan's attempt at humour failed. No one laughed. Not even Brandi.

Interlocking his fingers, Ed rubbed his palms together. "What time is it?"

Megan leaned back and, straining her neck, peeked at the digital clock on the stove. "4:45, or quarter to five if you're left-handed." She smiled. Then stopped, when she met her father's gaze.

Annoyed with herself, Valerie stared at Ed. She had forgotten to take something out for supper. The thought of money burst in amongst the absurd images in her brain. A few hours ago, she had promised herself there would be no more unnecessary spending. Money. It was always money. Valerie's hand slipped into the pocket of her sweater and touched the card.

She pushed away from the table. "I'll be right back."

She took two steps at a time. Once in her bedroom, she shut the door and dialled the number. Agent Vamozzi had a disturbing paternal effect on her, so she was glad it was Rostov who answered.

"I haven't made a decision yet, but I've got some questions," Valerie said.

"Yes."

"Does the defence know who I am?"

"No."

"If I testify, would they be told my name before the trial?"

An awkward second passed before Rostov spoke. "There will be a preliminary hearing to determine whether we have enough evidence. We'll instruct the judge and the defence that there is an eyewitness, but we have every legal right to withhold your name at that time. I'm not going to lie to you. If we can find Reynaldo Martinez and Lope Ramirez, the two men who were with DeOlmos, we might be able to deal. Bring you in later as a discovery witness. If not, the defence has the right to know who you are so they can determine what line of questioning to use. I can hold back your name until the day before you testify.... Mrs. McCormick?"

She doubled over on the bed, cupped the phone to her ear, and prayed silently.

"We will do everything to ensure your safety."

"My husband and my brother would like to accompany me, is that all right?"

"Of course."

Valerie tried to think of a way to broach the next subject. No matter how she put it, she'd feared she was about to sound pathetic. "We're not Americans. How can you protect my family?"

"We've been in contact with the Canadian Justice Department. We've been given a free rein as far as your protection is concerned. Our two countries will work together on this, Mrs. McCormick. You have to believe that."

"I'm trying. Tell me I won't regret this, but yes, I will testify. I need to know something, though. Why did he kill ...? I can't remember their names?" she said, ashamed.

"Special Agents Charles Onston and Gregory Vanderhal."

"He killed them himself, because ...?"

"I don't follow."

"Mr. Rostov, he went to an old wharf and killed them himself. Why? Wouldn't someone with his power have someone else do it?"

"Mrs. McCormick, I can't know why a criminal chooses to--"

"It's because he enjoys killing?"

Silence.

"Isn't that it, Mr. Rostov? DeOlmos kill those agents because he enjoys it? He killed the witness, too, Mr. Gordon? Because he likes to kill?"

"Yes, Mrs. McCormick. Anything else?"

Valerie cleared her throat and tried to sound brave. "He doesn't know who I am or where I live. Right?"

Rostov cleared his throat twice, a noise that sounded like gears grinding. "No."

CHAPTER 8

Nineteen hundred and ninety-six arrived during a record snowfall.

Valerie looked out the window over the kitchen sink and watched Brandi and Megan making angels in the snow out front. Their cheeks were red and their smiles clearly visible even at this distance. They climbed carefully out from the patterned cherubs to find fresh snow. They were safe and happy, and she knew she was right to pretend.

Brandi jumped up, ran a few feet away, and flopped backward to the ground. Her giggles sang on the wind, and Valerie laughed with her. She could still remember the first time Aidan had shown her how to make angels in the snow. That innocent act of lying on soft white snow with the clear sky overhead, made everything seem right with her world. That little girl with her big brother and parents nearby had felt very secure.

Megan, her red bob barely visible under the fluffy whiteness, caught sight of her mother and waved. Valerie smiled and waved back. Megan and Brandi gestured for her to come outside. She laughed and shook her head. Then spun around. Her father's presence was so powerful she could smell him; the way he smelled when they had been outside in the winter, and he would grab her and wrestle her to the ground.

No one was there. Her quiet blue kitchen was empty. Yet his presence ... she could feel it. Warm. Comforting. The way she used to lean on him when she was tired, ill, or sad. The way he used to explain why some people hurt others. He taught her and Aidan that dying was a natural part of life. But not everyone had a conscience. Sometimes things happened that hardened hearts against empathy and compassion.

She remembered when she was ten, one morning he told her that he and her mum were attending the funeral of a mother and two small children; victims of a drunken driver.

Valerie insisted on going. Begged even.

"Why?" her father had asked.

"I'm not sure exactly."

He studied her for a long time before he said, "Okay."

That funeral had been different. Maybe because she wasn't caught up in her own loss and personal grief, she remembered the scene better than any other funeral she ever attended. She had sat between her parents, leaning against her father, her mother grasping her hand. The giant of a man in front of her blocked most of her view, but when she stood to let someone in the pew, she saw the front of the church. A large white coffin sat below the altar ... with two tiny coffins on either side. Years later, Valerie realized the significance of that decision. She had wanted to witness firsthand the grieving of strangers. She needed to know that grief was universal; no one escaped it.

Valerie shredded two large carrots and threw them into the pot. The woman's youngest would have been thirty had she lived.

The timer on the stove buzzed; Valerie grabbed a mitt and pulled the tea biscuits, a Saturday baking ritual, from the oven. She arranged them on a towel over the counter top, then leaned over and inhaled the pleasant aroma. She knew she had made the right decision; no matter what Ed said, she'd testify.

A hand reached around her and snatched a biscuit.

"I saw that," Valerie teased.

"Is the soup ready?" Christine asked. She peered through the kitchen window and asked, "What are those two geeks doing? Are you sure somebody didn't make a mistake and I'm the one who's ten months older than Megan and six years older than the brat?"

"They're just having fun. Something you should do more often."

"I have fun. I just try to restrict it to something mature. Look at Megan, can you believe she'll be nineteen soon?"

"Not for eight months, thank you very much. I'd be out there with them if I wasn't a little under the weather."

"You're not feeling well?" Christine touched her mother's forehead. "Yecch! Are you ever warm."

"Really?" Valerie touched her face. Her temperature felt normal. "What are you grinning at?"

Christine wiped the smile off her face and planted her hands on her hips. "I know why you're not well."

Certain she shouldn't, Valerie said, "Really?"

"You were up late last night working on the article for that lady's magazine, right? Yesterday you said you had a deadline. You didn't get enough sleep. Go lie down, and I'll put these away." Christine reached for another biscuit.

Valerie smacked her daughter's hand affectionately. "As if." She laughed.

Christine giggled. "No really, I don't mind."

The telephone rang.

Valerie answered. "Hel--lo."

"Mrs. McCormick?"

The 'yes' barely escaped her throat. She regretted the sound of her voice, turned away from Christine, and leaned over the counter. A familiar sensation overtook her. The joy she'd experienced moments ago was replaced with dread.

"It's Paul Rostov. Hope this isn't a bad time."

"No." She waved goodbye to Christine, an indication she needed privacy. "I didn't expect the trial to begin so soon. I thought it would take months to pick the jury."

"We obtained an early trial date. This isn't your average case."

"Were you able to find those two men I picked out of your computer?"

"No."

"But Mr. DeOlmos is still in jail?"

His tone rose. "Of course."

She didn't appreciate the sound of his voice. How was she to know what their court system was like. "When do I testify?"

"I requested a week to confer with my witnesses. My request was denied. The judge adjourned court until Monday morning."

"This Monday morning?" It was Saturday afternoon.

"Yes."

The soup boiled over. With the phone jammed against her shoulder, Valerie turned off the burner, grabbed a towel, and pulled the pot to one side, scalding herself in the process. She flinched, wet a cloth under cold water, and pressed it to her arm. She didn't know which was worse, her flesh burning or the queasiness in her stomach. "Where are you calling from?"

"My office. Why?"

"I thought you might be here in Prince George."

"I know you must feel as if I'm invading your privacy, but I'm only doing my job."

"Does he know my name?"

"Yes, but that's all he knows."

That's supposed to be reassuring? "What happens now?"

"We'll send a plane for you Monday morning. You'll be taken to a hangar and will have an armed escort to the courtroom. Once there, you'll be placed in a secured room with maximum protection until you're called to testify. Afterward, you'll be flown home."

"My brother will be with me."

"Of course and your husband?"

Valerie saw Brandi help Megan lift the upper torso onto the base of the snowman. She had wanted Ed to go with her to the States, but when he refused to leave the girls, she felt ashamed. She hadn't considered they'd be left alone.

"Mrs. McCormick?"

"Yes." She watched her daughters.

"Mr. McCormick will be coming with you?"

"No. He's staying at home with our girls." She dropped the cloth and laid her palm flat against the cold window. She missed those flowery designs, frost etched on the windowpanes of her childhood. But modern conveniences, such as thick insulation, storm windows, and double paned glass, wouldn't allow for such artistry.

What a shame.

"When should I be ready?"

"A car will pick you up at six a.m."

Brandi centered a carrot below the snowman's black marble eyes. Megan set an old hat on top and tied a red scarf around his neck. "I'll be ready."

"Goodbye, Mrs. McCormick."

Brandi used small stones to make a mouth. A smile.

"Goodbye Mrs. McCormick."

She hung up at the mention of her name. His apprehension wasn't necessary; she knew what she had to do. "I wonder what the weather's like?"

"All you have to do is look out the window, and it's pretty obvious." Ed closed the back door behind him.

"Hi. I didn't hear you drive in?"

"That's because I was driving the Batmobile."

"Batmobile?"

Ed laughed. "Jimmy brought his son today, and the kid thinks I look like Batman." He removed his coveralls and stepped into the kitchen. "I saw you on the phone when I drove in. Anyone important?" He stuck his nose over the soup. "It wasn't another bill collector?" He stuffed a tea biscuit into his mouth.

"It was Mr. Rostov."

"Who?" Ed mumbled, chewing.

"The American--"

"Prosecutor?" Ed's face turned white. He pulled up a chair and sat down at the table, his back to her. "You have to go?"

"Yes. Monday morning. With any luck, I'll be home the same night."

Ed shook his head. "God, you're naive."

"What's that suppose to mean?"

"Just what I said."

Valerie ran her hands under cold water and dried them on the tea towel. "It's really great to have your support. I must say. I really feel like you're right there with me, all the way. Thank you so very, very, much!"

Ed pushed himself away from the table and stood. He turned and glared at her. "What the hell's wrong with you? Ever since you came back from Seattle, you've been acting weird. I think you better get your act together, because I'm not putting up with too much more of this shit." He stormed past and left the room.

And in the beat of a moment, she was alone.

Valerie closed her eyes, took a deep breath, and realized that was okay. Better to be alone than lost.

CHAPTER 9

Valerie, Aidan, and their armed escorts entered the courthouse in Olympia and went directly to the law library. It was an attractive room. Old and prestigious, it held the fragrance of cherry and maple and oak woods. Natural light from seven tall windows reflected off the parquet floor, enriching the assortment of area rugs. Two leather sofas faced each other in the center of the room with a handcrafted desk stationed behind each sofa. Four French crystal standing lamps threw soft light down the sofas and across the mahogany desk tops, and ceiling-to-floor bookshelves ran the complete length of the inside wall.

Valerie glanced at Aidan. He had his head stuck in some legal book while she could barely contain herself. Not sure why she bothered, she stood and paced along the bookshelves, the repository of knowledge she wished she were privy to. Instead, not able to ascertain anything except how physically ill she felt, she paced, fingertips grazing dustless leather bindings and gold print. Her shoulders slightly hunched, she pressed the palm of one hand against the knot in her stomach then turned abruptly and paced back until she reached the cornice window. Almost at once, one of the four agents in the room politely requested she sit down. But the deep chamois sofa was cold against the material of her suit and reeked strongly of leather. Unconcerned, he took a step forward and screened her from the view outside. Valerie looked up at the stone face, then sat down opposite her brother. The incessant flicking of Aidan's pen became an added irritation. She'd never seen her brother this nervous.

She reached across and placed a hand over his. "Please Aidan, you're driving me crazy."

"Sorry. Bad habit." He tucked the pen inside his breast pocket. "Don't worry, they'll call you soon."

Out of the corner of her eye, one of the large oak doors opened. Her chest pounded.

But they made no motion to summon her.

The unknown disturbed her. If only they'd allowed her one peek into the courtroom. Just enough to get a sense of the place. Where she would walk, where DeOlmos would be sitting, the number of spectators. Any visual aids would help steady her now. Rostov had apologized about that, saying if she'd lived closer, they would have taken the time to do a run-through inside the courtroom. Instead, they'd just bluff their way through.

Was that one more jab at her for taking so long to agree to testify?

Aidan scanned through one of the legal books while chewing on his lower lip. For a moment, she regretted him being there. His nervousness was contagious. She tore her eyes away and caught sight of a new arrival at the door. He handed something to one of the agents. Valerie didn't notice what it was because she couldn't take her eyes off the pistol snug inside his holster. When he shielded the weapon with his jacket, she switched to his face and caught him studying her. For a brief moment, their eyes locked. Then just as quickly, he turned to the agent beside him. Whatever he said caused a reaction; the young man shook his head and he, too, glanced at her.

The hair on the back of Valerie's neck stood up.

The older man's stern face, set brows, gave the impression of authority. He was maybe fifty. Not a large man yet built like a quarterback. Shoulders broad and strong. He stood approximately five-nine with blonde hair receding and a rugged complexion. His face intrigued her. Granted there was a certain male magnetism, but he was not handsome, nor did he look like a policeman. He pulled something out of his pocket, unwrapped it, and popped it in his mouth.

Valerie stared at the bulge where his gun was.

She hated guns.

"Excuse me," Valerie said to the agent nearby.

He approached and bent forward. "Yes, ma'am."

"The men at the door, the older one, who is he?" She inclined her head toward the door.

"The boss," he said and returned to his post.

Valerie slumped back against the sofa. That was the stupidest answer she'd ever heard.

Or was it?

She glanced back at the man. Once again, deep relentless eyes looked right through her. Valerie felt the heat rush to her face. She'd forgotten to check her imagination at the door.

Why shouldn't the boss look dangerous? Maybe that was a good sign. Matched opponents? DeOlmos versus 'the boss.'

Her attention diverted. The huge doors opened again. The boss stepped aside, said something, and four more agents swarmed into the room. Only these men were dressed in blue windbreakers, bullet-proof vests, and held automatic rifles.

"Aidan!" Valerie snapped, jumping to her feet.

He was already on his feet, gawking at the armed agents surrounding them. "What the hell!"

Rostov and Agent Vamozzi came in. The agents circled the room. They faced the windows and froze like statues.

Aidan moved in front of Valerie like a shield. Valerie's heart banged against her chest while her mind fought for control.

It's okay. It's okay. It's okay!

Rostov set his briefcase on one of the desks and avoided her eyes. An uncomfortable quietness fell over the room. Valerie glanced toward the door; 'the boss' was gone. Agents didn't budge from the windows.

"Mrs. McCormick ...?"

"What?"

"Unfortunately ... you won't be testifying today."

Aidan put a protective arm across Valerie. "What's happened?"

Agent Vamozzi ignored him. "Mrs. McCormick, everything will be done to ensure your safety."

"I don't understand," she said.

"What happened?" Aidan demanded.

Rostov put his hand into his pant pocket. He cleared his throat. "The defendant ... escaped."

"You mean you didn't have him in leg irons?" Aidan said, outraged.

Valerie pressed a hand to her heart. Air fought to get into her collapsing lungs. She sucked for air and stared at Rostov and Vamozzi, who simultaneously looked away.

"Look!" Rostov stammered. "I got enough personal problems without--" He shut his mouth. Vamozzi gave him a disgusted look.

Valerie moved from behind Aidan and took shallow breaths. She looked at Rostov. "You could take my testimony, then I could go home. I mean, couldn't I testify in front of a grand jury or something?"

"Valerie, don't you get it?"

"Yes!" she said, while the room spun. "Aidan, don't make matters worse."

"Worse? For Pete's sake Valerie, where do you think DeOlmos is heading? Back to Canada. Do you know what happens if he gets there? It'll take years before he's extradited to the States. If they ever find him. Besides, he knows who you are. His lawyer was given your name, address, occupation, next-of-kin, maybe even your frigging shoe size this morning. If you're killed, there's no frigging case."

Valerie stared hard at Rostov. "DeOlmos know I'm here?"

He didn't answer. Instead, his fingers brushed his thick eyebrows.

"He knows I'm Canadian?"

Rostov glanced at Agent Vamozzi, who showed little sympathy.

"He knows where I live?" Valerie asked, her voice rising.

Rostov muttered something, looked back at Vamozzi, while his fingers lifted and straightened his tie one too many times. "Mrs. McCormick--"

"We'll relocate you," Vamozzi interrupted, "to a safe house until DeOlmos is apprehended."

Aidan took a deep breath and flopped down into a chair. "I can't believe this."

Vamozzi gave him a look that showed the pain he felt at losing a man responsible for murdering two of his men. A pain that was without words.

Aidan's face softened. "I'm sorry about your men, but my concern is for my sister. She's ...." His voice trailed off while his chin sank to his chest.

"I want to go home," Valerie said.

"It's not safe." Rostov glared. "We can't protect you if you return to Canada."

"Mr. Rostov, by not answering my questions, you just admitted it's possible DeOlmos knows where I live. What you're going to do now is contact the Justice Department in Canada and have my family put under protection. I came down here in good faith. You owe me. If--when you catch him, give me a call, and we'll talk. That's all I can do."

"Mrs. McCormick, you can't walk--"

"Yes, I can." And not fast enough. She glanced at the closest armed agent.

Rostov shook his head, grabbed his briefcase, and steered Vamozzi toward the door, whispering something. Before leaving, he glanced back at her.

No, he did not look happy. Valerie didn't care. She watched Vamozzi walk back toward her.

He stopped a few feet away. "Are you sure about this?"

"Yes."

"Valerie?" Aidan said. "Maybe--"

"No." She tried to instil confidence through her voice. "I've got to go home to my girls."

"I'll have the jet prepped." Vamozzi turned to leave.

"Agent Vamozzi?" He stopped and faced her. At that precise moment, he may have looked like her father, but he didn't look like a friend. She cleared her throat. "During his escape ... did anyone ... get hurt?"

His stare was so intense Valerie wanted to look away. But her desire wasn't a strong enough persuasion. Vamozzi nodded then turned and crossed the room toward the nearest agent.

* * *

Miguel watched his first Lieutenant David Philips walk through his favourite Mexican bar, past the beautiful *señoritas*, the plates full of nachos and salsa and mouth-watering peppers, and move down the dark hallway toward Miguel. They embraced, slapped each other on the backs, then stepped back into the smoke filled office.

"*¿Amigo, que tal?*" Miguel DeOlmos returned to his desk and sat down. "*Me da gusto verle.*"

"I'm happy to see you, too." He sat opposite Miguel's desk. "I've got good news." Philips pulled a five by seven envelope from inside his trench coat.

DeOlmos yelled for drinks and food then sat down with his expected guest. "*Dígame?*"

"Sergeant Jackson came through. After the usual persuasion, that is. Your man was right about the name printed on her bag. Jackson traced her to a town in central British Columbia called Prince George." He laid a photograph on the desk.

DeOlmos smiled and looked down at the picture of Valerie McCormick. "Waiting?"

"Yes. Waiting and unprotected. You're pleased?"

DeOlmos picked up the photograph. "*Si, amigo. Estoy muy feliz. Pero,*" he said, his smile fading, "it's a shame. She is quite lovely."

Philips grunted. "Maybe so, but she has to die."

"Of course." DeOlmos glanced a moment longer at the picture.

CHAPTER 10

Valerie threw the folders against the wall. She looked to see Aidan's response. He didn't lift his head from the file he was reading at the desk across from hers. His finger incessantly clicking at his pen was the only noise in the office.

Valerie bent over the cabinet in her husband's office. Ten torturous weeks had passed since DeOlmos' escape, and her mood swings were worse. She pulled three more accounts payable folders and stacked them with the others on her desk. The stack toppled but blended with the new décor of disarray. Mess surrounded her. She couldn't concentrate on the daily routine of their dying business. Payday was a nightmare. To pay employees, they didn't pay bills. Overdue accounts filled the cabinet. In the past two days, she had found past due bills from vendors she hadn't known existed. Yet Ed expected her to keep on top of things. She looked around the office and felt the green walls closing in on her.

Why was she still alive? Despite assurances from Paul Rostov, Valerie knew DeOlmos waited. It was only a matter of time.

Valerie sensed the presence of a madness that wanted desperately to consume her. Their business was falling apart; they might lose the house. And DeOlmos, oh Lord, how that name could instil instant tremors, was out there somewhere. Would her luck run out?

Luck? Luck had nothing to do with it. Faith. It was faith that got her away from Lake Union. Faith that kept her alive before the trial. Faith that woke with her every morning.

She looked at the ceiling and wondered when it would come crashing down. Was she fooling herself? Had she misinterpreted faith for fate? Meanwhile, she'd signed those loan papers knowing it was a mistake. Scanning the bank's reconciliation forms proved that.

She was just scared. Stuck in the office was the last place she wanted to be. She looked at the forestry poster and calendar and the puke-green walls; the place was dilapidated and unpromising. But looking a lot better than their business. She tucked loose strands of her hair back into her bun. She lowered her arms, turned back to her desk, and the strands fell back out again.

Why didn't she just cut the damn hair and get it over with?

Valerie remembered why. Normalcy. Everything was supposed to continue as if nothing was wrong. After the shock of that day in the courthouse had worn off, the family agreed life should proceed onward as normal as possible. They couldn't let DeOlmos destroy the one thing that sustained them. Faith.

Valerie opened a white envelope tucked in amongst some maps and read of the ten thousand dollar loan she wasn't aware of that Ed had taken out

"Are you okay?"

She looked at the concern on Aidan's face. The worry had aged him. She couldn't tell him about Ed. "Yes." She stood and picked up the papers.

"Do you want some help?"

"Nah," she answered, just as the phone rang. She picked it up. "McCormick Contractors." She heard a click, and the line went dead.

"Who was that?" Aidan asked.

Valerie pressed star sixty-nine. A recording reported the caller as unknown. "I don't know."

Aidan got up from his chair and walked to the huge picture window next to the front glass door. Valerie closed the cabinet drawer, crossed the room, and stood beside him. Outside, motorists moved through the intersection. Large clouds of gray exhaust settled along the pavement as if held there by an invisible force. The iced sidewalks were empty. The air turned to a haze like the stills of an unfocused photograph. She glanced at the patrol car parked a few feet from the door.

Aidan threw an arm around her shoulder and gave her an encouraging hug. "We'll just continue to be cautious, and--"

"All that matters is that my babies are safe." Valerie pulled away then returned to her desk and sat down. "What's taking Rostov so long? I try to ignore the police car parked in my driveway every night. It's hard not to notice. Even so, I wonder if I made the right decision. But I couldn't leave them." She shook her head and leaned across the desktop. "Everything spooks me. The milkman, the furnace cutting in, the ice breaking off the eaves trough."

Aidan attempted a smile, and the effort made him look more worried. "We'll get through this.. Whatever it takes ... I'll protect you."

Valerie got up, went to her brother, and hugged him as tight as she could. "Protect my girls."

* * *

SAC Canaday yelled into the telephone. "Say what! Sir."

Tomlin's voice rang through the line. "You heard what I said. I pulled your undercover Agent Angela Parker out. She's on her way to Seattle. She'll brief you when she arrives."

"Brief me on what? She was in a position to crack this case wide open, and you pulled her out. Why?"

"Michael, I'm not about to explain my actions."

Canaday leaned his face in one hand while he cradled the phone in the other. "Tell me why, sir."

"She was spotted last night. She and DeOlmos's brother, Vincente, were at the La Fuente in New York. A woman working out of the DA's office, sitting a few tables away, called out her real name as Parker made her way to the Ladies room. Our people couldn't take the chance and grabbed her in the hallway."

Canaday smothered the desire to throw his desk clock through the window. It irked him to admit he was wrong. No case was important enough to risk an agent's life.

In a quieter voice, he said, "I'm sorry, sir. I shouldn't have yelled."

"We continue as planned," Tomlin said, seemingly oblivious to Canaday's apology. "Have you heard from your other undercover agent ... Ward?"

"No."

"Then we'll take no news as good news."

Canaday swung around and faced the American flag in the corner next to the window. The pencil in his fist snapped. Parker had been in a much more favourable position than Kyle Ward. If someone had to be yanked out, why couldn't that someone have been Ward?

"Son, I'm going to forget we had this conversation," Assistant Director Tomlin said. "But you remember this, I give the orders, you listen. Agent Parker is on her way. Contact me the second you hear from Agent Ward. That's all."

Tomlin slammed down the phone, and a loud crash echoed through Canaday's brain.

Canaday placed the phone gently back into its cradle.

Two hours later, he stood at the filing cabinet when Agent Angela Parker entered the offices on the seventh floor of the Federal Building. He watched her cross the room, nodding at a few agents as she passed. She wore a dark blue suit and long raincoat. The naiveté and enthusiasm he'd first seen a year earlier was gone. Her hair was thickly coiled in dreadlocks down to her shoulders, but her eyes looked weary. As if having opened them, she saw things she'd never forget. Canaday recognized the look.

Without speaking, he led her into his office and shut the door. He sat down at his desk and picked up a long, sharpened pencil. He hoped fidgeting with the pencil would disguise his disappointment at how this case was turning out.

She looked at him with her arms hung at her sides.

"Sit down, Angela."

"Thank you, sir."

Canaday didn't have to hide anything; Parker's face showed enough emotion for the both of them. It couldn't have been easy on her, getting the assignment of a lifetime, only to have the results mount to zilch.

"I know you're disappointed," he said. "Every agent who goes under takes the chance of being made. It happens to the best."

Full sensuous lips disappeared between her teeth, then reappeared in a pout. "You wouldn't have made the same mistake, would you, sir? You would have checked to see if there was anyone in the restaurant before leaving your seat."

"My first undercover assignment, I tripped over my Uncle Danny," Canaday lied, then changed the subject. "I won't keep you long. I imagine you need to be settled in your new assignment. Have you found accommodations?"

"Arrangements were made before I left DC."

"Good." He leaned back in his swivelled chair. "Tomlin mentioned you have vital information that shouldn't wait until a written report."

"Yes, sir." She pulled out a notepad. "Until Monday night, Vincente received no contact from the cartel's council. Then at 2015, he got a call, and the next thing I knew we were on his private jet to New York. We took a suite at the Plaza and remained there all day Tuesday. At 1800, one of Miguel's Lieutenants arrived, and I was ushered out of the room. Vincente had his men sweep the apartment every day for electronic surveillance. I was unable to record any conversations. However, I did overhear him saying something about the salmon fishing trip to Canada. Where exactly, I wasn't sure until last night."

"Did you see his brother?"

"No. Vincente said since Miguel was out of the country, he'd be running things."

"Was he?"

"I believe General Sanchez was in charge. The three had two meetings. Vincente's authority was minimal. I think he made the comment for my benefit."

"Did he say anything else about DeOlmos?"

"No, sir."

"He said DeOlmos was out of the country. Did he say where?"

"I suspect México, sir."

Canaday nodded. México made sense. "What happened last night?"

"Philips arrived at the restaurant, and the first thing out of Vincente's mouth was, 'Have you picked out a good fishing spot?' Then he suggested I go powder my nose. As I left the table, I heard Miguel's Lieutenant say 'Prince George was highly recommended', to which Vincente replied, 'You will have everything you need by the 19th.'

"Will that give you enough time, sir?"

February 19th was three days away. Canaday instinctively nodded to his subordinate while his mind started planning.

* * *

When General Sanchez entered the living room of Vincente DeOlmos, he saw a room that looked as if it had been hit by a cyclone. He looked past the unconscious Vincente to the bureau against the far wall. It had been swept clean. Remnants of a vase and fragments of broken crystal figurines were scattered across the tiled floor. One of the expensive paintings that had hung on the wall had been ripped down the center and draped over the sofa chair in the middle of the room. Sanchez assumed the other three were the bits of torn canvas and splintered boards hanging over the antique brass cloak hanger near the front door.

Vincente lay sprawled across the pink leather sofa, one leg flung over the back, while his left arm covered his face. The cracked glass coffee table was leaning on its side. From the evidence of powder on the floor, the origins of the white smudges on the glass were unmistakable.

Sanchez called for the houseboy, ordered strong coffee, and told him to prepare a bath and clean clothes.

"Vincente," Sanchez called as he approached. The stoned Vincente did not move. "Vincente. *¡Despierte, ahora!* Wake up!"

Still no movement.

He grabbed Vincente by the scuff of the neck, yanked him off the sofa, and dragged him down the long hallway leading to the bathroom. Vincente struggled until his panicky, bloodshot eyes showed recognition.

"*¡Dios Mio!*" Vincente cried. "¡He sent you to kill me!"

Sanchez ignored his whimpering and continued down the hallway.

"Tell me." Vincente bellowed. "You're here to punish me. And you should. I deserve it. *¡Es culpa mia!* Kill me! *¡No importa!*"

"*Cierra la boca.* Shut the fuck up. I'm here to make you presentable. Your brother wishes to see you." They entered the bathroom; the houseboy turned off the taps and left. Sanchez pushed Vincente toward the huge sunken tub. "Take off your clothes and get in."

"*Mi hermano* wishes … to see me?" Vincente's tears flowed freely, his pathetic face a mere shadow of a man. "*Mi hermano* ... wishes--" His words translated into bubbles as Sanchez, his patience worn, lifted Vincente, and dropped him fully clothed into the tub.

Vincente sprung from beneath the water, sucking for air, coughing. He inhaled deeply and looked up, his eyes clouded with fear. "My bro wants to see me?"

"*Claro.* And that doesn't mean tomorrow."

"It's 'cause of that FBI bitch. Miguel's angry." Vincente splashed his arms through the tub like a child. His face turned an ugly shade of gray. His eyes darted around the room until a sudden gulp of laughter erupted from his chest. "Why am I worried? In a few days, my bro will be free forever and all will be forgiven."

Sanchez remained quiet.

More tears poured from Vincente's eyes. "He's angry. *Dios mio, mi hermano* is angry with me." He sulked for a moment then looked up at Sanchez in compliance. "I deserve it." His tanned face drained of color. "What's my fate, Sanchez? *¿Qué mala cosa me sucederá?*"

Sanchez eyed the face of the boy hiding in a man's body and growled, "With any luck, he'll remove your tongue."

CHAPTER 11

Valerie went to Ed's study, knocked lightly, and opened the door.

He threw his papers to one side and rubbed the back of his neck. "Yeah?"

"Would you like something?"

"Where are the girls?"

"Ed, it's Sunday, they're gone till supper."

"Oh, right," he said. "Is there any cocoa?"

"No. I'll go to the store and get more."

"Don't. It's okay."

"We're short on milk and eggs. Anything else you need?"

"Some blades for my razor. By the way, where is my small power saw? I got to the site yesterday morning, and it wasn't in the back of my truck."

"I switched it with the larger in the garage. I didn't think you'd mind."

"Val, how many times have I told you not to use my saws? It's dangerous."

"Some of the logs you bucked are too long for the furnace. I wanted to save you the trouble."

"Please don't touch my saw. One of the girls comes home and finds you've bled to death. That's all I need. I'll buck them up for you later."

"Don't bother, it's done," she said, but Ed had resumed reading. Valerie closed the door a little too firmly.

She slipped into her boots, grabbed her coat off the hook in the mudroom, and slogged out to the van. The crisp winter air felt good against her face. She unplugged the block heater and started the engine. When it had warmed the van enough, she stomped on the frozen clutch, shifted into gear, and waved at the Constable parked in her driveway as she drove past.

When she arrived at the grocery store, five vehicles were in the parking lot, which wasn't surprising. People had better things to do than shop on a Sunday. She parked as far away from the store as possible. Since cancelling her membership at the gym, during the winter, walking was often the only exercise she got. She backed into an empty area that faced the sidewalk and the street beyond. She saw the constable drive past. When a pickup pulled in too close on her side, Valerie frowned. It wasn't as if he had no other place to park. She gripped the doorknob and looked into her side mirrors; his door opened. She waited. A paneled van backed in two spots over on her other side. The driver, fidgeting with his seatbelt, looked harmless.

She squeezed out her side and headed for the store. The pickup driver was halfway to the entrance. He had to be wearing cork boots, Valerie decided, just as a gray van pulled in.

Valerie trudged her way across the ice scarred parking lot. Her foot slipped, and she steadied herself. Maybe parking so far away wasn't a great idea. She glanced toward the entrance; twenty more feet to go. The pavement was sheer ice. She inched along and looked again toward the door--and gasped.

The man from the pickup had stopped short of entering the doors and was staring at her. Something in his expression left her feeling creepy. She glanced back to see where the Mountie had parked.

"You okay?" the man hollered.

Valerie sucked for air. She nodded, and the man entered the store.

"Get a grip, girl." She reached the shovelled sidewalk.

Indoors, she grabbed a cart from the entrance lobby. The man from the pickup had his head buried in a motorcycle magazine at the book section just inside the store. He looked even less friendly up close.

After wasting forty minutes wandering through the store, Valerie made her way down the aisle to a checkout, before realizing she'd forgotten Ed's blades. She whipped the cart around and almost ran into the couple following.

"Hi, Val."

Valerie froze. The shock of seeing them made her whole body feel like one big heartbeat. More to the point, a ruptured heart. Seattle FBI agents Peter Bailey and CT Kalamai stood before her. Valerie took a deep breath. Kalamai had a friendly smile on her face, like the young girls that had greeted them when their plane arrived in Hawaii for their honeymoon. Fake friendly.

Kalamai approached while Bailey, looking orderly in civilian clothes, surveyed the immediate area.

Kalamai gave Valerie an affectionate hug. "Peter and I have been meaning to get over to see you folks," she said, then whispered, "Listen carefully." Kalamai glanced at Bailey who nodded back. "Smile, your life depends on it."

Valerie couldn't smile. "My family?"

"They're fine. Just listen. Go directly to checkout. Don't go to your vehicle. Go to the restaurant next door, order a coffee, and take a seat. We'll join you in ten minutes."

"But --"

"Do as I say. I'm trying to save your life," Kalamai said. Then she and Bailey turned and walked away.

Valerie grasped the grocery cart. The aisle was empty. She glanced at the shelves and their many products. There was something more she was supposed to buy but she couldn't remember what. She pushed the cart and headed for the checkout. The girl at the cash register made the usual small talk. Valerie couldn't think straight. She nodded, unsure what the girl had said. She couldn't get the image of her daughters out of her mind.

"Mrs. McCormick?" the clerk asked.

Startled, Valerie snapped, "What?"

"Will that be cash or check?"

Valerie fumbled in her purse for her wallet. She couldn't find it. She rummaged again, yanked out her wallet, handed over the money, grabbed her bag, and rushed toward the door. The girl called out something about, "Your change," but Valerie kept moving.

In the restaurant, she sat at the table along the far wall and ordered a coffee. While waiting for her coffee to cool, she chewed on her cuticles and watched the door. She didn't know what else to do. She wanted to go to home to her children. Yes, Valerie decided, if the agents didn't show in ten minutes, that's exactly what she would do.

Eight minutes later Bailey and Kalamai sat across from her.

"Are my daughters okay?" Valerie asked after the waitress left.

"Christine's at her girlfriend's near the high-school, Megan's at the library downtown, and Brandi's at your neighbour's. Ed's at his office," Kalamai answered.

Valerie's panic subsided. "What did you mean about saving my life?"

Kalamai's eyes swept the room. "After you entered the store, a man wired a bomb under your van."

The news felt like a blow to her stomach. Then Valerie remembered that nothing DeOlmos did should shock her. "You're sure my girls are safe?"

Both Kalamai and Bailey nodded.

"Thanks for letting me know. I'll hitch a ride home with the Mountie outside. He'll call the bomb squad. I gather he knows you're here? " That was a dumb statement.

Kalamai leaned forward. "The Mountie's gone."

"Gone? I don't understand. Where?" Her underarms dampened.

"He's been pulled off. But that's okay. We have a plan."

"No."

"Valerie. Listen --"

"No," Valerie said. "I don't mean to be rude, but I don't want to hear your plan. Just go away. I'll ...."

"You'll what, Mrs. McCormick?" Bailey said.

Valerie felt the tears burning her eyes and hated herself for being weak.

Kalamai spoke up. "A man is sitting in a pickup in front of the hardware store. We've made certain he has an obstructed view of your van. If he doesn't see it blow up and we take him, DeOlmos will send someone else. Next time they'll blow up your home."

Valerie just needed a moment to think. "Okay ... I'll ... I'll get my daughters and I'll leave town. I'll hide where he can't find us. Agent Vamozzi mentioned something about the Witness Protection Program. We'll do that." She choked back tears and took two deep breaths, coaxing herself not to panic.

"We must act now," Kalamai said. "There is a way you can get out of this alive and at the same time keep your family safe."

Instincts warned Valerie that what she was about to hear would be BAD.

"There are agents outside preparing your van, and he can't see them," Bailey said. "When they're finished, come with us. We'll blow it up, and he'll think you're dead."

It felt as if someone had smacked her across the shoulders with a lead pipe. All her muscles knotted. A cold sweat shot in lightning speed down her body. Voices echoed in her ears until Valerie became faintly aware of her pulse. Which was vibrating through her body at an alarming rate. Not unlike an AK47. Valerie couldn't breathe. Thin, heavy air pressed hard against her chest. It wasn't a heart attack. A panic attack?

"If you come with us, your family will be safe. Val, are you listening?" Kalamai looked at Bailey.

"One day we'll arrest DeOlmos, and he'll be brought to justice. Then you can go back to the way things use to be," Bailey said.

Valerie blinked and felt her lungs expand. They didn't get it.

"If there was any other way, we wouldn't suggest you do this, but you mean nothing to DeOlmos. You're his connection to the electric chair. His brother Vincente would slit your children's throats before he would let you destroy his brother." Bailey wiped his brow with a tissue. "If you agree, you will proceed from here to your van. When you get behind the wheel, place the key in the ignition, but don't turn it. Two agents will assist you in moving to the van next to yours. When you're safe, they'll blow up the van. They'll drive you to a deserted part of the airport, where our plane's waiting. A body will be found, and the authorities in Vancouver will verify they're your remains. The DeOlmos Cartel will believe you're dead. DeOlmos will think it is all over, and he's without threat. He'll make a mistake. You have to believe that. When he does, we'll be there. And you can return to your family."

"I'll never see my girls again. Even if you catch him, they won't let me live."

"Mrs. McCormick, we have this situation under control," Bailey said. "We can't guarantee that'll be the case the next time. You have to come with us. If you don't, please believe me when I say he'll never stop hunting you. Come with us, and he'll surface. You must know this is your only chance. The execution of two FBI agents, with an eyewitness who's willing to testify, leads to a reasonable expectation of the death penalty. He's going to fry, Mrs. McCormick."

"You don't understand. You take me away from my daughters and I'm nothing." She smiled sadly and watched the surprised look cross his face. "But you've got me, don't you. If I don't do as you ask, my family is dead. Then I might as well be dead." She lowered her chin to her chest. "I give up." She lifted her head. "I'm tired of fighting."

Bailey pulled a small cellular phone from his pocket. He pressed a button and whispered, "Ready?" He nodded at Kalamai and folded his phone.

"You will remember to put the key in the ignition, but you won't start the van?" Kalamai said.

Valerie pushed herself away from the table and headed for the door.

"Val, your groceries," Kalamai said.

Valerie went back for her two bags, grabbed them off the floor then walked through the door and left the restaurant. Willing her legs not to collapse, she never took her eyes off her white van. It was in need of a paint job. Numerous niches and scratches remained from the rugged terrain it had traveled on over the years. She couldn't remember how many times she'd thought of taking a painter's course. The van needed painting; she'd learn how to paint.

It never happened. Like so many things in her life.

She stopped to let a '78 Rabbit passed, then continued to her van, unlocked the driver's door and climbed in. She tossed the grocery bags on the passenger's seat and ignored the figure crouching behind her. FBI or hired gun, what did she care? She was through trying to convince herself she was a good mother. It was time to prove it. She pulled the keys from her pocket and shoved one into the ignition.

"Ma'am, I'm going to open the van's side door. When I do, climb through to the other vehicle. Ready?" The young man didn't wait for her answer. The door opened and he left.

He was safe now.

Valerie's eyes filled with tears. She remembered her precious girls, Megan, Christine, Brandi, one last time. Would they understand it was the only way to save them? She gripped the key and stared out the windshield into the mist. She felt deadness approach like a dark cloud on a windy day.

"Lord, if you're listening. Please forgive me. I have to do this. I can't let him hurt them."

She started to turn the ignition key.

CHAPTER 12

Her van rocked. She wasn't alone.

"Please get out. Save yourself."

"It's too late. If your turn that key, you're killing the young agent in the van next to us." His deep voice cut through her. "What will they tell his mother? He lost his life because you gave up? Don't do this, Mrs. McCormick. You're not a killer."

She glared over her shoulder at him. He whispered something into the tiny mike hooked to his collar, gripped her right wrist so tight she thought it would break, then pulled her from her seat.

She didn't try to stop him; sure he'd be too strong.

"You don't have a choice," he whispered. "You must leave now." He scooped her into the van parked a foot from hers.

She flopped across the bench seat. The door slammed close. The van wheeled out onto the icy roads, and a second later, maybe two, the explosion behind her sent her sprawling to the floor. It felt as if a hundred pipe bombs had gone off next to her head. Pain centered inside her eardrums. She crawled to her knees. Looked out the back window. Flames shot like fireworks to the sky, and her van burned like an oiled log on an open barbecue. Thick black smoke coiled upwards. Across the street, people gawked; some ran toward the van, shouting, arms flying to their faces when the heat drew them back.

The vehicle turned sharply. Valerie slid to the floor. She crawled to the bench seat, sobbing like a baby. Her whole chest felt broken.

Despite the rough roads, for a long time Valerie didn't sit up. She couldn't. Grief had her pinned to the seat. She forced her eyes open and saw the lights on the dashboard, the young man driving, and the back of the head of the man in the passenger seat. His blond hair cut above the collar. He spoke into his tiny mike, but she couldn't make out his words; the heater blew loudly, but she was freezing.

She struggled to a sitting position. They were traveling southbound toward the river. Everything looked familiar, the Mr. G's gas pumps and convenience store, the hill descending toward the Nechako River, the turnoff to First Avenue. Houses disappeared, giving way to businesses then large stretches of thick bush and trees, until they climbed the steep hill to Jasper. She saw the whiteness covering vast expanses of bare land, the ranch district of Blackwater.

They were headed to the airport; they were taking her away from her children. Megan, Christine, and Brandi were in the opposite direction.

Oh, God!

He was right. She couldn't die. Couldn't leave her babies.

Her babies!

Who would hold them? Who would comfort them when they were sick? Who would listen when they had great news to share? Or make certain they ate a decent breakfast? Or hug them and say, "It'll be okay" while they were certain it wouldn't?

Tears pooled, but Valerie willed them not to fall. She forced herself to breathe. Deep breaths. In. Out. She squeezed her eyes shut. She thought she heard Brandi. "Ma!"

They turned onto a narrow gravel road on the right. They turned again. Five minutes later, the van stopped.

"Mrs. McCormick?"

Huddled in a corner of the seat, arms wrapped around her knees, chest heaving, she buried her head in her arms and wept.

The man from the van wouldn't go away. "Mrs. McCormick?"

She tried to speak. She wanted to say 'leave me alone'. She wanted to yell and scream, but only sobs formed. When she heard her name repeated she covered her ears.

"Give me your rings."

She looked up at the dark, imposing shadow. "What?"

"Give me your rings. Now."

She looked down at her wedding rings and let out a pitiful cry. "Why?"

"I don't have time to explain. Your family will get them back."

"Please," she begged, tightening her arms around her knees. She looked up at him, her eyes pleading. His face a dark shadow.

"Your life depends on this. Hand over your rings."

Valerie, alone and defeated, slowly pulled the rings from her finger and held out her hand. When he was within a grasp, she pulled back and threw them across the seat. They rolled onto the floor, the clanging noise biting at the madness eating up her brain.

He said nothing. After retrieving her rings, he leaned out the door and handed them to a man waiting. He leaned back against the passenger's seat and unwrapped a candy he'd retrieved from his pocket. "Mrs. McCormick, we have to leave now. The jet is ready."

"I don't give a damn!" She looked out toward the airfield.

"I know you don't. I also know right about now you're thinking you should run. But run to where? There's nowhere to go but to that Learjet waiting. In a few hours, you'll be safe, and we can talk."

Valerie covered her ears with her hands. "Please shut up! I can't think."

"There's no need to think. Get up. Move to the jet. If you don't, I'll carry you."

She thought of her daughters. Their faces so smooth, so perfect. Their eyes staring up at some stranger. A stranger who would tell them their mother was dead. Valerie gasped for air. "Why are you doing this? What have I done?"

She thought of her parents, the morning strangers came to her door, asked if she had a relative, someone she could call. Aidan had been stationed two thousand miles away; Valerie shook her head. Her eyes couldn't leave the officer's face, a face she could still recall. A face full of sympathy, a voice to match, a stranger's voice that chilled her skin, made her want to reach for a sweater even though she couldn't move.

"Mrs. McCormick?" the man in the shadows said. "You can't run from this."

Valerie snorted. But I'm a marathon runner, she almost said. Then her eyes dried up as one last sigh escaped her chest. He was right, she had nowhere to go, no one to help her. She rose to her feet and bent her head away from the roof. The side door opened. The only light came from the cabin of the plane fifty feet away. She looked down at the tarmac, across the darkened land to bright lights a mile away, the control tower. The man with his face hidden by night's shadows, the man with the cruel voice, held out his hand. She ignored him and stepped to the ground. He gestured for her to proceed to the jet, and Valerie did just that. There was nowhere else to go.

Agent Vamozzi wouldn't look at her as she walked past him toward the back of the cabin. Bailey, Kalamai, and two more agents she didn't recognize nodded. Valerie saw through them. She was nobody. Just an extra passenger. A witness. A means to an end.

She sat in the back and stared out the window. With no moon to reflect off the flat terrain, even the snow looked dark and dirty. She sank back. Her brain absorbed the darkness outside. She saw nothing but black, felt nothing but the beat of her heart and her shallow breathing. She concentrated on her chest rising and falling with each breath.

*　*　*

Canaday watched Mrs. McCormick's expression and remembered the loneliness he hadn't acknowledged in a long time.

After they landed in Nevada and the jet came to a complete stop, he stood and signalled to Bailey, who went to the back of the jet where Mrs. McCormick sat. He said something, and she stood. Canaday watched her approaching and empathized; she moved past him with unfocused eyes. Her being in shock was expected. What confused him was his reaction. He wanted to apologize for their incompetence at keeping surveillance on her eldest daughter. He wanted to apologize for taking her rings without an explanation, but his reason would have led to more questions he'd had no time to answer.

What confused him the most was apologizing wasn't part of his nature.

Canaday moved away from his seat and followed his people toward the exit doors.

"Mrs. McCormick, the car's here," Bailey said when they reached the bottom of the stairs.

Canaday stepped to the ground and stood behind her. Her scent, mixed with the cool night air, filled his lungs. He inhaled deeply.

Mrs. McCormick moved toward the first vehicle, stopped, and jerked her arm away from Bailey. "Don't touch me." She turned and faced the plane and the agents. "What have you people done?" Her eyes settled on Canaday.

He held her piercing stare. Her animosity tore through him. His intent had been to pull out the entire family. His intent… failed. "We saved your life, Mrs. McCormick. We're the good guys."

She didn't blink, but she heard him. The facial expression showed that and more.

"Would a kind word hurt?" Kalamai asked.

Canaday turned to Kalamai. His voice was as hard as he wished his heart were. "Don't ever address me in that tone of voice again, Agent Kalamai." His hand groped for a candy.

"Candyman, can't you at least show a little sympathy? The woman's been through hell."

Mike Canaday walked away. He wasn't interested in old news.

* * *

Valerie had always felt log homes and the golden color of honey oak flooring were warm and homey. This enormous log house should have been a dream, but instead it felt cold, empty, harsh. Oak tongue and groove. Large logs stretched across open ceilings. Hardwood floors felt like ice beneath her feet. From where she sat at the kitchen table, the large, flat backyard showed no trees, no shrubs, just miles of dry ground. Four feet away, the glass doors reflected the wide archway behind her that led into the living room. Periodically, muffled voices came from that room. On the far wall, twenty-five feet away, the double door refrigerator hummed, and the furnace vibrated through the floor vents. The house was fully furnished, yet there were no family pictures, no evidence people had ever lived here.

The man across the table wouldn't stop studying her. His eyes probed. She ignored him for a long time, but still, he wouldn't go away. Stark blue eyes cut into her. She felt naked, exposed. As if he knew all too well what was hidden in her soul.

His light hair was receding. The skin on his face was rugged. He wasn't a large man, but his upper body was solid. His tie, tight around his neck, looked as if it choked him. But it was his steel blue eyes that disturbed her. They looked ... omniscient?

"Who are you?" she asked.

"Mike Canaday."

"I've seen you before." She studied him, forcing her mind to remember. "The day I didn't have in court. You're ... 'the boss'. Who are you?"

He looked at her mouth, the top of her head, her eyes. "I just told you."

"Are you in charge of this elaborate plan, Canaday FBI?"

"Yes."

"Your plan sucks."

"You're alive, Mrs. McCormick."

"Like I said, your plan sucks." She snapped her head in the other direction and felt the strain in her neck muscles. She hugged her arms and cut her fingernails into her skin. "Where am I?" She looked back at him. He was still there, gawking at her, pulling the life from her.

"Elko, Nevada." Canaday pulled a candy from his pocket and offered it to her.

She shook her head. "Go away."

He didn't move.

Her gaze traveled away from him. She looked through the kitchen glass doors. What did he know that she didn't?

But even then, an effortless instinct abolished the question, sending it to a dry place, the place where God had once cast her demons; the place where all unanswered premises go. Instead, she focused through the acid etched glass to framed moonlight then to barren ground a few feet from the doors--rugged, dry, split terrain, deadened by the rainless clouds. She stared out at the wasteland while her pain, her daughters, and images of her parents fought for space in her mind. She forced them down. But new images blasted back. Bodies, smiling faces with black eyes, skinned knees, blood spurting through the air, brain cells splattering, thoughts vanishing; thoughts that had once contained sweet memories, sensations, wind touching bare skin, lips caressing a soft neck, laughter that sprang from down inside. Mud tracks through the kitchen, sunbeams marooned inside a crystal, dead eyes, cold flesh, the smell of damp puppy fur.

Valerie laughed, rolled her eyes, and knew now what DeOlmos thought when he pulled the trigger: 'Bang. You're dead. Bang. You're dead too.'

She knew how he felt. The power he had. Power to change a life. Power to take what no one had the right to take. DeOlmos. DeOlmos. Valerie wiped at her forehead. Was his name inscribed there?

Snow floated restlessly to the ground. She looked into an endless sky and waited. Soon the light specks turned to large, fluffy flakes. A light breeze blew. The flakes rode it, floating by the window in one direction then the other, before hovering, swooping back up to glide down once again. Free. When they reached the ground where they would not dissipate, she laughed. The simile was ironic: Snow freely covered the ground, Valerie forcibly trapped inside.

But her children were safe. She had to remember that, had to believe that. They were safe. She was dead, but they were safe.

Special Agent Canaday sat like a predator. Quiet. Focused. Eyes never shifting from his prey. Did he expect a prison break at any moment? Was she a rare commodity? She doubted that. He'd probably seen worse things than a woman falling apart.

Valerie blinked several times. Maybe that meant something? She recognized she was falling apart. Did that mean she wasn't? She wanted to laugh, to yell, and to cry, all at the same time.

She faced forward and looked at the agent. Her voice came out quiet. "You're destroying me."

"You think it would've been better if we'd died in that explosion?"

She narrowed in on his face. "You're the one who made me get out of the van. I know who you are. If I had a gun, you'd be dead." I don't mean that. Her lungs fought for air. She glared at him, hated him, simply because he was there.

"Yes, I'm sure I would."

All the muscles in her face tightened. Horrendous heat formed in her chest and worked upward. Her breathing quickened. She couldn't control the rage centered on this man. But part of her tried. "Go away," she whispered.

"Sorry, I can't do that."

"Please."

He shook his head, and Valerie sprang forward across the table, her chair falling with a loud crack to the floor behind her. Her eyes darted around the room and searched for a weapon, any weapon. Hurt him, a voice inside her said. It'll make you feel better.

Bailey and an agent name Hill rushed into the kitchen. Canaday motioned to them to halt. "Everything's fine. Mrs. McCormick was about to sit down."

Valerie rolled her eyes. "No, I wasn't."

"Fine. Stand."

She pulled the chair upright, flopped into it, while the rage continued to grow. If the sparks she felt in her eyes could kill, right about now bullets would have flown out of her eyes.

"You're no hero, Canaday. I would have been better off dead. You used your people to trick me. You think I'm stupid. You think not seeing my girls again justifies any of this? DeOlmos can fry in an electric chair. He can go free. I don't care. Do you hear me--Canaday FBI! You tricked me, he didn't!" She couldn't stop yelling. "You lied to me, he didn't. There's no way I'm ever going to see my children again. I don't give a shit if you captured DeOlmos. I'd rather be dead. Dead. Dead. DEAD!"

What's wrong with me? I don't mean any of this.

She collapsed backward pivoting the chair.

Canaday reached across the table and grabbed for her. Valerie lashed out at him.

He grabbed her wrists and pinned her while he kicked his chair away.

He reached around the table and swept her up; twisting her around until her back was against him, her feet barely touching the floor. He wrapped her arms across her chest and held tight. Bailey and Vamozzi watched from the archway.

She stomped her feet, yelled, and fought to escape. Her mind split in half and raced around her. She was losing ... losing.

"You want to fight," he said. "Okay, fight. Prove to me how tough you are. Show me what you're made of. I'm not going to let you die. You're not going to die."

"Sweet Jesus!" Valerie screamed, stiffening with madness.

"Scream. Fight. But I'm not going to desert you. I'm not going to let anyone hurt you again."

"Please. I need my girls. I can't make it without my girls." She breathed like a wounded animal. The pain in her heart unbearable. One more minute away from her girls was one more minute she couldn't bear. They were her life. They were her reason for living.

"Yes, you can. You've been through hell today. I know that. I've seen awful things happen to innocent people before. They survived." He shook her. "Dammit, Valerie, they were strong enough to survive." Then tenderly he added, "You are too."

"No!"

"You are. Trust me. Everything's going to work out. You're alive. Because of your sacrifice, so are your children. Keep remembering: Because of you they're alive."

Valerie cried in agony. "My babies. My sweet babies."

"That's right. They're alive. They're safe because of you."

Her legs gave way. Canaday loosened his hold. Valerie stopped fighting.

He turned her gently, lifted her into his arms, and carried her past the agents to the bedroom down the hallway. He laid her on the bed, unrolled the comforter at her feet, and covered her. He pulled a chair close to the bed and sank back, exhausted.

For a brief moment, Valerie looked at him through swollen eyes, before turning to face the wall.

CHAPTER 13

Aidan Roth heard a car pull into Valerie's driveway. He tossed the magazine onto the coffee table and stood up. He'd been waiting an hour for his sister, or for one of her family to return home. He stretched his neck and looked out the front window .... It wasn't Valerie. A 1996 blue sedan stopped a short distance from the front door. Aidan didn't recognize the vehicle, but the burly man crawling out from behind the wheel was his old boss; someone he hadn't seen in six months.

He rushed toward the foyer and threw the front door open. "Inspector?"

RCMP Inspector Banyan rubbed his hands vigorously then rechecked his notepad. "Aidan? You live here?"

Aidan yanked his collar away from his neck and fought to breath. "No. My sister ... does."

"Valerie McCormick ...? Aidan?"

"Huh?"

"Is your brother-in-law home?"

"He's at his office."

Aidan looked past the Inspector to the large front yard. From nowhere the wind had come, skimming off the snowdrifts outlining the driveway, twirling beads of crystallized moisture around him, his lungs gasping as the frozen air swept down his throat.

"Aidan?" Inspector Banyan gripped his elbow and turned him.

Aidan frowned at his old boss. Banyan said something weird. If only he could make sense of it.

He remembered the day his parents died. Remembered it as if it were yesterday. A rough dayshift. Difficulty sleeping. The phone rang at half past three in the morning. Then the empty, hollow feeling like the world had sucked him in and spit him out. The worst kind of worse imaginable. Where his whole being failed him. What was that? The Inspector repeated something. Had he replied 'what' to himself, or had he said it out loud as he intended?

"Let's go and sit down, okay? What's your brother-in-law's office number? Do you have someone you can call? Do you want me to fix some coffee?"

Then Aidan absorbed the words the Inspector had spoken and he whispered, "She can't be dead." He stopped short of sitting on the couch--sitting being a confirmation, and no way could he do that. No. "You're wrong, sir."

* * *

The conversation around the kitchen table continued, though Aidan was barely aware of it. For three hours, he'd been trying to hang on. One quiet Sunday afternoon he chose to watch the game, and DeOlmos won. Now, instead of grieving like the rest of his family, he dreamed of choking DeOlmos with his bare hands. The visions were so satisfying. His hands squeezing. Tightening around DeOlmos's throat. DeOlmos's eyes opened in horror. Pleading. Aidan's hands tightening. Squeezing.

Aidan grunted in a strange orgasmic delight. Then he looked around. Did they hear his groans?

Ed, Banyan, and Megan sat at the table with him. His wife Susan stood at the sink scrubbing the dishes. But that was Susan. Keeping busy to ward off the pain. His sixteen-year-old son, Trevor sat on the chair next to the back door. He was bent forward, steadily petting poor old Bethum. Trevor's older sister was upstairs comforting her two cousins, and Aidan's heart ached. Instead of supporting Valerie's family, he'd spent the last few hours contemplating murder. A scenario that had sprung out of guilt. He'd done the one thing he promised Valerie he wouldn't do. He let her down. Just like ... he'd let his dad down.

He remembered how she'd held onto him after their parents died. She looked to him for strength, for understanding. What could he tell her? How could he explain that life wasn't always fair? But she held onto him like he was all she had because that was the truth. He made sure she never felt alone. It had cost him, but he loved her. The cool kid that always made him laugh, no matter how angry he'd get. He felt like shit when he had to walk her down the aisle to that moron Ed. He couldn't talk her out of it. He tried.

"Ed won't die like mum and dad did. I'll make sure of that."

Only then had Aidan realized how much guilt Valerie carried. He'd been a kid himself. If he'd known before that, he'd have helped her. "I'll always be there for you, sis," was the best he could do.

What a fucking liar.

"They won't be shipping the body to Vancouver until tomorrow," Inspector Banyan replied in a voice that sounded like his nose was plugged.

"What was that?" Aidan asked.

"I was telling your brother-in-law the coroner's office would prepare the remains tomorrow and ship them out."

"Why Vancouver?"

"They're taking over the investigation. Remember?"

Yes, he remembered. But his head was so muddled it was difficult to think clearly. "Where is ... her body?"

"At the morgue."

Aidan cursed himself and sprang to his feet. "I've got to see her."

"Aidan?" Susan said.

"Uncle Aidan, you want to see my mum like that?" Megan asked.

"Aidan, what's the matter with you?" Ed snapped.

He ignored them all and looked at Banyan. "I have to see her."

"You know that's not necessary. Under these conditions, she'll be identified by other means than viewing by a family member. Besides," he glanced at Megan, "it won't be pleasant."

"I have to see her, Inspector."

"You can't," Ed demanded.

"Why?"

"Because ...." Ed didn't seem to know why.

"Dad, maybe you should think about this?" Trevor said.

Aidan rubbed his eyes and looked at his son then at the others. "Please understand even if I can't explain why, I've got to see my sister. I have to." He glanced at Susan; she nodded.

He got up and went to the mudroom off the kitchen. He looked around at the jackets hanging off the hooks and tried to remember, which one was his. The red plaid one? Aidan grabbed it.

"We'll take my car," Inspector Banyan said, two steps behind him.

Aidan didn't care. Outside the back door, he looked up at the clouded gloom, the darkness. Then he climbed into the passenger seat. Ten-fifteen p.m. He was amazed at how fast the day had gone. He couldn't remember most of it.

Downtown, Aidan accompanied Inspector Banyan through the basement of the Prince George Regional Hospital. Without saying so, Banyan seemed to understand why Aidan was there, even if Aidan wasn't sure himself. All he knew was he had to see Valerie. His little sis, who never once stopped believing in him, who never once stopped thinking of him as her hero.

Some fucking hero.

Inspector Banyan wiped his nose and pushed at the large door leading to the morgue.

Aidan's body temperature dropped at the same time his palms dampened. He dug his hands into his coat pocket and scuffed his shoes across the waxed floor. A familiar odour stung at his nostrils. The orderly handed them each a cloth. Inspector Banyan declined indicating his nose was already plugged.

"Sir, are you sick?" Aidan asked, while the phlegm in his throat moved upward.

"Allergies." Banyan's eyes settled on something behind Aidan. "You certain you want to do this?"

Grasping the fabric over his nose and mouth, Aidan turned around, looked at the slab, and squeezed his eyes shut. His heart told him to get the hell out of there; his head told him to open his eyes. He opened them and focused on the Gurney. A heap of burnt flesh and bones lying in front of him resembled no human being, let alone his sister. Nowhere in the deepest part of his brain could he summon her image, not in this ... ugliness.

Aidan moved closer. The scar on Valerie's neck, sustained in a childhood accident, was impossible to detect. Exposed cartilage and neck muscles were all he saw. This body held no existent skin. The top of the head reminded him of a festered scarecrow; burnt straw. Skin gone, bones blackened and stuck together by overcooked sinews of meat. The length of the corpse might be correct, but that wasn't enough. He studied the bone structure. He was surprised the body was still in one piece.

What am I thinking? This is my sister. Not some crime scene. What the hell am I doing here?

He moved closer to the gurney.

Because I deserve to be. I let you down little sis. I'm so sorry.

Aidan's teeth clamped hard on the inside of his cheek. The sharp piercing pain didn't help. His heart ached. Intense pain narrowed in and around his arteries. He could swear the blood in his heart had just thickened.

This couldn't be his sister. This corpse was grotesque. Nothing like his beautiful sister. Kind, sweet Valerie.

Aidan moved closer. He wasn't there when she really needed him; he owed it to her to be here now. To witness all of it. Every last inch of it.

The ring finger was thinner than the rest. But part of the gold band still glittered. Aidan pulled a pencil out of his pocket and carefully poked the lead tip into the tiny bones until he felt contact. He flipped the pencil around and with the eraser, rubbed gently. A thin layer of membrane, smudged with black soot, smeared across the diamond, then the gold band. Careful not to destroy the delicate bone, he twisted the rings until they were on the inside of the palm. Aidan's stomach flipped. They were Valerie's rings.

Aidan swept a hand through his hair. Of course, they were Valerie's rings. This was Valerie.

Sickened, Aidan took a step backward then he noticed something. Holding the cloth against his nose, holding his breath for a moment, he pulled his specks from his breast pocket, put them on, and bent over the hand. A faint line of flesh had wrapped itself up against the outside of the ring; as if the skin had pushed back. And the gold? There was enough heat to sizzle the flesh; yet neither ring had sunk into the flesh or melded together. What the hell did that mean?

Aidan straightened then remembered something. He took off his glasses and turned his attention back to the jaw. Valerie had a tooth removed shortly after Brandi was born. The day was still so clear in his mind. He had picked her up at the dentist because Ed had to work. She sat in the passenger seat and pressed her hand to the left side of her face.

Aidan inched his way to the other side of the slab. He grabbed a sterilized glove from a box on the counter and wrapped it around the lead. He inserted the pencil into the mouth and tugged at the swollen lip. The tooth was gone. He brought the cloth back to his face. But the ring?

"Inspector?"

Banyan stepped forward.

Aidan gestured toward the left hand. "The rings."

Banyan leaned closer. "Yeah?"

"There was enough of a blast to send parts of the hood across the parking lot. Yet the body remains intact. The bomb was stuck to the gas tank, right? The Coroner said the body was lying across the floor behind the driver's seat?"

"Yes."

"But her rings didn't sink into her finger. And ...."

"And ...?"

Aidan wasn't sure. He glanced at the attendant standing a few feet behind them. "I'd like my sister's rings, please."

The attendant shook his head. "Sorry, we can only hand them over to next-of-kin after the police finish their investigation."

Aidan nodded slowly. He was a cop for twenty years, of course he knew that.

CHAPTER 14

The first clear light of morning touched the night sky as Canaday spoke softly into his walkie-talkie. Kalamai and Bailey both responded with an all's clear. He laid the radio down and adjusted his shoulder holster. After twenty years, it still felt uncomfortable. God's way of telling him something?

The horizon lightened. In the distance red flashes peeked above the hills. Newly fallen snow glistened, untouched except for Agent Bailey's tire tracks. About two hundred yards out, they completed a circle around the entire estate.

Canaday heard footsteps behind him and turned.

Vamozzi threw his coat over the back of the chair and sat down. "How's she doing?"

"Sleeping."

"I talked to Griffith, and you were right, DeOlmos has a man watching Roth."

"Miguel is too cautious not to." Canaday rubbed a hand through his hair. "Unless I missed something in the RCMP file on her brother Roth."

"I don't think so."

Canaday lit a cigarette.

"Everything's quiet outside. Get some sleep if you like."

Canaday shook his head.

Vamozzi rose to his feet and stretched his arms. "In that case, wake me in two hours."

Canaday flicked his ashes in the ashtray. He lied; he was tired all right, but his mind wouldn't shut down. He took a deep drag, exhaled, looked at the cigarette, and saw, for the umpteenth time, what smoking really was: A coward's way out. He butted the cigarette in the ashtray, unwrapped a candy from his pocket, and stretched out farther.

He'd been given four days to plan for this diversion. Seventy-two hours of thorough preparation. Expect everything and anything, he had told his people. What he hadn't expected was Valerie McCormick. It had jolted him to see her sitting at the wheel, her fingers gripping the key. A mother ready to kill herself to save her children was the most powerful image he'd seen in a long--

The alarm system screeched. Pain shot through his ears.

Canaday flew over the back of the couch, gun extended. He raced for the hallway. Vamozzi was there, crouched low, magnum aimed. Canaday knew the agents outside were already circling the house.

Vamozzi signalled and moved to the alarm box. Valerie's bedroom door remained closed. If the noise hadn't driven her out of her room, that could only mean one thing.

Canaday straightened up and ran toward her door.

The alarms died.

Canaday nodded his intent to Vamozzi then kicked Valerie's door in.

"Don't say a word," she snarled. "Okay, so I opened the friggin' window. I wanted some air. I forgot there'd be some stupid alarm system. I JUST wanted to breathe."

Vamozzi laughed.

Kalamai appeared behind him and told Canaday, "Everything's secure outside."

Vamozzi followed Kalamai from the doorway and headed back to his room, still chuckling.

"This is funny?" Valerie glared at Canaday.

"Not particularly."

The bedroom window was closed. Faint light filtered through the lace curtains. Day began. He walked back into the living room; her bare feet patted across the honey oak floor behind him. He stretched out in the chair, crossed his ankles, propped them on the coffee table next to the full ashtray, and lit a cigarette.

"You smoke too much." Valerie sat on the couch across from him.

He glanced at her for a second then back to the window. Maybe if he ignored her?

"I can't sleep." She rubbed her forehead. "I have a headache."

No kidding. Canaday closed his eyes and hoped for silence.

"I'm sorry about the alarm. I wasn't thinking."

"It's okay."

"He's never going to believe it was me."

He peeked. "DeOlmos?"

"No. My brother. He's a damn good investigator. He understands and feels things most men never do. He's not going to believe I'm dead. He'll investigate, and he'll--"

"Lead DeOlmos right to you."

Valerie's eyes fixed on his cigarette then slowly rose to his face, her contempt obvious.

"Why did he quit the force?"

"What?"

"I saw your brother's record. It doesn't say why he resigned."

Valerie lifted her hands, then lowered them again. "It was a long time ago."

"He had a promising career with CSIS. Quit to move back home. Drove a patrol car for a year, then resigned."

"So?"

He saw the spark in her eyes and decided to change the subject; he'd find out about Roth through Bureau channels. "Later today we can go for a short walk outside. What size boot do you take?"

She leaned forward. "Are you married?"

The question disconcerted him.

"I bet you aren't. I bet you don't have children either. I bet you don't have brothers or sisters. Am I right?"

"Yes."

"Do you know how I knew?"

"No."

"Because you have no idea what you've done. You made a decision that took me away from the one thing...." She lowered her head. A tear formed in the corner of her eye. Her breathing quickened.

She was trying to hold on.

I'm sorry, he wanted to say.

"I keep thinking about my family." She looked at him, her blue eyes sparkling. She chewed on her cuticle.

She was fighting with a thought. But there was nothing he could say to make it all better.

"I'm trying to understand. I mean ...." She rubbed her eyes and leaned her head in hand. "What happens next?"

"Depends."

"You're making the rules. What do you want to happen?"

"We'll be here for awhile."

"What? A week? Month? Two months? Forever? What happens when I become old news? What if DeOlmos never surfaces? Please. You have my life in your hands."

"We'll take one day at a time. I wish I could reassure you, Mrs. McCormick. But the truth is it's up to DeOlmos."

Valerie slid down until she was stretched across the cushions.

His eyes, no longer responding to orders, wandered down her breasts to her legs, her small feet, and back to her neck, her face. Canaday wet his dry lips and turned away. After an excruciating silence, "We have a witness protection program. You're given a new identity, a new place to live, and enough money to start over."

"With my family?"

"Once the trial is over, you can go home." He set his cigarette in the ashtray and glanced at her face.

Her eyes moistened. "Don't lie. Even I know the witness protection program doesn't work that way. Once you're in, you're never out."

"If something should happen to DeOlmos, the threat to you would be gone."

She blinked and a tear touched her cheek. His cigarette smouldered.

"You're going to kill him?"

"I didn't say that."

"While you're at it, could you do me a favour and kill his brother, and everyone else who works for them?"

He didn't realize he was frowning until Valerie laughed. Then as abruptly, she stopped. The pain in her face made him uneasy. He'd seen suffering before. Worse suffering. He was sure of that; he just couldn't remember when.

"What do you suppose his last thoughts were?" she asked.

She was doing it again, dumbfounding him. "Who?"

"Special Agent Charles Onston."

"I don't know."

"It doesn't matter," she said then asked, "Is someone protecting my children?"

"Yes."

"Would you tell me if something bad happened?"

"They're safe, Mrs. McCormick. You don't have to--"

"Would you tell me?"

"Yes."

"Will you tell me how they're doing if I ask?"

"I'll try."

"What do you mean, you'll try? You're the FBI."

"Mrs. McCormick, I'm not going to make promises I can't keep."

Her face flushed. "But, you'll try."

"Yes."

Joylene Nowell Butler

* * *

Night's lights danced in swirls off the folded knife's blade laying like a gemstone across his palms. He dug his toes into the sand and watched Vincente weep openly while ten feet away, twenty members of their cartel stood in remorseful attention.

Miguel waited until Vincente ceased fussing. The two soldiers holding him down would not let go. It angered Miguel to think no one would raise his voice in defence of Vincente. If only one of them had, he would have reconsidered the action he was about to take. An action that seemed irreversible now.

He held his flat palms high above his head and cried out. With one swift motion, he flipped the knife into the air, grabbed the ivory handle, and brought the sharp blade down, severing off the three largest toes on Vincente's right foot.

Vincente screamed, the men released him, and he dropped his head to his knees. Hands moved quickly, wrapping white strips around his foot.

Miguel stood up and backed away. The prodigal brother had returned to face the wrath of his keeper. But Miguel felt no such anger. He looked upon his brother and felt only sadness.

His foot elevated, Vincente was lifted and carried to the limousine. Miguel looked to the night sky and wondered if his parents watched from heaven. Would their mother have accepted his actions, a sweet, gentle woman, who abhorred violence? Was he justified? Clearly, he was, yet that knowledge brought him no peace.

The ivory sculpted knife, cleaned, replaced in its protective leather pouch, was returned to him. He called out to Sanchez who appeared.

Miguel handed him the knife. "I must be alone with my brother."

"*Si, patron.*"

Miguel went to the limousine. Vincente was huddled in the backseat; his face twisted with pain. His bandages already showed stains of fresh blood. Miguel sat across from him. After a long deliberation, penitence for bedding an agent had been decided. If left unpunished, Vincente would become not only a liability but also an example others might follow. Surely, three severed toes attested to his authority and instilled unrelenting loyalty from his men?

"*Mi hermano, lastima malo?*" Miguel asked, knowing it had to be painful.

"No! *¡Si!*" Vincente stuttered, as if convinced a struggle for bravery was beyond his capabilities.

Miguel smiled secretly. Vincente was too predictable.

"But it's the pain in my heart that's killing me. I've dishonoured you."

Miguel shook his head. He searched the handsome, dark face. Maria, Mother of God, had blessed him with understanding and wisdom, while Vincente was blessed with rage and beauty. It pained Miguel to punish his brother for God-given traits.

"You've exonerated yourself. This saturated cloth will attest to that," Miguel said.

"I haven't tasted the blood of my woman."

"*Hermanito*, it's only been one week, you have to be patient."

"Senora McCormick?"

"She is no longer a problem," Miguel said, while an image of the lovely woman strayed too long in his mind.

"Yesterday, her death delivered your freedom. I rejoice with you. But I must hear you say you forgive me."

"You're forgiven." Miguel tried not to look at the red, soaked cloth.

"I would rather you had cut my eyes out. It sickens me to think I laid with that Parker bitch."

Indeed, it would have taken all his soldiers to hold Vincente down had that been the case. Miguel laughed softly. Vincente's verbal bravery amused him. To cover up his disrespect, he mused, "*Un perra de FBI.*"

"Yes, FBI whore."

They looked at each other and roared. Vincente held his sides then took a deep breath and squeezed his injured foot. "She was a beauty." He smiled at the memory of her. "She had a most pleasing manner. Miguel? I need to be with her at the end."

"You have my word."

"*¿Cuando?*"

"Patience. She has returned to Seattle. When the time is right, you may do with her as you please."

Vincente smiled. "That eases my pain."

"I'm glad." Miguel patted his brother's shoulder. "Now ... go home."

"And you?"

"Fishing is most relaxing."

"Good."

"But one must never forget the lessons learned," Miguel warned.

"Tell me your lessons my brother?"

Miguel smiled fondly at Vincente's beautiful face. "Caution. You must have many eyes to discover your enemies, because their numbers grow. Our *dos credos* in Seattle, they were an unfortunate mistake. But honour is always sacred. The fact they were FBI proves my point. Even *la policia* are greedy and corrupt. Had they offered a reasonable price for the guns they would still be alive." Miguel paused, reflecting on what might have occurred. "But, it's better they are dead."

"They should all be destroyed."

Miguel smiled at his little brother's sweet innocence.

CHAPTER 15

Aidan stopped outside the kitchen. His wife and son held each other, and he was stung with envy. They shared common grief, common belief. He was alone. He leaned against the doorframe and watched, unable to shake his uneasiness.

Eleven days had passed since the bombing, and everyone else had accepted Valerie's death. Members of his family reached out for each other while he could only distance himself. His son, Trevor, had become Susan's shadow, his daughter, Lydia, was a constant support for Christine, and Ed, who hadn't been to the office all week, refused to untangle Brandi from his side. They were all there for each other, supporting, clinging. Everyone…

Except Megan. She hadn't spoken more than a few words for over a week. Aidan tiptoed back from the doorway.

He found his eldest niece in her bedroom, a silhouette against her window. He gave his eyes time to adjust to the room's dim light before whispering her name. "Megan?"

"Come in, Uncle Aidan."

"How are you, Sweetie?"

She kept her hand at her back. "I never appreciated my mother. I loved her, of course, but I thought what she did in the scheme of things as unimportant. Trivial. I wanted to be more than just somebody's mother. That's why I studied so hard. At nineteen she was married. I'd be nineteen and attending UNBC in the Fall. How could being a housewife compare?" She slowly brought her hand from behind her back. "I was so wrong."

Aidan saw the flash of a white envelope in her hand. "What's that, Sweetie?"

Megan stepped forward and handed it to him. Aidan took the envelope and switched the desk lamp on. It was addressed to Ed from the insurance company. "Where did you get this?"

"In the waste paper basket in Dad's office. It says: Attached please accept a check for One Million Dollars. Uncle Aidan, why didn't he say something?"

Aidan read the letter. It was the standard impersonal correspondence. Aidan felt his blood pressure rise. "He was probably planning to."

"When? Today is Sunday. We don't receive weekend delivery." She looked down at the envelope in his hands. "Will you speak to him?"

"He's in his study?"

"Yes."

Aidan folded the envelope and placed it in his pocket. He hugged his niece, kissed her on the forehead then left the room and walked down the hallway toward the stairs. He paused at the top and took the envelope out of his pocket. A million dollars? He turned it over and glanced at Ed's name. His sister was dead, and now his brother-in-law was a millionaire. Suppressing the urge to rip it to shreds, Aidan folded the letter again and put it back in his pocket. Insurance companies never paid this quickly.

He reached the study door, knocked once, and stepped in. Brandi and her father sat together on the sofa chair in front of the warm fire. He took the chair next to them and stared into the flames. Ed had his arm around Brandi who slept peacefully.

"She didn't sleep well last night," Ed whispered.

Aidan glanced at his niece then reached in his pocket and pulled out the envelope.

Ed squinted at the return address then turned his attention back to the fire. "I was shocked when I opened it. It came on Friday. I'd forgotten we took out insurance when we first got married. Valerie had insisted." He smoothed the hair away from Brandi's forehead. "I was embarrassed. The check meant I wouldn't lose the business." He frowned at Aidan's expression. "You must have realized things hadn't been going so great lately. When I saw the check, I realized my wife had died ...." He wrestled with a thought. "The check is in the top drawer of my desk. I couldn't deposit it. I know she would want me to, but, if I do it means she really is ...."

Aidan stood up. The anger he was experiencing was too dangerous for him to stay put. Was the bastard lying? In order to claim the insurance, a death certificate had to be submitted. Aidan could hear Susan's calm voice in his head, 'He's in shock. He probably can't think straight.'

"What should I do, Aidan?" Ed asked.

"I don't know."

"You're investigating. You must suspect something."

"I'm tying up loose ends."

"I keep wondering why I didn't go with her to the store. I never thought about what kind of danger she was facing. Now I sit here every night wondering ... why didn't I go with her."

His anger seething, Aidan stepped toward the door and stopped. "Has Vancouver said when they're shipping the body back to Prince George for burial?"

"In a few days."

"Have you made arrangements for the funeral?"

"There won't be one. We'll have a memorial service."

"A memorial service? What about the gravesite--"

"Aidan." Ed's annoyance was evident in his low voice. "Val told me some time ago she didn't want to be buried; she wanted to be cremated."

"Cremated?"

"Aidan!" Ed growled. "Stop repeating everything I say."

Aidan gritted his teeth. "Is there anything else I should know?"

"I am honouring my wife's wishes. Why is that so hard to accept?"

Aidan raised his hands in defeat as he backed away from his brother-in-law. "Forget I asked. Let me know when the memorial service is."

He got as far as the front door when he paused. Valerie wanted to be cremated? You're lying, you, piece of shit! Valerie had never mentioned cremation to him, and they'd talked about everything. Ed was just too cheap to pay for a decent funeral!

* * *

A week later, Aidan drove to a secluded restaurant on the outskirts of Prince George. The Spruce Pine Lodge was an old log chalet converted to a restaurant in the early seventies. Aidan liked the rustic atmosphere. The second story held a galleried porch with a view of the lake and surrounding forest. The main floor had half the number of tables approved by the fire department, which meant that conversations were seldom overheard.

Aidan stomped the snow from his boots and removed his outer jacket. After shaking it vigorously, he placed it on a hook inside the foyer. Elsie, the owner, spotted him and approached with a large friendly smile.

"Aidan Roth, what a pleasant surprise."

"Elsie, I swear you're getting lovelier everyday."

Elsie giggled and ran old seamy hands through her hair. "You, my dear boy, need glasses. Go sit yourself down, and I'll be there in a sec'."

Aidan obliged.

Inspector Gary Banyan blew his nose and surveyed the room. "Roth," he said, looking back at him.

"How are you, sir?"

"Can't complain. I hope you don't mind, but I took the liberty of ordering two Halibut steaks for lunch."

"Sounds good." Aidan took a seat and looked around the half empty restaurant. He didn't recognize any of the four suits sitting at a table across the room.

Elsie brought him a coffee and refilled the Inspector's cup. When she was gone, Banyan offered Aidan a cigarette. He declined.

"Didn't your doctor say you had to give those up?" Aidan said.

"Sure, his greatest enjoyment in life is making certain I have none." He lit his cigarette and took a deep draw.

"What did you learn about the bomb?" Aidan asked, his voice a half octave lower than usual.

"Plastique. Connections to the ignition and the gas tank. Pretty simple, really."

"How'd they know the gas tank would be full?"

Banyan shook his head. "It wasn't. Besides it doesn't work that way. All they needed was to ignite a spark. It happens very quickly. The key turns in the ignition and .... There is one thing, though. The key wasn't turned. But the investigative report from E Division says it was."

"Could your investigators have made a mistake?"

"It's possible."

"But you don't believe that?"

"No, I don't."

"Could the blast have dislodged the key?"

Inspector Banyan shook his head. Elsie placed their steaks in front of them. When she was gone, Aidan continued, "What about my sister's rings?"

"I inquired about that with little results."

"What did the tests show? There must have been a reason why they were so perfectly preserved?"

"The rings are gone." Banyan scooped up a forkful of steak.

"What?"

"Ed McCormick requested his wife be cremated with her jewellery."

His fork slipped from his fingers; Aidan quickly picked it up. "Has an insurance investigator been assigned to the case?"

"He's already finished his report. Apparently not all the automobile owners filed a claim."

"Which ones?"

"The four most damaged by the blast."

"Did ICBC contact the owners?" Aidan shook his head. "That was stupid. I keep forgetting the Insurance Corporation is part of the government bureaucracy. Did your men get any license plates or registration off those four?"

"Aidan, you know the procedure," Banyan said, a mouthful of fish in his mouth. "Whether they claimed or not what's that got to do with this case?"

"Tell me this? Why has Ed already received my sister's death benefits?"

"They put a rush on it."

"E-Division?"

"Yeah."

"I need to see the criminal investigation files."

"Your Dad was a good guy, Aidan, but don't ask me--"

"I know what you're thinking, sir, but this is different. Yes, I messed up bad over my parents' murder, but I still live in a democracy, and I'm entitled to see that file."

"I've been ordered off this case. What do you think we're doing out in the middle of nowhere and me with a stack of papers this high on my desk." He indicated with his hand a heaping pile on the table. "I don't have a file. Everything was sent to Vancouver."

"Sir, I was on the force for twenty years, remember? I know there's an original in your cabinets."

Inspector Banyan retrieved his handkerchief and blew his nose like a foghorn. "They're photocopies. I was ordered to send the originals."

"Inspector--"

"Hey, wait one minute. I didn't say I was turning anything over to you."

"You know I wouldn't ask if it wasn't important."

"Ah, hell." Banyan sighed. "I think I'm allergic to something in my office. Maybe I should take my doctor's advice and retire." He frowned at Aidan. "What if you're wrong a second time? This case is pretty straightforward."

Aidan gave the Inspector a long and hard look. "Then why did you make photocopies?"

* * *

Directly above Aidan Roth and Inspector Banyan, the man on the second floor balcony with the tiny earpiece stuck in his ear and connected to an even smaller amplifier, pushed his empty plate aside. He pulled a clip of money from his pocket, selected a Canadian twenty-dollar bill, and placed it on the table. His boss's instinct for people was impressive. He'd suspected her brother would cause problems; and he was right.

The man mused over this revelation as he left the restaurant. Lucky for the cartel that DeOlmos was suspicious of everybody.

CHAPTER 16

Miguel DeOlmos took the cellular phone from his steward. "Thank you for returning my call. Your promptness is a pleasant reminder of why I allow you to live. Now, tell me. Have you prepared those dossiers?"

"I've done everything you said," Sergeant Jackson replied. "I placed the file in the deposit box this morning just like you told me."

"*Bueno.* You have a complete profile on each of them?"

"Everything I could find out."

"On whom?" Miguel asked, enjoying the frustration evident in the man's voice.

"What d'ya you mean? I got files on Vamozzi, Canaday, Tomlin, Rostov, Bailey, Kalamai, and Ed McCormick, just like you said. Look--it's not my fault I didn't know who she was when she showed up at the precinct. I gave you her name before anybody else."

"Don't panic, Sergeant. I'm sure you've done your very best. By the way, how is your family?"

"Look, I've--"

Miguel clicked off his cellular phone.

* * *

Two weeks passed before Valerie saw Elko, Nevada as similar to Cache Creek, British Columbia. Pretending to be closer to home was comforting except for one problem. When she looked through the windows, the steep, majestic Coastal Mountains weren't there. Neither were the trees. Nor the jagged cliffs, dynamited to make way for highways, roads, bridges, and railroads. All she saw were rolling hills Agent Bailey had referred to as mountains.

What did he say this morning? "The mountains are pretty here."

Valerie had bit down on her lower lip then blurted, "Those aren't mountains, you idiot."

Agent Bailey dismissed her rudeness and offered her a cigarette. Valerie retaliated by storming through the smoke filled rooms and gathering up all seven ashtrays in the house, dirty and clean. She marched to the back door and flung them into the snow. The agents' silent resignation only fuelled her frustrations further, until she flopped into the nearest chair and realized how silly she looked. Ten minutes later, she handed Kalamai a small dish for her cigarette. Kalamai smiled that Hawaiian greeting smile of hers.

Valerie went back to her spot at the front window.

An hour later, she heard her name and turned around. Vamozzi approached with a kitchen chair. She looked at him, at the chair, and shook her head. The cold hardwood floor beneath her feet stifled her temper. A temper, until a few months ago, she didn't know existed.

Or did she?

She'd lost her temper once when she was twelve. She punched the bully living on her street, square in the jaw. He deserved it. Her father wasn't so sure. Despite being a policeman, he abhorred violence. When Valerie explained that the little jerk killed a squirrel with a baseball bat, her father had agreed sometimes punishment was necessary.

For the next three days, Valerie stood at the window for hours without tiring. During the daylight, the sun's rays warmed her. The empty landscape soothed her. In the evenings, she watched the reflections of the agents behind her. The periodic glances, the soft whispers, meant nothing. What they thought or didn't think held no credence. Except for Canaday. Still half immersed in her own world, part of her cringed under his scrutiny.

He sat on the couch, body bent forward, hands locked, and he watched. And watched.

After supper on Sunday night, Valerie marched to her room, determined to stay there.

After a moment, the solitude of the freshly painted room, with its lace and bright colors made her cry. Everywhere she looked, she saw her daughters. The stuffed animal one of the agents had given her, his name escaped her, reminded her of Brandi. In the privacy of her bedroom, Brandi, the hardcore tomboy, cuddled Garfield to sleep every night. The thick duvet, reminiscent of Christine's, reminded Valerie of the many times she entered her daughter's room, looked at the mound on the bed, and wondered if Christine was actually in there. The small desk and reading lamp reminded her of the times she caught her eldest studying past midnight. "Go to sleep, Sweetie. You'll learn more if you're well rested." Megan, the compulsive learner, would answer, "Yes, Mum, just one more paragraph."

Valerie faced the room. Where were her daughters now? How did they cope through the funeral? It must have been a closed casket. Did they sit bravely, wondering what their mother looked like inside? Did they touch the shining mahogany wood, thinking they were touching her? Did they stand over the grave until the coffin descended into the ground? Did they look to Aidan for comfort, only to see a face filled with pain?

Once upon a time, Valerie had done all those things.

She squeezed the images of her parents aside and wondered if Ed was sleeping in their bed? Or had he taken to staying in the study?

Valerie threw open her bedroom door and went back to the living room window.

* * *

After speaking to Assistant Director Tomlin for almost an hour on the secure line in the sedan, Canaday entered the house through the backdoor. He approached the entrance to the front room, saw Valerie facing the window, and stopped. Kalamai and Vamozzi were leaning back against the outside of the wet bar a few feet away.

"She's thinking about her family again," Kalamai told Vamozzi. "She hasn't raised her voice in days. Have you noticed that strange look on her face?"

"She's in shock," Vamozzi said.

"We should have waited and pulled the whole family out when we had a second chance."

"It would have been too late. We had a perfect opportunity, and we were right to take it."

"I suppose," Kalamai offered.

Vamozzi sipped his coffee. Canaday stepped closer.

"She asked if Onston was a relative," Kalamai said. "When I said no, she asked me what I'd do if I were in her place. I didn't know what to say."

"You'd adjust, just as she will," Vamozzi said.

"I offered to put her hair up this morning, but she said no. She said things were different now and having her hair hanging loose seemed appropriate. What do you think she meant by that?"

"Her last connection to freedom?" Canaday interrupted.

"Candyman!" Kalamai swung around to face him. "Stop sneaking up on me. Otherwise, don't hold me responsible if I shoot you."

Canaday glanced at his watch.

"It's not my turn outside, already?" she asked. "Couldn't you send someone else; I'm freezing. Give me Hawaii anytime, but this place--"

"C.T., go outside."

She looked at him, her face drawn. "Yes sir."

Vamozzi went back to sipping his coffee after Kalamai left. "What did Tomlin say? Since it doesn't look like DeOlmos will surface, do we go back for the kids?"

"He says sixteen days isn't long enough."

"What do you say?"

"It doesn't matter what I say."

"Now, you expect me to believe you have no influence with the boss?"

Canaday turned sharply and gave Vamozzi a hard look. "You think I like what's happened to this woman? I don't. But I made a decision, and I'm carrying it through. DeOlmos isn't stupid. He's biding his time. Did you read that statement from the informer Jeremy Gordon before he died? He described DeOlmos as cautious, patient, and the most suspicious man he'd ever met. DeOlmos will wait until he's positive we haven't tricked him. Besides Agent Ward is still there. Maybe he'll finally meet Miguel."

"You just answered my question. You do still have influence with the boss. But the longer Ward stays undercover...."

"Saul?" He looked at one of the few men he could call friend and purposely didn't blink. "When I decide to switch strategies, we'll make a move. Meanwhile, we have a problem."

"What kind of problem?"

Canaday unwrapped a candy and stuck it in his mouth. He leaned his face on his hand and watched Valerie. She'd been standing at the window most of the day. Now with night fallen, she looked so small, like a young child wrapped in an adult's sweater. Corduroy pants folded twice at the ankles, feet covered by socks too big. She stood out against a curtain of silver tinted clouds. Isolated from them, slipping into invisibility.

"Tomorrow, send Kalamai to town for some woman's clothing." He looked at Vamozzi and sighed. "Roth's asking questions."

"What kind of questions?"

"What do you think?"

"How much time are they giving us?"

"As usual, Tomlin won't commit himself. Eventually she'll be set loose. Resettled in some city with new identification, money, whatever." He rubbed the whiskers on his chin. "She is stronger than she thinks. She'll survive."

"You like her, don't you?"

"Say what?" he snapped.

Vamozzi changed the subject. "What about Roth?"

"Agent Griffith and E-Division will keep an eye on him."

"If he discovers she's alive--"

"Don't you think I know what that would mean?" Vamozzi opened his mouth to say something. Canaday raised his hand palm out. "Saul, don't be my conscience today."

Kalamai stuck her head around the corner; her breathing was irregular. "There's a call for you." With afterthought, she added, "On the secure line outside."

Canaday followed her out to the sedan. He sat in the passenger's seat and switched on the interior light. He made a face at the stale luminous air and put the receiver to his ear. "Yeah."

"Our number two man arrived back last week minus three toes."

"Retribution?"

"Seems that way."

"What about his brother?"

"No sign of him. Nobody's talking, but it's rumoured he's fishing. Fishing for what I don't know." Undercover agent Kyle Ward changed the subject, "I hear Parker's back with you. Is she okay?"

"Yes, why?"

"No reason, except she's on Vincente's mind. Keep a close eye on her. You never know with this guy."

"Does he suspect Parker knows about Prince George?"

"If he did, I think there'd be more panic."

"Is your cover secure?"

"Vincente doesn't know I exist. I'm just another soldier. As long as I keep my ears out of range and obey orders, and don't get caught making these calls, it's cool. *Hasta luego, adios, amigo.*"

Canaday hung up the handset. Smoke from the chimney billowed, curled and coiled, ascending away into a dark haze. Valerie stood at the window, her face devoid of all expression. She looked fragile, beautiful, despite the invisible scars. He knew he should relay Ward's message on to Tomlin, but he couldn't tear his eyes off her.

She hugged her arms across her chest, and he involuntarily shuddered. One night, hell--one hour alone with her would--Canaday shook his head. Get a grip, asshole.

For over four decades, he'd managed to elude the emotion he felt now.

After two tours in the Nam and twenty years with the Bureau, he'd seen it all. Yet nothing he'd witnessed or done prepared him for Valerie McCormick. The worse part was he didn't understand why. She was under his skin. She was in his dreams. She was in his head even when he couldn't see her. Why? He'd been with women more beautiful.

Canaday shook his head in disgust. Did he want her because he couldn't have her?

If only it were that simple.

He took the pad from his pocket, scribbled a long note, and dialled Tomlin's number in Washington. When he had the Assistant Director on the line, he put the note through the fax machine next to him. Following that, he called another secure line. This time to a car phone parked near the McCormick house.

"Griffith, it's Canaday. How's it going?"

"The Canadian Justice Department won't authorize a phone tap."

Why isn't that surprising? "I'll call back tomorrow." He hung up.

He rolled down the window and spit his candy into the night. Kalamai, standing at the back door, took that as a signal and walked toward the car. He got out, walked past her, and went into the house without saying a word.

"Good evening to you too," Kalamai yelled.

CHAPTER 17

Twenty-five days after the bombing, Aidan spoke to the car rental owner about the men who'd rented three of the four vehicles most damaged in the bombing. The owner was about as helpful as a hole in a gas tank. He couldn't remember what the customers looked like; the address he gave Aidan was bogus, and the purchase order recorded a full payment in cash. Disgusted, Aidan drove to the grocery store and parked on the edge of the road, six feet from where Valerie had parked her van that day. He flipped through his small notepad full of scribbles. He clicked his pen.

Two rented panel trucks and one pickup rented from the same company, along with a '78 Rabbit purchased privately, surrounded his sister's van the day of the bombing, February 20.

Bad timing?

Ed said Valerie left the house at three p.m. Witnesses said the bomb exploded at 4:15. She was in the grocery store for over an hour. Plenty of time for vehicles to surround her van. Why? The Cartel doesn't worry about innocent bystanders. They certainly don't spend exorbitant amounts of money to get rid of a witness.

Aidan tapped his pencil against the steering wheel. Two panel trucks and one pickup. He looked out over the parking lot and repeated the information. He continued tapping his pencil. Finally, he closed his eyes.

I'm about to kill a witness. I rent a bunch of vehicles to protect the innocent. Four days later, I attach a bomb to her ignition and park close enough to witness the explosion.

His eyes still closed, Aidan shook his head.

I don't care about the innocent. I'm there to do a job, quickly, neatly, cheaply.

Why four days?

A fluke? Opportunity?

The man at the car rental said they'd been out-of-town executives.

Not good enough.

Aidan flicked through his notebook to the details for the other vehicle most damaged by the bombing. He rubbed at the sore muscles in his neck.

The address was for an apartment across from him. He decided to check it out. Sitting in his car wasn't getting him anywhere

A kid, twenty-something, dressed in jeans and a worn tee shirt answered the door. "Yeah."

Aidan handed him a business card. "I'm looking for the owner of a '78 Rabbit. His name's...." Aidan glanced at his notes.

"It was mine, but I sold it."

"To whom?"

"Geez, man, I don't remember."

"That was January 20th?"

The kid leaned against the doorframe. "No way."

"The transfer papers say ... January --"

"It was February 20th. I think I'd remember selling my first car."

"Can you remember anything about the buyer? This is important."

The kid scratched his head. "He was just a regular guy. He was walking through the parking lot when he stops and asked me--I'd just finished jumping my car. He asks me if I'd sell it. He hands me four hundred bucks. I thought of asking for five, but it wasn't worth three. I guess he must have gone for groceries right after. You remember the bombing. But hey, it's not my fault what happened."

Aidan rushed toward the exit sign and headed back to his sister's house.

* * *

"Where have you been?" Susan wiped her hands on the towel and stepped away from the sink.

Aidan leaned over Valerie's kitchen counter and fidgeted with his car keys. "I went home to surf."

"I was worried."

"Sorry." He continued to twist the keys in his hand.

"There are leftovers in the microwave."

He shook his head.

Susan reached across the counter and took the keys. "What's wrong?"

Aidan tried to form the words.

"Aidan Roth, if you have a problem, it's my problem. And vice versa, remember?"

"I think Valerie's alive."

She gave Aidan back his keys. "Are you sure?"

"Yes--no. I don't know." He reached for her hand and held it gently. "I believe the FBI has her. I found out today the same dummy corporation from the States rented vehicles surrounding Valerie's van. I checked it out on the Net and found zilch. I contacted an old friend with the GIS in Ottawa; he found nothing. I called a buddy in Virginia, and a strange thing happened. The file existed, all right, but somebody sealed it three weeks ago. So, yeah, you could say they were rented by the FBI."

"Don't get angry with me, but how does that prove Val's alive?"

He gave her a summary of what he knew. "What are the chances of that happening without deliberate planning? Agent Vamozzi said he'd do everything in his power to protect her. I believe the FBI faked her death to fool DeOlmos. Only trouble is, if I can figure that out, why can't DeOlmos?"

Susan walked around the counter and hugged him. "I want to believe you, Aidan."

"I know." He held her tight. "When it comes to my family, I have a tendency to screw up bad."

"I didn't say that."

He pressed his lips to her temple. "It's the truth. I threw away seven years on the Force because I was so sure my dad's death was a contract killing. I know what I did was--"

"Don't you dare say that. You loved your dad."

"I also ruined a promising future."

"Aidan, stop. The ruined future you're talking about has been great. Fabulous, in fact. What happened after you came out here could have happened to anyone. How many members saw the evidence you'd accumulated and believed you were right? Six. Don't forget that they were just as convinced as you."

"They didn't jeopardize their careers. They didn't have to resign."

"It wasn't their parents who were murdered."

He pressed her hand against his face, smelling her scent, and feeling the hard texture of her rings against his cheek. "I love you so--" He leaned back stared at Susan's rings. "They didn't look like that."

"What didn't?"

"Valerie's rings. When I went to the morgue, they didn't look like that. Your band is first then your diamond. Is that traditional?"

"Yes. The band first then the engagement ring. Why?"

"Valerie's rings were the other way around."

"She wouldn't have worn them that way." She backed up to look up at him. "You're sure?"

Aidan nodded. "I think they were put on by a man."

"Are you going to tell Ed and the girls?"

"Christ--no!"

"Why?"

"Susan, Valerie's life depends on us keeping this information to ourselves."

"Except, since the memorial you haven't been around much. You're not here during the day and rarely at night. This family is falling apart, Aidan. I don't know how much longer I can watch."

He saw tears coming and pulled her into his arms. "I'm not going anywhere."

* * *

The following week, after exhausting all his contacts with the highway patrol and the Canadian Customs officials at the border, Aidan drove to the Prince George Airport. He parked outside the security doors, stuck his pass upright on the dash, and took the steps two at a time. Manny Carleton sat behind his desk with a pen in one hand and a coffee in the other. He was studying the huge manifold binder stretched across his desk; his glasses were perched precariously on the tip of his nose.

Manny was Aidan's oldest friend in Prince George. After his parents' deaths, Aidan's first assignment had been patrolling the airport. He and Manny hit it off straightaway. Manny said he became Aidan's friend because he was the only one Aidan could beat at golf. Aidan said they became friends because any poor shmuck who played golf like ET deserved a friend.

The air traffic supervisor looked over his horn-rimmed glasses and smiled. He stood and extended his hand. "Where the hell you been?"

"Working."

Manny took off his glasses. "Sit down. This isn't a social visit, is it? The last time I saw you, you promised you'd let me bust your chops at golf the following week. That was eight months ago. Judging by the snow outside, I'm guessing you're not here scheduling a new game?"

Aidan scratched his head and sat down. He could hear the hum of voices in the control tower next door. "At the risk of abusing our friendship, I need a big favour. Would you check your log entries for February 20th?"

Manny got up and went to the filing cabinet. He pulled out a folder and placed it on his desk. "What am I looking for?"

"Any small planes coming in from the States prior to 1600? Particularly any plane not on a regular schedule?"

Flipping to the back cover, Manny went through the last few computer printouts. "I've got a Learjet, identified as--"

"Do you have the flight plan?"

He guided his finger across the page. "That's strange."

"What?"

"It was left blank."

"Is that normal?"

Manny scratched his head and frowned at Aidan. "It should've been filled in."

"You have no idea where they headed?"

"Sorry, Aidan."

Aidan stood up and put his note pad away. "It's okay."

"How's the family?"

"Fine." He paused at the door.

"I'm sorry about your sister. I looked through the papers for a funeral date."

"The memorial service was closed."

"Do you need anything else?"

"No."

"You in some kind of trouble?"

"No. I'm working on a case."

Manny nodded. "I mention no heading, and the blood drains from your face. That explains a lot. You want to talk about it?"

"Can't. Do you know who the jet belongs to?"

"Gates Learjet, Series fifty, longhorn, model 54. Belongs to the United States Justice Department. Better known as the FBI."

"How do you know that?"

"Remember that case you worked on where that kid went missing on his way down from Alaska, and they found his truck burnt, stuck in some carwash downtown?"

Aidan nodded.

"It was that same jet." Manny continued, "Remember? They landed here with a special forensic team. They went over that truck for almost two days."

"They found the killer in California," Aidan said. "Any way of finding out where they were headed?"

Manny shook his head. "Aidan, those babies have a range of 4,000 kilometres."

He knew it was a long shot, but he had faith in Manny, and this was the closest he'd ever been to finding anything. "What's the passenger allowance?"

"Two crew and up to eleven passengers."

"Speed?"

"A walloping 1384 km an hour, give or take a kilometer." Manny frowned at the glum look on Aidan's face.

"Don't you think it's kinda suspicious that the FBI lands in Canada and doesn't file a flight plan?"

"Give me a couple of days. I have a few pals in the States. I'll see what I can come up with."

He reached down, grabbed Manny's hand, and shook it wildly. "I owe you. If anyone asks--"

"Yeah, I know, you weren't here."

Aidan left. He spent six gruelling days waiting for Manny to call. He caught up on his other cases and checked his messages every hour on the hour.

"Sorry for the delay, I was waiting on a friend from Las Vegas," Manny said when he finally did call.

"How'd you put it? The guy's wife was …?"

"Dog-ugly but built like a brick shithouse." Manny laughed.

"Why Las Vegas?" Aidan asked, cutting into their small talk.

"They left here and flew directly to Elko. Which is weird considering Elko ain't exactly metropolitan."

"Did they take off again?"

"A bunch debarked first."

"Thanks, good buddy."

"I wish it was more."

"It's okay, Manny. It's somewhere to start. One more question. Who's got access to your records?"

"I've got bosses like everybody else, Aidan. It could've been anybody connected to the airport. Anybody from Ottawa."

"GIS?"

"Them, too."

CHAPTER 18

Vincente DeOlmos grabbed the prostitute by her ankles and yanked her from the bed onto the floor. Naked, sweaty, and feeling meaner than usual, he kicked her twice in the stomach and yelled, "Shut up!"

The girl sobbed, curled up in a ball, and tried to protect her face. She had made the mistake of calling him "Mommy's boy".

He wanted to kick her again but unfortunately, balancing on his deformed foot was difficult. "Get on the bed," he ordered. "Now do what you're paid to do. Spread your legs." He picked up the knife next to his bed and crawled across the bottom of the bed toward her. She clapped both hands over her mouth to stop the guttural sounds. The cell phone on the bedside table rang; Vincente cursed loudly. He picked it up and screamed "What!"

"*Jefé*, Roth is going on a trip."

Vincente sat on his bed and faced away from the cringing whore on his bed. "Where?"

"Elko, Nevada, *jefé*."

"Elko?"

"*Si*, Elko."

"Call me as soon as you get there."

"Si, jefé."

"Remember, you tell my brother, and you're dead. ¡*Muerto*!" Vincente slammed the phone down.

He'd find out what Roth was up to, then show Miguel how much of an asset his *hermanito* really was.

* * *

After two hours of counting sheep, summarizing Chaucer's 'Canterbury Tales' then in a desperate attempt, listing Canada's ten provinces and their capitals, Valerie finally succumbed to sleep, only to have her comforter plucked off her face.

"Val? Get up. We're history," Kalamai said.

Valerie struggled to open her eyes. "What?"

"We have to leave ASAP."

Special Agent Kalamai pulled a bag from under the bed and stuffed in the few clothes purchased a week ago. In seconds, the top drawer and the closet were emptied. Valerie rubbed her eyes and squinted. The clock on the bedside table showed 6:15. She didn't know how much longer she could survive without a decent night's sleep.

"If you take off that thing, I'll stuff it with the rest of your laundry," Kalamai said.

Valerie stretched her legs over the side of the bed. "I can manage by myself."

Kalamai hesitated, her teeth clamping down on her bottom lip. She looked as if she'd been coerced into disobeying a direct order. "Yeah, sure ... I'll get your things from the bathroom. Be up and ready to go when I come back."

"After 28 days in captivity, where am I going now?"

"I don't know. All I was told is it's imperative we leave."

Moments later, Kalamai hustled her outside to the sedan. Valerie climbed into the backseat. Kalamai slipped in beside her and signalled to Vamozzi at the door. Two cars left with one remaining behind.

"Why aren't the others following?" Valerie asked.

"When the house is swept down, they'll leave. Probably ten minutes," Kalamai answered.

As they sped toward the highway, Valerie looked back at the log house. From the ensuing distance, it no longer resembled a prison, simply a house with four walls, and a roof. The car behind closed in and blocked her view. She faced forward and looked out at the miles of deserted road ahead.

"Where are we going?" She glanced from Bailey behind the wheel to the back of Canaday's head.

"We're off to another safe house, Val," Kalamai explained.

"Why?"

"Because that one," she gestured behind her, "isn't safe any longer."

"From whom?"

Kalamai looked toward Canaday, who seemed to be either ignoring their conversation or oblivious to it. "I'm not sure."

C.T., are you lying? During the past month, Valerie had had the impression giving her even a tidbit of information was against the rules. Unless the rules had changed?

She hesitated a moment, then taking a deep breath, leaned forward and tapped Canaday lightly on the shoulder.

He looked back at her.

"Why are we leaving?"

"Your safety has been compromised." His tone was gentle.

"How?"

"It may be nothing, but someone was spotted at the airport in Elko. We can't take a chance." He glanced at her mouth, her hair, her eyes, then blinked. His expression changed from warm to cool. He faced forward.

His shoulders looked strong, as if they could carry the weight of the world. He smelled like pine soap. Valerie closed her eyes and inhaled. When she opened them, she noticed how his hair curled in waves behind his ear. She wet her dry lips. "Where are we going?"

Canaday stayed face forward. "Back to Seattle."

An hour later, in the middle of nowhere, they turned off the highway onto a dirt road. Ten miles further, they approached an unused airstrip and deserted hangar. Neglected and wind plagued, the building leaned to one side. Valerie wondered if one good push would topple it over.

They stopped. Bailey left the car and with an effort, opened the large hangar door. When they were parked inside, Canaday picked up the telephone receiver next to him and repeated a numerical code three times. He replaced the receiver and instructed Bailey to remove the luggage. The rest climbed out of the second car parked beside her and attempted to secure the building. They looked like little boys playing a grownup game.

Kalamai went to the far end of the hangar and stood near a small window. Canaday pushed his door open, planted both feet on the ground, and stopped.

"Do you want to stretch your legs?" he asked, his face turned away.

Because she was the only one left in the car, Valerie assumed he'd spoken to her. "I'm too tired to move."

"I heard you pacing last night and the night before ... and the night before that. Nightmares?"

"Yes."

He lowered his head. "I'm sorry." He rose and walked away.

He passed through a streak of sunlight and went to the second vehicle. He reached in through the driver's open window and pulled out the handset. She was too tired to care about whom he was calling. Another concern bothered her. She watched him through heavy eyes and wondered why she cared what he thought.

His brows set into a deep frown. He swept a hand through his hair and looked across at her. She lowered her eyes, counted to five, and looked back at him. His arm stretched across the roof, his fist thumped to a slow beat. He said something, his frowning face turning bitter, while she sensed the anger he fought so hard to control.

At that very instance, Valerie understood why she'd been so angry with him back at the safe house. She'd been redirecting her rage. Yes, Canaday had given her an ultimatum. But she was the one who had accepted without question.

She should've never left her children.

A tear rolled down her cheek. Valerie had no energy to wipe it away. She had grown up without her parents; she knew the damage inflicted by such a loss. It didn't matter if she was alive; her children were motherless.

What do I do now?

Deal with it.

* * *

Canaday walked out into the morning light. He changed the frequency on his radio and summoned Vamozzi. They were finished and would meet as planned, Vamozzi reported. At that, Canaday turned the radio off and proceeded to the far end of the hanger. He stood a few feet away from Special Agent Kalamai.

"How many were spotted at the airport?" She looked at something behind him.

Canaday looked over his shoulder and followed Kalamai's gaze. Valerie's head was tilted back, her eyes closed. "Three."

"How did DeOlmos know we were there?"

"He didn't."

"Huh?"

"Two of DeOlmos' men are following Roth."

"Val's brother? How did he know where we were?"

Canaday heard the sounds of an airplane overhead. "I don't know." He headed for the side door. "But I'm going to find out."

* * *

Valerie took a seat inside the jet's familiar cabin. Canaday sat opposite her. Their eyes locked, and for a split second, she felt as if he could read her thoughts. She tore her eyes away.

Outside, the barren land passed quickly as the plane taxied to the end of the unkempt runway. They made an about-face, and soon the ground beneath them fell away. The sun, now fully visible, glared through the tiny window.

The worse part, she realized, were the mood swings.

"It's the usual routine, Mrs. McCormick?" Canaday said.

"Ah, yes, the routine. Stay in my seat with the seatbelt fastened until we come to a complete stop."

She buckled up her seatbelt and watched him do the same. This wasn't the alert and focused agent she was used to. Now that they weren't making direct eye contact, he looked exhausted. He took a deep breath, leaned his cheek against his fist, and glanced out the window. His eyelids lowered, as if given the chance he'd nod off right there in front of her.

If only sleep would come as easily for her.

He loosened his tie and leaned his head back, his eyes still directed toward the window. His chest rose and fell slowly. His lips parted while his arms lay comfortably along the armrests, his biceps bulging against the inside of his sleeves. Strong weathered hands hung limp. No wedding rings.

She slowly raised her eyes and scanned his face. Was he single or did he simply choose not to wear a wedding ring? He was definitely different. And it wasn't because he was American. His very manner procured respect. But that wasn't it either. He had the kind of eyes that could look straight through you, see all your secrets straight away, and then pretend he hadn't.

"Canaday?" Valerie whispered.

He gave her his full attention.

"I need to ask you a question."

He waited.

Valerie's reserve faltered. She didn't want another confrontation. Still she had to ask. "Why didn't you send agents back for my girls? The authorities could have made up some story about the girls moving east to live with relatives."

"You don't think DeOlmos would have checked that out?"

"The relatives could have been undercover agents."

Canaday shook his head. "It wouldn't have worked."

"Why?"

"Mrs. McCormick ...." He paused, crossed his arms, placing his thumbnail to his lips.

"It's not too late. You could arrange to have them moved. You could talk to the Canadian authorities."

He shook his head.

Valerie clenched her fists. "Why not?"

Instead of answering her, he stared with such intensity to her left that she turned to follow his gaze. Beside her was nothing but an empty seat.

"Why didn't you pick them up when you saw that man put a bomb under my van?"

"You die and your children disappear. Does that make sense?"

"It makes more sense than this." She raised her hand to the air. "You must be tired of hearing the same questions over and over. I'm sick of asking. But since you continually refuse to answer, I'm going to presume either you left my children behind because it's cheaper to guard one person than an entire family, or you left them behind because it never occurred to you to take them. Which is it?"

"No matter what I say, it won't be the right answer."

She sat up straight. "Try me."

"I'm not going back for your girls."

"Answer the fucking question!" Dear God! She squeezed her eyes shut then opened them and saw Canaday gawking at her. Equally disgusted? "I'm sorry. I swear--I promise I won't ask again if you could please tell me why. I don't care how bad your reasons are, but I have to know. Not knowing," her eyes moistened, "is killing me."

"We lost Megan." His expression changed to something recognizable. Those steel blue eyes cut right through her. "We had everyone under surveillance, but Megan slipped out of the basement of the Prince George Library. The RCMP didn't find her until thirty minutes after we'd left."

Valerie's hand automatically covered her mouth. A terrible sorrow sprang up from her stomach, through her heart, and tried to escape out her mouth. She clenched her jaw tight, pressed her hand over her lips as hard as she could, folded almost in half, and cried until it felt as if her heart would break. Fate was an ugly, ugly thing.

CHAPTER 19

Aidan arrived in Elko and straightaway visited the Elko Chamber of Commerce. Then he went to every realtors and car rental in town. For five days and four nights, he made the rounds of all the grocery stores, casinos, and fast food restaurants. On the fifth night, he sat at the bar in an out-of-the-way casino, and watched the gamblers come and go. At two a.m., he declined another soft drink and ordered Canadian Club. He asked the waitress if there had been any strangers in town.

She looked at him, at the crowd behind her, and laughed.

Aidan laughed too. Then he leaned forward and banged his head on the tabletop.

The waitress, probably thinking he was a nut and for good reason, disappeared. When his drink was empty, the bartender served him, leaning forward from a safe distance to set his drink down.

Aidan sipped that drink. Two, thick necked Latinos, about as inconspicuous as two ducks wading amongst a bunch of swans, sat down at the bar, their profiles to him.

The bartender poured two highballs, while the eight-hundred-dollar suits sucked on fat cigars and tried real hard not to look at Aidan. Their huge diamond rings glittered against tanned, smooth hands. The gold chains around the closest guy's neck probably weighed more than all Susan's jewellery put together. They downed their drinks in one gulp and ordered two more. When the bartender offered them chips instead of their change, the first guy growled.

Mistake number two. This was a casino; people didn't come here to drink; they came here to gamble.

Aidan stretched out his arms and faked a big yawn. He had a good idea who they worked for, and he had to lose them quick.

He slapped two five-dollar chips down on the table and walked out into the lobby. He bought yesterday's paper from a coin operated machine then strolled toward the front doors. As he passed by the half partition separating the bar from the lobby, he glanced at the spot where the men had sat. They were gone. Aidan reminded himself to expect the worse. Then he prayed Valerie was already gone.

Except for a few tortured gamblers, the street was quiet. Aidan headed north. His rental was east two blocks. After walking the roundabout way, he'd lose them before heading back to his car.

Fifty feet up the sidewalk, he saw a shadow; a few more feet and he smelled the distinct odour of cigar. He automatically touched his holster, which of course wasn't there. He was in the States. His gun was in Canada. You brainless prick. He searched the sidewalk for a weapon. A stick. A loose piece of concrete.

He cursed himself for not purchasing extended medical just as the two men walked out from a side alley. They leaned up against the storefront window and leisurely puffed on their cigars. Aidan tossed the newspaper in the garbage bin. Slapping them silly with the paper didn't work for him. He stuck his hands in his pockets and gripped a recently purchased butane lighter in his right fist.

"Hey, mister," the guy wearing the gold necklaces said. "You know where the Manhattan Bar is?"

Aidan slowed down and stopped within ten feet. He put his left hand to his head and made out like he was thinking. This was proving difficult. "Sorry, can't help you."

"Maybe you show us where it is? We make it worth your time." The guy with the chains smiled. Obviously, he had a hearing problem.

"Sorry, fellas, but I'm new to town. I don't know where anything is."

"C'mon, mister, try harder." The guy stepped forward and swung.

Aidan ducked and then hit him in the head. He flew back. Aidan spun around and kicked the second guy in the nuts.

The guy with the necklaces, got to his feet, staggered, his hand reached inside his jacket.

Aidan drove a fist into his jaw. His head lolled backward, but he recovered quickly; he clobbered Aidan in the stomach. The air gushed from Aidan's lungs. He punched the guy in the head then the stomach then the head.

Out of the corner of his eye, he saw the second guy rise, shake his head like a dog. With the lighter clutched in his hand, Aidan beat his fists into the first guy's nose, again and again; he felt his knuckles crack; but the guy wouldn't go down; he staggered backward.

Aidan whipped around to face the second guy. He swung at his head; the man ducked then rammed a fist into Aidan's side. Aidan couldn't breathe. He blocked the second shot then fell to the ground.

The first guy bashed him in the kidneys. Aidan's face smacked into the sidewalk. A tremendous pain targeted his back. A metal lid smashed into his head.

They picked him up by the lapels of his jacket. Aidan needed to throw up but not enough that he would. Too bad. He could have given these guys something to remember him by.

They dragged him by his arms. His muscles wouldn't respond. He shook his head to remain conscious. They hauled him into an alley. They twisted him around and pushed him against a building. They let go. He slid down the rough wall into filth.

"Now, this is how it works. We ask questions, you give answers."

If his back didn't ache so much, Aidan might have laughed. He loved the way the jerk came right to the point.

"Why're you here?" the gangster asked.

Aidan couldn't help himself. "Dah, I like gambling."

A fist rammed into his stomach. Aidan doubled over then roughly straightened.

"Mister, you got balls, but your smartass mouth is gonna get you dead. What're you looking for?"

"A good time."

The little prick's fist felt like a battering ram against his stomach. Aidan gasped and bent forward at the waist. The thought of dying thousands of miles from home left more than a bad taste in his mouth.

This had gone far enough. Aidan rocked backward, grabbed the clump of gold chains, twisted, and pulled then upward, two knuckles cracking against the base of the man's nose. He swung at the gangster and missed.

Ah shit.

He was on the ground, curled up in a foetal position, trying to protect his head. He smelled boot leather and dog shit. A rib snapped, sending a jolt of pain to take away his breath. A blow to his head. Wow, neat stars. A sharp blow to his tailbone, and he was definitely more scared than pissed.

Aidan heard a loud thud. A man groaned. Aidan was pretty sure it wasn't him.

A body dropped to his right. Another body dropped near his head. He felt his own body being lifted.

"You okay, man?"

Aidan tried to focus on his new 'best' friend but his eyes wouldn't open. "Yeah, sure," he said and passed out.

* * *

Miguel DeOlmos rested his arms along the back of the velvet couch in his stateroom and looked out over the Sea of Cortez. Sunbeams flickered off the calm water, interrupted periodically by the smooth surfacing of quaking humpbacks. He marvelled at their majestic presence. Soon they would take their pups from the protective surroundings of their nursery and head to open waters. Until then Miguel would sit and watch as these gentle beings coursed the sea.

Not only was Los Cabos where his mother came from, it was a place as dear to his heart as any place he had been. The quiet people, simple ways, brought him peace. Power allowed him to prosper, and he felt it only right to pass on some of his good fortune. He employed many people from Baja. Their loyalty was profound and uplifting. It made up for the lack of family. Although he adored his little brother, it was a lonely life. He had no true friends. His associates were polite because that was good business practice. The childhood friends he'd grown up with in Toronto were either dead or subordinates. His distant relatives in Colombia had treated him as an outcast when he was young. As if he and Vincente were to blame for his father seeking refuge in a foreign country. A place where the mother tongue was French instead of Spanish.

Ses parents furent des idiots, he thought in French. In Spanish: *Sus parientas fueron badulaques*. In English: His relatives were fools. His father had done well in Canada.

In Los Cabos, the people were kindred spirits. As always, when the matters at hand grieved Miguel, he retreated to this solitude to regain the perspective he needed. For the first time in his life, he had to admit having removed Valerie was not something he enjoyed doing. Her death was necessary. And painless. He had made certain of that.

He caught sight of the small zodiac approaching. He rose to his feet and saw the face of his brother. Miguel smiled. Vincente was a pleasing sight.

The two men embraced on the foredeck and walked back to the stateroom. Miguel poured his brother a tall Pina Colada and sat at his side. Together they admired the view of the sea. Sunshine and blue water surrounded them.

"How's the fishing, *hermanito*?"

DeOlmos laughed. It was a family secret; he never kept what he caught. "*Va bien*. A great challenge. You, my brother, look well mended."

Vincente's face beamed. "Business is good. Our associates in

Colombia have expanded their orders."

DeOlmos knew that. "I think my time here must end. Tonight we feast, tomorrow it's business as usual."

"Miguel, I have more good news. The Canadian authorities have finished their investigation. The case is closed. Now we can go home to Canada."

Miguel contemplated Vincente's news while pushing back the cuticle on his left index finger. Miguel understood the wisdom of instinctive reaction. His reaction to Vincente's news prompted caution. He heard voices. The messages in his head warned of betrayal. The FBI had tricked him before.

"How is Valerie's family faring?" Miguel masked his face against the shock he felt at using her first name.

"They mourn, of course," Vincente said, frowning.

Miguel looked down at his manicured nails. "Her brother, Roth, how is he?"

"He's on a business trip to Nevada."

"When did he leave?"

"Seven days ago."

"What for?"

"He's working for the Air-Traffic Controller from the Prince George Airport. It's about money."

"You're certain it has nothing to do with us?"

Vincente squirmed. "I'm sure, brother. Even so, nobody's going to listen to him. He pissed a lot of people off when he was a cop."

Miguel already knew about Roth's father. But the voices inside Miguel's head were too important to dismiss. "You didn't order the men back to Florida?"

"No, I wait for your orders only."

Vincente's expression was one who knew fear and disapproval. Miguel sensed his brother's body tensing. He decided not to ease his doubts. Vincente, regardless of how much assurance he received, would always feel inadequate.

Miguel stood and walked to his desk. The dossiers were in the top drawer. He flipped through and pulled one out. "You sent a man to follow Roth?"

"Of course." Vincente appeared physically wounded.

"He understands it is most vital Roth must not spot him?"

Vincente grabbed his glass and took a quick gulp. "Yeah."

"Good." Miguel pushed the button on top of the mahogany desk behind him. Within seconds a man appeared. "A change of plans, Tomas. Return home immediately."

"*Si, patrón.*"

Vincente wriggled under Miguel's scrutiny. "Have I displeased you?" He rubbed his deformed foot along the back of his left leg.

"Not at all." DeOlmos glanced out the port window just as a gentle giant surfaced through the tranquil water and blew a gush of air from her spiracle.

CHAPTER 20

On April 9, Aidan left the Prince George Airport terminal and came out into a scene of gray skies and dull light. The snow, all but melted, was replaced with puddles of muddy water. It was the time of year he hated most. The mud season. That period after winter and before spring. The dirty, ugly few weeks of gloom.

Twelve days after he had left this airport, he returned worse off. He wondered now what it was he had expected. Some stupid miracle? Valerie standing on a street corner, guarded by inept agents no smarter than the rookies the RCMP graduated each year? A glimpse of her passing by in an unmarked car? He shook his head at his stupidity. He'd promised himself he'd stop acting like an amateur; that was weeks ago. When would his promise kick in?

His body ached. Without thinking, he almost turned west on Fifth Avenue and headed toward his home on King Drive. He caught the mistake at the intersection as the light turned red. Home wasn't where he wanted to be. Without Susan there, it was only a house. When the light turned green, he headed north.

Twenty minutes later, he dropped his bag inside the back door of his sister's house, and entered the kitchen. An aroma of tomatoes, garlic, and Italian spices swept under his nose. Trevor sat at the table; Susan stirred something in a pot on the stove. He stood for a moment until Bethum spotted him and wagged his tail.

"Dad!" Trevor yelled.

Susan turned away from the stove, and before Aidan knew it, they were both hugging him. Then Lydia was there, struggling for a spot. Not too tightly, Aidan almost said.

He kissed Susan, smelled the sweet scent of his daughter's hair, and patted Trevor on the back. For a moment, he wished his arms were longer and stronger. He'd hold onto them forever if he could. But his family had stepped back, and now they all stared at him. Aidan tried to smile.

"Oh, my God! What happened?" Susan asked.

"Honest, it looks worse than it is. I got into a fight."

"Poor Dad." Lydia examined his face and his hand.

"What happened to the other guy?" Trevor smiled. "Dad, you look like shit."

"Trevor, please." Susan stepped closer to Aidan. "Are you okay?"

"I'm fine. Honest." Aidan gently removed his hand from his daughter's grasp. "It was no big deal. Two punks jumped me. You'd have been proud of your old man."

"Oh, Aidan." Susan hugged him.

Aidan moaned.

"What's that?" She touched his shirt, the bandages underneath, and took a step backward.

"Enough already. It's nothing. I cracked a rib and got a small scratch."

"How was your trip, Aidan?" Ed asked from the dining room doorway. "What the hell happened to your face?"

"My trip was unproductive, I'm afraid. I did manage to meet some real friendly folk." He kissed Susan again and felt his family moving away from him, slipping away.

"Your timing is perfect," Susan said. "Supper is ready."

"I'll call my girls." Ed left.

"Is everything okay?" Aidan asked.

His family looked at him, then Lydia and Trevor glanced at their mother.

Susan returned to her spot in front of the stove. "It's been nice staying with the girls, but I want to go home first thing tomorrow morning."

"Has something happened?"

His eldest child shook her head. His son said nothing.

Susan stirred the spaghetti sauce then poured the drained pasta into a large bowl. She faced him. "We'll talk about it later."

The two families gathered at the table.

When the meal was over, Ed rose from his chair. "Susan, the meal was delicious. Aidan, when you've got a minute I'd like to see you in my study."

"Sure."

"Daddy? Wait for me." Brandi pushed her chair back and rushed to catch up with Ed.

"Peanuts, I'm not changing my mind. You're going to school tomorrow."

"But Daddy ...."

Aidan listened as his niece's voice faded toward the back of the house. "She hasn't been to school?"

"Not for a week," Megan answered. "It's hard for her. Christine and I at least are in the same high school. Brandi's alone."

Megan rose from the chair and started clearing the table.

"Leave it," Susan coaxed. "I need the exercise."

Megan attempted a smile then followed her sister and cousins into the living room.

The kitchen was quiet. Susan reached across the table and touched Aidan's good hand. "What happened?"

"Nothing. It was a waste of time."

"I can't believe that."

"Believe it."

"Did their jet land in Elko?"

"No."

"I thought Manny said--"

"They might have landed on a private strip, or they might have gone to another state."

"What are you going to do now?"

"Talk to Manny tomorrow. Maybe he can think of something."

"You still believe she's alive?" Susan asked, her voice low.

"I don't know. Yes, I think so. But I'm not handling this properly. I've got to distance myself." He leaned over and kissed her. "Meanwhile, I'll go and talk to Ed."

"You're all right with us going home tomorrow?"

He kissed her gently on lips that were moist with a taste of tomato paste, savouring the sweetness of her being so close, and understanding his need for her. "What happened?"

"Ed snapped at Trevor yesterday over nothing, and it was all I could do to keep my tongue in check. I don't like feeling that way. For the girls' sakes, I'd like to go home before I say something I'll regret."

Aidan nodded. He cleared his throat. "My trip ended up costing a little more than I'd planned."

"Why?"

"I had to spend a few days in the hospital." He paused, hoping Susan's expression would remain sympathetic. "I forgot to renew our extended medical."

"You're alive," she said. "How much?"

"I'll show you the receipts later, but that's not the bad news. The guys who whopped my ass work for DeOlmos."

Susan's mouth dropped open. "They could've killed you."

"Some guy helped me out. That doesn't matter. The point is they weren't there to kill me. If so, I'd be dead. They were looking for information."

"Do they think Val's alive?"

"Let's face it, my trip raised suspicions."

"Then it's good you didn't find her. You would have led them straight to her."

"After I got discharged from the hospital, I checked around. They were gone. If they're out there somewhere, I promise you, it'll be different next time. I'm home now."

"Next time?" Susan repeated. "What do you mean 'next time'? Aidan, it's too dangerous." A sudden thought turned her face white. "What if they come after the girls?"

"I'll speak to the Inspector. Don't worry, I won't let anything happen."

"Should we even be talking about this? What if the house is bugged? They must have been watching you for some time. They followed you to Nevada."

Aidan nodded. "Has anything out of the ordinary happened? Anyone from BC Hydro or Inland Gas hanging around? Or someone working on the telephone lines out front?"

Susan shook her head.

"Tomorrow, while Ed's at work, I'll have someone come over and check the house. I'll have our house swept, too. Maybe what happened in Nevada is a blessing in disguise. I know I'm being watched." He pushed himself away from the table. "I better go find out what Ed wants." He reached the doorway and looked back. Susan was slumped over, with her face in her hands.

Ed was where he said he would be. He and Brandi were sitting in the sofa chair in front of the fireplace.

"It's time for your bath, Peanuts," Ed said.

"Ah, Daddy, I had a bath last night."

"It's time again. Go to it," he ordered gently.

Aidan threw his niece a kiss and sat down in the chair next to Ed.

Ed spoke as soon as the door closed. "I haven't been much help to you since ... you know. I guess I haven't been much help to anyone. I wanted to apologize. I also wanted to thank you and Susan for everything. I don't think we would have gotten through this past month without you both.

"I've run into friends downtown, I've even stopped and talked to the neighbours. After only a month, they all act as if everything is back to normal. As if I should get on with my life. I felt like yelling 'hell, the first two weeks were the easy part'."

Aidan stared into the fire and wondered if anything Ed said was true.

"I wake up at night," Ed continued. "I walk through the house. I think I see her standing at the window, waiting for the girls to arrive home from a date, or a party, or .... "

Pausing for effect, Ed? Aidan wondered.

"Aidan, I know you've been investigating that day, but maybe everyone's right. Maybe it's time to put what happened behind us."

"Would that make you feel better?"

Ed turned toward him. "What good has it done you, Aidan? You're exhausted. Your family hardly sees you. I realized because you were once a cop you feel the need for closure, but ...."

"But what, Ed?"

Ed shot him a strange look. "I don't know." He shook his head. "Forget what I just said. I can't let go." His gaze wandered to the fire. "Part of me says it's the best thing to do. But I can't."

"Why did you have Valerie cremated with her wedding rings? Didn't she want to leave them to one of the girls?"

"Her rings?"

"The coroner's report says she had her rings on when she was shipped down to E-Division."

"I forgot about them. Jesus--Aidan. I had other things on my mind. When they asked if I wanted them back, I realized I had three daughters. Which one was I supposed to leave Valerie's rings to? I couldn't decide because they didn't belong to any of them. They were Valerie's rings. I bought them for Valerie."

Aidan rubbed his eyes. Now, not only was he tired, he doubted himself. Had he been wrong about Ed? "I gotta get some sleep. We'll be leaving first thing in the morning." He rose slowly.

Ed gazed at the coals. Aidan sidestepped past the wastepaper basket, stopped, and looked down. He recognized a purchase slip from Ritchie Brother's Auction. He couldn't make out what Ed had bought, but the balance was… Twenty-eight thousand dollars.

"Was there something else?" Ed asked.

"Nope." Aidan left the room.

* * *

Vincente DeOlmos paced across the ceramic tiles from his front glass wall back to the bar at the far end of the room. His stomps echoed throughout his glass and steel house and bounced off the twenty-foot ceiling. Outside, birds sang. He paused and touched his holster. He was on his way outside to kill the whole mite infested bunch, when his cell phone rang. He yanked it from his pocket, ripping one corner off his shirt.
"What!"

"*Buenas tardes, jefé.*"

"It's been over a week. *¿Dónde estás?*" Vincente asked.

"As you ordered we are back in Prince George."

"And?"

"*Nada, jefé.* Roth returned this evening."

"I know that, you piece-of-toilet-shit! What did you find out?" Vincente barked.

"He's stopped the investigation."

Vincente calmed down. "Keep watching. If he does anything suspicious, call me at once."

"*Claro, jefé.*"

"Under no circumstances do you say anything about what happened in Nevada. If it gets back to my brother--you're dead. *¿Comprendes?*" Vincente slammed down the receiver and yelled for his man on the patio outside.

The glass doors opened, and a soldier stepped inside. "Yeah, *jefé?*"

"Take one man and go to Seattle immediately. Contact me the second you find the FBI agent Parker."

"Okay, *jefé.*"

"If," Vincente said firmly, "anyone learns of this, your tongue comes out. *Comprendes?*"

"*Si, jefé.*"

CHAPTER 21

Sounds of rain tapping on the patio doors pulled Valerie like a kingfisher to water. After the first two dry weeks of April, the rain cascading down the concrete structures and the darkened glass, made everything look untarnished. Traffic moved below, and people scurried down the sidewalks like ants searching for spilt sugar. Beyond mankind and his impressive towers were things more regal: hazy-gray sky, fir trees, ocean, and snow-capped mountains.

The city was beautiful. Valerie hated it.

" ... insane ... " somebody behind her said.

Insane?

Her level of irritation was at an all time high. Though she tried to conceal her glumness, she could feel the infection growing. Bizarre scenarios kept popping into her mind. One that almost made her laugh. Big-time FBI agents try to explain how their passive little Canadian witness managed to kill herself while they watched. "But dah, boss. How was we to know she'd take poison? Dah. We treated her like she was a sister."

Valerie glanced at the gun inside Kalamai's holster and felt the tears. None of this was funny, and no, she didn't want to die. She wanted her children safe.

Security was as tight as it had ever been. She was never alone. Meals were brought in. Kalamai arrived each morning with clean towels and even took to changing Valerie's bed.

Her jaw relaxed. Agents moved back and forth behind her. A door opened and closed. Agents Vamozzi, Bailey, Hill, Kalamai, and Canaday, mumbled.

As usual, life went on behind her, as if everything done was important, every thought compatible. They were a team. A unit. She was the outsider. Not privy to the inner comradeship that nurtured their every step.

She heard a door close and turned around. Everyone was gone except Canaday. He stood at the stove in the small kitchenette and stirred something in a pot.

He saw her watching him. "Are you hungry?"

She turned back to the window. "No."

Her reflection in the glass startled her. She saw madness in its raw form. Eyes, unblinking, glaring, a mouth twisted open as if it had devoured something foul. Yet, a weak, tiny voice whispered 'hang on'. Valerie turned away from the face and blinked. Bitterness transgressed to numbness.

"I'm heating tomato soup. Are you sure you're not hungry? Or would you prefer something from room service?" he asked.

"I need a drink."

"Water or a soft drink?"

"No, Canaday FBI, I said a drink."

Like an obedient puppy, he walked to the phone and lifted the receiver. "What would you like?"

"Two Screwdrivers. That way I'll get my quota of vitamin C for the day."

He cracked a brief smile and placed the order.

When he hung up, she asked, "Why are we alone?"

"I thought you could use some space." He pushed aside the files on the table, went to the cupboard, and pulled out a bowl then a spoon from the drawer. Next, he poured the soup into the bowl and grabbed a package of crackers from a box in the cupboard.

Everything he did reminded Valerie of something a normal human being would do. Still, seeing Canaday as normal was difficult. Could he iron, too? She tried to picture him standing at the ironing board, iron in hand. Could he do menial chores? Did he keep his holster on while he performed these simple but important duties? An image of him taking a shower with his holster still strapped across his chest sprang to mind, and Valerie laughed.

He glanced at her and sat down at the table. For reasons she wasn't sure of, she joined him. He grabbed a handful of crackers from a package next to him, broke them up, and sprinkled them over his soup.

"Who *are* you?" she asked.

He brushed the crumbs from his hand. His blue eyes looked questioningly while his eyebrows creased.

"Where did you grow up?"

"Chicago."

"Is your family still there?"

"No."

"Are you married?"

"Once. We were kids then the war came."

"Vietnam?"

He nodded and stirred his soup. She took his silence to mean he didn't wish to answer more questions. She was wrong.

"I did two tours. It was an ugly and insane war, but I went back because so many kids were dying." He shook his head. "That's not true. I had nowhere else to go." He ate some soup. "After I left Nam, I joined the Bureau. That was twenty-three years ago. After a marriage that lasted eighteen months, I decided it would be wiser for me to stay single. I wasn't husband material. Every chance she got, my wife told me I was a cold son-of-a-bitch. With those attributes, I figured I'd make a good agent." A sad smile briefly crossed his face. He ate his spoonful of soup.

"So." Her voiced was laced with sarcasm. "You've seen it all."

"I've seen enough. Stuff that haunts my sleep. The hardest part is when kids are involved. I've seen ...." He set his spoon down and looked straight at her. "Maybe I haven't seen it all, maybe I haven't experienced it all, but I've seen more than most. One to ten, ten being the worst, you're a seven."

"You'd base that on what?"

"You haven't lost a child."

"I lost three!"

"You didn't see someone you loved brutally murdered with an axe. You weren't privy to witnessing the dismemberment of your husband, sister, mother, or father. You saw two strangers shot. They didn't suffer. They didn't scream for mercy. They were probably dead before you exhaled."

"Interesting." She felt sick to her stomach. She laid her hands flat on the table and started to rise.

"They meant nothing to you."

Valerie sat down.

"On the other hand, they were my colleagues. Onston's oldest boy is my godson. I made the decision to pull you out because I believe in 'Cause and Effect'. Your life and your daughters' lives were in danger as long as DeOlmos believed you were alive."

There was a knock on the door. Canaday put a finger to his lips and stood. "Yes."

"Sir, it's your order."

Canaday crossed the room, opened the door, took the two drinks from Bailey, then shut the door without speaking. He set the drinks in front of her and continued as if nothing had interrupted him. "The fact you were there is a blessing to those two men's families. Without you, this crime would have fallen through the cracks. Because of you, those families know Vanderhal and Onston died with dignity. That means everything. You eased their pain by coming forward, and they are more grateful than you'll ever know." He grabbed his spoon.

"The night before my dad was supposed to take mum and I up in our first helicopter ride … my parents were murdered. I was fourteen." Out of the corner of her eye, she saw him turn slowly and gaze at her. "It was their 25th anniversary, and they parked outside their favourite restaurant. A carload of kids drove by. Someone pulled out a gun and shot them both in the back. They died on the sidewalk. It turned out the shooter recognized my dad as the policeman who arrested him after a fumbled break-in at a garage downtown. He said he didn't mean to kill them; only wanted to teach my dad a lesson. To scare him."

They looked at each other; Canaday's eyes sad. Valerie sipped her drink, coughed, then wiped the condensation off the brim with the tip of her finger. "The next day I slipped out of the house and took a cab to the restaurant. I stood on the sidewalk and looked down at the dried blood. I could still see the faint chalk lines. Did you know chalk doesn't cover bloodstains very well? Yes, I suppose you do."

"I'm sorry."

"The police report said the boys didn't leave right away. That's how they caught them. Somebody wrote down the license plate number. If they hadn't…."

Canaday was right. She had done the same thing for the agents' families as that witness had done for her.

Valerie took a quick breath, fingered the file on the top pile then flicked open the cover. A photograph of a man lay on top. Thirty-something with jet black hair, penetrating eyes; someone Brandi would refer to as 'a hunk'.

"Who's that?"

"Vincente DeOlmos."

Valerie flicked the file closed and realized she was no longer afraid of the truth. "How did you know they'd try to blow up my van?"

"We didn't. All we could do was prepare for every possible scenario. A bomb was one of those scenarios."

"What exactly happened that day?"

Canaday wiped a hand across his mouth. "Why ask now?"

"Because it's the right time." She laid her forearms on the table and grasped her drink with both hands. "Maybe because I'm ready to listen."

He leaned his head on his hand and gazed at her with those steel blue eyes. The hub of Seattle murmured around them. Sirens, eighteen wheels gearing down on the highway, the soft buzz of traffic on the street below. The outside world carried on as if what happened between two people had no significance.

Valerie couldn't believe that.

"Members of E-Division in Vancouver," Canaday finally said, "plus a few of us from the Bureau had you under surveillance as usual. When the man in the pickup parked on your left attached the bomb, Agents surrounded your van with enough vehicles to take the brunt of the explosion. A car was even purchased across the street from the store."

"How did they gather enough vehicles on such short notice?"

"They sacrificed the ones used to follow and protect the girls. Seattle sent the Learjet with a body from Washington."

"I still can't believe the RCMP went along with that."

"They have their own reasons for wanting DeOlmos stopped. I'm not privy to their investigation, but I'm guessing he's had his hands on a lot of people's lives."

Valerie believed that, too. "What happened next?"

"We waited while they searched for Megan. We couldn't wait any longer. I made one final phone call, and obtained permission to proceed. Agents followed the bomber back to the States. He's under surveillance. As soon we apprehend DeOlmos, he'll be arrested, too."

Valerie got up, grabbed her two drinks, and went to the sofa. She was very tired. Depression could do that.

Canaday went to the kitchen counter. She heard running water, the fridge open, close, and the sound of dishes being scrubbed. She sipped her drink slowly. When he was finished, he sat down on the other end of the sofa. His sleeves were rolled to his elbows, and his hands were still red from the hot water. He sat forward and placed his cup on the coffee table in front of them. Except for the humming of the refrigerator, the room was silent.

She emptied the glass in her right hand and set it on the coffee table. She switched to the second glass and took a quick swallow, without coughing this time. The exploding warmth in her stomach moved upward into her chest.

It was early in the evening. Maybe six o'clock; she wasn't sure. But it felt early. Spending the rest of the evening beside him made her uncomfortable in a way that surprised her, yet, she didn't move. She sipped her drink without glancing at him. He was still. She listened for sounds of his breathing. "Where are your parents?"

"Haven't we lingered on this stuff enough?"

He looked sad, and the ugly part of Valerie couldn't resist. "Oh, c'mon. I told you about mine, the least you could do is to tell me about yours."

"It wouldn't help."

She liked the hurt look on his face. It made him vulnerable. More human. "Maybe hearing about their good fortune will make me feel better."

"I found my mother." His eyes stared straight ahead. His fingers locked together across his lap, and his shoulders slumped forward. "She was in the bathtub. It was the first dead body I'd ever seen. I was only eleven. Her knees were propped up, and her head was under water. Her eyes were opened. Her lips were blue. There was a rubber hose and a syringe on the floor beside her, along with a spoon and a lighter."

"Canaday, I'm sorry." Valerie took another sip then handed him her glass. It was still half full. She wasn't certain she wanted to hear more, but something kept her quiet.

He lifted the drink to his lips, took several long gulps, and set the empty glass on the coffee table. "I pulled the stop in the tub and gave her mouth to mouth. I'd learned the procedure at school. I tried for a long time to get her to breathe. I couldn't lift her out of the tub. Finally, I pulled a blanket off my bed and covered her. Then I sat down on the toilet seat and asked dumb stupid questions. Like why? What would happen to me now? Where would I go? Stuff like that. Then I called the police."

"Wow, we're quite the pair," Valerie blurted and felt the heat coming in waves off her face. She glanced sideways at him, terrified he'd taken her comment the wrong way.

His face set into a short and brief smile, and his eyes fixed on hers. Valerie tried to move. His eyes lowered to her mouth. His lips parted. Warmth passed down her neck, through her chest, until every inch of her skin tingled. His eyes lingered too long, uninhibited, wandering slowly, caressing her face, her mouth, her neck. Valerie's stomach felt like mush. She imagined his mouth, his soft mouth giving so much pleasure.

Valerie blinked and sprang to her feet. "I'm very tired. I'm going to bed--I mean ... goodnight Agent Canaday."

The next morning, she found him asleep on the sofa, faced toward the back cushion with his gun still in its holster. She had heard him many times during the night. The balcony doors opening, closing, and the noise in the kitchen while he made more coffee. The last sound had been about two hours ago, around four in the morning.

His cigarettes were on the coffee table. Without making a sound, Valerie reached down and took one then grabbed his lighter and the full ashtray. She sat down in the chair across from him. She put the smoke in her mouth. It had been twenty years since she'd done that. After lighting it, the first drag made her nauseous and dizzy. She took another drag. The taste in her mouth was disgusting. No wonder people referred to it as 'licking a dirty ashtray.' She took another drag. Her head felt light.

Canaday stirred. She froze. He mumbled something and placed his hand over his holster. She wondered what he was dreaming. Maybe about his mother? Or his friend, Agent Onston? He moved suddenly and rolled onto his back. Even in sleep, he looked ready to strike.

Valerie glanced at the cigarette then butted it in the ashtray. She crept across the carpet to the bathroom and closed the door quietly. She put the stop in the tub and turned on both faucets. After brushing her teeth, she tested the water's temperature, adjusted the hot faucet, and stripped off her nightshirt. When the tub was half full, she turned it off, climbed in, and sank lower until the water rose to her shoulders. Her eyes closed. What would Kalamai say if she asked for sleeping pills? Valerie almost smiled. Under the circumstances, it was unlikely she'd be given any drugs, even ones to help her sleep.

Sleep. Valerie eased back in the tub. She couldn't remember the last time she'd slept the entire night. Despite the two drinks, last night was worse than ever. She couldn't stop thinking about Canaday, about her girls, and about Canaday again. His eyes were incredible. And the way one glance could make her feel warm all over was ... disgusting! She was married!

The knock on the door startled her.
"Mrs. McCormick?" Canaday called. "Are you all right?"
"I'm fine."
"Are you hungry?" His voice calm.
"No."
"You didn't eat supper last night. I could send Kalamai--"
"Canaday?"
"Yes."
"Do you mind if I soak for awhile. I need some time to myself."
"Of course, Mrs. McCormick."

She heard him move away from the door. "Canaday?"

"Yes."

"I borrowed a cigarette. You were sleeping, or I would have asked." She waited for a response. "Agent Canaday?"

"Yes."

"I borrowed--"

"I heard you, Mrs. McCormick. Don't worry about it."

He moved away from the door. Valerie heard the television blast through the silence. Commentators discussed the strategy of a recent basketball game.

Something weird was happening. It was a comfort knowing he was close. She liked that. Actually, she liked many things about Canaday. The sound of his voice. The way others responded to him. The way he moved, even the deep frown that seemed to grace his face most days. She leaned her head back, closed her eyes, and reassured herself feeling something for him was normal. He paid attention to her. Given the same situation under different circumstances, Ed would be doing the same.

Valerie sat up, rose from the tub and grabbed a towel. Her psychoanalysis didn't explain last night. The two drinks? Loneliness? Hell, whatever it was, from now on she'd avoid alcohol and Canaday.

* * *

Canaday stood where Valerie stood most days and looked out over Seattle. The celestial lights faded as the sun rose to meet another day. He could hear the tub draining in the bathroom and wondered which was worse for her: Daylight or evening? The company of agents during the day had to help but the activity outside her window? Ten floors below, people going through their daily routines; men and women off to work; mothers performing endless errands; children window-shopping. But at night, cooped up in this apartment, her imagination had to run amuck. Either way, it had to be hell. You do the right thing and where does it get you?

Her reaction to them losing track of her eldest daughter still wrenched his conscience. His intent had never been to cause her unnecessary grief. The situation had called for a quick decision and no time to think of the consequences. They had to leave. They couldn't wait to find Megan.

He stuck his hands into his pockets and for the first time in weeks, faced the truth. He cared about this witness. He experienced her pain, and it bothered him in a way he'd never felt before. He went back to the sofa and concentrate on the latest sports statistics on TNN. That worked for about ten seconds.

Lesson number one: Better he stayed clear of Mrs. McCormick.

* * *

Formerly undercover, now office confined, Special Agent Angela Parker tied back her dreadlocks with a white scarf and checked her watch, 0730. She grabbed the Nevada file off her kitchen table and slipped it in her briefcase. She unlocked her front door. Once in the hallway, she double-checked the dead bolt then ran to the elevator. She had thirty minutes to meet ASAC Vamozzi and hand over the file. Hearing how Aidan Roth had jeopardized his career by accusing high-ranking RCMP members of covering up his parents death would surely lighten Candyman's mood. If the RCMP considered Roth a hot-head without credibility, why should the Cartel take him seriously?

Parker was in her car, three blocks from her apartment, when she spotted the tail. A black Mercedes, following at a reasonable distance, turned onto every road she did. A coincidence? Her neighbourhood wasn't the kind that harboured Mercedes Benz. She turned onto the exit to Redmond, swerved over into the outside lane, and glanced in her rear view mirror. The Mercedes was gone. Parker laughed aloud.

At the all-night gas station, she turned around and headed back. She glanced at her watch and reprimanded herself. Her jolt of nervousness would cost ten minutes; she was going to be late. That wouldn't get her back on the streets. Stuck in the office all day was driving Parker loony. The DeOlmos Investigation was important, and she wanted to be in on it again. At least being assigned to protect Mrs. McCormick would be an improvement.

Near the turnoff, Parker's car died. She coasted to the edge of the road and, brushing aside a sausage curl of black hair, frowned at the dashboard. The gas tank was empty. She'd filled the tank two days ago; there was no way it could be empty. The nearest garage was one block.

Parker locked her gun in the glove compartment, locked the doors, and grabbed the gas can from her trunk. She sighed. Vamozzi would be kept waiting, and she'd be stuck at a desk for the rest of her career.

Parker froze.

The Mercedes pulled onto the shoulder and moved toward her. Her gun was in her glove compartment. She inched backward, fumbled for her keys in her jacket pocket, unglued her eyes from the Mercedes, and ran to her door. Oh Christ! A car had pulled ahead. Two men she recognized from Vincente's crew were walking toward her.

CHAPTER 22

At precisely 0758, Canaday unlocked the dead bolt, and Special Agents Peter Bailey and CT Kalamai entered.

"Has she eaten?" Kalamai carried fresh linen and clean towels toward Valerie's room.

"No." Canaday followed Bailey to the kitchen table. "Where's Vamozzi?"

"He's waiting outside for Parker. She's bringing the report from Nevada." He glanced toward Valerie's closed door and whispered, "Roth is out of the hospital and back in Canada."

Canaday nodded and sat down. As soon as Vamozzi arrived, he was out of here. Since Aidan Roth's mugging, things had been quiet. Too quiet. Undercover agent Ward described Vincente on the verge of busting wide open. While Miguel was nowhere in sight, Vincente took to shouting most of his orders. Still, the SAC in Miami, Fredericton, had nothing new to report. With Roth back in Canada, tension was subdued. Which played like an alarm in Canaday's head. Something was bound to happen.

Twelve minutes later, he heard a knock on the door then two short taps. Even though he knew it was Vamozzi, Canaday looked through the peephole. He unlocked the door and Vamozzi walked in. Something in his expression set off an alarm inside Canaday's head. "What's wrong?"

"Agent Angela Parker's missing."

Canaday stifled his shock. "Tell me everything."

"Downtown paged me. I've already processed what I know. Fredericton's been alerted in Miami. Her car was spotted near the turnoff to Redmond."

"What was she doing there?"

Vamozzi shrugged.

"Ask Mrs. McCormick to pack," Canaday instructed Bailey. "We'll leave as soon as she's ready. Tell Kalamai to call for backup. I want two extra teams." He turned to Vamozzi. "Is the file missing?"

"No, it's in my briefcase. Nothing was touched in the car. It's at the compound. They're testing for prints and will get back to us if they find anything."

"Do you think they left the file behind to throw us off?"

"It doesn't matter. Nothing in it specifies Mrs. McCormick is alive. All it proves is we're watching them watching Roth."

What about Parker? She knew Valerie was alive and that knowledge might be her only leverage.

"With Agent Ward's help, we'll find Parker in time," Vamozzi said, as if reading Canaday's thoughts.

"Ward isn't due to call in until tomorrow. Which might as --" He stopped short; Valerie stood at the edge of the room.

"Why are we leaving?" she asked.

The expression on her face was stern and fixed on him. They'd been through enough for him to know he'd need to give her a reason this time. "Our location might have been compromised."

"By whom?"

Vamozzi stepped backward, out of Valerie's line of fire. Canaday gave him a look that spelled "Thanks buddy". "One of the agents assigned to this case is missing."

"DeOlmos …?"

"We're not taking any chances."

"Do I know this agent?"

"No."

"His name?" she asked softly.

"It's a woman. Special Agent Angela Parker."

"Parker's trained for situations like this," Vamozzi injected.

"Why her?" Valerie asked.

"She worked undercover in the DeOlmos Cartel for six months," Canaday answered. "She was close to Vincente. She warned us about the bomber. After her cover was blown, she came back here to help find Miguel."

Valerie turned without speaking and went back to her room. An eerie silence proceeded.

Canaday looked at Vamozzi's drawn face. "We'll move out within the hour. Tell Kalamai we'll need an arsenal. I'll leave for Miami first thing tomorrow."

"Parker's been trained for this," Vamozzi repeated.

Canaday didn't answer. He saw the remark for what it was. A feeble attempt to believe in the good guys.

* * *

Canaday checked the clock for the seventh time in an hour. 16:35.

Ward was two and a half-hours late reporting in. Canaday fidgeted in his chair. He tried to control his anxiety and avoided looking at Assistant Director Tomlin. Undercover agent Kyle Ward had been late before. Hell, Ward was usually late.

The Miami Office had set up surveillance of Vincente DeOlmos' home weeks ago and still no news. The large white hacienda was invisible behind the thick row of Eucalyptus trees. During the day, Wolf's ears were ineffective, and at night, the infrared scopes picked up nothing. In fact, their entire arsenal of sophisticated surveillance paraphernalia seemed useless. Vincente must have had the wall constructed with lead because the word fortress was an understatement. Canaday thought of Miguel DeOlmos and realized the estate was probably one of several, or maybe a fake. There was no proof that Vincente even lived there.

Canaday had earlier requested all calls be forwarded to Tomlin's office in Washington. He had wanted to fly directly to Miami, but Tomlin wasn't convinced that was where Parker would be. Canaday gave up arguing. The likelihood of finding Parker alive wasn't good no matter where he waited.

Canaday stared at the phone, willing it to ring. Ward was their only link to the cartel and to the possible whereabouts of Parker. It was a long shot. They had no idea Vincente would transport Parker back to Miami. Though, it did fit the profile. Vincente was vicious and vengeful. He'd feel more secure on his turf.

The phone rang. Canaday lunged forward as Tomlin reached for the handset. He listened then without replying, handed the phone to Canaday.

"Yes?"

"*Buenos tardas, Amigo,*" Ward said.

"Kyle, listen carefully. Parker went missing this morning."

There was a pause on the other line. The cheerful voice was replaced by a serious tone. "That explains the slight breeze in the air. A party's planned but not sure where. Wait. The pieces fit now. I would have called earlier but my normal routine was cancelled. I was lucky to get a connection. Someone's coming. Midnight at the playground. Join us." The line went dead.

"Well?" Tomlin asked, exasperated.

"He said the playground."

"That warehouse outside of Miami?"

"Yeah. Last year we had surveillance teams on it for over three months. The cartel brought in a large shipment, and we stormed in. Only the cargo was highly sophisticated exercise equipment."

Assistant Director Leonard Tomlin grabbed the phone, almost yelling into it. "Prep the Lear. Canaday and I are on our way. I need clearance immediately. Contact Fredericton in Miami. Connect him to the jet as soon as we're aboard. I need two SWAT teams on the ground at Miami Airport and contact the DEA for backup. Got that!" He slammed down the phone.

Canaday had his coat on and was heading for the door.

* * *

When she wasn't crying, Special Agent Angela Parker screamed. The warehouse was empty except for her, tied to a chair, and six ugly, sneering men; her agony seemed to give them much joy. Through her tears, she saw yellow toothed grins and glittering black eyes. Each time another toenail was ripped from her foot, they cheered.

She couldn't believe she was going to die in this desolate place, miles from home. She thought of her mother who at forty-two had died simply because she was Black and vulnerable. Parker joined the Bureau right after that. Dying alone and defenceless was never going to be her fate. Parker had planned on leaving this world gun in hand, while fighting it out with some bank robber, or taking a bullet for an innocent victim, someone like her mother. Alone and vulnerable. Oh, sweet Jesus.

Vincente whispered something, and another nail was ripped from her foot. Parker screamed into oblivion.

Ice water crashed into her face, waking her to more pain. Blood ran from her toes to a large puddle on the floor. Ropes cut into her wrists. The room spun. Indescribable pain crawled its way up her legs. Pain so paralyzing she couldn't breathe. Couldn't think. She slumped forward.

Please God, no more. No more. If dying will make them stop then please let me die!

Someone leaned toward her foot. More pain. Excruciating pain; like a wild animal was chomping at her! Angela screamed. She was afraid to look down. Afraid her foot was gone. Afraid to see the ugly stump.

Laughter erupted around her, then nothingness.

* * *

Undercover Special Agent Kyle Ward followed his two companions into the warehouse. He was not prepared for what he saw. Angela Parker was in the center of the room slumped over in a wooden chair, moaning.

Her white blouse, dirty and spotted with blood, was torn at the front and across one shoulder. She was stripped of her skirt. Her underpants were saturated with urine. Blood dripped from the bare patches on top of her head; her coiled black hair was saturated in blood. Her face was bruised and swollen with knife marks along each cheek. Shallow knife wounds ran down both arms. The guy holding her chair grabbed a handful of locks and pulled her head back, forcing her to look into the eyes of Vincente DeOlmos.

Ward couldn't risk moving closer. If she saw him, if she cried out, they'd both be dead. He set his face in a stupid grin and prayed Candyman would reach them in time.

In addition to the two companions he'd arrived with, Ward counted Miguel DeOlmos' right hand man, General Sanchez, Vincente DeOlmos, one man carrying an AK47, and another with a pistol in his shoulder holster. Vincente's driver stood guard outside. Seven men.

Sweat dripped down Ward's back. What if Candyman didn't reach them in time? Ward figured he could take out three, four maybe? But what about DeOlmos and Sanchez? And the man outside? Ward studied his surroundings; damned if he'd give up without a fight.

"¿*Como estas*, my sweet?" Vincente cupped Angela's chin in his hand and turned her head from side to side. His bloodied knife dangled in his hand. "Oh, but you look terrible. To think, I once thought you too beautiful for words. That is simply no longer the case. You are ugly. And you smell. But worse, you are a whore and a liar. I can abide whores but liars? You dishonoured me. You betrayed me. Now you will suffer more pain than you can possibly imagine. My men are going to rip off your fingernails next. They will rip out your tongue, so you can tell no more lies. Then your eyes, so you can tempt no longer."

Vincente leaned over, came within an inch of Angela's face, and sneered. "Or maybe I'll blow you to smithereens like I did to that McCormick bitch."

Angela mumbled something, and Vincente shot up; his smile turned to a scowl as ugly as anything Ward had ever seen. He grabbed the soldier closest to him, yanked the switchblade out of the man's inside pocket, bent down and dragged the blade across her ankle.

Parker screamed. Blood poured out.

"Take this whore to the Everglades. Make certain the crocodiles smell her blood." He rose and limped back to the door. Sanchez followed.

Ward stepped aside and tried to mask the surprise on his face. Though the odds were improving, he had to get Parker out of there, or she'd bleed to death. One of the men cut the ropes wrapped around her ankles and wrists. Vincente paused, apparently surprised to see Ward standing there, noticeable by his lack of enthusiasm.

"¿Que esta?"

Ward thought quickly. "With all due respect, does it really take five men to kill one girl?"

Vincente studied Ward's face. The two men, gripping Parker's arms and dragging her feet across the grimy floor approached, while her blood continued to flow from her wounds.

"You wish to prove yourself, please do," Vincente said. Sanchez started to object but was quickly cut off. "Enough," Vincente growled. Without taking his eyes from Ward, he snapped his fingers at the two remaining men carrying the AK47s. They went outside.

Ward bowed respectfully. He and the two men dragging Parker left the warehouse. Sanchez climbed in beside his patron's brother in the back seat of the limousine under the bright yard light. The limo sped off, throwing dust in its wake. The car Ward arrived in was gone. Only the Pontiac remained.

"Let's get out of here." One of the men gestured toward the Pontiac.

"What's your hurry?" Ward winked and nodded toward Angela.

The two men grinned down at the unconscious agent.

Ward shot the first man through the left eye.

The second man dropped Angela and ran for cover behind the Pontiac.

Ward fired his gun with one hand and dragged Angela toward the warehouse door with the other. He got as far as the dumpster. Bullets zinged past his head and dug into the ground behind him. He couldn't reach the door. He dragged Angela as far as the east side of the dumpster.

The second man fired over the hood of the car. The third man climbed out of the driver's side. Rapid fire from his machine gun flew within inches of Ward's head.

Ward fired at the gas tank. Cursed. Then fired at the men.

The second man peeked over the hood.

Ward leaned out and fired. He hit DeOlmos's soldier in the head. The man went down.

The third man continued to fire.

A bullet ripped through Ward's shoulder. Bone splintered. The force spun him around. He fumbled his gun into his left hand. He fired until he clicked air.

* * *

The lead car held Canaday in the front seat with the SWAT driver, plus three SWAT members in the back. More SWAT accompanied Assistant Director Tomlin in the chopper above and behind them. Canaday glanced over at the speedometer. 90 MPH. Ahead, he saw the warehouse, heard the sound of automatic fire. He urged the car onward. The warehouse zoomed in before them. Canaday yelled, "Hit the Pontiac," then he braced himself.

The driver swung at the wheel, tore off the Pontiac's door, and then smashed into the front bumper.

Canaday jumped from the car.

SWAT members followed.

The man from the Pontiac swung around. He fired his machine gun at the SWAT members. They dove to the ground. He raced toward the dumpster.

Canaday caught sight of a figure crouched low beside the dumpster.

The man from the Pontiac opened up. Sparks ricocheted off the metal container.

Canaday sighted two feet in front of the runner's head and fired.

His brain splattered. His body hit the dirt.

The figure hiding beside the dumpster jumped up. Supporting his shoulder against his chest, he stretched his other arm high in the air. He shouted, "Don't shoot! Don't shoot!"

Canaday, recognizing Ward, yelled into his radiophone, and notified Tomlin. The chopper swooped down over the gravel road one hundred feet away.

Canaday ran toward Ward. "Where's Parker?"

"Angela's here. She needs an ambulance. She's lost a lot of blood. A convoy is headed to Vincente's. The chopper can catch them. Hurry. My cover's blown anyway. But, sir, Angela needs that ambulance now."

The Assistant Director jumped from the chopper and ran the remaining distance toward them.

Damn, Canaday thought, the old man's liable to have a heart attack.

Tomlin reached them. His face flushed. "Where's Vincente?"

"Sir," Canaday yelled over the rotors, "Parker's in trouble. If we use the chopper to go after Vincente, she won't make it."

Tomlin glanced once at the chopper, then signalled the SWAT

Commander. "Take both vehicles. I'll send the chopper back to you ASAP."

Parker was transported onto the helicopter's stretcher and secured. Supporting his injured arm, Ward climbed in, followed by Tomlin. Canaday hesitated. He needed to be there when they captured Vincente. He looked across at Parker laying on the stretcher, hesitated a moment longer then climbed aboard. The chopper took off.

Parker's eyes stared out from her bruised and bloodied face. An attendant checked her vital signs and inserted a needle for an IV bag. Ward looked at Canaday with a tortured expression.

"What?" Canaday hollered over the rumble. He secured his headgear.

Ward stared anxiously at Parker. "She mumbled something to Vincente."

The chopper trembled through turbulent air. Ward braced his right arm.

"Agent Ward, do you believe Agent Parker told Vincente that Mrs. McCormick's alive?" Canaday asked.

Ward adjusted his earpiece. "I don't know, sir."

"But it's possible?"

Ward looked torn between his conscience and his loyalty. He glanced at Parker then looked Canaday square in the face. "Yes."

Tomlin pressed a button on his mike and spoke directly to the pilot. "Contact the tower and have an ambulance waiting when we arrive. Then contact Washington and have them notify the Canadian authorities ASAP. Tell them we advise they tighten surveillance on the McCormick family pronto!"

"There's something else, sir," Canaday said.

"What else could there be?"

"Tell them to sit on Roth. After what's happened, Miguel might start to take Roth seriously."

CHAPTER 23

Aidan stuck his key in the front door and caught sight of the next door neighbour shovelling snow from his lawn back to his driveway. It wasn't anything strange; Aidan had participated in the same ritual many times. It was one more thing Valerie liked to rib him about. Every time she caught him, they'd have the same silly conversation.

"What are you doing, you nut?"

And he'd give her the same answer. "I'm making the snow melt faster."

"Actually, big brother, it means more work. You remove the snow, the sun shines, the grass grows, and you know perfectly well what you'll end up with."

Her summation would be longwinded to the least. "The coast can have its blossoms and its flowering lilac bushes. Because, dear brother, it doesn't matter if my birch trees are still naked, or if my bulbs don't bloom for another three weeks, or if all my flowers are dead long before the end of *their* summer. I've got eight weeks less lawn mowing to do."

He could still hear the sweet sound of her laughter. She loved to tease him. In truth, spring was her favourite season. "Another beginning", she would tell him; as if their enduring one more winter was some great unobtainable feat. Like a delicate tree surviving to see another spring.

Aidan looked toward the front yard and fixed his attention on the cherry tree he and Val bought and planted for Susan's birthday last May. They had driven out to the tree nursery early in the morning. Valerie dragged him down rows and rows of plump Spruce shrubs to the patch of dwarf trees at the field's edge. Aidan picked the finest tree there. He looked up for Valerie's approval, but she was nowhere to be seen. He found her several rows over, admiring a skimpy, fragile looking cherry tree. He screwed up his face and tried directing her back to the one he had found. But Valerie couldn't be swayed.

"Oh, Aidan," she exclaimed. "This one needs a home. It's so delicate, so perfect."

"No, Val, there's one right over here." He looked back into those sad blue eyes and knew it was useless. "Val, it won't survive the winter."

A strange sounding laugh escaped his throat, and Aidan thought about grabbing his axe and chopping the tree down. He opened the front door instead and jumped at the sight of his wife.

Susan jerked back. "Honey, I'm sorry. I was coming out to the shop to get you. That friend of yours, the air traffic controller, is on the phone."

Aidan trudged toward his office at the back of the house. He sat down at his desk and grabbed the phone. "Manny, please tell me you've got good news."

"You were on the mark. Right about the time you arrived in Elko, your friends were grabbing airtime over Nevada. They headed, get this ... to Seattle."

"Did they hang around or fly out again?"

"They shut it down."

Possible conclusion: They took Valerie back to Seattle because they knew he was coming? But why Seattle? They weren't given enough time to prepare another safe house, so they returned to familiar ground? Maybe.

"Thanks Manny."

"I hope this pans out. Just remember what a sweet guy I am the next time we're on the golf course."

Aidan hung up, waited a few seconds, and was about to pick up the phone to dial out when it rang. "What?" he asked annoyed at the interruption.

"Aidan Roth?"

"Yes."

"Your son is Trevor Roth?"

The air in his lungs burst out of his chest as if a Mac truck had hit him. "Yes," Aidan said, so softly he wondered if the man heard him.

"Trevor is here at the detachment. He was picked up for shoplifting. Maybe you better come down."

"I'll be right there." He hung up the phone and took a deep breath. Trevor was okay. "Thank God." Then Aidan remembered Susan. No way was he going to tell her because no way was their son a thief. He calmed himself and went into the kitchen.

Susan was chopping celery into a salad bowl.

"I have to go out for a little while. Do you need anything from the store?" he asked.

"Apple Crumb or Bread Pudding for dessert tonight?"

He grabbed his jacket and avoided Susan's eyes. He'd explain later. "Apple crumb sounds great. I'll pick up ice-cream."

"Good idea."

Aidan was in his car, on the road, and through the intersection at 15th before he realized there was a patrol car behind him. The thought of the faces he'd see in a few moments, of the whispers that would generate through the detachment, made him cringe. Young and old, Aidan knew every cop in town. Except for the voice on the phone. He dismissed his lapse in memory and tightened his grip on the steering wheel. It didn't matter what any of any of them thought. Trevor was no thief.

When he turned onto the block toward the police detachment and the patrol car continued to travel further down Victoria Street, Aidan was grateful. Now wasn't a good time for small talk.

He parked, then entered the station and went to the window. "I'm here about my son."

The officer behind the glass looked him square in the face, smiled, and pressed a button; there was nothing uncomfortable in his gaze. "The Inspector is waiting for you in his office."

Banyan? He was the last person he wanted to see. Aidan stepped through the door. He walked past several desks, nodded at each officer present, then approached the inspector's office. He reached out to knock. The door opened.

"Aidan," Inspector Banyan said, "Come in."

He bypassed his old boss and saw two men rising from the small leather sofa against the wall. One was dressed casual in windbreaker and jeans; the other wore a blue pinstripe suit. GIS, Aidan thought. He faced Banyan. "Where's Trevor?"

"Trevor's not here. I'm sorry for dragging you down here on false pretences, but they needed to insure you'd come without raising suspicions."

Banyan's 'they' stood out like a 30-foot billboard. It sounded like a 'they' as in the entire police force 'They'.

"Is something wrong?" Aidan asked.

"Sit down, Aidan," Banyan said.

"No thanks."

The guy in a blue pinstripe suit stepped forward. "It's about your recent actions into the death of your sister."

"Come again?"

"Don't waste my time, Mr. Roth. We know you've been investigating, and you must cease and desist at once."

Aidan looked at Banyan and stopped himself from laughing. "What's he talking about?" Banyan shrugged. Aidan glanced back at the two men. "You come to town, order me off a case that's been officially closed, despite the fact there were never any arrests, and you expect me to understand what you're talking about? You have no jurisdiction over private citizens. I'm not breaking any laws."

"You're endangering the lives of your family," Pinstripe said.

"Where is my son?"

The other man, with his faded jeans and a windbreaker with a 'Winter Games' insignia stood. "He's washing his truck in the car wash across from the Parkhill Mall. I'm sorry we had to use that as an excuse to get you down here. It's crucial you stop your investigation."

"Why?"

This man's face showed no discernible emotions. "I think you know why, Aidan. May I call you Aidan?"

"No."

"Okay." Windbreaker seemed mildly amused. "Hear us out. Sit down."

Aidan felt his blood pressure rising. This guy had him good, and they both knew it. Aidan couldn't walk away now. Still, he couldn't remember being more terrified. Except the night his parents died. He sat in the chair across from Banyan's desk. "Okay. Let's talk."

Windbreaker nodded to Pinstripe, who pouted for a second, then sat down on the couch.

"Is my sister dead?" Aidan hardened his stomach for the blow that was sure to come.

Pinstripe smirked, "Man, you're as nuts as they say. Didn't you hear? She died in an explosion."

Aidan sprang off the chair, grabbed Pinstripe by his lapels, yanked him from the couch, and slammed him into the wall. Pain ripped through Aidan's ribcage and hand. "Look, you little weasel. I've had a real bad week and a terrible fucking year. If you don't shut the fuck up, I'm going to rip off your fucking head and puke down your throat. "

Banyan and Windbreaker had already jump to their feet and each grabbed one of Aidan's arms. He fought to restrain Pinstripe.

"Aidan!" Banyan said. "This isn't helping. Let him go."

"He's out of this room as soon as you let go," Windbreaker said. "You have my word."

Aidan glared at Pinstripe for one full second longer before releasing him.

Pinstripe pushed himself away from the wall and struggled to stay balanced. He tucked at his tie, which looked to be choking him. "I'm going to have you up on charges, mister. You'll be lucky --"

"Shut up and wait for me outside," Windbreaker said.

"You expect me to walk away after this bastard --"

"You're not helping the situation. Leave us alone."

Pinstripe frowned at Windbreaker, glared at Banyan, then hissed at Aidan, who would have laughed if he hadn't been more interested in wiping the smirk off the man's face.

When Pinstripe was gone, Windbreaker sat down. "Can we start over?"

"Has something happened to my sister since the FBI took her out of the country?"

Windbreaker chewed on his lip and looked at Banyan. "No."

Aidan gasped and sank to the chair. Hot tears spilled from his eyes. A hot flush rose in his face, and he fought the dizziness. "Is she okay?"

"Yes."

Aidan closed his eyes to tears he couldn't stop. Valerie WAS alive. Valerie IS alive. Thank you God!

"Are you going to tell Mrs. McCormick's family?" Windbreaker asked.

Aidan wiped his face. "You know I won't. But what I really need to know is why?"

Windbreaker frowned, and then his gaze cleared. "The plan was to remove the entire family. When that wasn't possible, your sister allowed the FBI to fake her death. She did it to save her children. We could sit here all day and rehash where we went wrong, what we could have or should have done, but it won't change anything, Mr. Roth. We need you to stop your investigation. We're doing everything in our power to secure the whereabouts of Miguel DeOlmos and his organization. Twenty-three years ago, you gave up seniority at CSIS to come back here and take care of your sister. Nobody doubts how much you love her. We need your cooperation."

Aidan scowled at Windbreaker. "Why didn't you come to me? I could have helped round up the girls. I could've made sure the FBI's plan worked, instead of screwing up by going to Nevada."

"You won't get an argument from me."

Aidan took one look at Windbreaker's face and understood. They didn't ask him for help because of the reputation he'd acquired after his parent's death. "Are you sure she's okay?" he finally asked, his voice neither forceful nor confident.

"She's safe. While I'll accept the fact we should have done more at the onset of this investigation, I can assure you we are in constant contact with the FBI. We stay apprised of the situation, and it's our contention that they're doing the very best they can to find DeOlmos. I promise … if we hear anything, you'll be the first to know. You have my word on that, Mr. Roth."

Aidan pressed his lips together and tried to form the word 'thanks'. The effort was impossible. "Call me Aidan. Everybody does."

CHAPTER 24

The day after Parker's rescue, Canaday knocked on the door to Valerie's suite. When the door opened, he barked, "Who the hell are you?"

"Special Agent Simpson, sir. It's an honour --"

"You check for ID before unlocking the deadbolt. Understand!"

"Yes, sir. I --"

"Never mind." He swept past him. "Where's Vamozzi?"

"He had personal business downtown, sir. He should be back any --"

"Where's Mrs. McCormick?"

"In her room."

"You can go."

"But, sir --"

"Son, getting on my bad side wouldn't be smart at this point." Canaday surveyed the room.

"Yes sir. I mean if you need anything, please don't hesitate to ask. Sir."

Canaday unlocked the door and opened it. "You're still here — why?"

The young, flustered agent stammered then stepped through the doorway. When it looked as if he was about to say something more, Canaday slammed the door in his face. He turned to see Valerie leaning against the doorframe into her room. "What the hell was Vamozzi thinking? That kid would shit his pants if somebody said boo."

Valerie pressed her lips tight and looked as if she was struggling not to laugh.

Sure his face was red, he asked, "How are you, Mrs. McCormick?"

"I'm fine."

"Where is Vamozzi?"

"His wife was stranded downtown. He said he wouldn't be long."

"Have you had dinner?"

"Yes."

Canaday nodded, feeling like an idiot. He stuck his hands in his pockets and walked as casually as possible to the living room sofa. "Would you like to watch TV?" he said then wanted to kick himself. Two days away from her and he was acting like a bumbling teenager. Who was wasting valuable time. The next few moments were crucial. Vamozzi being away was perfect. This might be the last few moments he'd have alone with her.

"I surfed the channels, and there wasn't much on."

"It's probably a good time to talk then? I need to discuss something with you."

She sat down in the sofa chair. "Sounds serious. Is this about Agent Parker? Saul said she's recovering in the hospital. He also said DeOlmos's brother got away."

"It's not about that." Canaday stared at the blank television screen and thought of the chopper. If Parker hadn't been dying, they would have caught Vincente. Saving Parker was worth it.

Canaday realized something, then glanced at Valerie. She'd called Vamozzi by his first name. How had that come about? They both agreed? Or was it her idea?

"What did you want to talk about?" Valerie asked.

God, she was beautiful. Her skin looked incredibly smooth. He longed to reach out and touch her face.

Only in your dreams, pal.

He looked at the television. "Remember I mentioned witness relocation?" When she didn't answer, he was forced to look at her. "The Witness Protection Program?"

"Has it come to that?"

"I've been ordered to hand you over to them first thing tomorrow morning."

Valerie shook her head.

"Mrs. McCormick, I know this seems extreme, but it'll be safer for you."

Valerie's head lowered.

"We have no other choice," he continued. "With a new identity, at least you'd have a life. You wouldn't be cooped up inside some hotel room. You'd have your own place."

By the look on her face, Canaday knew he'd gone too far. "It wouldn't be forever. And it'd be a lot safer. Only two agents would know your whereabouts, instead of every agent in the Bureau."

"No."

Canaday exhaled deeply. "Mrs. McCormick, please."

"Go back and tell your boss, no way am I going to be shuffled off on some strangers. If they want me in the Witness Protection Program, fine. But I won't go unless you and Saul are assigned as my contacts, or whatever you call it."

"They'll never go for that. Members of WPP are specifically trained for any unforeseen problems."

"It took me a long time to trust you, Agent Canaday. If they don't agree, then I'll go home."

"This has been in the works for a long time. You don't have a choice." Shit. He did it again, said the wrong thing.

Valerie's face reddened. She opened her mouth to speak, hesitated, then after what seemed deliberated consideration, said, "If they don't agree, I'm out of here. Okay?"

"Yes ma'am."

"Don't call me ma'am."

"Sorry."

* * *

Three days later, the black Buick squealed out of the underground parking lot and twelve minutes later, arrived a few feet from the Lear jet. Valerie hesitated at the bottom of the steps leading to the plane then turned and took one last look at agents Kalamai and Bailey.

Kalamai stepped forward and shook hands with Valerie. "Take care."

Feeling sad, Valerie nodded, turned, and climbed the boarding ramp to the plane's cabin. She took her usual seat.

Canaday sat across from her, grabbed a candy from his pocket, and offered it to her.

She declined.

He reached into the folder on his lap and retrieved four pieces of identification. "This is your medical insurance card. It expires April of next year. This is your credit card; there's a five thousand dollar limit." He handed them to her. "The check book is in your bag. It has a balance of three thousand. There will more when you need it. Here is your California driver's license, good for five years. And lastly your birth certificate. Your background info and social security card are in your bag. I suggest you memorize the number. Any questions?"

She smiled. "They expect people to believe I'm American, born and bred?"

"Locals will think you're from the north. The house in Santa Cruz is under a five-year lease. The car in the carport is registered in your new name, Katrina Sands. The car insurance has been paid for a year. After that --"

"I know. I'm on my own."

"I was going to say ... maybe you'll be home by then."

"Canaday, I thought you and I had an agreement. No lies. Remember?"

Canaday loosened his tie. "Here's your address and keys. Try to remember the address. When we arrive at the airport, you'll mix in with the crowd and hail a cab."

"You two aren't coming with me?"

He had that look again, as if he was certain she was afraid, and somehow he had to reassure her. "You're on your own from here on. That's for the best, remember?"

Valerie nodded.

"Have the address memorized before you reach the house. If you need to get in touch with Vamozzi, or myself, this is the number --"

"Memorize it?"

"Yes. Never speak to anyone else. If we're not available, leave a short message, 'Kat called.'"

Valerie laughed. Canaday didn't.

"Don't deviate from any of my instructions and don't take any chances. If there's anyone hanging around, anything suspicious, call."

Valerie saluted.

"Candyman, how many times are you going to go over this stuff?" Vamozzi took a seat next to Valerie.

"Until I'm sure she's got it straight."

Vamozzi smiled at her. "You've got it straight, don't you?"

"Of course."

"You're ready for this, aren't you?"

"As ready as I'll ever be."

"If worse comes to shove, you're strong enough to start a new life, right?"

Valerie cringed. Why did they continue to do that? Hit her with reality. Wasn't it kinder to avoid mentioning certain things? Like the fact, she'd been a total jerk when they were only trying to help. "If you're worried I'm going to jeopardize your case, you needn't. I would do nothing to put my children in harm's way."

Vamozzi secured his seatbelt. "I may not know a lot of things, Valerie, but that's one thing I'm sure of."

CHAPTER 25

Valerie set her suitcase and purse down in the front hallway, slipped off her shoes, and walked through the small one-bedroom house. Sunlight beamed off the walls. All the rooms had recently been painted white, casting a hint of pink. The floor tiles were pale rose and in excellent shape. Valerie liked their cool touch on her bare feet. The bathroom was equipped with a deep pedestal tub and a painted white pipe leading up to the antique showerhead. A white flowered curtain hung against the wall. Valerie turned the faucets. They worked.

The tiny kitchen had plenty of cupboards. No possible space had gone unused. She checked the cupboard doors, there were no unpleasant squeaks, and their contents included staples, dishes, olive oil, sugar, flour, all the essentials for a happy home.

A happy home?

Pretty flower designed lace curtains hung over the window above the porcelain sink. Behind them, closed rose-coloured Venetian blinds. The same rose-colored blinds hung throughout the house. Valerie was surprised how well decorated the little bungalow was. These would have been the colors she'd have chosen if asked.

A happy home?

In the middle of the kitchen, Valerie looked for a moment around the sun drenched room and spotted the telephone on the desk next to the counter. She froze, her eyes glued to the phone. She could call her children. In thirty seconds, she could hear Brandi's voice again then Megan's and Christine's.

Valerie hung her head and cried. Her arms limp at her sides, she cried until her legs felt weak, and she slid down on one knee. She was still crying when she heard a distant chime. The doorbell. She wiped at her eyes, stood up, and darted back into the front room. She couldn't see anything through the closed blinds. She crept to the door and looked through the peephole.

Canaday.

Valerie threw open the front door. "What's wrong? Is it my girls?"

"No! They're fine. I'm sorry. I should have called." He glanced at the

Joylene Nowell Butler

neighbour's yard. "Can I come in?"

He looked different dressed in a white silk shirt and pale green dress pants. "Sure." She stepped aside. When he was through the door, she took a step outside and blinked into the sidelong sun. "Where's Saul?"

"Back at the plane."

Canaday set a paper bag on the coffee table and went into the kitchen. He came back with two crystal tumblers. He pulled a bottle and a jug of orange juice out of the bag and unscrewed the cap. He handed her a full glass.

"What's this? A drink before noon? Is this part of the program?"

"No. I just thought ...."

"What?" Valerie took a small sip. "Ah, Vodka. The good stuff."

"I thought you might need something to help you relax."

"Why? Do I seem uptight?"

Canaday scrutinized the room and chose the wicker couch. "I know this must be hard on you. I thought--"

"You think too much, Canaday."

He leaned forward. "Are you okay?"

"Sure." Her red, swollen eyes must have made that comment odd.

Valerie sat down in the chair. It felt strange seeing him this way. He sat on the edge of the couch and rested his drink on his knee. He had recently shaved. His shirt was unbuttoned at the neck. His tan looked good against the white silk. But when did he have time for the sun? What she'd seen of his life didn't suggest such indulgence.

"How do you like the place?" Canaday asked.

"Just tickidy boo."

Canaday smiled. "Tick-idy-boo?"

"It's a ... northern expression." She expected him to suggest she lose it. He didn't.

"Have you checked out the view?" He gestured toward the back.

"I barely had time to walk through the place before you showed up." She was glad not to be alone. And the drink did go down smoothly. "What happens now?"

"I'm not sure, Kat."

Valerie smirked.

He smiled. "Did I say something funny?"

"Who dreams up these names?"

"Probably somebody's mother."

"You mean there actually is a Katrina Sands?" She found that very funny, in a sad way.

"Died at birth. No living relatives."

"Great. What does that make me? A dead witness?"

Canaday added more to her glass. "You don't look dead."

Valerie prayed to God she wasn't blushing. "What are you really doing here, Canaday?"

"Call me Mike."

"What are you doing here, Canaday."

"I wanted to make sure you were okay." Under the short sleeved shirt, his tanned arms looked muscular.

"Is that the truth? Or were you worried I might skip out. Turn away from this wonderful life you've given me and go back to my family?"

"Never occurred to me."

The expression on his face was difficult to discern. Was he telling her the truth? Maybe. "Have you got any candies?"

"No, sorry. I decided to give them up. But, if you needed something from the store …."

"Giving up candies, won't that infringe on your nickname?"

"I hope so."

He was relaxed now. Valerie sat up straight. "Have you got any leads on DeOlmos?"

"No."

"His brother?"

"No."

"If your people had found Megan that day, what would have happened?"

One eyebrow shot up and he smiled. "I've never met anyone who could throw questions out from every direction like you can." He grew serious. "Your daughters would have joined you at the store. The news would have reported four deaths instead of one. Later, your grieving husband would have relocated, along with your brother and his family. Never to be seen again."

Valerie clenched her fists. She wanted to hit him. "Why didn't you tell me this on our flight from Elko to Seattle? You could've--"

"I know."

Valerie saw regret in Canaday's face. "How are my girls?"

"They're okay."

"Do you know what tomorrow is?"

"April 19th."

"Brandi's twelfth birthday."

He looked embarrassed. "I didn't know."

"Why should you? She's not your daughter. You don't have children. You don't have anyone."

He looked down at his drink.

Valerie set her drink on the coffee table with a loud thud. "I'm sorry, I shouldn't have said that."

"It's okay."

"No. I'm in a lousy mood. The truth is ...." Valerie squeezed her eyes shut. She hated that her emotions took control so easily. "Let's start over." She opened her eyes. "Tell me everything you know about Miguel DeOlmos."

"He'll kill you if he can." Canaday put his drink down and stood. "I should go."

"How many men work for him?"

"Fifty, maybe."

"Where does he live?"

"If we knew, do you think he'd still be out there?"

"Mr. Rostov said DeOlmos had associates throughout North America. You must know where 'they' live."

"Believe it or not, we do know how to do our job."

"Is DeOlmos married?"

"No."

"No children, no family, other than his brother?"

"That's right."

"Does he have any legitimate businesses?"

"Valerie--I mean Kat-- "

"This man wants me dead. Is it so strange that I'd like to know something about him? Saul told me about an informer. Before that man died was he able to tell you anything?"

"Nothing we can use now." He sat down, irritated that she and Vamozzi had become friends while they couldn't have a conversation without arguing.

"Canaday, why are you being so evasive? Your people must have a file a mile long. Tell me something."

"Why?"

Her back stiffened. "Why do you always read an ulterior motive into every question I ask? Are you so warped by your job you can't see me--"

"I see you."

"I was going to say ... are you so warped you can't see me as someone other than a witness."

Canaday bowed his head. "I don't want to argue."

"Then tell me about DeOlmos."

"First tell me why you want to know."

"God, you're stubborn."

"I'm stubborn? You're the one who's been making demands the last few weeks. When I first read your report from Seattle, I wondered how a passenger could talk a professional bus driver into stopping during a tour with a busload of seniors. I'm not wondering anymore."

Valerie, at a loss for words, had to think for a moment. "I didn't talk him into doing anything. Saturday morning we all agreed we'd make a list of stops." She caught the lack of interest in Canaday's expression and threw up her arms. "Canaday, why do you insist on bringing out the worst in me?"

"It's a gift?"

"You're not only stubborn, you're smug."

"I'm not telling you anything more about DeOlmos."

"Why?"

"Because ... I don't want you doing something stupid."

"What the hell can I do? I'm not a cop. I'm living in a foreign country. What could I possibly accomplish? Do you even understand what you're doing? Every time you refuse to answer my questions, you make my determination to know much stronger. What have I ever done to deserve your distrust? I didn't ask for this to happen. I tried to do the right thing. I was screwed. Now I'm angry. Angry with my parents for dying on me. Angry because their killers were just kids. Angry because my life has spun out of control. And now, to top it off, you keep pissing me off."

He looked at her for a long, hard moment. "DeOlmos is a killer. He was born in Toronto forty-seven years ago to Anton and Bolina DeOlmos, originally from Colombia and México. He was educated in Europe. He speaks English, Spanish and French fluently. He likes the water. It's our guess he has homes in Canada, the States, México, and South America. He's an avid collector of fine arts. He has expensive tastes. He enjoys sports, fishing; fine wines, classical Spanish music. He's not clinically classified as a psychopath because he exhibits empathy for his victims. He kills for a reason. It's a sick reason, but to him it makes sense. He's donated to several charities. Save the Whale. Greenpeace. Cancer research. He owns four hotels on the Baja and is reputed to pay his employees well.

When one of his bellhops from Del Cabo needed a kidney transplant, DeOlmos sent him to the States and paid all expenses. He's revered, respected, and feared. Those who do turn on him end up like our Gordon. Dead. Anything else you'd like to know?"

"Damn, you make me want to ... punch you."

Canaday bowed his head. She saw a trace of a smile and wanted more.

They sat for a long time without speaking. She sipped on her drink and thought about DeOlmos. Most of what Canaday had said she'd already overheard. Her father told her once that all races had one thing in common: Their humanity. He said even killers were entitled to be treated as human beings. The world would never be rid of them. Most of them would never be rehabilitated. What separated them from the rest of society was they acted upon their impulses instead of stifling them. Her father didn't believe in capital punishment. "They should be incarcerated and studied for the rest of their lives," he once told her.

Sure, Dad, unless one of them is trying to kill you.

"What about DeOlmos' younger brother?"

Canaday shot her a suspicious glare. "What about him?"

"Oh, geez, I don't know, Canaday. From what I've overheard, he's not a very nice person."

"No kidding."

"Why did you send one of your undercover agents to get close to him?"

"Parker is a trained professional."

"I heard Vincente doesn't like women. Weren't you worried about her safety?"

"Of course!"

"How do you train a woman to deal with a psychopath?"

Canaday's face turned red.

"I--I'm not trying to put you on the spot. Really. I just wondered how she coped."

"Unlike DeOlmos, who prefers gentility, Vincente is attracted to sensuous and aggressive women. He took one look at Parker and fell hard." He searched his pants pocket for something, (Valerie guessed candy) then gave up and sipped his drink.

"I had the option of accepting the prize money."

Canaday shrugged. "I bet it'd be a real trip to be inside your head. What are you talking about?"

"When I won the trip to Seattle ... I had the option of taking the money instead of the trip."

"You can't keep blaming --"

"Winning that trip was a big deal. I'd never won anything before, and I needed to go. I love my family more than life itself, but I needed to experience, just once, the aftermath of doing something right. I wrote that article. I won that contest. I accepted knowing Ed wouldn't come, knowing I couldn't take the girls. For the first time in my life, I had no responsibilities. No errands. No demands for my time and my energy."

"What did you do with that freedom?"

"I spent an entire day traveling around Seattle, taking in the sights, admiring the beautiful city, yet at the same time, experiencing a discomfort I couldn't explain. Minutes before I saw your friends die, I realized that a long, long time ago, I'd lost part of myself. The part I respected. Over the years I'd become passive. Accepting my fate as if interfering was unacceptable. Unthinkable. It wasn't until I met you that it dawned on me: A person should be careful what they wish for."

He looked at her for a moment. Did he understand she needed something from him. She wasn't certain what. Encouragement? Wisdom?

When he spoke, his voice was low and husky. "It was Divine Providence. You didn't wish for this to happen; it was just timing. You were at the wrong place at the right time. This isn't over. After what you've been through, don't let it beat you. Being accountable isn't a bad thing."

His moist lips parted, and his eyes ... they were doing it again. Making her insides turn to mush. If he reached out for her at that moment, she didn't know what she'd do.

Fight it. Say something. Anything. Before all there's left to do is to rip off his clothes.

She switched the subject, and they talked for another hour. Nothing important. Baseball, hockey, and the kind of sports they liked to play as kids. Where they both were the day McGwire then Sosa beat Maris's record. When Valerie yawned, Canaday rose and walked to the door. They stood together on the porch and admired the quiet neighbourhood; the sounds of children playing in the distance; the scent of orange blossoms. Canaday stepped off the stoop, retrieved his sunglasses from his pocket, and reached his rental car without speaking.

Before he got in the car and drove away, he turned to her and said, "Be safe, Katrina."

"You too, Canaday."

* * *

    Miguel DeOlmos stood behind his marbled desk and looked through his bullet-proof window to the Caribbean Sea. His heart wouldn't allow him to do what his mind said he must. Vincente was his brother, and Miguel swore an oath at his mother's deathbed to protect him.

    He turned into the room where his General waited for a response. Mother's pleas were strong in his mind. She understood that Vincente would always need protection; desire ruled his simple mind, not reason. But now, too many associates lurked in the background, waiting for Miguel to slip. Too many rumours circulated saying Vincente was the one weak spot in an otherwise powerful armour. Mother wasn't here, and a loss of authority would crumble the DeOlmos Empire.

    Still, Miguel knew he would obey Mother's wishes. The empire that had taken so many years to build was at risk, but the empire was built for family. Not respecting Mother, disgracing Vincente, wouldn't benefit this empire. Better for it to fall with honour.

    Miguel considered his position one last time before committing himself to Mother's wishes. It was strong. Those four who disappeared in Miami and who were no doubt dead, served as a testament of what would happen if his enemy were not taken down. No one disappears without a trace unless they were careless or disloyal.

    He opened the top drawer of his desk and glanced down at the photograph of Valerie McCormick. She wasn't the beauty his mother had been, but she was lovely in her own way. The eyes of a lady, gentle and kind. It seemed sad in deed that fate had shortened her life, just as it had shortened his mother's. Fate had a cruel side. But Valerie McCormick's death ensured the prosperity of many good and loyal servants. For one to die so that many could prosper was a noble death.

    Still uncomfortable with possessing the photo of a dead woman, Miguel pushed the drawer closed and locked it. Perhaps he kept her photograph as a reminder of the difficult decisions he would always need to make.

    He glanced up at his most trusted soldier.

    Sanchez folded his hands in front of him and took a step forward. A sign he wished to speak.

    Miguel nodded his consent.

    "The men know you have suffered." Sanchez's voice was deep and respectful. "Perhaps if you sent Vincente somewhere safe? *¿Quizás Baja*?"

Miguel stepped from behind his large desk, his heart lightening. In Baja, Vincente could be kept happy without impairing business.

He stood with his hands on each side of Sanchez's shoulders. "Thank you. Yes. Indeed, you have the solution my old friend. Make the arrangements; provide him with enough working girls so he doesn't bother the locals. Then bring him to me so we may dine together before he leaves."

"But first come and sit, I have something to discuss."

Sanchez followed him to the long curved couch at the other end of the room. He sat only after Miguel had done so.

"The abrupt end to the investigation into Senora McCormick's death is unusual. It's my understanding the RCMP would leave it open because it is unsolved. They haven't done this. *Por qué*? Because she's still alive?"

"Vincente believes the young woman spoke only to anger him?"

"But if this *puta* spoke the truth? What if the FBI are involved, and the Senora's brother isn't the fool we were led to believe?"

"Then we have been tricked."

Miguel stood and walked to the window. Crystal blue waves hit violently at the edge of his home. Pounding their presence, they flipped and returned to the brilliant blue sea. On the east side, sand sloped gradually. Guards walked back and forth, their pants rolled up. One guard propped himself high atop a huge granite stone. Miguel watched him carefully. When the guard's head moved slightly, proving he was neither asleep, nor hypnotized by the sea, Miguel turned from the window and made a mental note to give more responsibility to the young man. Diligence should always be rewarded.

He walked through his room, stopping periodically to admire a Ming sculpture. As a young boy, he had spent hours with his father as he painstakingly described the differences of the Renaissance Painters. While boys his age were battling on soccer fields or hitting home runs, Miguel had experienced all of life's beauties.

"The world is full of wonders. *El mundo es lleno de maravillas*," Papa would tell him. "But these things created by man, they are the real miracles. Rub your hands down the smooth form of this sculpture. Close your eyes and feel the sensation. Absorb its beauty until it becomes one with your body. An extension of you. Then open your eyes, my son. Take in the spectrum of hues, the fine strokes. Let your spirit go. Let it entice you to experience the true wonders of the world. For only through the Grace of God could man set hands to clay, brushes to canvas, and create such miracles."

Miguel mused on the words of his papa. As a child, he thought him the wisest of men. So strong. So fearless. If he were alive now, he would have marvelled at the possessions in Miguel's magnificent home. Anton DeOlmos was a great lover of Art, but even he had never laid eyes on most of the pieces Miguel now had harboured in his home.

Your enemy still lives.

Miguel heard the voice but felt no stirring of conscience. Revenge brought Agent Angela Parker to the brink of a horror she would not soon forget. A small tinge of regret surfaced. Had he been there, she would have told him everything. Then she would have died. Slowly. *Muy lentamente.*

He pulled the cellular phone from his pocket and turned to Sanchez. "His number?"

Sanchez, at first confused, hesitated then quickly retrieved the small business card from his pocket and handed it over.

Miguel dialled the number.

"*Señor*," Miguel said. "You sound surprised to hear from me. I would have thought after your wife's wager mishap last summer, you'd be expecting my call. This is all very much your fault."

Miguel smiled at Sanchez while loud cursing could be heard through his cellular. He placed the phone back to his ear. "Are you finished? You have twenty-four hours to do whatever's necessary to determine whether Agent Angela Parker spoke the truth." He listened to pleas then interrupted. "Twenty-four hours, or I'm afraid I'll have to call in your wife's marker. Think what that will do to your career. Twenty-four hours or I'll send Sergeant Jackson to collect."

Satisfied by the silence, Miguel clicked off his phone.

CHAPTER 26

Canaday stood at the door of his office and watched Special Agent Ward steer Parker through the exterior office toward him. He stepped aside as they moved into his private sanctuary. Parker's face was drawn and ebony gray. Ward set the wheelchair's brake, sat on the couch, as close to his partner as possible, even leaning in, protecting her.

As far as Canaday was concerned, Ward had just gained new respect.

Canaday kept his smile ready in case Parker looked up at him to receive it. "I'm sorry for what you went through." He caught her eyes as they darted up at him. "If it wasn't vital to our case, I wouldn't have asked you to come in."

"It's all right, sir." Her full sensuous lips disappeared inside her mouth, then reappeared into a slight pout.

"No, it's not. But I do need your help."

She scrunched her shoulders. "What can I do?"

"In the middle of torturing you, Vincente got up and walked out. Why? What did you say to him, Angela, to make him so angry?"

"I don't know." She dug her fingers into the arm pad of her chair and glanced nervously at Ward. "He's a psycho; how could I know how his mind works? I was hurting bad."

"Would you submit to hypnosis?"

Parker tried to raise herself off the chair and instead sank lower. "I have to live through that again?"

"I wouldn't ask if it wasn't important." Canaday stood, moved to the front of his desk, sat on the edge, and looked down at her. He was ashamed of his intimidating pose, but it was urgent. "Are you certain you didn't say anything to impede our case?"

"I swear I don't remember. Maybe you would have handled things differently, sir, but I … just wanted it to end."

"For more wars than I can count, better men than I have broken under torture, Angela. You have nothing to be ashamed of. And I promise you, you have nothing to fear from me."

"Fine. Hypnotize me."

Canaday leaned back and pressed the intercom. "Send in Fielding."

He ignored the look of surprise on Parker's and Ward's faces, went to the window, and looked down on Seattle. The city buzzed with activity as if everything about life was normal. He thought about Valerie McCormick. He thought about Charlie Onston. He didn't look back at Parker. When Fielding arrived, he shook Fielding's hand and returned to his chair. "You remember Special Agent Ward?"

Fielding shook Ward's hand.

"And Special Agent Angela Parker?" Canaday said.

"It's truly good to see you again, Agent Parker."

Canaday's secretary peeked in. "Mr. Rostov's on line two."

"Is it urgent?"

"He didn't say."

"I'll call him back." Canaday turned his attention to Parker, who looked scared. "Let's get started."

* * *

Angela Parker lay on Canaday's office couch and cried. Fielding, speaking in a soothing voice, assured her that she felt no pain. Parker's breathing slowed. She stopped moaning and lay back against the couch.

"Your body is numb. You feel nothing. Vincente DeOlmos is standing over you. You whisper something. He asks you to repeat it. He leans over, and you say it again…. What did you say, Angela?"

"She's alive. Asshole."

"When I snap my fingers, I want you to wake up. Angela, I want you to remember that none of this is your fault. You're guilty of nothing." Fielding snapped his fingers and Parker's eyes opened.

She cried.

Ward and Fielding looked away.

Parker glanced up through her tears at Canaday. "How did you know?"

Words seemed inappropriate, and Canaday stayed quiet.

"He was bragging about taking Mrs. McCormick out. Like he was some big bad wolf." Parker wiped her nose on her sleeve. "I wanted to mess with his head one last time. I wanted him to know he wasn't fooling anyone. I'm sorry. I've let you down. Twice."

"You did what any of us would have done," Fielding said.

"Ward will take you home," Canaday said. "I want you to see Doc on a regular basis. As soon as she says it's okay, I want you back in this office."

"I'm ... not fired?"

Canaday handed her a tissue. "Angela, you have my word, when I'm finished, you'll be one of the finest agents the Bureau has ever seen."

When they were gone, he turned to Fielding, "Will she be all right?"

"Let's monitor her progress for a few months and then hear what the doctor has to say. Her body will mend, but her psyche .... It's anybody's guess if she'll ever be able ready for another field assignment."

"There's plenty here to keep her busy." He saw the look on Fielding's face. "She meant to piss Vincente off, and it worked. But why don't I feel better?"

"Because you and I both know Miguel isn't that naive."

CHAPTER 27

Valerie opened her eyes. Something felt wrong. She reached across for Ed, but that side of the bed was cold. She listened for the sounds of her daughters laughing, arguing, the phone ringing off the wall while each of them yelled it was the other one's turn to answer. Then Valerie remembered recent events, and with her memory came the recognition that Vamozzi, Bailey, Kalamai, and Canaday had become her second family.

So this is my new life, Valerie thought, lifting her head off the pillow. Abruptly, the pain came. Her brain felt as if it were being crushed from all sides by a thousand pounds pressure. Her eyelids hurt, and when she moaned, her throat ached.

She had the flu.

It had been ten years since she had felt this sick. In the last few weeks, she'd seen news reports about dangerous viruses popping up throughout the United States. What if she caught something deadly? What if she died alone, apart from those she loved, not to be found for weeks? She was Katrina Sands now. A woman with no friends, no family. Just Canaday, who hadn't said when he was coming back.

What if a month passed before he found her? What would he tell her family?

He wouldn't tell them anything. To them she was already dead.

Valerie found some aspirins in the medicine cabinet, a hot water bottle under the sink, and a box of tissues in the hallway closet. She made tea, took the pills, and filled the hot water bottle. She wobbled back to bed, where she spent that day and the next before surfacing.

On the third morning, the toast she had for breakfast stayed down. She drank a half gallon of water, thought about going back to bed, but searched for the car keys instead. She needed to find the nearest drugstore. No way would she stay put until she was too sick to move.

She found brochures in the top drawer next to the kitchen sink, spread them across the table, and mapped out the shortest route to the shopping mall. By eleven in the morning, she felt strong enough to tackle the drive. Sweater and bank passbook in hand, she went outside to the carport. A while later she found the bank. She held her head intact while standing in line behind four other customers. She withdrew one hundred dollars and asked the teller for directions to the drugstore. Turned out it was next door.

The stationary shelves were full of notebooks, journals and diaries, and Valerie wondered if she'd ever have the heart to write again. She stopped in front of the beauty department and browsed over all the fancy hairpins and latest makeup products her daughters would surely love. Her heart ached. In the non-prescription section, she grabbed cough medicine, antihistamines, and something to calm her stomach. She paid for her items and reached the exit doors when she caught sight of a small alcove of computers to her left. The sign above the entrance said INTERNET CAFÉ--ONE HOUR TEN DOLLARS. She hesitated.

The Internet?

Why not? Maybe she'd find something that would give her back her life. She and Ed had purchased their first computer in 1986, ten years ago. She wasn't incompetent when it came to online research; she knew a thing or two.

The lady at the counter took Valerie's ten dollars and told her to pick any computer she liked. Valerie eased herself down at the computer in the corner one, determined to find some lead before heading back to--it felt strange to think of it as her new home.

Her 411 search for *DeOlmos* gave her nothing. She tried locating his name in Toronto, then South America. Nothing.

She leaned her chin in her hand, stared at the screen. She gripped the mouse.

A global search using Dogpile for South America, Cartagena, and Miami displayed zero.

Valerie wiped her nose then used a string consisting of *DeOlmos, Baja, Hotels*. One of the links revealed a URL for a map search of Baja, California.

She clicked the icon.

A small square appeared with an aerial photograph of the coastline.

She typed in *hotels*.

Nothing.

She slid forward on her elbows, covered her face with both hands, and realized she was burning up.

These weren't FBI files; she'd learn nothing here. It was hopeless. She was out of her depth. To find information, required skill, expertise, the genius of a computer nerd. All of which eluded her. Damn!

The store was packed. Everyone looked suspicious. Even the old man sitting on a stool at the lunch counter. She caught his eye, and he smiled. His eerie expression left her uncomfortable; his lingering gaze was uncalled for. Valerie wanted to leave. No. She wanted the old man to leave. She wiped her nose, twirled her seat back around, and frowned at the screen.

Go home, Valerie.

At that instant, a voice inside her head said, "I didn't raise you to be a quitter. Use your brain. Think!"

How!

She closed her eyes. She was tired. Tomorrow was another day; she could come back, try again.

The coastline of Baja lay across the screen. Valerie wondered how many Canadians visited each year. Hundreds. Probably thousands.

That was it!

She pulled the keyboard out and typed _Travel Agent_. Blew her nose. Then did a hotel search for Baja. The screen came alive. Five, ten, fifteen, twenty-seven hotels.

Valerie sat up straight, wiped her nose, then stood up and draped her sweater over her stool. She borrowed a pencil and paper from the lady at the counter, then rushed back to the computer. She jotted down all twenty-seven hotel names and addresses. Excited, breathing through her nose for the first time that day, Valerie logged on to California's Land Offices. She did a search for all the Land Registries until locating the one for Baja, then typed in one hotel at a time. She wrote down each owner whether it was private, commercial, or a holding company. When she was finished, she studied the list. None of them showed the name Miguel or Vincent DeOlmos. Pacific Cortez Industries owned four hotels and three golf courses. Could that be one of DeOlmos's companies that Canaday spoke of? He said DeOlmos owned four hotels on Baja. Why hadn't she asked, which four?

Oh, sure, Canaday would have thought that was a normal question.

The Senez Brothers owned three hotels. Bolina Holdings owned four more hotels. An overseas company from Japan owned five. An American based corporation, along with a Mexican partner, also owned four. The rest were under individual ownerships.

Valerie rubbed her eyes and the back of her neck. She felt miserable, cold, feverish, and ready to give up. The thought of laying her head on a soft pillow grew very desirable. When her flu was gone and she was back to her old self, then she'd try again. Meanwhile, she'd go back to the house

and mother herself back to health.
Mother.
Valerie opened her eyes and looked at the screen. Canaday had said, "DeOlmos ... born in Toronto fifty-three years ago to Anton and ... *Bolina*... DeOlmos."
Bolina Holdings ... from San José del Cabo ... owned four hotels on Baja.

* * *

Aidan sat down at his desk and checked his watch. Thirty minutes had passed since he spoke to the Valley Ridge Crematorium. He couldn't understand why they were taking so long. All he wanted to know was whether Ed had told the truth about Valerie's rings. He said that although he'd had her cremated with her rings by accident, it was for the best.

Aidan glanced at the clock. How long could it be to trace one file? They must have upgraded to computers. It was a simple matter of looking up the name McCormick. The phone rang. He checked the view window on his telephone. It was the crematorium. He let it ring twice.

"Good afternoon. Roth Investigation Services."

"Sorry for the delay, Mr. Roth," the director said. "My assistant found the file you requested, and you were correct. Mrs. McCormick was not cremated with her jewellery. Her husband changed his mind, and they were sent Priority Post to him the day before the cremation. I hope that helps."

A sick feeling settled in the middle of Aidan's stomach. "Yes, that does help. Thanks."

He hung up and laid his head in his hands; an invisible weight lay heavy on his shoulders. He'd known for years that Ed was a weasel, but he just hadn't realized what a prick he was.

That McCormick Contractors had been suffering for months was no secret. Every other small logging company was having the same problems. It proved nothing.

Then why did Ed lie?

And if he lied about her rings, what else had he lied about?

He sold Valerie's rings. That had to be it.

Aidan fingered his wedding band, flung open his desk drawer, and grabbed the cheque Valerie had given him for office supplies he'd picked up a few days before the bombing. He grabbed his jacket off his chair and headed for the door. He found Susan in the kitchen. "Want to go for a drive?"

She wiped her hands on a tea towel. "Sure. Where are we going?"

"To Valerie's."

They arrived at his sister's door and were greeted by Megan, who was home alone and so pleased to see them she hugged them both for several awkward seconds. Then she made coffee and summarized the week's events. "Brandi goes to school as long as Dad drops her off, and Christine or I pick her up. Christine's trying. She's been cooking a couple of times a week. I don't know how long it's going to last, but I'm enjoying the extra freedom. This 'running a household' is hard work."

Susan grinned.

Aidan pushed away from the table. "Sweetie, is it okay if I use the phone in your dad's office?"

"Of course, Uncle Aidan."

Aidan ignored Susan's puzzled expression and left the room.

He stared at the four-drawer filing cabinet in Ed's study, used for home use. He pulled open the top drawer, spotted the Utilities file, then searched for the phone bills. He glanced back at the door, listened, then continued reading.

February showed no out-of-country calls. He grabbed the phone bill for March. Regular calls to up north, likely business related. Aidan counted six to Fort Fraser alone. Why use his home phone if these were business related? He spotted the two calls to Florida. Both on the same day: March 30. The day Aidan arrived in Elko. He pulled the notepad from his breast pocket and copied the number. He stuck the phone bills back into the Utility file and grabbed the bank reconciliation file. The file showed no bank statements after February. He grabbed the telephone book off Ed's desk and flipped through to the yellow pages for the bank's telephone number. When he found it, he pulled the cheque Valerie had written to him out of his pocket and noted the account number. He called the bank.

As soon as the call was answered, Aidan asked, "May I speak with your accounts supervisor?"

The receptionist connected him.

"Yes, I need verification on a check from McCormick Contractors."

"Go ahead," the supervisor said.

Aidan recited the numbers off Valerie's check. The supervisor asked him for a specific amount. Without hesitation, Aidan came up with a nice round figure of forty thousand. Seemed credible considering most logging equipment, even second-hand equipment, cost double that amount. The other end of the line was silent. Aidan waited. Then the supervisor spoke matter-of-factly and told Aidan the cheque would be covered.

Forty thousand dollars, Aidan wanted to shout obscenities at Ed. Instead, he thanked the accounts supervisor and hung up the phone.

"What are you doing?"

Aidan jumped. Susan stood in the doorway. "You scared me, babe."

"What are you doing, Aidan? Why are you checking Ed's finances? You already know Val's okay." She glanced over her shoulder then whispered, "What does Ed have to do with what's happened?"

"Susan, I'm relying on strangers to tell me what's happening with my sister. How do I know they're telling me the truth?"

Susan shut the door. "You think Val's dead?"

"No! But what about the men guarding her? We don't know these agents. We don't know if we can trust them. I already know Ed's a liar. He told me he had her cremated with her wedding rings. They sent them up to him the day before she was cremated. The call I just made confirms Ed cashed the insurance check. We're talking about one million dollars, Susan. When Val comes home, the insurance company is going to want their money back. Where will that leave my sister and her children?"

"Why do you think they call it *insurance*? You shouldn't be investigating your own brother-in-law. It's not right." Susan's eyes widened. "Please tell me you don't think he had anything to do with… I'm not even going to say it aloud. Aidan Roth, what in heaven's name is the matter with you?"

"Ed's a weasel. He's capable of anything. I found a strange number on one of his phone bills. I'm not going to sit by and watch him destroy what little--"

"Don't say it." Susan turned to leave the room. "Ed may be a lot of things, but he loves Val. He adores those girls. I came in to tell you Megan wants us to come for supper on Sunday."

Susan left. Aidan rubbed at the ache in the back of his neck. He wanted to kick something. He wanted to bust the phone into a thousand pieces. Damn! How much longer could he face Megan, Christine, and Brandi, and remain silent. The girls were suffering, and he had the means to change that.

To hell with E-Division. He'd tell the girls the truth. He'd explain to them they had to playact. They could do that.

Visions of Brandi skipping out the front door, a smile so bright that the sun reflected off her braces, clouded his mind. He clasped his hands together and lowered his head. He calmed his breathing. He tried to reason like his father. His father? Twenty-three years ago, their parents had died leaving Aidan as Valerie's guardian. He raised her as best he could. He tried to be both mother and father. If they were alive today, would they blame him?

    Aidan knew one thing for sure, neither one of them would have endangered the girls.

    He left Ed's study and went into the kitchen. "I'm sorry, sweetheart, but Aunt Susan and I have to leave."

    "Will you come for supper on Sunday?"

    He kissed Megan's forehead. "Maybe you should check with your dad first. Otherwise, sure."

    When they were in the car and headed downtown, Susan asked, "What's your hurry?"

    "I've got to find a payphone."

    "What for?"

    "I need to call Agent Vamozzi."

CHAPTER 28

May 1st, thirteen days after placing Valerie in her new identity, Canaday left Vamozzi at the federal building in San Jose, California, and told him to call when he was through giving evidence in a capital case. He then rented a car and drove to the tract house in Santa Cruz. When he arrived, he found the blinds closed and the house quiet. Parked out front, he watched the windows and tried to think of another excuse for being there. The one he'd dreamed up, _'I had some free time before heading back to Seattle, and I thought I'd see if you needed anything.'_ that was the excuse he'd told Vamozzi, sounded as stupid now as it did then.

Canaday climbed out of the car. The walk to the front door seemed a lot further than he remembered.

He knocked.

No response.

He knocked again, louder.

Nothing.

He tried the door handle.

Locked.

Her car was still in the carport. Canaday unclipped the clasp on his holster, crept to the back of the house, and what he saw calmed him instantly. Valerie sat at a glass sculptured table, on the back patio, a glass and a pitcher of iced tea in front of her. She was watching something across the yard. If Canaday had been a religious man, he would have thanked God that she was okay. He did anyway. Then he opened the gate and approached. The smell of orange blossoms drenched the surrounding area, rose, and mixed by a breeze that didn't exist in the front yard. It swirled around his neck to cool and dry the sweat there.

Valerie rubbed at her forehead; Canaday hesitated. The neighbour's cat walked along the picket fence toward the rock cliff and stopped under the shade of the orange tree. It glanced at Valerie, lifted his paw, and began a vigorous wash, then stopped, and glared at Canaday.

I belong here as much as you, pal.

Valerie turned her gaze from the cat and spotted him. Her serenity vanished. "What's wrong?"

"Nothing." He moved closer. "I had some business nearby and thought I'd stop for some iced tea."

She made a move to rise.

"I'll grab a glass from the kitchen. Don't get up."

"They're in the cupboard next to the fridge."

In the kitchen, he found a glass with a Mountie stamped on the side, frowned, then grabbed two ice cubes from the freezer compartment, and went back outside. Valerie poured iced tea into his glass while Canaday stripped off his jacket. He rolled his sleeves to his forearms and sat down. They sipped their tea. The breeze found Valerie. Canaday watched it sweep loose hairs across her cheek. The movement mesmerized him, and he wondered what her hair would feel like sweeping across his skin. She brushed the hairs aside, and he looked at her more closely. Dark circles outlined her eyes. The moment was still soothing, the silence still comfortable, but Canaday felt a growing unease.

Looking at the cat, he said, "Are you okay?"

"Yes."

"You sure?"

"I have a cold, but I think it's almost gone."

"Did you see a doctor?"

"No. It's not serious. I'll be my old self in a few days." She looked at him. "I've been taking medicine. It's only a cold."

Canaday let it go. Behaving like a mother hen wasn't part of the program. His fingertip outlined the scalloped design of the table's top. The silence between them grew stifling. He loosened his tie. That didn't help. The sun's heat stuck his shirt to his chest, and he could feel the sweat seeping down his armpits.

"How's my family?" she asked softly.

"They're safe."

Her detached manner surprised him. After their last meeting, he'd hoped they were past indifference. Apparently not. His eyes grazed her face.

"And DeOlmos?"

Canaday interlocked his fingers. "I wish I could say ..."

"Never mind. I don't want to know."

"The minute we arrest him, I'll call."

"Of course." Her voice was flat.

Canaday wiped the sweat from his brow. He shouldn't have come. But hell no, he had jumped at the chance to see her. Why? So he could experience the void deepening?

He pushed his chair back. "Is it okay if I wash up?"

"There's a clean towel and face cloth behind the bathroom door. Help yourself."

Canaday left her gazing off at nothing in particular and went inside. In the bathroom, he filled the sink with warm water, peeled off his shirt, and lathered a cloth. When he was finished, he dried off and threw the towel and facecloth into the clothes hamper. Valerie was sick. Of course, her mood would reflect that. He walked down the hallway to the living room, whipping his shirt through the air. She wasn't distant because he had no right to be there.

Canaday studied the living room. The way she'd switched the furniture around was nice. The wicker couch separated the room from the dining area while two wicker chairs sat in front of the window. Some type of huge potted fir tree stood in the corner. Stacks of paperbacks covered the glass table between the two chairs. The bookshelf was on one wall, the stereo on the other. Canaday put on his shirt and buttoned it. A small variegated pink rug lay in the middle of the room. Covering it was a large, fat pillow and a stack of magazines. The coffee table was overlaid with brochures. Canaday stepped closer and tucked in his shirt. The brochures showed photographs of Los Cabos. He sat down on the couch and fingered through the pile. San José Del Cabo. Cabo San Lucas. What the hell? He grabbed a handful and stormed toward the back door. He stopped at the entrance to the kitchen and thought for a moment.

Canaday threw the brochures back on the coffee table and went into the kitchen. He peeked through the blinds; Valerie still sat at the patio table. He pulled the cell from his pocket and dialled. When the connection was made he said, "Are you finished?"

"Just now, why?" Vamozzi asked.

"Grab a cab and I'll meet me at the end of Kat's road in an hour."

"Why?"

"I'll explain when you get here." Canaday hung up and went out to the patio. He sat down, thought for a moment, and said, "Would you do me a favour?"

"What?"

"Don't go after DeOlmos on your own."

"What are you talking about?"

He shifted his legs out in front of him and glanced around the yard for sight of the cat. "I saw the brochures."

"You were *snooping* through my house?"
"Promise me you won't do anything stupid."
"Leave me alone, Canaday. I owe you nothing."
"Promise me. You can't fight him. DeOlmos isn't about to let you destroy everything he's worked for. You'll be dead before that happens."
"Instead, I should sit here day in and day out and wait? No thanks."
"Get a job."
"Go to hell."
"You're not a cop. You're not equipped to deal with him."
She pushed her chair back and stood. "I've got some brochures. Big deal. It means nothing. You think I'm stupid? Go away, Canaday." She marched into the house; the screen door slammed behind her.

* * *

Valerie eased her finger down on one of the Venetian blinds above the kitchen sink and peeked out. Canaday sat at the patio table. He gripped his glass in both hands; his head was down. He made no attempt to leave. She jerked her finger away, and the blind snapped back to shape. Crossing her arms, she swung around and leaned back against the counter. She counted to ten. When she looked back, he was still there.

What's he waiting for? An apology? Valerie reminded herself never to underestimate Canaday. He's no fool. Up to this point, she had been an open book to him. He wasn't going anywhere until she convinced him there was no way she'd screw up his investigation. She glanced at her watch. She had one hour to get rid of him.

It'd been a shock to see him standing there. Of all the days for him to show up, today was the worst. He'd done enough for her already. No way was she going to jeopardize his life. He must have thought her change in mood strange, particularly after his last visit, but no way was she going to give him any reason to hang around. She knew he couldn't stop her from going to México, but she also knew she couldn't stop him from following her. He was too stubborn not to.

She walked briskly outside to the patio table and sat down. Her tea was now lukewarm, but she took a sip. "I've been on three job interviews this week alone," she said quietly. "I'm either totally unqualified, or I'm the wrong age, or the wrong type, or ...."

"I'm frustrated, Canaday. Can you understand that? Grabbing those brochures was a reflex action. I thought if I looked at them long enough something would ... I don't know. My whole life has been flipped upside down, and it infuriates me that I can't do anything about it." She glanced at him and wished to God she knew what he thought. As usual, his face gave nothing away. "I'll throw the brochures in the garbage. I'll stop whining and get on with my life. Maybe I'll go back to school. I've always wanted to be a paramedic. All those years of First Aid courses should count for something. Don't you think?"

His chin lifted. His head turned in her direction, steel blue eyes so intent she almost blinked. He was doing it again, delving into her soul. Valerie didn't move but instead made her mind go blank. With her eyes glued to his, she concentrated on the small black dot next to his left iris. She'd never noticed it before. A tiny black spot not much bigger than a petunia seed.

"I should be going." He rose from his chair. "Thanks for the drink."

Valerie's mouth fell open. Canaday grabbed his suit jacket, hooked his finger in the collar, and swung the jacket over his shoulder. He stepped off the patio, walked toward the gate, and disappeared around the side of the house.

Gone. Just like that.

Valerie sat still. In the distance, she heard the faint sound of a car starting. She glanced at her watch and stood. She had less than an hour. Gripping the pitcher in the crook of her arm, she stuck her fingers inside the two glasses and rushed into the house. She set the glassware on the counter, darted to the front window. No sign of Canaday. She rushed to her bedroom. Her two suitcases sat against the wall on the other side of her dresser. If he'd peeked into her room, he wouldn't have seen them. If he had, the way they were positioned looked innocent. For all he knew she could have been storing them there. Unless he lifted the one she had packed. Valerie flopped down on her bed. She grabbed the phone. The hell if she'd let self-doubt stop her now.

After the dispatcher assured her the taxi would arrive at her door in twenty minutes, Valerie hung up the phone, stripped off her clothes, tossed them to the closet floor, and dug out her new sleeveless, blue, ankle length dress. She brushed out her hair, swept it up into a tight, flat bun, and pinned it securely. In the mirror, she adjusted the black shoulder length shagged wig, inserting the dark brown contact lens, applied dark mascara, and finished with mauve platinum lipstick. She blinked several times, stepped back from the mirror, and studied her image. What she saw was the perfect illusion.

"Hello, Mr. DeOlmos," the image whispered, "my name is Katrina Sands."

Valerie took a deep breath and moved away from the mirror.

* * *

"There's a cab," Vamozzi said from the passenger side of Canaday's rental. "What the hell ...?"

Canaday squinted at a brunette leaving Valerie's house. Dressed in a pretty summer dress, dark glasses, carrying a suitcase, Valerie was almost unidentifiable. He had to smile.

"Where is she going?" Vamozzi asked.

"To the airport."

"Are you going to tell me what's going on?"

Canaday started the engine and inched away from the curb. Staying at a distance, he followed the cab. "She's going to Los Cabos to find DeOlmos."

"You've got to be kidding? Why are we following her? We should be stopping that cab."

Canaday didn't answer. He knew Vamozzi would figure it out soon enough; he wasn't looking forward to the confrontation. "I've got some leave coming."

"I don't think I like this," Vamozzi said. "Actually, I'm positive I don't like this. I've covered your back on a lot of stuff, but this is crazy."

"If Tomlin barks, remind him I'm entitled to a few days off. That way his ass will be covered."

"Nobody's going to believe that. Candyman, you don't take time off. I've known you for twenty-five years, and you've never taken a holiday."

"Good time to change." He glanced at Vamozzi's glum face. "I have no choice. I can't let her go alone, and I can't officially interfere."

Vamozzi's beeper alerted him to a call. He pulled it off his belt, looked at the message, and swore, "Damn."

"What?"

"If I'd known the day was going to turn out like this, I'd have stayed in bed. It's an urgent message to return Aidan Roth's call."

"What would he want?"

Exasperated, Vamozzi rolled his eyes.

Canaday took the turnoff for the airport. "Do you recognize the number?"

"It's not his home or the McCormick's, but it's definitely a Prince George number."

"Call him back and find out what he wants." Canaday could see the airport's control tower. "Better hurry. I've got to catch that plane."

"Why do you do this to me? You like adding to my stress level? If you screw up my retirement, I'm going sic my wife on you. You can't let Val leave the country. We're supposed to protect her. Instead of you taking off, we should haul her back to the safe house and have a good long talk."

"Then what? As soon as we're gone, she's on the next plane out? No. She has to discover for herself that she's not equipped to find him. Like the reports have speculated all along, DeOlmos is in Cartagena." They were almost at the terminal. "I can't wait. I'll contact you tonight, and you can tell me what Roth wanted."

"What if it's important? Are you sure you can afford to leave not knowing?"

"You read the FBI report on Roth. He's loony tunes. He accused the rank and file of assassinating his father. He had to resign. Why would anyone take anything he says seriously?"

"He's Valerie's brother and he loves her?"

Canaday pulled up in front of the airport terminal and slammed the gearshift into park. "Make it quick."

Vamozzi dialled the number, listened for several seconds before commenting. Then he and Roth talked back and forth while Canaday stewed.

"What'd he want?" Canaday asked when Vamozzi hung up.

"He wants a number in Florida checked out. He also wants a meeting with Assistant Director Tomlin. On friendly ground."

"What for?"

"He wants Tomlin to convince the RCMP to put a tap on Ed McCormick's phone. He thinks Ed may be up to something. He found a Florida number on the McCormick phone bill. One other thing ... he knows his sister's alive."

"Rostov told him?"

"No. The Mounties did."

"Well, don't this just keep getting better and better," Canaday said. "Why would they do that?"

Vamozzi shrugged.

"Has Roth got a case against McCormick?"

"I don't know, but there's something about Valerie's marriage that I can't put my finger on. I know it ticks you off that Val and I talked a lot, but not once, and I mean NEVER, did she mention Ed. Is that natural?" Vamozzi frowned. "When did Rostov find out?"

"He didn't say. He called to ask if it was true, and if so would she still testify." Canaday stared at the terminal doors. The urgency to leave was powerful. But what was its source? He was ninety-nine percent certain that Miguel DeOlmos was in Colombia. It was the other one percent that nagged at him. "Check the number he asked about."

Vamozzi put in the request. Canaday unwrapped a candy and stuffed it in his mouth. A terrible dread soured the taste.

During a ten-minute wait that felt like thirty minutes, Vamozzi made three phone calls. Canaday's right leg twitched the entire time. He popped another candy in his mouth.

"It belonged to a manufacturer of greenhouse kits," Vamozzi said, after hanging up.

"Any links to DeOlmos?"

"They don't know. The number's been disconnected. What do you want to do? Even if she goes to Los Cabos that's not where DeOlmos is."

Canaday watched a plane ascend to the heavens and dug another candy out of his pocket. He had probably already missed that fucking plane.

CHAPTER 29

Valerie moved through a room decorated in soft peaches, grays, and pinks, dropped her suitcase to the floor, tossed her key card on the desk, and headed for the French doors leading out to the balcony. Moist heat flooded her lungs and assaulted her face and bare skin. Valerie relished the sensation.

A small table and two chairs were positioned near the wrought ironed railing. She pulled out a chair, sat down, and was immersed in a heat wave. She looked out at the unspoiled beach. The turquoise and aqua blue waters of the Sea of Cortez rolled onto shore, exposing clusters coral beneath their deep waves. Below her balcony to the right, tourists stretched out on padded lounge chairs arranged around the blue pool. Others sat at the poolside bar, their bodies waist deep in water. While still more lazed under the shade of *paraguas*.

Beyond the pool, shielding the hotel from the beach, tropical gardens spread out past the edge of the courtyard. Hibiscus, laden with large, bright purple scarlet flowers, nestled in alongside the well raked paths. Crushed cobblestones, dried by the sun, made a trail through the Eucalyptus trees to the white beach.

San José del Cabo was indeed aesthetically satisfying. The air, mixed with a vibrant blend of exquisite scents: cinnamon, papaya, and vanilla scented Genista trees, also carried an aroma of sweet rolls, coconut, rum, and oranges from the lunch area somewhere below. Yet, on the cusp of such palatable scents, she detected an unpleasant taste and a familiar smell. She heard an unusual sound below and to her left.

Valerie dragged her chair to the other end of the ten-by-five foot balcony. Resting her forearms on the railing, she leaned over as far as she dared. Around the side of the hotel to the courtyard partly obscured by the balcony next door, at the center of the U shaped hotel, before the huge doors, lay an outside dining area laid with powdery pink ceramic tiles. Long tables, filled with foods, fruits, and various sea lion ice sculptures surrounded a water fountain in the center of the yard. Pinks, blues, and greens reflected out of the flowing layers of water.

The strange noise grew closer. Valerie looked out at the waves pounding to shore. It wasn't that. The sound mimicked a ... bus.

Again, the smell hit her, harder this time. She sniffed the air, tasting more than smelling. Exhaust fumes ... Gladiola ... sea salt. Her heart thumped. She saw the agent knocked back by the blast of DeOlmos's gun. She heard the shot. She saw his smile. The charming, trusting smile DeOlmos gave the agents seconds before --

A lawn tractor came around the corner of the building, under her balcony. Valerie collapsed back against her chair. She breathed deeply, acknowledged the scents, and reasoned away their significance. It was her mind playing games. Creating fears that could cripple her.

A lot had happened since that morning in Seattle, the morning Valerie promised herself she'd listen to her instincts. It was time to act. Time to influence her own fate, not sit back while others continued to do it for her. DeOlmos owned this hotel and one more on Carretera Transpenninsular, one on Carretera Cacto, and one on Boulevard Océano. She wasn't going to confront the man. She'd just do a little detecting and find out where he was. Then she'd pass along the information to Canaday who, she was certain, would do whatever he had to do to bring Miguel DeOlmos down. It wasn't that she thought the FBI incompetent. Their plan wasn't working. DeOlmos was an intelligent man. He wouldn't just surface. He would show himself only to his people, people he trusted. Like the employees of his four hotels.

She'd start with this one.

Valerie hoped that posing as an American freelance writer would squash any misgivings his employees might have. She wasn't a threat to anyone. She knew how to make people feel comfortable. If anybody did check her résumé, they would discover that she'd published many travel related articles under the pseudonym of Bridget Spenser. Luckily, the woman existed, was credited with writing various pieces for popular travel and women's magazines, and was presently on an undercover assignment for a famous travel agency.

Valerie laughed at her naivety.

All right, so maybe it wouldn't be that simple. But sitting in a tract house in Santa Cruz certainly hadn't helped. She'd pose as a journalist, find out any snippet of information she could on Miguel DeOlmos, pass it on to Canaday, and prove to him that she wasn't useless in contributing to the welfare of her family.

There it was again, her need to prove something to him.

Not to mention the fit he was certain to have when he learned his accusation over the brochures was partially true. But the man had a bark worse than his bite. She'd let him sound off, then she'd stand tall and remind him that she had at least found something out.

Why the need to prove anything to Canaday?

Valerie didn't answer that. Instead, she practiced her first line of defence; verbal lies. "Hello, I'm doing an article for an American teenage magazine, and I was wondering …?"

The hard part would be lying.

But, if she wanted her life back, she'd better get over it. Nothing else had worked.

Valerie stood up, and the trembling in her legs made her grope for the door.

"No more fear," she whispered. She was too close and had come too far to quit.

She retrieved her camera from the suitcase, gathered a notepad and pencils, and checked the mirror to insure no blonde hair was peeking out from beneath her brunette wig. She opened her eyes wide. The contacts were in place; both eyes were brown.

The lobby buzzed. Tourists wore bright, florescent shorts, tops, and big floppy hats. Their broad smiles depicted their exhilaration. Under different circumstances, Valerie would have felt the same way.

She passed through the lobby and headed toward the patio out back. She needed time to clear out the random spurts of fear. To approach employees, sounded so easy when she was sitting at the Internet café. Her faith made it sound easy. She stepped through the patio doors leading out into the hotel's courtyard and into a different heat wave. Without the slight breeze from the sea, nothing was the same at this end of the hotel. Even the quality of sound was different. A couple laughed, raced along the edge of the pool, and dove in. They came together under the water and embraced. Valerie tore her eyes away and kept walking. She shrugged off the loneliness in her heart and saw a young woman approach; she wore the customary dark suit jacket with the hotel's crest just above the heart. Valerie pulled the notepad and pencil out of her pocket.

The assistant manager grinned widely when Valerie explained her assignment. While they made the rounds, she offered to introduce Valerie to many of the younger staff later that evening. Then she spotted a waitress through the restaurant's windows, waved, and jabbed a finger in Valerie's direction.

Valerie had noticed an outdoor area affixed to the front of the dining

Joylene Nowell Butler

room when she'd first arrived. On the same powdery pink Italian ceramic stones was a long brass sculptured bar surrounded by intimate arrangements of wicker sofas and round back chairs. Valerie took several photographs of the girl, promised to meet her at this same outside bar at seven o'clock, and joined the waitress in the informal restaurant facing the courtyard at the back of the hotel.

The waitress, named Rosa, listened as Valerie explained her assignment. She directed Valerie to a table beside the window and answered as many questions as possible while attending to other customers. When her break came, she asked if she could join Valerie. Valerie couldn't agree fast enough.

"How would you rate your employer?" she asked, after the girl had answered several non-essential questions.

"She is a kind supervisor."

"Are the owners nice people?"

Rosa nodded hesitatingly.

Valerie's sixth sense stirred. She sketched a Happy Face on her notepad. "Do they live here at the hotel?"

"No."

"That must be a comfort?"

The young girl looked confused.

"To have the boss, always peeking over your shoulder, would make it difficult to concentrate."

Rosa smiled politely. "He is a very busy man."

"He probably spends most of his time in his office at one of his hotels?"

"No. He is at his more important office in Cartagena."

Valerie's pen slid through her fingers; she fought to control her frustration. "I was hoping I could ask him some questions for my article. Do you know when he'll be returning?"

"No."

"But he does visit periodically?"

"Oh, yes." The waitress mimicked Valerie, "Periodically."

Valerie stuffed her notepad and pencil back in her pocket and snapped several photos of the young girl, much to the amusement of nearby patrons. When Valerie asked if she would join her at the outside bar in three hours, Rosa nodded tentatively. Valerie, wondering if her own expression had changed to reflect her mood, remembered to smile. The girl's hard stare softened, and she smiled in return.

Walking back through the restaurant, through the lobby, Valerie's legs continued toward the elevators, seemingly unaware that her brain didn't know where to go. What had she thought? That Miguel DeOlmos would be wandering around one of his hotels while the American authorities wanted him on seven counts of murder. She laughed softly, then ducked into the elevator behind four tourists. Their voices filled the small space with high-pitched squeals. Laughter, giggles, assuasive sounds that reminded Valerie of part about what was good in the world.

It didn't matter if Miguel DeOlmos was in Cartagena. All was not lost. Somebody had to know something. She could still find something to help Canaday's investigation.

The elevator door opened, Valerie stepped out and walked a few feet. To her right was Room 339. She halted. She was on the wrong floor; her room was one floor down. Goodness, Valerie thought, laughing at her blunder. Maybe she was suffering from sun deprivation.

Valerie made an about face and strolled past the elevator to the exit door. The best medicine would be to sunbathe for the rest of the afternoon. Taking the stairs back to the lobby three flights down would do her good. Clear her woolly thoughts. She secured the camera over her shoulder and swung her free arm. Her footsteps were virtually soundless.

Her spirits lifted, she descended the stairs in no time, and entered the lobby. Three employees stood behind the front desk. Two young men and a girl. Bright, crisp suits. Mannerisms and charm essential to the job. One of them would know where the bathing suit shop was.

Valerie approached the counter and glimpsed a man out of the corner of her eye. He was talking to Rosa, the waitress, outside the entrance to the restaurant. Rosa's shoulders were slouched, as if to ward off an attack. Even from this distance, Valerie saw the fear in young girl's eyes.

The man looked familiar. Bile rose in Valerie's throat. It was the man from the yacht. The man who worked for DeOlmos. What was his name!

Rostov had repeated the two men's names enough times during the investigation. Reynaldo Ramirez and Lope Martinez. Or was it Ramirez? Maybe it was the other way around, Reynaldo Martinez and Lope Romarez?

Valerie spun around, anxious to distance herself, caught her heel in a wide crack in the ceramic tiles, tripped, and landed in the arms of a stranger. She laughed. Embarrassed, confused by the strength of his arms, she dislodged herself from his grip, straightened up, and adjusted her sunglasses. She looked up at his face.

Joylene Nowell Butler

"*Señorita*, are you all right?" Vincente DeOlmos asked.
Valerie's heart stopped.

CHAPTER 30

Survival instincts took over straightaway. "My shoe caught on something." Valerie glanced at the floor as if searching for the culprit. "Forgive me for barging into you like that." She inhaled and glimpsed up.

Vincente, who looked exactly like his photograph, spread his arms and smiled. "*Señorita*, a feather would have inflicted more damage. I am only glad I was here to save you. You could have injured yourself."

Valerie backed away. "Thanks again."

He bowed his head. Valerie turned. The elevator bell rang. She floated toward it, at the same time compelled to glance back. He continued smiling. His teeth were as white and as perfect as God intended. His black eyes twinkled. His white tailored suit, white shirt, and pink tie, made his tanned skin look bronze. He was a Greek deity. A deadly, repulsive deity.

Valerie stepped into the elevator, pressed the second floor button, and turned to face the lobby. He was still standing there. Her eyes wandered across the floor to his white leather shoes, his white trousers. The elevator doors closed. Valerie gasped for air.

Her key pad was ready before she reached her room. Her hand shook. She managed to unlock the door and stepped inside. Her legs gave out. She collapsed against the wall and grabbed the doorknob to stop from falling to the floor. She gasped for breath, the noise in her head compounding the urgency for silence. Her hands reached upward, climbing the metal door until she was pressed against it, her ear straining to hear. But the noise in her brain spoiled any attempt at recognizing footsteps, soft whispers, or sounds of men gathering in the hallway.

She backed into the bathroom and locked the door. She turned on the cold water and struggled with her black shagged wig. Yanked it off. Splashed cold water on her face. The dizziness wouldn't pass. She turned off the tap and flopped onto the toilet seat. "Holy Mother of God!" Valerie cried then she moved aside, lifted the toilet seat, and vomited.

Later, in the shower, she felt embarrassed for overreacting. Vincente had surprised her. It wasn't as if she'd walked into Miguel.

She thumped her head against the fibreglass shower wall.

Goodness to Gracious--what was wrong with her!

Miguel was a killer, yes, but Canaday said Vincente was a psychopath. "Get a grip, Valerie."

God gave you a brain. Start using it.

Valerie stepped out of the shower and took the edge of her towel to wipe at the condensation on the mirror. The color in her face had returned. She had been shocked to see Vincente, but still a test she'd passed. Maybe running into him was a blessing in disguise. She knew two things for certain. She could face these men. And, they wouldn't recognize her.

Valerie smiled at her reflection in the mirror. The fact her stomach was doing somersaults meant nothing.

Though the air conditioner chilled the inside of her room, she chose a cool cotton skirt and a white corset top. Lace covered the smooth skin of her breasts with a slight show of flesh visible above the lace trim. She grabbed the shawl from her suitcase, stepped back, and studied her image in the mirror. Seductive without appearing vulgar. She put the black wig back on and tugged hard. It would take more than a good pull to lift it off her head.

In the restaurant downstairs, she ordered dinner: Filet mignon, refried beans, salad, and breadsticks, with a tall glass of iced tea.

Word about her article must have spread, because her waiter and waitress smiled every time she looked their way. When she'd finished her dinner, the waitress asked that since Valerie still had an hour before their important rendezvous in the outside bar, would she care for dessert. Valerie ordered one slice of chocolate cake. A moment later the waitress returned with a piece of cake that could have easily fed three, covered in thick, rich chocolate, and surrounded by grapes and strawberries. She couldn't finish it, but she did manage to down two tall bottles of Perrier.

Her thirst satisfied, her stomach full, Valerie left a tip and deciding to walk off her meal, wandered through the gardens down to the beach then stood and listened to the pounding surf. Behind her, the hotel lit up. Pink, blue, and green lights from the fountain shone brightly, and soft yellow lights outlined the courtyard. The air smelled of coconut, papaya, and fuchsias. It reminded Valerie of coco butter and cold cream. In the distance, she heard Spanish guitar music from the outside bar. The next hotel was a mile down the beach on the north. To the south, nothing ... but shadows.

Valerie headed back.

The bar was packed with tourists filling the cozy sofas and round back chairs. In the background, Gloria Estefan's voice serenaded from one of her tapes. Groups of young people were gathered at the bar. A cook, still dressed in his white tunic jacket, spotted her. He waved. The others turned and smiled. One young man rushed forward to greet her. "*Buenas tardes, Señorita.* Please join us." He nodded toward his friends.

Rosa slipped off a stool in amongst the group. "Here, take my seat." She grabbed another stool from behind the bar and sat next to Valerie.

Introductions were made.

"Bridget, what is your pleasure?" the lanky bartender asked.

Valerie asked the girl two stools over, "What's that you're drinking?"

"Pina colada and grenadine."

Valerie scrunched up her nose; the group laughed. "A diet coke, please. And drinks for everyone."

"Is it true you work for an important American magazine?" the boy on her left asked.

"Not really, I freelance."

"What's that?" someone said.

"She writes for whoever pays the best," someone answered.

The group laughed.

"What would you like to know, Bridget?" the bartender said. "We are your servants. Ask and it shall be answered."

Everyone, except Rosa, nodded in agreement.

Valerie pulled out her notepad and pencil. "I'm doing a piece on the young employees working in five-star hotels. My theme will be to compare the differences between the working conditions in México verses the United States."

"It sounds most titillating," someone said. The group laughed.

"Don't mind Juan," the bartender said. "Studying English for 5 years has given Johnny a fat head."

"It does sound boring," Valerie answered. "But hopefully, one of you will be able to add an interesting angle. What if it turns out that working here in Baja is far more exciting than working in hotels… say in Florida or Hawaii, or even California. Either way, I'll try to make it interesting. Who wants to go first? How do you find working in this fabulous hotel? Is it fun? Is the work extremely hard?" She glanced at the smiling young woman seated on the other side of Rosa. "Or is all the hard work worth the chance of meeting Mr. Rich and Dreamy only to live happily-ever-after?"

"Hasn't happened so far," the waiter sitting at the end of the bar, replied sadly.

More laughter.

"Tell me about your employer. Is he a good man? Does he give salary raises on a regular basis? Do you receive many benefits? Such as health insurance, dental, lots of sick leave?"

The ten young faces looking back at her were blank, though the bartender did appear sympathetic. "Bridget, who would care whether my teeth get fixed for free?"

"Okay, so maybe dental isn't so glamorous. You'd be surprised how interested American readers are in their neighbours, though. Particularly the beautiful and the handsome from Baja."

The desk clerk to her right blushed; the rest remained quiet. Valerie tried another tactic. "How do you like working in a big, fancy hotel versus say ... one of the budget hotels downtown?"

"The money is *mucho* better here than anywhere else," the girl with the weird drink answered.

"But money isn't everything." Rosa fidgeted with the straw from her drink. "Money won't buy you safety and the love and security of a family."

While the rest seemed to ignore Rosa, the bellhop, sitting between Rosa's friend and the waiter at the end of the bar, smiled as if he alone understood the true meaning between those who say and those who do.

"What do you think?" Valerie asked him.

"He doesn't speak English," Rosa answered, her voice flat.

The bus boy from the indoor restaurant said, "My mother worked two jobs until I was hired here. Now my wage covers the extras and she has only to work one job."

"I noticed on the trip in from the airport that there's no neighbourhood segregation," Valerie said. "No class distinctions. I passed a lovely white Spanish style home, and right next door the house looked to be four pieces of plywood stuck together."

The group grew quiet.

"It must be difficult to see firsthand how the rich live. Judging by the grandeur of this hotel, the owner must be living like a king."

"There will always be those who have and those who have not," the housekeeping supervisor replied.

"What's he like?" Valerie asked, "This owner who *has*?"

The bartender shrugged.

"Bridget?" the desk clerk to her left asked. "You must meet interesting people while doing these assignments. Rich single men."

The girls giggled, all but Rosa who seemed lost in her own world.

"Rich men seldom like reporters." Urged on by the opening, she added, "I did see a gorgeous man in the lobby today. Judging by his clothes, he is very rich. White satin suit, white silk shirt, and--"

"Pink tie?"

"Yes." Valerie looked to her right. She wasn't sure, which one of the four girls had spoken, but everyone was studying their drinks.

Rosa twirled around on her stool and looked up at the stars, then at the tree lined highway in front of the hotel. Traffic whizzed past. Rosa's face was gray, her eyes appeared glazed over, and an incredible misery clouded her features. She glanced at Valerie then looked away. She was the one who had spoken.

The bellhop next to Valerie took a long swig of beer then set down his glass. "I wonder if it will rain tomorrow. You cannot trust the weather people. They are seldom correct."

Valerie smiled at him. Not exactly subtle, but his intent seemed reminiscent of the entire group. Especially Rosa, who twitched once then blinked twice before coming alive. "We have the same problem where I live," Valerie said and the air around her warmed.

At ten o'clock, the group dispersed. The couples were drawn to a favourite club downtown; while many others said work came too early in the morning.

Valerie approached Rosa, who was finishing her drink. "Do you work tomorrow?"

"No, tomorrow is my day off."

"I don't feel like going to my room, and I don't want to stay here by myself. Would you stay for awhile?"

Rosa smiled sweetly. "All right, *Señorita*."

"Please call me Bridget. Otherwise I feel like your mother."

Rosa laughed. "You are a child next to my mother."

Valerie smiled. "I knew I liked you for a reason." She ordered them another drink.

They talked about girl stuff, clothes, swimsuits, movie stars, and rock music, had a second drink, and continued to make light conversation. At midnight, Valerie thought of asking Rosa straight out what was wrong. Her intuition said 'Mind your own business.'

She took a long sip of her drink and knew one thing for sure. Something bad had happened to this young woman. Valerie hoped it had nothing to do with Vincente. That would be too horrible to imagine.

As the evening progressed, Rosa had more drinks, until finally Valerie had difficulty discerning Rosa's words. Several times Rosa slurred something, they giggled, and Valerie said she had no idea what Rosa had just said; then Rosa attempted to articulate slowly in English, until they laughed so hard the other patrons scowled.

Despite the gloom that had settled over Rosa earlier in the evening, the young woman soon bloomed like a delicate rose, sweet, mysterious, with a soul that was meant to be cherished. It saddened Valerie to think that something bad had happened to this gentle girl.

The atmosphere seemed more relaxed with each passing hour. Valerie clasped her hands together on the table and smiled at Rosa then looked toward a couple dancing on the lawn. "This is such a beautiful place; I can't believe I'm here because of work. If I had half a brain, I'd forget about my assignment and just enjoy it. But," she stopped to yawn. "I can't afford to be lazy." She yawned again. "I'm not as young as I used to be. I haven't been up this late in years."

"Two o'clock in the morning is early," Rosa slurred.

Valerie laughed. "I seldom see midnight. Unless I have to pee."

Rosa giggled.

"I'm beat. Think I'll call it a night and see you tomorrow."

"I will walk you to your room, Bridget."

Valerie stood and stretched. "Don't be silly. You stay here and have fun. I can manage."

Rosa frowned. "No. I would be a terrible companion if I didn't see you reached your room safely."

Valerie looked toward the entrance and was grateful Vincente hadn't appeared. He was definitely someone to fear. "Fine. Who I am to argue." Valerie left a ten-dollar tip on the table and stood up. "I want to ask you something, but it escapes me at the moment. Maybe while we walk, my memory will return."

Rosa accompanied Valerie back into the hotel. As they walked down the long, quiet corridor to her room, Valerie tried to recall what it was she'd wanted to ask. Something about Baja, more specifically: San José del Cabo… oh yes, now she remembered. "Rosa, how do I go about renting a house for a few days?"

"There is a business in town around the corner from the ice-cream pallor. They would help you. What type of house do you want?"

"Small, cozy, something on the beach. Something… cheap."

Rosa grinned. "My aunt has a little white house up the road. It has a private terrace in the back. The front entrance is protected from the wind by beautiful fuchsia bushes. She usual rents by the month, but I'll speak with my aunt."

"It sounds perfect." Somewhere she could regroup, forget about the danger ... in between searching for news of Miguel DeOlmos.

Valerie slowed her pace. Her door was a short distance away. She pulled the key card from her pocket. She glanced at Rosa. The girl looked pale. Do I really want to know what's wrong? Valerie wondered. She did and she didn't. She unlocked the door. "Would you like a drink or something? Maybe a juice?"

"Okay." Rosa followed Valerie into the room and went directly to the couch and sat down. "I don't really want something to drink. Could I sleep here?" She smoothed her skirt down over her knees.

Valerie grabbed a diet coke from the fridge and fumbled with the bottle cap remover. "Of course you can stay. I have an extra nightie you can borrow."

Rosa nodded and produced a strained smile.

Valerie pulled the San Jose Sharks nightshirt from the drawer, sat down on the edge of the bed, and faced Rosa on the couch. She sipped her drink.

Rosa fingered the nightshirt and kept her head bow.

Something was wrong. Whether she actually wanted to know, still plagued Valerie. She sensed pushing the issue might frighten Rosa further. But she also sensed the girl needed to tell someone.

I understand how that feels, Valerie wished she could admit.

"Do you have children?" Rosa asked with her head down.

Valerie's heart ached. "No."

"But you have a family?"

"No."

Rosa looked up, her eyes shiny. "You have no mother, no father?"

"They died."

"I am so very sorry."

"It's okay. It was a long, long time ago."

"You have no brothers, no sisters?"

Valerie shook her head.

"How did your parents die?"

Valerie sipped her pop. "A car accident."

"What were their names?"

"Serg--I mean... Johnathan and Bibiane ... Spenser." She gulped over her near mistake. It was so natural to say Sergeant Johnathan Aidan Roth. But it was a mistake that could get her killed.

"They are nice names. I asked because you can tell a lot about a person by how they are named. Most of the time." She smiled briefly and then frowned. "You must be so lonely. I have my mother, many aunts and uncles, and cousins. My father is also dead."

Valerie wondered when it stops? The need to say I'm sorry.

"At least, I believe he's dead. But we're not sure."

"You mean he's missing?" Valerie sipped her pop.

"Yes."

"That must be terrible."

"Yes."

"How long?"

"Since September sixteen, nineteen ninety-five. My father has--had a good name: Lope Esau Ramirez. "

The acid in Valerie's stomach jumped to the back of her throat. The words stammered off her tongue, "How can you be sure of the date?"

"He told my mother that morning that he would call after dinner. He didn't. Never did my father miss calling. I asked her where he was. She didn't know. The man he worked for said he drowned. They could not find the body."

"What did the police say?"

Rosa shook her head and laughed in disgust.

"You mean going to the police wasn't an option." Valerie wet her dry lips and wondered if she was even more foolish than Canaday thought. She should never have left the States. She faked a yawn. "I can't stay awake any longer, Rosa. I'll get you a blanket. We'll visit some more tomorrow, okay?"

Rosa stood up. "I talk too much."

"No you don't. I'm just jet lagged. We'll talk more tomorrow."

"I'll show you the white house on the beach."

"Great," Valerie said, on her way to the bathroom.

She closed the door and collapsed against it. She buried her face in the crease in her elbow. Caution screamed at her to get out of there, board the first available flight back to the States, and get as far away from this hotel as possible. The place was likely crawling with cartel members. Vincente was a maniac. If he discovered who she was, she'd end up like Lope, gone without a trace.

Yet, even as she stood there saturated in sweat, her imagination conjuring up horrific scenes of torture, Valerie knew she wasn't going anywhere. She couldn't. Go back to her new house and wait until Canaday told her she might see her daughters again? No.

She already knew more than she did when she'd arrived. One of the men from the boat, Reynaldo Martinez was there. Lope Ramirez was missing. Miguel DeOlmos was in Cartagena, and as far as Vincente was concerned, she was merely another brown eyed, dark-haired tourist.

Then why did she feel sick to her stomach?

Because Rosa's father died after Valerie had escaped the marina.

Did his death have anything to do with her getting away?

God, she hoped not.

CHAPTER 31

Aidan sat in the civic center watching the Zamboni sweep over the hockey rink. Chopped ice in front of the machine became a mirror smooth surface once it passed. It was mesmerizing to watch. But Aidan was only killing time.

A man appeared at the end of the row and waved him forward. He pointed to the door marked *Maintenance* and left. Aidan knocked. Another man let him in.

Inspector Banyan, Special Agent Vamozzi, and an older man Aidan assumed was Assistant Director Tomlin were inside the room. Banyan made the introductions, and Aidan shook hands.

The old man scrutinized him. "I've heard of you, Mr. Roth, and I don't mean that as a compliment."

"I don't care what they told you about me, sir. I'm here to help end this so my sister can return home."

"I've come a long way, Mr. Roth. This better not be a waste of my time." Tomlin sat down on the bench under the window.

"My brother-in-law cashed a hefty insurance policy after my sister's fictitious death. His phone bill shows two calls to Miami. He has one incoming call from an unknown source. Wouldn't surprise me if it were a scrambled cellular phone. I'm going to guess you already know the calls to Miami belonged to a greenhouse manufacturer that's since evacuated the premises with no trace." Aidan propped his hip on the corner of the table. "Maybe it's me, but I find that peculiar, considering my brother-in-law has never taken an interest in growing anything. One call could be explained, but he called Miami twice. He's not a stupid man, sir. He knows if Valerie comes home he'll lose everything. Insurance companies don't like being deceived. If I can find out about his finances, so can DeOlmos. It makes sense to me that they'd both be a lot happier if Valerie didn't return home."

"Those are strong allegations. With little facts. Believing his wife is dead would explain cashing her life insurance."

"It would also give him additional reason to talk to DeOlmos."

"You're suggesting one man, with no investigative skills or connections, managed to locate a man law enforcement agencies in both countries can't find?"

"I'm saying DeOlmos contacted Ed, a man who had recently received an insurance check for one million dollars. My brother-in-law is a simple man with big dreams. I'm asking for a phone tap. If nothing comes of it then no harm done. If something does ... then all our problems are solved."

Tomlin turned to Banyan. "Wouldn't this request be better coming from you?"

"Let's be honest. You know your government has pull in Ottawa. Have you ever put in a request that wasn't honoured?"

"Actually, yes."

"I know my sister's alive, sir. I could do this alone. Find Valerie, then take her away where you'd never find her."

"A threat, Mr. Roth?"

"It's not a threat, sir."

"You're asking me to influence a foreign agency with unsubstantiated evidence. What if you're wrong? What if you don't know Mr. McCormick as well as you think? He could be trying to cope in his own way. Maybe your sister always wanted a greenhouse. It's not unheard of, a grieving husband making an effort to achieve his dead spouse's dream."

"Ed told me he had Valerie cremated with her rings on. I called. They have the paperwork to prove that at Ed's request, they shipped her rings up the day before the body was cremated. I'm guessing he sold them."

"To whom?"

"I don't know. I checked the pawnshops...."

"Why would DeOlmos risk contacting him?" Tomlin asked.

Aidan lowered his eyes. He pulled a chair out from a rickety table next to a battered filing cabinet. He tested the chair by pressing down on the back then deeming it safe, sat down. "My trip to Elko raised suspicions that DeOlmos couldn't ignore. I'll have to live with that. Because of me, DeOlmos did some checking and came up with the same conclusion I did. All it took after that was a simple phone call. Once DeOlmos realized Ed didn't know anything, maybe he put the fear of God in him, I don't know. But I think Ed should be watched, and if he does talk to DeOlmos, he should be nailed to the cross."

"I didn't come thousands of miles to discipline one of your family members, Mr. Roth. I'll make the call, but that's all I can do."

Aidan rubbed at the stubble on his face. Four months ago he would have presented himself to the Assistant Director of the FBI clean shaved. Now he didn't give a damn what he looked like. "There's one other thing.

If Ed's willing to deal with DeOlmos, then there's a good chance he'll deal with anybody for the right price. What if he were persuaded to help set a trap?"

Tomlin wrinkled his lips and tried to look unimpressed. It was too late. "As I said, Mr. Roth. I'll call Ottawa. That is all I will do."

"Thank you, sir."

* * *

Rosa slept on Valerie's sofa until ten a.m. As soon as she was ready, they walked the few blocks to town. Valerie made some excuse about not getting enough exercise.

In town, while Rosa was occupied visiting with a clerk at the drugstore, Valerie walked across the street and rented a car using her Katrina Sands American Express. She had no choice. They required a credit card, and she had none under the name Spenser.

Rosa's aunt gave Valerie a receipt for two weeks in advance. Valerie took the key, thanked the woman, then drove with Rosa back through town. They traveled the coastal highway toward San Lucas. A few miles past her hotel, they pulled into a long gravelled driveway.

The adobe styled home sat on a small bank overlooking the Sea of Cortez. They walked up the path, and Valerie opened a wrought iron gate. She crossed the flagstone patio. Shrubs, palm trees, and large bushes, bordered the yard, hiding it from the highway.

The house had no running water and was tiny inside, but the bright yellowy white walls created a pleasant atmosphere. Valerie remarked on how lemony the place smelled, and Rosa smiled and said that besides being a good businesswoman, her aunt was a good housekeeper.

They left the sitting room light on, went out the back, and Valerie locked the door behind them. They drove back to town.

"What else can I do?" Rosa said.

"You've done plenty. Where shall I drop you off?"

"Do you remember the ice-cream parlour? There will be fine. My house is a few doors away."

"I can drive you home."

Rosa's eyes sparkled. "My mother loves maple walnut ice-cream."

"Me, too. But won't it be melted by the time you get home?"

"That's why I walk. My mother always worries about her weight. If I say I can't finish it, then she'll scold me for wasting good money and take the ice-cream." Rosa's face beamed.

Unsure how to broach the subject, Valerie smiled. "Could you do me one last favour?"

"Of course."

"If anyone from the States should ask about me ... particularly a grumpy looking man, don't tell him where I'm staying. Okay?"

"You wish to hide from your boyfriend?"

"Not exactly. I just need time to think."

Rosa's eyebrows arched and she nodded, as if the mystery of men knew no language barriers. "I understand."

Do you? Valerie wondered; and knew of course that Rosa didn't. Not really.

Two miles down the road, Valerie pulled the car to the curb. The ice-cream parlour lay forty feet away with customers standing in line, most of whom were fanning themselves under sun bleached umbrellas. Valerie's stomach growled. The sun's hot rays drained the energy from her body. She needed food, yet something told her not to rush Rosa.

Rosa stared at the children playing at a table near the booth. She took a deep breath, continued to watch the children, and told Valerie about a terrible evening in August.

Valerie knew Rosa meant Vincente even though she never mentioned him by name. Unspeakable words came out of Rosa's mouth. He not only raped and humiliated her, he used a knife to carve his initials on her breast. Then he threatened to cut them off if she ever showed anyone.

What Rosa said next was worse. "I waited a whole month before I told my father --and that was the last time I saw him."

Valerie felt an anger and repulsion growing like none she'd ever known. She stared at the girl, sickened, terrified, and more determined than ever to go back for her girls. "Has he bothered you since?"

"No."

"Then he's no longer around?"

"He's around, but pretends he doesn't know me. It's as if that horrible night never happened." Rosa wiped away the tears.

"I'm very sorry for what he did to you, Rosa. Please don't let him ruin what could be a wonderful future."

Rosa stared at Valerie for a long moment, then slipped out of the car and walked toward the parlour.

At her hotel, Valerie had lunch in the outdoor restaurant. Revitalized, but still saddened by what Rosa had shared, she went up to her room, had a quick shower, and changed into a white cotton top and a short, finely embroidered skirt. When she was ready, she checked out. She locked her belongings in the rental outside. Back at the poolside, the lounge chair positioned in the shade beckoned her. She stretched out. A short time to rest was all she needed before moving to her new accommodations. Just a short siesta ....

* * *

Canaday took his coffee and wandered away from the restaurant of the Hotel Santa Maria. He pushed his sunglasses further up on the bridge of his nose and sipped his coffee. Tired and sore from sleeping on a soft bed, angry at having missed the plane Valerie had taken, he walked through the courtyard and settled into a chair near the pool. A crowd of tourists passed. Canaday watched the door. After spending yesterday at the Hotel Playa then at the Westerner Hotel, he felt edgy. Valerie wasn't as easy to find as he'd hoped. Still, Canaday decided he'd wait before moving on. The desk clerk had said there was no one registered by the name of Katrina Sands. But what if she'd been switching hotels, searching for DeOlmos, like Canaday was searching for her.

Canaday waited another hour. He thought of the defining moments in his life: his mother's death, his first kill in Nam. He thought of the choices he'd made since. Giving up on his marriage. Deciding to hunt bad guys instead of raising a family. Decisions and choices that in no way prepared him for Valerie McCormick.

He got up, went into the hotel, and asked the desk clerk for a brochure of Baja. A young woman handed him three. Canaday thanked her and headed out to his car.

One of the maps named all the hotels from Cabo San Lucas to San José del Cabo. He marked off the three he'd already checked. Opening his cell phone, he pressed Vamozzi's number. The phone rang four times before Vamozzi answered.

"Where are you?" Canaday asked.

"Back in Seattle."

"Has Valerie used her credit card?"

"Not yet."

That's because she's too damn smart for her own good, Canaday thought. "What did you learn from Roth?"

Vamozzi relayed yesterday's conversation at the civic center. "Tomlin spoke to Ottawa this morning. They've reluctantly agreed to the taps. So far nothing. Any trace of Valerie?"

"No. What's your opinion of Roth? Do you think he's paranoid?"

"Nothing he's said checks out. RCMP looked in Ed's safety deposit box and didn't find Val's rings. That doesn't prove anything. He cashed the insurance check. But that's no crime. When you find Val, you're not going to tell her, are you?"

"You said yourself her brother has no evidence. I'm not telling Valerie that Ed's a scumbag without proof. Get me some proof."

"It'll destroy her."

Canaday grimaced. "You don't know that. Maybe the news will give Valerie the perfect reason to behave herself."

"She might think your intentions are questionable."

"Say what?"

"Candyman, I know how you feel about her. I'm only suggesting she may see an ulterior motive."

"I'd turn her against Ed so I can have her for myself? Is that what you think?"

"No. But that doesn't mean Val won't see it that way."

"Get me the proof. I'll call later."

"Hold on a second. What am I suppose to tell Tomlin?"

"The truth. I'm trying to stay one foot ahead of this mess we call a case."

"I haven't said anything. Nobody's asked, so--"

"Look," Canaday said, aware he'd stretched the lines of friendship far enough. "Don't cover for me."

"You okay?"

"Yeah, why?"

"This infatuation of yours is turning you into a nice guy. It's shocking."

"Saul, you're real funny."

* * *

"*Señorita?*"

Valerie's eyes snapped open. The rest of her body froze. Vincente was sitting on the lounge beside her. He wore green khakis, yellow tee shirt, a white jacket. Heavy rings covered two fingers on both hands. His hair was slicked back with gel, his eyes were concealed under sunglasses. He smiled, exposing his perfect white teeth.

"You are burning." He pointed to her neck and chest, coming within an inch of touching her. "If you do not go in soon, you will be in much pain."

Valerie sat up. "Thank you. I must have drifted off." She forced herself to smile. Politely.

He extended his hand. "I am called Vinny."

Valerie hesitated for one full second. Then something snapped her out of her shock, and she placed her hand in his. He pulled it to his lips and planted a feather light kiss. Valerie's breath caught in her throat. She wanted to smack him. Instead, she calmly said, "My name is Bridget."

"Bridget," he repeated, kissing her hand again. She saw her reflection in his glasses. "Bridget ...?"

"Spenser." Valerie pulled her hand away, scared to death.

But what could he do? They were in a public area surrounded by a hundred tourists. Calm down.

"Thank you for waking me up. I should probably get going. I doubt the hotel would like it if --" Valerie's heart fluttered. When would she learn to SHUT UP!

"If what, Senorita?"

"I checked out. It just occurred to me that I'm no longer a guest."

"You are leaving? But we've only just met."

Valerie tried to think quickly. She had the edge here if she used her brain. Vincente didn't know who she was. "I've rented a house down the road. It is beautiful here, but I prefer the quiet. It gives me the peace I need to write."

"You are a writer? Fascinating. What do you write? Novels?"

"I freelance for women's magazines. My dream is to write a novel. Someday ...." She forced her voice to remain light. "Maybe I'll write about this exotic place with its beautiful people."

"Ah, so you lay in the sun doing research?"

Valerie was surprised at how easily she laughed. "Sort of. Today I'm being lazy."

"But soon you will go to your little house where you will be alone to contemplate the prose needed to tell an extraordinary story. I envy you your passion."

"I don't know about passion, but I like what I do."

"Will you stop for food? Or do you plan to languish over a laptop all night and all day?"

"I'll eat ... eventually."

Valerie was surprised at his gentlemanly nature. This wasn't the Vincente she'd expected. Which set alarms off inside her head.

"I have a solution if I may be so assertive. Would you allow me to prepare you dinner tonight so you do not have to interrupt your creativity? Well, you would have to stop long enough to eat, of course."

Valerie smothered the urge to laugh. This was not the man she'd expected. Not at all.

Remember what Rosa said.

What if she wasn't talking about Vincente? Maybe she was talking about the Reynaldo Martinez character she been speaking with yesterday?

It doesn't matter. This man is a killer.

"I don't want to put you to any bother." She could learn a lot from Vincente about his brother. She was a born listener.

"What time should I pick you up?"

Oh my goodness, Valerie thought, removing her sunglasses. Had she accepted? If he picked her up, did that mean she would be going to _his_ place. Not good. Too many guards and too many guns.

"Would it be ... rude if we dined at my place? I have to go into town and fax my article. Around 8:15? I could pick you up on my way back. If it's not inconvenient."

He studied her, and the creases around his mouth deepened. His eyebrows furrowed. Because he was wearing sunglasses, she couldn't decipher the look. Doubt? Confusion? But at her place, at least she'd be ... what? Safer. Valerie thought of shaking her head and politely declining. But something told her it was too late for that. Better if he came to her. She'd have her car. The highway was close. If something went wrong, she could outrun him. She was a marathon runner for heaven's sake. Canaday said Vicente was a coke addict. How good of shape could he be in?

"Seems fair. You cook. I chauffeur. Unless ... that's rude. I'm not sure what's proper here."

Vincente looked at his manicured fingernails and took off his glasses. Without moving his head, his eyes rose and met hers. "I shall be ready at half past the hour. Will that give you enough time?"

His smile was alluring and deceiving. How many women had he harmed because they believed that smile? A smile that hid an ugly secret. This attractive, sexy, and powerful man hated women. Hated with such depth that he could torture them without hesitation and kill them without conscience.

Fully aware of that, Valerie was more disturbed by the fact she wasn't as frightened as she knew she should be. Was that because she really was the stupid woman Ed had accused her of being too many times? Every instinct she possessed warned her to stay alert.

"More than enough," she said and smiled. "Vinny, I don't make it a habit of inviting strangers to my home. But there's something gentle and kind about you. I'm guessing you have a very good and decent soul."

Vincente bowed his head.

Valerie swallowed the vomit in her throat.

* * *

She opened the back door and hid the key under the flowerpot. She set her packages on the floor and went through the yellowy white kitchen to the sitting room. She checked the front door and every window; the locks were in working order; the windows all had latches. She entered the kitchen. The oven worked. She walked out the front door. Fifty feet below the yard, the desert disappeared into the sea. Pounding waves drifted onto shore, striating the sand. Five seagulls flew in close formation three feet above the shoreline. The moon lay low in the east, while the sun began its western descent. Darkness would arrive shortly after she returned with Vincente. Acres of desert lay south side. Trees, bushes, and cacti bordered on the north. No sight of another house for miles. Complete solitude.

Valerie went back inside. She took her groceries and water, plus a bottle of Pina Colada to the kitchen. Grabbing her beige sweater off the backseat, she went to the front patio and sat down at the table. Her stomach felt queasy, and when she stood to put on her sweater, her knees wobbled. She sat back down and looked out over the Sea of Cortez. An empty, raw feeling developed around her heart.

CHAPTER 32

At 8:30, Valerie drove up to the entrance of the hotel. An attendant rushed toward her vehicle and as soon as she stopped, opened the passenger door. Valerie didn't have time to turn off the car. From nowhere Vincente appeared. He flipped the passenger seat forward and placed a picnic basket in the back.

He sat in the front. "You look lovely, Bridget."

Valerie drove away from the entrance. "Thank you. Dinner smells wonderful." She glanced back at the basket.

"I hope you will find it equally delicious. They are my favourite dishes. Food my mother loved to prepare."

"If they taste anything like they smell, I'm sure I will." She pulled onto the highway and headed west. "My place is just a few miles up the road."

Vincente seemed content to gaze out of the window, though occasionally Valerie could feel his eyes on her.

They sped down the highway; Valerie followed suit when Vincente opened his window. The air whipped at her snug black wig and bit at her cheeks. Her hot skin cooled. A mile straight ahead, beyond the stretch of desert to her left, she saw the lights from the adobe house. It was like a lighthouse in a storm, sending a calm to envelop her. The moon lay low behind them; the road curved, straightened, curved again. As she pulled into the long driveway, she looked upon the house and suspected she'd remember it always.

Valerie parked the car and turned off the engine. Without looking at him, she reached for the door handle.

"It suits you," Vincente said, as they both climbed out.

She walked beside him toward the back door. They entered. She slipped off her sandals then walked through to the kitchen, listening to the sounds of Vincente's footsteps behind her. Her earlier bout of nervousness returned. A repeated thought kept her pulse racing. One wrong move and she was dead.

"Would you like a drink?" she asked.

"No, thank you." His eyes settled briefly on her cleavage then to the basket of food.

"I took the liberty of asking the bartender what you liked, and he said Pina Colada and rum."

"You did that for me? That was sweet." He gave her a haughty smile. "Pina Colada and I have a special relationship."

"Then you will have a drink?"

Vincente laughed. "Maybe later. I'm not thirsty now. Perhaps after dinner. Which reminds me, may I use your oven to warm our meal?"

"Of course."

He set the basket on the table, and Valerie turned on the oven. Her hands shook. She set the temperature at 350 degrees. Had she made a mistake offering him a drink? Behind her, tin foil crackled. She turned to face him. He balanced an aluminium covered plate in each hand while his eyes traced the outline of her body. Every muscle in her body tensed. Canaday had said that it was _Miguel_ who preferred gentle women — not Vincent. He liked his women aggressive. Maybe that meant she was safe.

Vincent had raped Rosa. Valerie knew she had to speak. "It was kind of you to do this, Vinny. Do you cook often?" She moved aside and glanced down at the oven. "It may take a few minutes to heat up."

He smiled, the plates balanced atop his fingertips.

The air around Valerie thinned. Her throat constricted. "I suppose a few minutes won't make a difference." She opened the oven.

While dinner warmed, Valerie grabbed a diet coke from the fridge and asked him if he would like to sit out front. Vincente nodded then followed her. She turned on the garden lamps and waited for him to sit down before taking the chair opposite him. He continued to make light conversation. She scarcely heard, though she nodded and smiled whenever appropriate. Instead, Valerie wondered how this gorgeous man with his perfect white teeth, had become a monster.

"Bridget?"

"Yes."

"Our dinner should be warm enough."

"Oh, right." She stood.

He rose to his feet. "Why don't I get our food while you set the table?"

"Is it all right if we eat here?"

"That would be nice."

Valerie moved into the house.

She set the table and cursed herself. She hadn't thought of wine. A toast at dinner would have been perfect. Vincente set the plates on the table and waited for her to sit first. Too late now.

* * *

Canaday parked in front of the hotel next on his list and finished his burrito. He checked his watch, 20:05, and entered the hotel. Ten minutes later, he walked back to his rental and stood next to the driver's door. The desert across the street, thanks to modern technology, was turning into green lawn and a gardener's paradise. A large billboard at the edge of the highway showed a future gulf course surrounded by pink condominiums. Canaday shook his head and climbed into his rental.

Dressed like any other tourist, bright printed shirt, casual pants, sunglasses, he walked into the next hotel and went to the desk. Three young people looked up and smiled.

"*Buenas noches, señor*," the young clerk said.

"Good evening. I was wondering if you could help me." Canaday smiled warmly. "I'm looking for a friend. Katrina Sands."

All three of the employees smiled. "Sorry, but there is no one by that name registered at our hotel."

Canaday remained focused despite the urgency to curse. But then realizing what she had probably done, he unclenched his jaw and forced himself to smile. "I had the privilege of sitting beside a very attractive woman on the flight in yesterday. She was dressed in a blue, sleeveless dress. Black, shoulder length hair. Very beautiful. I should have asked her name, but I couldn't imagine a nice girl like her interested in an old warhorse like me."

The young man standing in the middle smiled, then immediately looked sad. "You must mean Miss Bridget Spenser. Sorry, but she checked out this morning."

"Too bad," Canaday said, meaning it. "She was the kind of girl that made time stand still, if you know what I mean?" Feeling suddenly old, he turned toward the doors.

"Excuse me, sir."

He turned back. The girl standing behind the counter stepped to the far end. Her two coworkers were busy conversing with new guests.

"I saw Miss Spenser leave with Rosa Ramirez. Perhaps Rosa will know where she is?"

"Do you think so? That would be great. Really, really great." Coincidence, Canaday wondered? Ramirez was a common name.

"One moment, please. I will telephone her."

"Thanks. I really appreciate this." He tapped his fingers on the counter and glanced around the lobby. The girl dialled a number, spoke Spanish then handed the phone to him. He stepped away from the girl and spoke quietly. "Miss Ramirez?"

"Yes."

"My name is Mike Canaday. I'm a friend of Bridget Spenser's. Do you know where she is ...?" No answer. "Maybe she told you about me? Canaday? Mike Canaday?" Silence. Canaday lowered his voice, "It's very important I see her. Urgent, in fact."

"Why? Rosa said you didn't know Bridget; you sat beside her on the plane."

"It's complicated. I couldn't tell Rosa everything. I have to find Bridget."

"Are you grumpy?"

"Beg your pardon?"

"She said the man in her life was grumpy."

Grumpy? Was that how Valerie saw him? "Can we meet somewhere? I have to find her."

"I'm sorry, I can't help you."

"Miss Ramirez, Bridget is very important to me. If you know where she is, you have to tell me. Her life is in danger."

More silence.

"Please ...."

After a few rapid heartbeats, she finally spoke. "Do you know where the ice-cream parlour is?"

"No."

Rosa gave him directions then asked to speak to the girl behind the desk. Canaday handed back the phone. The girl listened for a few seconds then replied in Spanish that yes, Canaday looked grumpy, but harmless. He had to bite his lip to stop from smiling. He mouthed a *Gracias* and though she at first declined to take a tip, he insisted then walked outside to his car. A few moments later, he pulled up to the curb in front of the ice-cream parlour. A young girl sat at the picnic table. Canaday got out of his car and approached. A man of about fifty stood next to the building. Insurance? "Miss Ramirez?"

"Order something."

He walked to the opened window and ordered an ice-cream cone. He walked back to the table and handed it to the girl; she shook her head.

"Why must you see Bridget?" Rosa asked.

Unsure how much the girl knew, Canaday remained cautious. He glanced back at the man who scrutinized him; he was probably a relative of Rosa's. "Bridget came to Baja without letting me know. The last time we spoke, she was upset. She wouldn't tell me why. I'm worried. She means a lot to me, and I don't want anything to happen to her."

"You are her lover?"

"No."

"She is not able to take care of herself?"

"I hope she can. Look, I don't have time for this. Please tell me where she is."

Rosa searched his face. "How do I know you are her friend?"

"You don't. You'll have to trust me."

"How many sons does she have?"

"None."

"Where are her parents?"

Here goes nothing, Canaday thought. "They're dead."

She studied his face. "I'm sorry, I can't help you. I promised I wouldn't."

"So she did tell you about me?"

"She said she needed time to think away from you."

"We're not lovers, Rosa. She's ...." How could he explain to this young girl something he couldn't explain to himself? "Bridget is an investigative reporter. She's investigating the disappearance of ..." he was taking a chance saying this and hoped to hell he was right. "Lope Ramirez."

Rosa's eyes watered instantly.

He was right.

"She came here to find the man who killed ... your father."

"She said she was a writer. I don't understand. Why didn't she tell me?"

"She wouldn't risk your life."

"What happened to my father?"

"She's investigating his death, Rosa. If she didn't tell you that's because she probably doesn't know enough. You obviously talked to her. You must have realized she's not the type to speak without thought. Now, please help me. I have to find her. I have to make sure she's okay."

"Did Señor Vicente DeOlmos have anything to do with my father's death?" Tears rolled down her face.

"Why do you suspect him?"

Joylene Nowell Butler

Rosa gulped for air. "I told my father he raped me, and I never saw my father again."
The man watching over Rosa approached. Canaday detected the bulge in his jacket. The man asked Rosa in Spanish if she was okay.
"*Si, Tío.*" She wiped her eyes and looked at Canaday. "If you are lying to me, I will tell my uncle, and he will shoot you."
Canaday looked over at the three locals ordering ice cream.
"No one will help you," Rosa said.
"Does your uncle work for DeOlmos?"
"He does what he must to survive."
Canaday swore under his breath, pulled out his ID wallet, placed it on the table, and slid it toward her.

* * *

The meal was hot and spicy, and Valerie savoured every mouthful. "The food is wonderful. What is this called again?" She pointed her fork at the chicken.
"*Mole poblano*. This," he scooped up a forkful of chili peppers, "is *chiles en nogada*. And this ...." He chewed what was in his mouth then stuck his fork into the tortilla. "This is *huevos rancheros*. It's not usually served with this particular meal, but I hoped you would enjoy it."
"It's delicious. When did you learn to cook?" Did he even know where the kitchen was?
"My mother taught me when I was a boy. I suppose it began solely as entertainment. Gradually, it became a ritual, assisting my mother in the evening meal, hearing her laughter as I dug my hands into whatever task she gave. Usually ending up with more food on me than in the bowl."
"She sounds wonderful."
"Would you like to see her photograph?"
"Yes, please."
Vincente pulled an expensive Italian leather wallet from inside his jacket and slipped out a small photograph.
A constellation of stars glittered in his mother's black eyes. Her satiny, olive skin glowed with life. Valerie touched the photograph expecting to feel her warmth. This woman, with her black hair swept up into a loose bun, was a study in grace and gentility. "She's lovely. No, she's exquisite." Valerie meant it. "She looks kind and gentle."
Vincente smiled. "Yes. She was a beautiful woman. Very patient. I miss her very much. She died when I was ten."

"That's sad."
"God's angels needed her more than I."
"That's a nice way of looking at it."
"Bridget?"
"Yes."
"May I have that drink now?"
"Of course."

Valerie went to the kitchen, grabbed the jug from the refrigerator, and set it on the counter. Reaching for a glass, she could feel the calmness absorbed by every muscle in her body. Regardless of what type of woman Vincent preferred, she'd found the key to her success. Being herself and pretending Vincente was a man worthy of her respect. Simple. Now all she had to do was ask a few innocent questions.

Valerie stuffed the keys to her rental in her sweater pocket, as a precaution, and went outside. She set the glass down in front of him, then took her seat and finished the last few mouthfuls of food. The air had begun to cool, and it was soothing. Even Vincente's sudden quietness was okay. A good sign that the evening was progressing as planned. The time had come to break the ice. He was full, relaxed, and ready to talk about family. She would pose innocent questions. Not too many but enough to show her interest. Then she would suggest they go on a picnic tomorrow afternoon. Instead, first thing in the morning, she would board a flight back to the States, and never see Vincente again. Except in court.

Vincente rose. "May I use your washroom?"
"Of course. *Mi casa es su casa.*"

She watched him cross the flagstone patio and enter the house. While he was gone, she rehearsed some of her questions to make sure they sounded casual.

'Do you have a large family?'

That was an innocent enough, considering he was left without a mother at the age of ten.

Or maybe, 'It must have been lonely without your mother. Do you come from a large family?'

Yes, that sounded more natural. Then he might or might not mention his brother. Probably he would. If not, perhaps after she suggested they do something together tomorrow. A picnic ... yes, Valerie decided. As soon as he returned, she would mention a picnic. Her treat ....

Enfolded by a wave of dizziness, Valerie raised a hand to her head. She squeezed her eyes shut briefly. Everything spun, the house, the table, her glass.

Certain all she needed was a cold glass of water, She pushed away from the table, stood up, and made it to the backdoor, into the living room, into the kitchen. She groped for the dishcloth and soaked it under the cold water.

"What is wrong, Bridget?"

Valerie pressed the cloth to her cheek. "I ...."

"Are you ill?" Vincente took her by the arm and led her outside.

"Fresh air, good idea. All of a sudden I feel very dizzy."

He helped her into the chair, took his own, and gave her a ghastly grimace. "Are you sure you're okay?"

Sweat seeped down her neck. Heat targeted her face. "I think so." More dizziness assaulted her. "I'm not sure." It felt as if the vertebras in her back were knotting. Valerie stretched her shoulder blades.

Vincente rose. "We'll go for a walk."

"All right. But I don't have my shoes. Still, a walk would be nice. I love walking in the moonlight. Where I come from either it's too cold or the mosquitoes drive you mad." She clamped her mouth shut, shocked by her sudden burst of chattiness.

They walked down the path to the small bay. Her footsteps, uneven, wandered to the left then the right. Valerie let Vincente grasp her elbow. She focused her attention on the moon. A perfect moon that streaked across the bay, laying out a perfect invitation: A swim. A cool breeze swept through the bangs of her wig. Her wig. She raised a hand to touch it. She wanted desperately to take it off. No, not a good idea. She laughed. "Look at that spectacular view. Moonlight glistening off the water from high above, shining like a street lamp, lighting the entire playground." She giggled. "No, I will not dive through the waves. Oh, Pyracanthas." She looked at the abundance growing among the shrug grasses and cacti. "And there's some Hollyhocks and Love-lies-bleeding. Oh, and see how the soft moonlight makes the violet blues, reds, yellows and pinks take on the texture of velvet and silk. So lovely. My goodness it's beautiful here. No fancy hotels, no elegant homes. No one for miles."

"That's right." Vincente held her by the waist while she leaned forward to smell the flowers. He pulled her upright.

Valerie squished the sand between her toes and looked out at the bay. "This looks like those magazine pictures I've been drooling over for years." She flapped her arm against her side. "This is virgin land, untouched by man's feeble attempts at prosperity. Crystal blue water, unpolluted by man's greed. Air, fresher and cleaner than anything in the north." Her head spun.

Vincente laughed.

"What?" She grinned at him.

"You sound like a writer."

She laughed.

Vincente cupped her face. "I'm glad you're happy. But I'm afraid you may be angry with me when I tell you what I've done."

Strange, she thought. His accent was gone. "What?"

He kissed her hard.

She wanted to push him away. She couldn't raise her arms. They were heavy.

Vincente bit her lip. Valerie grimaced with the pain. He withdrew his teeth then sucked the blood and licked the corner of her mouth.

"Don't," she mumbled.

"Do you feel strange?"

"Yes."

His hands traveled down the front of her blouse.

Valerie could barely stand. Her legs rubberized beneath her. But she didn't fall. His arm held her, while blazing images, unshakable images, swirled inside her head. Images of Rosa crying. Images of Vincente carving small cuts into Rosa's flesh. Rosa screaming!

"Oh God," Valerie whispered.

"Did you enjoy the meal? I added something special. Go with it and enjoy. Let it take you on a journey."

"What?" Something was wrong. Valerie sensed it at the center of her being. Something was deadly wrong. She focused on her arms. Willed them to rise, to push him away. His mouth was on her neck, sucking, biting. His tongue moved upward. "What have I done? What did you put in my dinner? Why are you doing this?"

"I must, Katrina. Or should I say Mrs. Val McCormick."

"McCormick ...?" She wanted to tell him her name was Bridget Spenser, but she couldn't. "How did you --"

He silenced her with his mouth.

With every inch of strength she could draw from, Valerie pushed against his chest. There was something hard at his side. A gun?

He grabbed her wrists.

"What did you put in my food?" she mumbled.

"I don't want to hurt you, my sweet Mrs. McCormick. Please

understand I must surprise my brother. Even though I don't want to do this."

"Then don't."

He pulled her top from the confines of her waist.

She grabbed the lapels of his jacket. Her legs wobbled. "I have to go back. I must return to the rental. My key --"

"Not yet," he whispered and pulled her top down over one shoulder. "I must ask you some questions." He kissed her earlobe. "I hate to waste valuable time but answer my questions quickly, then we shall make love."

"I don't understand. I was very nice to you, and now you're being so mean."

He touched a finger to her lips. "Listen carefully, Val. Your answers are very important. Do the Americans know you're here?"

"No." She struggled to twist away.

He grabbed her shoulders firmly, looked into her face, his breath smelling of cayenne. "Does your family know you're alive?"

"No, they --"

"Good. My brother will be pleased. And because you were so sweet, I'm glad I didn't tell Miguel you were here. And I won't tell him about Rosa helping you. Yes." He moved in too close. "I have loyal *empleados* everywhere. Miguel called me, of course. Right after his mother-in-law rented you this house. You were watched from the moment you left your room this morning. Of course, at the time I had no idea who you were." Vincente laughed. "My suspicions arose simply because Rosa stayed with you last night. I'm sure she told you of our special relationship. I think she's angry at me for losing interest in her." He laughed again. "My brother called me last night. He told me of your new name. I cannot tell you how surprised I was when you rented that vehicle under Katrina Sands, especially after introducing yourself this afternoon as ... Bridget Spenser. You can also imagine my embarrassment. Ah, but you're a blessing in disguise. You've made my life much easier." He grabbed her head and tugged. The black wig lifted off, floating to the ground.

Her scalp hurt. Her vision blurred. "I want to go home." Gathering her strength, silently praying, she forced her eyes wider. "I'll take my girls and disappear. No one will see me again. Tell your brother I will not --"

"Too late." He freed her hair from the bun and pushed her backward.

Valerie flapped her arms to balance herself from falling. Waves pounded against the shore, intermixed with the sounds coming from her mouth. "No wait. You mustn't do this." She stepped backward and steadied herself. The space between them had grown to eight feet. "Let's talk. If there's a problem, I'm sure we can work it out. I don't want to hurt you."

"Hurt me?" He laughed and approached. "As soon as you are found, my brother wants you in Colombia as quickly as possible. So it's very important that I have you first."

Valerie waited until he took one more step toward her. Despite not wearing shoes, she kicked him in the groin as hard as she could. Then dodged his collapsing body, grasped her hands together in a fist, and clobbered him across the neck as he went down.

She ran toward the path leading to higher ground. It narrowed then widened and ended back at the beach. She didn't look for Vincente. But she could hear him. Stumbling, moaning, yelling, screaming at her. Then silence. Valerie tried to run harder. She spun around, confused as to which direction she should go. Streaks of light swirled in front of her. It's the drugs. She ran harder. Fighting it, fighting the urge to lie down, to give up, her legs staggered. No! She had to fight, had to get away. He couldn't--he wouldn't catch her.

Valerie saw a clearing up ahead. Then a small granite mound. A hill. Her lungs burned. Her legs ached, but she could make it. Just a little farther. Up the slope four hundred feet--house lights. Yes!

Valerie gasped for air. Her legs flew out from under her.

CHAPTER 33

Valerie fell to the ground, knowing in that instant that Vincente had tripped her from behind. Her contacts popped out. Her face crushed into the sand. Her skin burned. His hands grabbed her ankle.

Valerie kicked. Her fingers thrashed through the sand ahead of her.

He gripped both ankles tightly and flipped her over onto her back. "Silly girl." He sucked for air. "You got turned around. I would have never caught you otherwise." He laughed. It was an ugly sound. "This is going to be better than I hoped. By all means, struggle. *¡Si, lucha!*"

He stretched her arms above her head and lay on top of her. His weight crushed her. His hot breath disgusted her. She inhaled quick breaths and tried to think.

But Vincente straddled her, pinning her hands under his knees. He pulled the gun from his holster and laid it on the ground next to her head. "Guess what, Val." He hovered over her. "My brother has given explicit orders that he be the one to kill you. But, do you know something? I don't care. I'm gonna fuck. I'm gonna cut you. Then I'm gonna blow a big hole in your little brain."

"Vincente, listen. My children need me. I want to go home. Protect them. I won't testify. Please. Get off me!"

"You shouldn't have kicked me." He ripped her bodice. "That wasn't very nice." He leaned over her.

"I know. You're right. I shouldn't... No--don't! Vincente, listen. I know Miguel is disrespectful. To you. He embarrasses you in front of others. Come back to the States with me. You could.... Get off me!"

He sat up again and tugged at her skirt, bringing it high above her waist. "Tell me." He contemplated her body. "Are you excited?"

"No!"

He laughed. "What do you feel at this precise moment? Please, you must tell me. I need to know."

"Get off me!"

"Ah, c'mon."

"You make me want to puke!"

Vincente laughed loud. "Val, you're so funny. I'm really going to enjoy this." He leaned back and laughed.

Valerie felt his body relax. She reacted quickly. With all her strength, she rolled as she flung her hips into the air, sending Vincente sprawling into the sand next to her. Her hand flew out for the gun. It wasn't there. She kicked Vincente in the head with her bare heel. Pain shot up her leg. Her foot throbbed. He groaned and hunched forward.

She scrambled backward, tried to stand. Her head spun. Her eyes adjusted, while her brain registered a sudden stillness. Except for the pounding of waves, the silence was unnerving. She twisted around, ready to strike him again. But when she looked up, she didn't see a wounded Vincente. She stared down the barrel of his gun.

It took a second to see past that to the sneer and to the deadly, ugly, evil.

Although the gun made her aware of her imminent death, Valerie knew an anger, not spawning from hatred alone, but from a hatred and fury that reached down inside the deepest part of her. It boiled from her lips. "Kill me. I don't care. Go ahead--you pig!"

Except for his lips moving into a smile, Vincente stood still. A sickening, ugly smile.

Valerie, preparing to die, slowed her breathing.

Vincente lunged toward her.

Valerie gasped.

He punched her in the face.

She hit the ground.

He flew on top of her. His fist rammed into her sides.

She sucked for air, the pain paralyzing. She tried to flip him off, tried to punch him back, but his fists wouldn't stop. A blow to her head sent her mind whirling.

He ripped her underwear off with one quick yank. He stood, towering over her. He held the gun at his side and unsnapped his trousers.

Valerie blinked aside the blackness. She heard a sound. Saw Vincente's chest exploded in red. She tasted the salt of his blood. He fell on top of her. Knocked the wind out of her lungs. Warm liquid oozed from his body and flowed down her sides. Her mouth opened. A wretched sound sprang from her throat. She was still screaming when Vincente's body flew off her.

Canaday swept her up, and she clung to him; her cries muffled by his chest. He lifted her into his arms. She dug her fingers into his back, determined to never let go. Never!

He carried her back up the steep hill. He lowered her feet to the ground, held her tight then opened the passenger door, and set her in the seat. She grabbed for his arms to keep him from releasing her. He bent over, folded what was left of her top across her chest, and wiped something off her cheeks.

"Valerie, it's over. He won't hurt you. I have to go back to the beach, but I want you to stay here. Lock the door and wait for me. Can you do that?"

"Canaday?"

"Yes, Valerie."

"He's Vincente."

"He was."

For a brief second Canaday's remark stirred a reaction Valerie was incapable of understanding. Her eyes saw nothing, but her mind registered: Vincente, dead. Then she understood. Understood that it horrified her to acknowledge she wanted to be the one. Repeated gentle squeezes on a cold steel trigger.

"I'll be right back. Wait for me here." Canaday punched the trunk lid button.

Valerie leaned her head back against the seat. It seemed only seconds before Canaday appeared on the top of the hill, something over his shoulder wrapped in black plastic. Vincente?

He carried the body to the trunk. The car rocked. Canaday passed by her window and went into the house. Valerie closed her eyes.

She heard something and opened them again.

Canaday came out of the house. He went to the back of his car hauling a large garbage bag in each hand. The car rocked again. He walked to her rental, leaned into the passenger side. The trunk's lid rose. He lifted out her suitcase and returned to his rental. He opened her door. "I got all the dishes, the food, the bottle. I'm going back for your purse and shoes. Is there anything else in the house? Where are the keys to your rental?"

She tried to think. "They're ...."

"Where, Valerie? We have to hurry."

"My pocket." Her head hurt. There was something else she had to tell him.

He patted her sides. "There're no pockets."

"My sweater ... on the beach." But that wasn't it, either.

She watched Canaday disappear over the hill then closed her eyes. Her body floated, lower, lower, descending into ....

Valerie snapped her eyes open. The interior lights of her rental, parked a few feet away, were on. Canaday sat in the driver's seat. He was wiping the dash, the steering wheel. She closed her eyes.

The interior lights inside Canaday's car blinded her. The car rocked.

"Are you okay?"

"I'm gonna be sick."

* * *

"Canaday!"

"I'm right here. Wake up." He leaned over her. "I got us a room. Can you walk?"

She tried to answer, but the stench of blood muddled her thoughts. He slipped her shoes on her feet. She wanted to say something, but his rubbing her hair, as if something was stuck to it, distracted her.

He gripped both her hands and gently pulled her from the seat. Leaning her against the outside of the car, he asked her not to move then he went to the trunk and returned with her suitcase. He put an arm around her waist and led her to the side door of a motel. The soft glow from the desk lamp streaking across Canaday's face comforted her. Still, there was something she wanted to tell him. Maybe if she tried very hard, the answer would come.

Canaday's smile reassured her. He guided her forward. Her feet touched the carpet. What a nice smile.

She tried to smile back, but her whole body was limp, unresponsive, as if only her brain was still alive. Her torn camisole and skirt were stripped off. She felt the touch of his hand on hers. She walked with him, still unable to feel her legs, winced as the first shock of water hit her face.

He held her away from the shower wall, washed, and scrubbed her hair.

Valerie felt like a rag doll, but the thick towel rubbing against her skin, warmed her. She leaned on him as he took the same towel and rubbed her hair. The shivers traveling down her back were pleasant. It felt nice to be clean, but ... how did she get dirty?

He wrapped her in a clean towel, and placed her clothes and his own in a plastic bag, then hid it in the bottom of his overnight valise. It seemed a strange thing to do. He put on a new pair of pants and smiled again, encouraging her with a kind voice to sit on the bed. Willing and curious, she flopped down.

He stuck a lacy pair of underwear over one foot then the other, sliding them up her legs, laying her back on the bed, lifting her buttocks, and uncovering the towel, pulling the panties higher. Her skin tingled. Her fingers, no longer lifeless, touched his face. He winced.

"Your skin is rough, but I like it, Canaday."

She touched his mouth, and he pulled away, lifting her by the hands until she sat upright. Helping her to raise her arms, tossing the towel aside, he pulled a light cotton tee shirt over her head. It grazed across her face, her nipples. Before she knew it, her fingers, as if under their own control, reached out to touch his lips. She needed to feel their soft texture again.

"Valerie, don't."

"I want to feel your mouth."

His face looked sad. "You have to get dressed, Valerie. We have to go."

"I want to kiss your mouth."

"Look ... it's the drug talking, it's not you. We have to go. I'll help you with your jeans. Point your toes." He crouched at her knees, one hand behind her calf, lifting her foot, the other holding her jeans.

Her body felt hot and fearless and strong enough to do whatever she bade. She had the power, and it was centered in her hands, hands that were now touching both sides of his face. And her body, hot and out of control, ached for him. She leaned forward and licked his mouth. She was right, it was soft, sweet tasting. Nice. She slid her tongue over his upper lip then closed her mouth over it, sucking. Her hand moved behind his neck, forcing his mouth harder. She felt his moan, and her power surged, the pulsing heat escalating between her legs.

He gripped her under the arms and lifted her higher up on the bed. He lay on top of her. His hands moved down her body, caressing the contours of her breasts, his mouth devoured hers. Valerie's body tingled between a pleasurable prickling and waves of burning fire, aching and throbbing for him. She wrapped her arms around his back. Her tongue sought out his, her legs spread, and her hips rose--

Canaday sprang off the bed. "Get dressed. We have to get out of here."

CHAPTER 34

Canaday headed north, glancing often in his rear-view mirror. He shifted his body forward, away from Vincente's gun snug in the small of his back. Baja was as far away from his jurisdiction as he could get, but if necessary, he'd kill again. He'd do whatever needed to protect her. He glanced over his shoulder into the backseat. She was curled up underneath his jacket, sleeping soundly. Her shallow breathing soothed the silence. How close Vincente had come to killing her still left its mark. The sensations in his heart, his body, his mind, confused him. Terrified him. The memory of her mouth, her body under his, lingered.

Canaday rubbed at his eyes and glanced at the rear-view mirror. He felt as if he was split in half. One part of him wanted to stand his ground and kill every bastard that came near her. Another part of him wanted to take her as far away from all of this as possible. His head ached. He had to admit one more entry into this split personality. The part that wished he'd never met her.

"Canaday!"

He slowed the car, pulled to the side of the road, and stopped. He jumped out and opened the back door. He wrapped her up in his arms. "Wake up, Valerie. It's a dream."

She pushed against him. "I have to go home! I have to get my girls!"

His held her tight. "It's okay. You're safe."

"No. You don't understand." She pushed him away. "DeOlmos knows I'm alive. Vincente called me Valerie McCormick. He said Miguel called him last night. He told him I was Katrina Sands now. If Miguel shows up, he'll know I was here."

Canaday flopped back against the seat. "Okay. Let me think …. He doesn't know Vincente's dead. We still have time." He pulled the cell phone out of his pocket and pressed the redial button. "It's Candyman."

"Where are you?" Vamozzi asked.

"Heading toward Site 42."

"She's with you?"

"Yeah, and so is our friend."

"Miguel?"

"No, Vincente."

"Alive?"

"No. Listen. DeOlmos knows who Katrina Sands is. Contact the Mounties. I want every available man at the McCormick house--Now."

"How did Miguel find out?"

"I don't know," Canaday said. "Our ETA is twenty minutes. Send the jet and a cleanup crew. Send Bailey, Kalamai, Griffith, and Hill on the next redeye to LA."

"Orders?"

"I'll pass out instructions when we arrive."

"You okay?"

"Fine." Canaday clicked off the phone.

Valerie didn't move. In the darkness, he could see the outline of her head and shoulders. "Do you want to sit up front?"

"No."

"Are you okay?"

"My face hurts. He punched me."

Canaday wanted to kill the sonofabitch all over again. "In a few days the bruises will disappear. There's another one on your side, but your ribs weren't broken." He returned to the front seat, shifted out of park, pulled onto the road, and stomped on the accelerator.

It was hot in the car; at least Canaday felt as if he was suffocating. He glanced at her in the mirror. He decided to keep silent and opened the window instead of asking if it was okay first. A thousand thoughts and fears swam through his mind. The only ones who knew Valerie was Katrina Sands were Rostov, Tomlin, Vamozzi, himself, and the Director. He couldn't believe it was one of them. Not those men. Somebody with witness relocation?

He reached the deserted tarmac ten minutes early. He parked the car on the edge of the road adjacent to the landing strip. After opening the window further and turning off the engine, he lit a cigarette.

"Where are we?" she asked.

"Nowhere in particular. Our plane will be here soon."

"The world won't stop spinning."

"It'll wear off by tomorrow."

She shifted forward, her hand resting on the back of the seat beside him. "One minute I was talking non-stop, the next I couldn't raise my arms. Then I felt as if I could fly. My right foot hurts. What did he give me?"

"Without a blood test, it's hard to tell. Sodium amatol. Laced with mescaline, maybe. I don't know."

"Did you and I ...?"

Canaday swallowed hard, his eyes glued to the mirror. "What?" he asked, nonchalantly.

"I remember ... at least I think I remember ...."

"What, Mrs. McCormick?"

She sat back. "Nothing."

"Did you find out anything about Miguel DeOlmos?"

"He's in Cartagena. He called Vincente last night and told him my new name. How'd he know that?"

Canaday clenched his fist resting over the steering wheel and glancing up into a deep blue-black sky, saw the flashing lights of the jet overhead. He opened his door. "Our ride's here. I'll be back for you in a minute."

He waited for the plane to land then met Vamozzi at the bottom of the stairs. "I've changed my mind. Take Valerie back to the States while I--"

"Written orders." Vamozzi handed him an envelope.

Canaday tore it open, read the note from Tomlin, and swore under his breath. He was being ordered to return stateside. A code name for the safe house in Berkeley was inserted in the note. "What about DeOlmos?"

"My friend, you are in so much trouble, he's the least of your worries. Give me the coordinates. There's a team moving in."

Canaday reread the note then crumpled it in his fist. "I'm supposed to just leave it at that?"

"I guess Tomlin knows you better than you think. This isn't the time to bend the rules, Candyman. This isn't our land. We're going to get him, but we're going to do it on our own turf."

Canaday looked back at Valerie in the backseat of his car. "Vincente's body is in the trunk." He handed over his rental keys then pulled a folded piece of paper out of his pocket. "Here are the coordinates for the house. DeOlmos may not be far behind. How many are coming in?"

"Two have already arrived." Vamozzi reached into his inside pocket and pulled out his cellular phone.

"They understand there's to be no trace?"

Vamozzi nodded.

"There's one more thing."

Vamozzi gave him his full attention.

"I want Vincente's death kept a secret. And from now on, only you and I and Tomlin will know where Valerie is."

"Agreed."

"Anything come of Roth's phone taps?"

"Nothing so far. Did you tell Val?"

"No. And no one else is going to either."

Vamozzi looked despondent. "You know something? You should think about seeing a doctor. You keep forgetting who your friends are." He turned, climbed one step then stopped. "One more thing. Tomlin wants a report faxed to him by morning."

Canaday dismissed his shame, searched his pocket for a candy that didn't exist, and watched until Vamozzi ascended the plane and disappeared inside. He went back to his rental.

Once inside the plane, Valerie walked on her own to the back of the cabin, dropping into the first seat facing the front on the starboard side. Canaday sat on the bench seat against the port side in the middle, opposite Vamozzi. Valerie curled up into a foetal position and fell asleep; her chest rose and fell with each shallow breath. He watched her while his heart ached. Studying her every feature, memorizing every line, every curve, he knew he could close his eyes and see her. He rubbed his fingertips together and remembered the feel of her skin. The smoothness. The soft texture of her neck, her shoulder. He clenched his jaw. He had committed a grievous sin. He had done the unthinkable, falling for a protected target. His instincts were being corroded by his need for her; he had to find a way to smother the feelings.

His whole life had been spent living with violence. First on the streets of Chicago then in Vietnam. It was crazy to believe he could change now; he was a fool to even think it. No more. He tore his eyes away from Ed McCormick's wife. Smother it; kill it, he warned himself. Then he damned Tomlin.

Had the choice been his, Canaday would have stayed behind. Vincente's sudden disappearance created an opportunity too important to ignore. DeOlmos would look for his brother. For all Canaday knew, he was in San José del Cabo now, frantically searching for Vincente. A brother he'd never find.

Canaday closed his eyes and visualized Vincente's dead body folded in the trunk of his rental. He almost wished DeOlmos could see him like that. He envisioned the pain in DeOlmos's face. The agony of losing someone he loved.

Retribution.

Canaday shook. The hatred eating at him was emotionally and physically crippling. Also dangerous. He wondered if he was still suited for this job. For the first time in over thirty years, his emotions were surfacing. Love and hate were separated by a thin line.

He pulled out his cigarettes, caught the look on Vamozzi's face, and put them back in his pocket.

"Bailey and Kalamai will be waiting for us when we reach the airport. Hill and Griffith are one hour behind them," Vamozzi said.

Canaday nodded. "Have Hill and Griffith diverted to Valerie's place in Santa Cruz. Bailey and Kalamai can join them later. Has Tomlin given them access to additional men?"

"Yes, but they've got to make it look convincing. Any more than four inside the safe house may look suspicious."

"They'll need them on the outside." Canaday glanced at Valerie. "Kalamai will need a blonde wig."

"In the meantime, we have to get Val new papers. It won't take DeOlmos long to dope it out that we know he knows."

"We'll go on to Berkeley and see what happens."

Vamozzi got up from his seat. "I'll make arrangement for two cars fully loaded to meet us when the chopper lands. And I'll position the SWAT team at the top of the hill from the Santa Cruz safe house."

"Contact the Justice Department in Canada. They had better be prepared for anything."

"Tomlin says it's already done." Vamozzi walked toward the communication center.

Rubbing the whiskers on his rough face, Canaday glanced once more at Valerie before resting his head back against the seat and closing his eyes. He didn't bother opening them when Vamozzi took his seat. There was nothing more to say.

When the jet landed, Canaday lit a smoke as soon as his feet touched the ground. While Vamozzi helped Valerie into the helicopter, he grabbed the M-16 from the rack behind the pilot, and walked toward Bailey and Kalamai. They stood waiting near their car a short distance away.

"Keep alert. Don't underestimate this man. He knows she's alive." Canaday handed Bailey the rifle. "Don't think of taking him down alone. The SWAT team will be in a paneled truck at the top of the street from the safe house. Don't make any contact with them unless it's a go. We'll assume DeOlmos is capable of intercepting our transmissions. Besides, surveillance will have their Wolf's ear pointed at you. Don't contact me on my cell phone. If you need me, call Tomlin. He's the only one who knows the number." He threw his cigarette to the ground and crushed it under his shoe. He looked at his agents, compelled to say something else but uncertain what that was. "Go now and remember what I said. Keep alert."

* * *

Miguel DeOlmos shouted so loud it felt as if his neck vertebrae had snapped. He grabbed the man's shirt collar, pivoted on his right heel, and flung him across the top of Vincente's desk. The man pleaded, cried. No, he did not know where *Señor* Vincente was. He had left several hours ago with a woman. No, she was not blonde. DeOlmos threw the man to the floor and yelled for Sanchez. The man crawled to the door and escaped down the long staircase. Miguel, furious and frightened, nodded to Sanchez to leave. If anyone could locate Vincente, it would be Sanchez.

Sanchez left with three men while Miguel buzzed for the hotel manager.

The manager appeared a few minutes later, leaned over Vincente's desk as instructed, squinted at the name Bridget Spenser on the register, and shook his head. "I am sorry, *Señor* Miguel, but I do not know this woman."

Miguel pulled a handgun from inside his jacket and with his arm stretched straight out in front of him, pointed it at the man.

"But *Señor* Vincente was seen talking to a woman in the lobby yesterday. She was a beautiful brunette. Perhaps you should check with the other hotels."

"Perhaps, you should." Miguel kept his arm extended.

The manager left and returned five minutes later. "*Señor* Vincente was seen leaving the hotel with a woman early this evening. The receptionist said she checked in yesterday but stayed only one night. Yes, she was the 'Katrina Sands' you mentioned."

Miguel picked up the telephone, dialled a US number, and signalled to his man to remove the manager. When his call was connected, he spoke in a quiet and calm voice. "I want to know everything about Katrina Sands, and I want to know within the next two hours. Do you ... u n d e r s t a n d?"

"You bet."

* * *

At dawn, near a deserted hangar at the San Francisco Airport, Miguel looked out from his private jet and assessed the man standing beside the plain sedan. He was still young enough to mould, and Miguel was certain this ambitious man would serve him well. Miguel stepped down the stairs toward the waiting messenger.

"I have the information."

"Do you? Because I should warn you that if your news is not conclusive ... you die."

Paul Rostov's face paled. He removed his leather glove, dug into his pocket, and handed over a small slip of paper. "Her file was inactive. It showed no trip to Baja, just the usual: address, telephone number, driver's license. They didn't know she was out of the country until yesterday. And as far as I can tell, she's still in México."

"Is that what you believe?" Miguel asked, narrowing in on Rostov's face.

"No. I think she would return to her new home as quickly as possible. Where she believes she's safe."

"*Bueno*. Because, dear sir, I want that woman. If I must kill you to get her, I will."

"That won't help you get her."

"Perhaps not. But it'll make me feel *much* better."

CHAPTER 35

Aidan Roth slumped forward, his forearms planted firmly on Inspector Banyan's desk, the earphones to his ears, the tape recorder humming softly behind irrelevant and unimportant conversations, his finger flicking his pen to the beat. He was bursting inside. No contact between Ed and DeOlmos. No coded messages. Nothing. He crammed his neck forward and rested his chin on crossed hands. He listened to the sounds of Brandi's voice doling out orders to her best friend then pressed the fast-forward button. He heard Christine's giggle over some stupid joke from some punk kid. Aidan fast forwarded the tape. The calls Ed made were to employees, the guidance counsellor at Brandi's school, the library to see if his request for a manual had arrived. The calls to his office were business related. Nothing calls.

Aidan was wasting his time. Inspector Banyan had already told him there were no calls to or from DeOlmos. Still, he'd had to hear it for himself. He clicked off the tape recorder. A knot in his gut told him the call would come eventually; he needed patience.

Banyan was at the front desk when Aidan entered from the main office. He waited until Banyan finished scanning last night's dispatch.

"Heard enough?" Banyan looked up.

"Uh-huh."

"I'm sorry."

"Don't be, sir. It'll happen. Any word from the FBI?"

"No."

"Then, I guess I'll be seeing you tomorrow."

Banyan lowered his voice. "You okay?"

Aidan rubbed the back of his neck. "Yeah." He grabbed the door to the waiting room. "It's a feeling. I can't put my finger on it."

"Get some rest, Aidan."

Aidan nodded then left the building.

His car was parked on the other side of the street. He waited for two cars to pass then walked across the road. He rubbed at the back of his neck. The knot in his stomach tightened. Scanning up and down the empty, quiet street, he reached into his pocket, pulled out his keys, and--reared forward. A pain, more fierce, more unbearable than anything he'd ever experienced, ripped through his back, shortening his breath, until all he was aware of was the cool damp blacktop beneath his cheek.

Strange, Aidan thought, lying perfectly still. He heard a gurgling noise coming from his chest, listened to the thundering echo of a rifle shot close by, and realized ... there was no more pain.

* * *

Situated on a large lot in the heart of Berkeley, the Victorian house was spacious and comfortable. The living room was over four hundred square feet, the ceiling ten feet high, the walls a warm yellow, and the trim a clean white. The large window awnings kept the inside cool while creating an ambiance of sophistication and charm. Broad expanses of glass facing the deep, south veranda not only added light but also brought the outdoors inside. Although trees crowded the street, from every side of the house she had a clear view of the landscaped yard. No one could approach without being detected. Even so, Valerie was persuaded not to venture out to the protected covering of the front veranda.

She sat on the ottoman in front of the living room window. Low gray clouds moved in from the north, leaving a crack of light streaked across the horizon. She glanced at Canaday and shivered. He wouldn't look at her; not that she blamed him. Going after DeOlmos was ... beyond stupid.

Canaday looked glum. And he had to be tired. As far as she knew, he hadn't slept in two days. Looking at his face, she couldn't imagine life without him.

But he was pulling away from her. She could feel it. Her conscience told her that was for the best, but ....

But what?

He was vulnerable, but he was strong too. He was the kind of man a woman couldn't help wondering about. Not just sexually. Though, she'd had a dream about being with him. Kissing him. God, she'd almost asked him if it had been real.

Twisting around so her side was to him, she continued watching him out of the corner of her eye. It was embarrassing to think he'd catch her. Yet, she couldn't stop. Looking at him made her feel warm. A warmth that seeped into her muscles, sending a flush through more than just her body. He'd killed to save her. He'd endangered his life and his career by following her. Nobody, except Aidan, had ever risked anything for her. Ed wouldn't have. She couldn't imagine why she'd ever married him. No, that wasn't true. She married him because once upon a time he had worshipped the ground she walked on. Or so she'd thought. But she was young then, inexperienced, mistaking lust and possessiveness for love. She was an object, the picture perfect wife. Duty bound, passive, obedient, a young girl void of backbone. Willing to be led because the path ahead seemed dark and threatening. But what had she feared? The unknown? Her parents must have turned over in their graves. They had raised her to have a voice, and yet she gave it away.

Valerie squeezed her eyes shut. She had to stop dwelling on the past. She had three beautiful daughters. Her life was not a waste. She wasn't that young girl any longer. Now she had to protect her children. Soon enough they'd leave, choosing their own paths. She had to be there to make certain they believed in themselves. They had to know what she'd done in the past was wrong. They had to know that no man could create their destiny. Sharing a life with a man was not the same as giving up your life for him. She had to make sure they understood the difference.

She glanced at Canaday and knew, faced with the horror of the last few hours, she could handle whatever happened next. It was as if the whole world had opened up before her. She stood on the threshold of the unknown and felt no apprehension for herself. Eventually this whole situation would end. She'd either get back to her children or die trying. No matter how hot Canaday made her feel physically and intellectually, she'd pass him over in a second for a glimpse of her girls.

He sat across the room, his head low, his expression troubled.

Valerie trembled.

* * *

Canaday sat at the dining room table and faced the front room. Valerie's thin summer dress, one of the few clean items left in her suitcase, pulled tight over her round breasts, leaving the upper slopes bare. The pale rose colour in the dress illuminated the flush to her cheeks. Thick blonde hair fell past her shoulders and covered the soft texture of her neck. She shivered and wrapped her arms across her chest. The cut on her lip was mending, and the swelling had gone done. When asked earlier, she'd flexed her foot and said it felt better.

Valerie shivered again. Vamozzi, the consummate gentleman, handed over his large pullover. Valerie put it on and looked even more seductive. The sleeves reached past her knuckles, while the neckline plunged. She sat back down on the ottoman and pressed her hands between her thighs, forcing the sweater lower and the dress higher. Even from across the room Canaday could feel the smooth touch of her thigh, the curve of her back. He imagined her body beneath his. When she glanced his way, he didn't smile. It was his only defence. Once they got DeOlmos, Canaday knew she'd leave him. She was different. The eyes of the victim were gone. And she wasn't simply a survivor he saw across the room. Her spirit was gaining strength. He could see it in her posture, her face, the strength to stand alone.

Valerie's eyes drifted in his direction. He lowered his head, closed his eyes, and chewed on his thumbnail. He didn't have to look at her to see her. He could see her clearly on the back of his eyelids, her breast shiny with the wet. Her nipple, solid between his fingers for a long moment before he could force his hand away. Canaday's eyes popped open. He wanted her so badly he ached. And not only physically. The lust part he could deal with. It was her passion. Her belief in herself. It had taken a lot of guts to go to Baja. Sure it was a dumb move. But ... her courage. He ached for that. Truth be known, he was still as scared today as he'd been the moment he stepped foot in Nam. He'd learned how to hide it. Hunting killers was a way of hiding. Consumed by his job, he'd shielded himself from the one thing Valerie thrived on. Living and loving.

Vamozzi signalled from the kitchen; lunch was ready. Canaday stayed where he was.

* * *

When the lunch was over, Valerie rose and began clearing the table.

"Leave them, Val," Saul said.

"It's my turn."

"I know. But I can't sit and watch a woman work. And I don't think I could help you right now. I ate mine plus Candyman's share."

Valerie sat across from Saul. "What's bothering him? He hasn't said a word since we got here. Is it because of what I did? Does he think the silent treatment will help?"

"He's not acting any different than usual. The talkative side you witnessed wasn't normal. Though I imagine he is wondering what you'd hoped to accomplish."

"Desperate people do stupid things."

Saul toyed with the place mat in front of him. "Tell me about Prince George. Do you like living in the Canadian wilderness?"

Valerie laughed. "Maybe it's not the urban jungle you're accustomed to, but it's not exactly the wilderness either. There are over ninety thousand people. Before you met me, had you heard of Prince George?"

"No."

"Had you ever been to Canada before?"

"No." He grinned. "I grew up in Chattanooga and never saw Rock City until a few years ago. I've always wanted to see Canada though."

"Saul, it hurts to talk about home."

He tilted his head to one side. "I imagine it does." He smiled. "I had trouble picturing you slinging a power saw over your shoulder until I saw you at the airport. Going to Baja was a courageous move."

"It was stupid."

"Did you learn anything about Miguel?"

"No."

"Vincente?"

"Only that he was crazy. And capable of doing anything."

"What does that tell you about Miguel?"

Valerie thought for a moment. "To put up with Vincente's antics, Miguel must have patience. I think his family means everything to him. When Vincente talked of his mother, his face lit up. I imagine she had a similar impact on Miguel."

"Does that bother you?"

"That Mrs. DeOlmos was a good mother? Yeah, I suppose it does. She was loving and kind, and they still turned out the way they did."

"Maybe it had nothing to do with her?"

"I can't accept that. Being a mother has to count for something."

"And the father?"

"Vincente didn't speak of him. I don't know if he's still alive."

"He's not." Saul glanced around the bright kitchen and rubbed his palms together. "I understand your husband owns some kind of contracting company?"

"And?"

"I'm sorry, I wasn't trying to pry."

"Yes, you were."

"I'm just curious what life must be like up there in northern B.C."

"Saul, if you want to know something specific, ask."

"You and I have spent a lot of time together, yet you never speak of Ed."

"We own a contracting business. More specifically, a logging company. Do you know anything about the forest industry?"

"Not much."

She frowned, trying to imagine what had prompted his question. Curiosity, as he said? "What do you want to know?"

"You're right, I'm prying. But I do know a bit about the situation in your country. I know the forest industry has suffered the past few years. I was wondering if you've felt the effects. Now you're suspicious of my reasons." He smiled. "I'm fond of you, Val. I shouldn't have pried."

Valerie's body stiffened. "Don't!"

Stunned, Saul leaned back in his chair and gazed at her ... just like her dad used to do when she was a bit too spontaneous.

"Don't what?"

"Stop playing games with me, Saul. If we're friends as you say, then why haven't you told me what's going on since we got back? What's happening with your investigation? What leads do you have? I don't know any of this. I'm not FBI. If you have a specific question, ask. Don't beat around the bush and try to psychoanalyze me." She whipped her hair to one side and smoothed the placemat in front of her. She was as surprised as he was by her outburst.

"Is the business failing?"

"Yes. Now, tell me why you wanted to know that?"

"It places Ed in a vulnerable situation."

"Which means what exactly?"

"DeOlmos knows you're alive. If he thinks he can get to you through Ed, he'll try. I guess what I want to know is what will Ed do?"

"You think DeOlmos will threaten my children? I thought the RCMP were watching them?"

"Your children are protected."

"Then you think Ed will give me up for money?" She couldn't believe her ears. The horror of what he suggested made her lunch rise to her tonsils. She swallowed hard. "Ed may be a lot of things, but he's a proud man who loves his family and only wants what's best for them. No, he would not take DeOlmos's money. Besides, he doesn't know I'm alive." She leaned forward and looked Saul square in the face. "Can DeOlmos get to my girls?"

"The RCMP has round-the-clock surveillance."

"Why don't you pull my daughters out?"

"As hard as it might be to believe, they're safer where they are."

Valerie hung her head. They were doing it to her again, only now her family was in greater danger. She raised her chin high enough to look into

Saul's face. He held her gaze for a moment then started squirming, as most men did when dealing with an irate woman.

She blinked several times, inhaled deeply, and stood. "I'm out of here."

As she swept by the table, Saul reached out and grabbed her wrist. "You can't."

Valerie glared down at him. "Oh, yes I can. You think I'm going to sit by and wait for him to go after my children. I'm not." She tried to pry her hand free. "Let go."

He stood up and grabbed her other wrist. "Val, I can't let you do this."

"Let go!"

"I can't do that."

"My girls! DeOlmos will go after them. You have to let me go home." She struggled but his grip was too strong.

"Let her go." Canaday stepped into the room and moved toward her. "Listen to me, Valerie. You remember I made that call? Your family is safe. The RCMP moved in as soon as DeOlmos learned you were alive. There's no chance of him getting to them. His only hope is finding you. We have reason to believe he's got someone on the inside. We don't know who, yet. That's why we can't interfere in the protection of your family. Nobody knows where you are except Assistant Director Tomlin, and it'll stay that way until DeOlmos is apprehended."

"Why didn't you tell me this before?"

"I was trying... I don't know."

She glanced at Saul then back to Canaday. "I saw the two of you outside this morning. What were you whispering about?"

"Bailey, Kalamai, Hill, and Griffith have moved into your house in Santa Cruz. They're decoys. Word's out that you're there, and we're hoping DeOlmos gets wind of it and tries something."

"They've put themselves at risk for me?"

"It's their job. And they're not alone. The SWAT Team's close."

She moved toward the sink and stared out the window. The sky was full of black clouds threatening rain. She turned and faced them. They were watching her, waiting.

"Why this place? Who else knows about it?" she asked.

"It's not a regular safe house. It belongs to the Assistant Director's brother-in-law. They're in Europe for six months. There's no way anyone can trace you here."

Shoving her hands behind her, Valerie supported her back against the sink. "One of my pet peeves is those scenes in movies where the child is drowning in the ocean, and the mother runs up and down the beach screaming. People come running to see what's wrong, and she points toward her drowning child. 'Save him', she screams."

Valerie squelched her panic and smiled at the two men. "I can't count how many times I've seen that on TV. But every single time, I wanted to stick my fist through the screen and punch that woman right in the head. But," she choked by the tears. "I was that woman. I sat back and expected someone else to protect my children. No more."

Canaday approached slowly. "Valerie?"

She held up her hands. "Don't. Better yet ... please ... stay away from me." She looked him square in the face. "I appreciate everything you've done, but please, stay away from me."

The phone rang behind her. Valerie ignored it, swept past Canaday, and left the room.

* * *

Canaday stared after Valerie while Vamozzi picked up the phone.

"Hello," Vamozzi said.

Canaday wondered if he should go after to her.

And say what?

"Is he alive?" Vamozzi was saying.

Canaday turned.

Vamozzi's eyes were wide. "Yes .... She's fine .... Yes, please keep us informed."

Vamozzi hung up then gestured for Canaday to follow him outside. They went to the back hallway, through the back door to the veranda.

"What?" Canaday asked.

"Aidan Roth's been shot."

A pain targeted his temple. "Will he live?"

"They don't know. What are you going to tell Val?"

Canaday sat on the edge of the railing, closed his eyes, and rubbed his forehead. "Did the airport's surveillance cameras pick out anybody?"

"No. What are you going to tell Val?"

"What about the border crossings?"

"Tomlin says the Mounties found no evidence to prove it was DeOlmos's men. It was a .303 with a steel jacket. Not exactly standard sniper issue."

Canaday looked up. "Doesn't prove it was DeOlmos?"

"No, but that doesn't mean it wasn't. He could've told whoever to use the steel jacket simply to throw the RCMP off track."

"But there were no sightings?"

"What difference does it make? Roth's been shot. You have to tell Val."

"Why?"

"What do you mean 'why'? Mike, she's got a right to know."

"And then? Tie her to the chair so she doesn't take off the first chance she gets. She's not going to sit still for this. Her brother's been shot. He may die. What am I suppose to tell her? Gee, sorry, Valerie, but no you can't leave. But, hey, don't worry; I'll let you know if he makes it? Sonofabitch!"

"Okay, we talk Tomlin into sending her back, and we concentrate on finding DeOlmos."

"Are you nuts! Miguel will kill her."

"We don't know that."

"Saul! He shot her fucking brother!"

Vamozzi turned toward the house. "She'll hear you. Of course, that's one way of letting her know."

Canaday stiffened.

Vamozzi lowered his voice. "You don't have a choice. It doesn't matter who shot him. For God's sake, he was a cop. We don't know how many enemies Roth has. Stop and think with your brain for a second. What would you feel like if you were in her place?"

"Tomlin said what exactly?"

"Nothing. He didn't volunteer any advice."

"Well, there you go. Our own chief doesn't think she should know."

"Mike, this is wrong. You're letting your lust, or whatever the hell you want to call it, interfere with your judgment."

"She's our witness--Remember? We don't have a case without her."

"Bullshit."

"Saul?" He raised his hands, palms out. "Tomlin said he'd keep you informed, right? So, we wait."

"This is wrong."

Canaday walked back into the house.

CHAPTER 36

Huge impressive elm trees sheltered his black Mercedes from the rain's downpour. Miguel watched the young man approach then stop a few feet from the dark tinted glass.

Miguel lowered his window. He removed his gloves, but didn't look at the young soldier. "You will send three men to the Savings and Loan on Marsh Street and four more to the Bank of America on Chestnut Street. Make certain they are heavily armed and highly profiled. Tell them their sacrifices will not be in vain. Their families will be well taken care of." He slipped the package through window's opening. "Here is her address and photograph." He handed the young soldier a money envelope. "I can't emphasize enough how disappointed I shall be if my instructions are not carried out to the letter. There must be no witnesses. But--do not kill the woman. Bring her to me unharmed."

* * *

Ten minutes after finishing the Chinese food that he, Kalamai, Griffith, and Hill had order for dinner, Peter Bailey stood on the back stoop of the safe house in Santa Cruz. He yawned, stretched, and smacked his face lightly. He couldn't fathom why he was so tired. He yawned again and heard a twig breaking in the bushes beyond. Then a footstep. He tried to spot the source. His eyes wouldn't focus.

The sky opened up.

A low click. A blast of gunfire. Peter flew backward. Slammed up against the house.

More shots inside the house.

His chest burned. His senses scrambled. His body slid downward.

More shots rang out behind him.

He thought of Kalamai.

CT Kalamai.

CT....

Calani Tia ....

* * *

Joylene Nowell Butler

Valerie sat across the room and watched Canaday clean his gun. She could almost feel his body relaxing. He avoided looking at her, which was good. His eyes made her uncomfortable. As if he knew stuff _she_ wasn't willing to admit. He switched on the TV and rested his legs on the ottoman. Vamozzi, having made a routine walk around, came in the front door. He hung his jacket on the coat tree and nodded at Valerie then sat down next to Canaday. Neither of them spoke. Valerie imagined they'd been working together long enough that small talk wasn't necessary.

Canaday switched to the local sports channel and reached for a cigarette. He looked at it for a second then put it back. Was he quitting? Good for you if you do, she wanted to say; but couldn't. Though she was no longer angry, words eluded her.

Noise from the television caught her attention, and for a brief second while the pictures flashing across the screen registered, Valerie was grateful for the distraction.

Until ….

Both Canaday and Vamozzi leaned forward. Valerie strained to hear what was being broadcast while breathing became difficult.

A reporter stood in front of the safe house in Santa Cruz and spoke as police and detectives moved behind her, in and out of the house. The house Valerie had lived in.

Two people were confirmed dead. Two more were wounded, one of them critically. No names were mentioned. Canaday sank back into the couch and rubbed a hand over his hair. Another nightmare had come true, and she didn't dare take her eyes off him. She swallowed the acid accumulating in her mouth, while praying the news reporters were wrong. They'd been wrong before. They'd reported she was dead.

The phone on the coffee table rang. Vamozzi, closest, answered, listened then hung up. "Tomlin's on his way to Santa Cruz. He doesn't know which two are … gone."

Canaday jerked forward and grabbed the phone.

Vamozzi laid his hand over Canaday's. "What are you doing?"

Color rushed into Canaday's face. He tossed Vamozzi's hand away. "Don't make me pull rank. I'm going to Santa Cruz."

"To do what? Our assignment is here."

Canaday ignored Vamozzi and dialled what Valerie assumed was the nearest FBI office. He requested a priority flight to Santa Cruz. He would be at their headquarters in five minutes, he said, then hung up.

Valerie lowered her chin to her chest. Out of the corner of her eye, she saw Canaday hand Vamozzi an extra magazine. She looked away. Her eyes watered. Something told her it was not the time for tears. It was better to become invisible. To sink back into the chair and hope neither man looked at her. Because all this was her fault. Agents were dead. Maybe CT. Or Peter. And Canaday? What was he going to do? What if...? No, please God, she prayed. Don't let him go.

Canaday pulled at his collar as if he were suffocating. He looked from Vamozzi to Valerie. She couldn't read his expression. Was he close to exploding? Or simply planning?

With no warning, he stomped across the room, grabbed her arm, and pulled her from the chair and toward the privacy of the first bedroom. He shoved her into the room and slammed the door.

Valerie looked at his face and took a step back. He had frightened her, yet she was sure that was not his intent. Maybe part of him was fighting to stay. Maybe if she could open her mouth, the words to convince him to stay would come.

His breathing slowed. "Do you trust me?"

She nodded.

"Stay in here until I return." He spoke above a whisper. "If you hear anything, get under the bed and don't come out until Vamozzi says otherwise. Understood?"

She didn't move. The only sound was the knocking of her heart. He was within arms length, close enough to touch. He turned toward the door and froze. She tried to will her mouth to open, but he turned back, moved toward her, and pulled her into his arms. She wrapped her arms around him and held tight.

He gripped the back of her neck and whispered, "I don't expect anything from you, just do as I ask. Stay here until I come back. Please." He unwrapped her arms and pulled a gun out of his holster. He handed it to her without saying a word. Then he turned and left the room.

The door crashed against the inside wall, reverberating through the quiet room.

* * *

An hour later, the cab dropped Canaday at the end of the driveway to the Santa Cruz safe house. He saw Tomlin on the sidewalk. For no other reason than Tomlin was in the direction of the front door, Canaday approached. Tomlin patted him on the back. Canaday stiffened. The Assistant Director withdrew his hand. They faced the house. The wide louvers on the front window were closed. The street behind him hummed with the questions and comments neighbours shared amongst themselves. He glanced toward the crowd, searching, yearning ... but DeOlmos was never that stupid.

Canaday clenched his shaking hands, ducked under the police tape, and crossed the lawn toward the front door. He gritted his teeth and focused his train of thought. This was just another crime scene, no better, no worse. Police barricades stretched around the perimeter of the yard, just like any other crime scene. Forensic teams moved inside ... just like any other crime scene.

"I'm waiting to speak with the coroner. We're here as observers. Remember that," Tomlin said.

Though he had a few choice comebacks, Canaday held his tongue. He shoved his ID into the face of the officer positioned at the front door and followed Tomlin inside. The first thing he saw was Special Agent Stan Griffith slouched against the front hallway, with a large cavity in his chest. The coroner, squatting beside him, exchanged words with the detective in charge. Canaday froze. His shame and guilt felt like a burning coil in his gut. Griffith's head tilted downward, and his eyes remained opened. Canaday looked upon a face that displayed the shock of death and attempted to remember what professional objectivity felt like. He pursed his lips and tore his eyes away.

When a grunt died in Vietnam, the only thing left to do was give your respects and carry on. Canaday ignored the creeping sensation on his skin, stepped aside, and went into the living room. The sweet smell of blood still lingered in the air. Investigators brushed at the fingerprints along the windowsills, coffee table, and the wooden arms of the wicker sofa and chairs. Plastic envelopes filled with shells. Bullet holes laced the walls, and everywhere Canaday stepped were more shells. Officers gathered samples of blood along the walls and floor leading to the kitchen, while others lifted gunpowder residue. Beyond them, he saw the outstretched legs of Dick Hill. He took a step forward.

Then another.

And another.

Hill was sprawled across the floor with his torso propped against the lopsided table. Canaday felt the hatred pulsating from his temples. There was a bullet hole in Hill's right forearm and kneecap, and half his face was gone. A trail of blood led from the living room. Shot twice, Hill must have crawled from the living room to the kitchen, where he was shot again. The wound to his face had been inflicted by a different calibre, and at point blank range, powder burns confirmed that.

Canaday twisted around and gripped the edge of the sink. He blinked several times and reminded himself, again, that he was a veteran soldier and cop. This was a crime scene, and he'd seen thousands of them. Children beaten until their faces were pulp. Victims dismembered by bombs, by blunt instruments. Crime scenes where the head could be found fifty feet away.

The officer, who stood close by, gave him an angry scowl then glared down at the additional prints on the sink. Fingerprints that shouldn't have been there.

Asswipe--my fingerprints are all over the fucking place, Canaday thought, while he held the man's eyes.

The officer turned away.

Canaday straightened himself and went to the bedroom. He hesitated at the doorway.

Blood. Kalamai's blood had splattered from a trajectory point on the far side of the bed, upward across the wall and the shear curtains. A blonde wig lay at the end of the bed. Shell casings were scattered across the rumpled comforter and the left-hand corner of the sheets. The walls were splattered with holes, gouges, splinters, with feathers stuck to the globs of blood. She'd been lying down.

Why?

Shot once, Kalamai dove across the bed to the floor, where she was pinned down until she ran out of ammunition.

Why was she lying down?

Canaday dug his hands further into his pants pocket and backed away. With his right shoulder, he pushed at the screen door and stepped outside. Blood coagulated on the patio and up the back wall of the house.

They attacked from the front and the back, and Bailey went down within seconds of Griffith?

Canaday looked back at the porch light and up at the cloudy gloom. Bailey heard a noise, stood under an illuminating light.

Damn!

Peter wasn't an amateur; none of them were. Then how did this happen? They were surprised and ambushed without taking anyone with them. It wasn't possible.

Back inside the house, Canaday found Tomlin quietly conversing with the Lieutenant and the Coroner. He walked past them and out the front door. He lit a cigarette, his eyes wandered to the gray Escort. If he had stopped Valerie from going to Baja, would any of this have happened? Of course. Somebody sold her out.

Tomlin approached from behind. "I'm on my way to the hospital."

Canaday flicked his long stub to the ground. He pressed his shoe into the glow and rubbed hard on the flesh of his left forearm. It felt like something was crawling on his skin. "What have they got?"

"The Coroner suspects the food was tampered with. They're testing the Chinese cartons for prints. They think four, maybe five gunmen. Came in through the back and front. Griffith and Peter were shot. Then Hill. Kalamai tried to hold out as long as she could. One of the neighbours had the good sense to call it in. One squad car arrived, and a chase ensued. They lost them five miles down the road. I have no idea why they didn't set up roadblocks, but I'll find out. So far all they know is the plates were stolen. The police didn't ID the victims as FBI until an hour later. Nobody ventured out of their houses, so no identifications were made. But they're still canvassing the neighbourhood."

"How did this happen? We baited this trap."

Tomlin didn't answer. Instead, he opened the back door of the Chrysler Seville and got in; Canaday followed. Tomlin's driver drove south toward the city.

"I read the report from San José del Cabo. You didn't mention how they learned Mrs. McCormick was there?" Tomlin asked.

"For the same reason you offered up the house in Berkeley. There's someone on the inside, isn't there, sir. Where was the SWAT Team?"

"They were called downtown earlier this afternoon to two bank robberies, both involving hostage situations." Tomlin looked out the side window. "Agent Kalamai is in stable condition. One bullet grazed her head. Another one lodged in her cheek. She has a punctured spleen and a hit to the right shoulder. Two headshots and she's still hanging on. They don't know if Bailey's going to pull through. He had multiple wounds to the chest. He's in surgery, probably for several more hours."

With Tomlin adding nothing more, Canaday concentrated on his directive. Stay calm. Stay focused. While the words sounded good, the images in his head were waking nightmares. But the worse part, the part that cut up his insides and made him want to puke until he couldn't puke anymore, was he was so grateful that Valerie hadn't been the one lying in her own blood.

Twelve minutes later, the driver pulled up to the entrance of the

Dead Witness

hospital and parked. Canaday, feeling like an obedient puppy, stared at Tomlin's back as he followed him into the hospital. Not only was he following the man, he was showing the same face. Indifference.

Special Agents and uniformed officers filled the waiting room. Tomlin nodded to a few men along the corridor to Kalamai's room. Canaday barely acknowledged them. He went to Kalamai's side and lifted her limp hand. Her eyelids fluttered at his touch.

She moaned then opened her eyes and struggled to speak. "Is Bailey ...?"

Canaday squeezed her hand. Weary and angry, he tried to smile. "He's in surgery. That's all I know."

"I couldn't ... get to him."

Canaday nodded. It seemed the only thing to do.

"I was napping. Gun shots everywhere. I emptied my gun. I yelled their names. But .... Oh God, I was napping." She coughed and struggled to breathe.

Canaday leaned closer. Tomlin faced the window. "Take your time, Kalamai." He held her hand, rubbing the top lightly. "Did you see DeOlmos?"

"No," she mumbled.

"Did anyone call you Valerie?"

"No."

"Did you recognize any of them?"

"No."

"Did they use names?"

With an effort, Kalamai shook her head.

"Did they think you were Mrs. McCormick?"

"No."

"It's all right. Rest now."

"Candyman?" she whispered.

He leaned closer. "Yes."

"The SWAT team."

"I know."

"No. DeOlmos is smart."

He nodded his head. Yes, DeOlmos could've had the SWAT team called off.

A small tear ran down her face. "Candyman?" she pleaded. "I'm sorry."

Canaday swallowed hard. "Did everybody eat the Chinese food?"

Kalamai's eyes squeezed shut.

"You were drugged," he said, not caring whether it was true or not. "I'm the one who's sorry." He brought his mouth next to her ear and whispered, "I'll get him."

Back in the hallway, Canaday walked to the nearest plainclothes officer. He showed him his ID and asked for information concerning the hostage situation at the bank earlier that evening.

Instead of answering, the detective gave Canaday the once over.

Canaday stared straight through him. He visualized ripping the officer's face off and could feel the rage sucking the blood from his own face.

"The perpetrators were killed at the scene." The detective cleared his throat and scanned the hallway. When he looked back at Canaday, his eyes widened. "Are you okay?"

Canaday couldn't answer. All he could think about was he had to get back to Valerie. Now!

CHAPTER 37

Valerie heard something. Lights reflected through her bedroom window and across two walls. She threw back the comforter and jumped from the bed in time to see a car pulled into the long driveway and stopped. The engine died. Valerie held her breath. The door opened and the interior was bathed in light; Canaday got out of the car slowly and walked toward the front of the house. Saul appeared on the front veranda. They faced each other. Canaday said something. Then he walked past Saul and entered the house.

Valerie wrestled into her housecoat, dancing in a circle before she had it on. She heard muffled voices outside her door. First Saul's voice. Then Canaday's. Then the door opened, and he stayed in the shadows. Still. Silent.

"Is CT okay?" she whispered.

"She's alive." His voice was so low she couldn't tell what he was feeling.

"Peter?"

"I don't know." He sounded numb.

"Agent Hill?"

Canaday shook his head.

"Agent Griffith?" Valerie whispered.

"No."

Tears came. She tried to stop them. "It's my fault," she exhaled. "I shouldn't have gone to México. I should have stayed in Santa Cruz like you said. I'm so sorry. I was trying... If I could only...." Her voice cracked. "I don't blame you if you hate me. They'd be alive now if... Dear God! I'm so sorry."

He stared at her. Not moving. Saying nothing. Then he took one step forward. Valerie couldn't stop the tears. She was to blame and now people were dead because of her utter disregard for the consequences of her actions. Actions that would never have occurred to her four months ago.

He moved closer. She wished he would say something. Anything. She cried without sound. Canaday's face remained indecipherable.

"Please, Canaday, please believe me, I would never intentionally hurt anyone. I'd rather be dead than--"

He grabbed her, pulling her into his arms. "Don't say that. Don't ever say that. I couldn't stand it if something happened to you. Don't say that ever again. It's not your fault. It's not." His hand cupped the back of her head. His lips, brushing against her cheek, moved to her mouth, kissing her. As if this moment was all they'd ever have.

Valerie wrapped her arms around him and kissed him back with a passion that had been smothered all her life. This man, this kiss, meant everything.

He broke away, lifted her, carried her to the bed, lay her down, his fingertips lingering on her face, her lips. Her skin tingled. He pressed into her. He rolled onto his back, pulling her with him, kissing her mouth hard. Sucking, pulling at the sleeves of her housecoat. He slipped it off her shoulders, while his mouth moved down her neck, burning a path. She rose above him enough to free herself from the confines of her robe.

Cool air touched her back. Her head spun. Heat gathered like a pool at the base of her belly. Her thighs trembled. Quivered. She undid the buttons on his shirt, her fingers grazed his chest, his warm chest, so full of life it beat a rhythm beneath her touch. He tugged at her nightshirt until it was over her head. He rolled her onto her back. She drew a quick breath. His tongue caressed the skin between her breasts, moved slowly, torturing her then finding her swelling nipple, sucked gently until she thought she would go mad. His tongue stroked back and forth in a slow circle until his lips closed in, sucking, nibbling, draining the sanity from her.

Valerie closed her eyes and cradled his head in her hands. And while her body was as hot and as full of rapture as she thought possible, only one word came to mind. Over and over. Yes.

Yes.

Oh God, yes.

His hand moved down her thigh, gripped the back of her knee, and spread her legs. His fingers working. Exploring. Touching her in a way that sent shock waves from the tip of her head to the tip of her toes. Pulsating rushes that cultivated in the center of her being, lifting her, as if she was a cloud bursting with electricity. Her back arched. She gasped.

Canaday moaned softly. His tongue moved down her body, tracing a path that was plundering her straight into pure ecstasy.

* * *

He was gone when she opened her eyes. Her bedroom filled with the morning sun. The clock on the side table showed 7:15. She rose then threw on a pair of white pants and a yellow cotton tee shirt. She tied her hair into a ponytail then went to the kitchen. Saul and Canaday were on the south veranda out back. She glanced through the window above the sink and saw them standing together. Saul propped one foot on a small stool, while Canaday stood beside him, hands in pockets, and faced the yard. She backed away from the window. Suddenly dizzy, she gripped the counter for support. Heat rushed to her face.

Something was wrong.

Of course, something was wrong. Last night she'd slept with an FBI agent. Last night agents had died.

That wasn't it.

Valerie took a deep breath. Her body wouldn't cooperate. She licked her lips and knew that she was responding to this man like an adolescent. All she wanted was to make love with him, again.

The calendar on the side of the fridge showed a picture of a little girl playing with a puppy. She was sprawled on a lawn surrounded by flowers and big maples. A golden puppy jumped up to lick her face. The yard didn't resemble Valerie's. The child was five years old with no similarities to any of her daughters. But at that instant, Valerie felt a horrendous guilt.

What am I doing? I have a husband, children, an entirely different life waiting for me.

Still she couldn't shake the feeling of Canaday so near. She closed her eyes and imagined his strong back. His skin had been so smooth and hard. The muscles in his thighs were like rock. He moved in her slow then fast until she thought she'd go mad, and then he'd slow again, daring her not to move, but to let the heat propel her toward him.

Total madness, Valerie thought, and hot tears burned her eyes.

Was this what it felt like to be totally controlled by one person? Was this even worse than Ed's control over her?

She couldn't imagine Canaday conversing with her children. The thought of Brandi cuddled up to him on the couch made Valerie want to laugh. It would never happen. He wasn't their father and could never be expected to act as one. Besides, he was American. He wouldn't move to Canada just to be near her. He thrived on his job and the danger connected to it.

Then what am I doing?

Loving Canaday was comparable to winning a million dollars, only to have them come back the next day and say, 'Oops, sorry we made a mistake. This money isn't for you.'

She leaned over the sink, turned on the tap, and splashed cold water on her face. Raised voices prompted her to look up. Canaday still had his back to her. Saul looked angry. Valerie went outside.

"What's the matter?"

Canaday glanced at her over his shoulder then faced Saul again.

"Val," Saul said. "Peter died early this morning."

Brooding heat waves struck her face. "Oh Jesus, I'm sorry.... Is CT okay?"

"Yes." Saul stared back at Canaday, who still had his back to her.

"What?" she asked, frightened.

Canaday cleared his throat. "Saul? Can I speak to Valerie alone?"

Saul walked to the back door. "Sure. I'll be in the house."

Canaday didn't move. Valerie stepped closer, reached out to touch his back, hesitated then lowered her arm.

"Let's go for a walk." He stepped down to the lawn.

Valerie followed.

The midmorning clouds had dispersed. New blossoms sprouted through the flowerbeds. The lawn looked emerald green after the long rain. Sunlight, doing its part, evaporated the water leaving the grass with a velvety texture. Soft. Beckoning. A light breeze swept through the sycamores, while small birds took to flight.

Everything was so perfect that it terrified her.

He strolled across the grass, around the side of the house, past the huge sycamores sheltering them from the neighbours. She followed until they were standing at the front stoop. Canaday flexed his jaw and sat down on the step. He patted the spot next to him.

She felt ill. She eased down on the wooden step unable to take her eyes off him. She didn't know if she was ready to hear what he had to say. By the look of despair on his face, she knew it was bad. Trying to prepare was impossible. Just tell me, she wanted to yell.

Canaday lit a cigarette and gazed toward the street beyond the front yard, two hundred feet away. The trees blocked most of his view and yet his eyes were fixed in that direction. He seemed disassociated, as if what had happened between them hadn't. Making love hadn't changed anything.

They sat quietly.

After awhile he said, "It's nice here." He tossed his cigarette to the ground and stepped on it. "Your brother's going to be all right, but he's in the hospital--"

"Huh."

"He's doing well."

"What!"

"He was leaving the police station in Prince George, and someone shot him."

Valerie jumped to her feet. She covered her mouth with both hands. An insurgence of panic struck her hard. She felt Canaday touch her shoulder, trying to turn her around, trying to hold her. "No!" she snapped, twisting away. "Just tell me what happened."

"He was crossing the street outside the detachment. An ambulance was on the scene in minutes. He was operated on. He's in intensive care."

"When did this happen?"

"Yesterday morning."

"Will he ... live?"

Canaday nodded. His expression showed guilt and remorse. But he wasn't responsible. It wasn't his fault. He didn't ....

"How long have you known?" she asked in a low, quiet voice. His gaze stayed locked on her. "How long have you known?" Her voice rose. "Yesterday? You've known since yesterday?" Before she could stop, she hit him across the face with the back of her fist. Stunned, she grasped her hands together, afraid he might strike her back, or worse she might hit him again.

Canaday stood like a stone statue.

"Who shot him?" she asked, her voice controlled.

"They don't know."

"Was it one of DeOlmos's men?"

"It was a .303 with steel jacket."

"That proves what?"

"It's not something a professional would use."

"Do they have armed guards posted at the hospital?"

"Yes."

She laced her hands behind her neck, touched her elbows together, and rocked. Images she couldn't ignore played through her consciousness like a movie set in slow motion. "You made love to me knowing my brother might not make it through the night?"

He opened his mouth to say something but nodded instead.

"Why?" she asked.

"Selfish reasons, Valerie."

Joylene Nowell Butler

She flung her arms to her sides. "You were going to tell me today whether he was dead or alive, right?"

He pressed his lips together.

This was getting worse.

"You only told me Because Saul threatened to? Canaday, say that's not true."

"As soon as I heard, I promised myself I wouldn't say anything until I had good news."

"Good news?"

"He's going to make it."

"You should've told me this yesterday."

"I didn't know if he was going to make it yesterday."

She glowered at him.

"I was afraid you'd leave. I know how close you are to your brother. I was afraid you'd go home, and DeOlmos would find you."

Men were pathetic creatures.

"Let's go inside, Canaday. You and I and Saul have something to discuss."

She marched up the steps, across the veranda, opened the front door, and waited for Canaday to go first.

Saul was sitting on the sofa when they entered the living room. He regarded them with a frown.

"Saul, that briefcase full of files you keep, I want to see it," Valerie said.

Confused, he glanced at Canaday.

"Now," she said. "I'll make coffee."

When the coffee was ready, Saul accepted the cup Valerie offered, set his briefcase on the table, and sat down. He took several small sips, which seemed to agitate Canaday further, then opened his briefcase, reached inside, and pulled out a folder. Canaday grunted, sat across from her at the table, and folded his arms across his chest.

"Val, if you find anything out of the ordinary, God Bless you. But I doubt you will. Though, you might find this interesting." Saul pulled a photograph from his briefcase and handed it to her.

"Mrs. DeOlmos." Valerie's eyes transfixed on the photo. "Vincente showed me one taken a few years earlier."

As Valerie stared at the photo, a foreboding sensation vanquished any trace of self-doubt she might have had. They had never met, but she recognized the type of woman Mrs. DeOlmos was.

"Bolina DeOlmos at the age of forty-two," Saul said. "It's the last picture taken of her."

Valerie couldn't speak. Her body trembled, and she felt like dancing. This woman was the key, and she had been all along. Mrs. DeOlmos may have died when Valerie was a small child, but still, Valerie knew her. This woman's spirit was recognizable. Her character emulated everything Valerie understood, and she was surprised Canaday hadn't realized that. Bolina's eyes registered grief. Her expression signified the love and devotion of a mother. Someone who would love unconditionally. Without prejudice. Without judgment.

"Canaday, I need to borrow your cellular phone."

"What for?"

"I have to call my sister-in-law, Susan."

"What for?"

They regarded each other for a moment. A word, a sound, a look from him could send her to jelly land. But not this time. Her eyes cut into his. He didn't back down. She knew he wouldn't.

"What are you thinking?" he said, very low. Then his eyes widened, and he sprang from his chair. "Forget it! You're not getting involved. And that's final."

"We'll get him, Val," Saul said.

She glanced at Saul. "No, you won't." She looked back at Canaday. "Let's face it, your plan didn't work. It's never going to work. DeOlmos knows I'm alive."

Canaday's eyes softened, ruining his momentum. He, sat down, pressed the bridge of his nose, and looked across the table at her. "I've been there for you, haven't I?"

Maybe it was to appease him that she nodded.

"And we both agree you're in my territory. This is a world I'm familiar with. I know these people. You don't. Correct?"

Nothing she said would stop him now, so again she nodded, if not to allow him his peace, then the respect of letting him say it out loud.

"I've spent my whole life surrounded by men like Miguel DeOlmos. I exist on a battlefield. It's where I belong. But, Valerie, you do not. And it's not because you're a woman or that you lack courage. You're one of the bravest people I've ever known."

Nice speech. Corny, but nice. "I appreciate that, Canaday, but hear me out."

His eyes grew enormous, and the hardness returned to his face. "This isn't a game. You don't know what the hell you're doing. I'm making the decisions." He jabbed his finger toward her. "You're not going anywhere."

Valerie rose off her chair. "Canaday, read my lips. Nothing you say is going to change my mind. On February 20, you took control of my life. I want it back. No buts, no arguments. I want it back."

He rushed forward, and she dropped to her chair. He rested his palms on the table and towered over her. "Charlie Onston is dead. Gregory Vanderhal is dead. Stan Griffith is dead. Dick Hill is dead. Peter Bailey is dead. Five custom officers are--"

"Candyman--Stop it," Saul said.

"Why?" he glared at him. "How many more dead agents does she need to prove she's not equipped to do this? I'm not handing over a phone, and she's not going anywhere. "

"I'm sorry for all those people," she said, "but I'm not your dead witness any longer. You said it yourself that DeOlmos doesn't know Vincente's dead. I can use that to bargain with. I want to call Susan, get my girls out of my house then I have to go back. But Canaday, I need your help."

"What the fuck is wrong with you?" he said, his voice too loud. "Are you stuck on stupid or what!"

All the heat in her body rose to her face, tightening the veins in her neck, making her eyes twitch. She looked up at him while the muscles in her back ached under the strain of knotting. "Don't talk to me like that. Ever. Either you help me or you don't but I'm going. One way or another, I'm taking back my life, and nothing you or anybody else can say will stop me. Those are my children, and I'm going back. And that--Agent Canaday, is final."

CHAPTER 38

That time a perp stabbed him in the chest during an altercation didn't feel this bad.

That night when the girlfriend of that drug dealer Aidan had pinned to the floor, whacked Aidan over the head twice with a whiskey bottle, didn't feel this bad.

And that time in Toronto when a suspected rapist drove over Aidan's foot while he clung to the truck's side mirrors as they sped down the highway, didn't feel this bad.

This time his torso burned like a huge mass of raging fire, scorching through what had once been his chest and his back.

Maybe it was Because those other three bastards ended up behind bars.

The buzzer lay beside him within easy grasp of his hand. All he had to do was press it and the nurse would come. Only, along with the vanishing pain came hallucinations. Like the time a biker rode past the end of his bed, glanced at him then kept going. When Aidan looked to see if anyone else had noticed, the nurses went about their business, oblivious. Nurses who all looked like Valerie. He couldn't stand that. And every time Susan came to visit, minutes passed before Aidan could remember her name. She was his wife, and he couldn't remember her name. That was when he decided no more drugs. At least not until he couldn't stand the pain any longer.

But they came anyway. Those nurses that looked like Valerie, their morphine filled hypodermic needles pricking into the IV bag above his head. Making the world spin out of control.

He opened his eyes and tried to find something to focus on, something to alleviate the pain. A nurse approached. A nurse with those same dark turquoise blue eyes. Dressed in a white uniform. White cap. White facemask. But Valerie was dead. When they peeled him off the pavement, rolled him into the ambulance, he knew his sister was dead.

The nurse stood over him. Her fingertips grazed his arm. Her soft eyes filled with tears.

Go away. Go away and stop torturing me.

She bent forward and kissed his cheek through the cloth covering her face. "I love you, big brother," she whispered. "I missed you. The doctors say you're going to be okay."

Valerie?

"Everything's fine now, Aidan. You don't have to worry about me anymore. I'm back. I'm not going away again. I'll let you rest now, but I'll return tomorrow."

Don't go!

She dabbed at the cloth over her face. The wet spot was real. "Maybe I'll stay until you fall asleep. You must rest now, Aidan. You have to get your strength back."

Is it really you?

"Rest now," she whispered, laying her hand over his.

Aidan closed his eyes and smiled. He welcomed the dwindling pain, his body and mind slipping away to a better place, a quiet and serene place, a place drifting toward greyness.

* * *

She asked the taxi driver to drop her off at the end of her driveway. He glanced in his rear-view mirror and gave her a strange look. "Sure lady, whatever you say." He pulled to the side of the road, flicked the trunk open, and switched off the meter.

After he left, Valerie stood at the edge of her driveway, three large bags in hand, a suitcase at her feet, and slid her running shoe across the black pavement. Her eyes scanned along its surface all the way to her front door. Three hundred feet. More specifically, three hundred feet of new blacktop, valued at probably five thousand dollars.

A brand new Ford van was parked in the opened garage, and in front of the door was a brand new Ford 4x4.

Valerie frowned at the blue metallic truck. Had they won the lottery?

What was she thinking? She was home. Back where she thought she might never be again.

Gripping the bags in her left hand, she picked up her suitcase with the other, and trudged toward the house. Among the spruce and fir trees surrounding their ten acre lot, the birch and cottonwood sprouted a rebirth of bright green leaves. Tulips, daffodils, crocuses, and wild flowers crowded her flowerbeds. The lawn had been recently mowed, and the air was laced with pollen and wet grass cuttings. She walked down her long driveway and steadied her heart. In the distance, she heard traffic on

Highway 97, a dog barked from somewhere across the road, and high above her, ravens squawked.

Loose hairs from her French braid whipped across her face. She set her suitcase and packages on the front step and stared at the door. Her whole body trembled, and her stomach wrenched. She swallowed three times before she was convinced her lunch would stay down. She looked back at the road, at the quiet neighbourhood, and faced the house again. She reached down for her luggage. The front door flew open.

"Valerie!" Ed ran toward her and lifted her into his arms.

He crushed the air from her lungs, and Valerie let out a sharp laugh. He let go and smiled down at her. Although she could see the flash of his smile, the expression in his eyes showed something else. He looked old. The wrinkles around his eyes were deeper, and the rugged tan he usually wore was gone. His skin was pasty with a tinge of gray.

"God, it's good to see you." He reached down for her suitcase. "Come in and ...." He groped for words, laughed, and stepped through the door. "It is so wonderful to have you home. So wonderful. God, I was shocked when Inspector Banyan said you were alive. Can't tell you how happy I was, though. So happy, Val." He set her things on the floor of the foyer and smiled back at her. He dug his hands in his back pockets and glanced toward the kitchen. "Are you hungry?"

Valerie shook her head and peeked into the front room. Her blue gray chesterfield was gone, replaced by a large, tan leather sectional. The carpet was different, too. A multitude of brown shades replaced the soft blue carpeting she had chosen only three years ago.

She caught sight of the large television screen. How could she have missed it; the huge bulky presence took up one corner of the room. It was ugly.

She turned back to Ed. "Where are the girls?"

"They're with Susan and the kids. They came for them this morning. Susan wanted them altogether for the weekend. The Inspector said you knew about Aidan."

"Yes."

"They're probably at the hospital. I could go get them. Or maybe you need to get your bearings first?"

Valerie nodded.

His face expressed fatherly concern. "You must be scared, Val. But you needn't be. They understand everything."

Valerie walked into the kitchen. She was relieved to see nothing had changed. She sat down at the table. "I was so terrified that this day would never happen."

"Would you like a coffee?"

She watched him pull a mug from the same cupboard where she had always kept them. He pulled the pot from the coffeemaker, still positioned in its familiar location, and filled the cup.

He sat across from her; his smile seemed strained. "What would you like to do? Would you rather spend the day together, alone? We could spend tonight alone, and I could get the girls tomorrow?"

"I would like that very much. We need to talk."

"Yeah ... sure."

She cupped her hands around her mug. "But first, maybe we should discuss the insurance money?"

His face dropped. "I thought you were dead."

"I know. But when they find out I'm still alive, they'll expect reimbursement."

"We're not responsible for our conniving government. The authorities and the FBI deceived us. Surely that counts for something?"

"We should have our lawyer look into it."

His face brightened. "I'll call him first thing Monday morning. Maybe we have grounds to sue." His eyes refocused on her face. "What would you like to do this evening? Whatever you want."

"A quiet dinner."

"Sure."

"Cocktails in the front room."

"Okay. Hey, we could watch a movie. I bought a satellite, and it's got over a hundred channels."

"Still a video means we can watch whatever we want when we want."

"I'll go to the video store, and after dinner, we can curl up together in front of the TV like old times."

Valerie stopped herself from correcting him. They had never curled up and watched anything together. "What I'd really like to do is take a long bath."

"You do that. I'll go to the store and buy their best steaks and maybe some lobster. I'll check to see if there's propane in the barbecue. I'll cook," he said rising. "In fact, I'll take care of everything, you just relax. Don't worry about a thing. I'll buy the fixings for a Caesar salad, garlic bread; all your favourites. I should be back before you get out of the tub, but if not, maybe you should have a nap. I'll wake you when I return."

He seemed eager to leave, but that was okay.

Ed grabbed the keys off the hook near the back door and went outside. A few seconds later, she saw him cross in front of the window then heard the truck door open and the soft growl as the engine started. She leaned across the table and peeked out the window in time to see him driving away; his tires squealed onto the road, and then the truck sped past their house.

She left the kitchen and wandered through the first floor of the house. The den looked much the same way it had the day she asked Ed what he wanted from the store. Valerie shook her head and went to the next room. The main bathroom sparkled, and Valerie could see Megan's touches. Small, delicate soaps in a dish on the counter. Pretty pink and rose towels folded perfectly. She went upstairs. Brandi's bedroom was the first door on the right. The patched quilt was spread over the bed in a thin disguise of having been made. Valerie sat down and smelled her daughter. Bubble gum, soap, chocolate. Clothes were strewn over the dresser and stuffed animals lay everywhere like always. But the Disney posters had been replaced with posters of teen idols. Valerie raised herself off the bed slightly and pulled Garfield out from under her. She brought him to her nose, sniffed at the sweet scent of her youngest daughter, and realized Brandi was stuck halfway between that awkward place. No longer a child and not yet a woman.

Valerie left the room.

Christine's bedroom was tidy and looked much the same as it had the last time Valerie saw it. The lace curtains were drawn to each side of the window, the bed was made, and four fat crocheted pillows adorned the pink duvet. On the bureau were the same two jewellery boxes spilling over with items.

To an outsider, this room would appear alluring and feminine. To Valerie, it was the room of a young woman who desperately yearned for order in her life.

She left Christine's bedroom and walked past the staircase toward Megan's room at the other end of the house, over the kitchen. She smiled when she stepped inside. Books were scattered everywhere, across the made bed, the dresser, on the floor, and tucked on the window ledge. She turned toward the door and caught sight of the bureau. Taped to the mirror was an old photograph of Valerie washing their white van. Her sleeves were rolled to her elbows, her hair was strewn every which way, but the smile on her face outshone the sun streaked across the side of the van.

Joylene Nowell Butler

Valerie tried to remember that day, a day like every day before her trip to Seattle. She couldn't.

She stepped out into the hallway and listened. The house echoed an eerie silence. She walked past Brandi's room, Christine's room, and entered the bedroom she had shared with Ed for over eighteen years. She didn't look around, didn't pause to reflect on anything. She went directly to the bathroom and turned on the shower. She undressed, flinging her clothes to the floor.

Ten minutes later, Valerie searched through her closet, didn't dwell on the fact that her clothes had been recently dry-cleaned, and instead picked out her long white dress covered in lace. The neck dropped off the shoulders, and the sleeves reached to a v-shape past her wrists.

She slipped the dress over her head and looked in the full-length mirror. She undid her French braid and brushed her fingers through her hair. Her toes peeked out from underneath the dress, and when she turned from side to side, the skirt danced back and forth across her legs. She had bought the dress under protest while shopping with Susan one day. She was convinced an appropriate occasion would never arrive, but Susan was adamant. "The dress was made for you," she had said.

It looked like a wedding dress. Valerie frowned at the image and realized in many ways it was a dress appropriate for a new beginning. Running her hands over her stomach and hips then twirling the skirt again, she knew she was overdressed. But the allusion was fitting; she looked like a woman in a soft tissue commercial. Valerie smiled again. Ed would think she'd gone mad.

She didn't care. She'd wear the dress every night if she had to.

Valerie found her mother's-in-law small pearl handled gun where it had always been, in the drawer of Ed's night table. She took out the magazine and placed the gun back in the drawer. She hid the .22 calibre bullets in one of his shoes in the closet. She went back downstairs, gathered up her parcels, hiked up the front of her dress, picked up her suitcase, and once again climbed the stairs to her room. She found the .38 Special that Canaday gave her when they reached Vancouver in her suitcase and glanced around the room for a suitable hiding place. She looked at the pillow on what used to be her side of the bed, at the bedside table, and then back to the bed. She placed the gun in the deep pocket of her dress while continuing to stare at the bed. A long time had passed since she and Ed had slept together. Eight months since they'd made love. Tonight, would he want to make love? Could she? Memories, not unpleasant, convinced her she could. It would make saying goodbye easier.

Valerie sorted the clothes she had bought for her daughters, during her short stay in Seattle, and took each bundle to their respective bedrooms. In Brandi's room, she made the bed first then lay the clothes across the quilt. She arranged the articles as if they were on display in a shop and stepped back to admire her effort. Two long baggy shirts, two formfitting skirts, one leather vest. She thought of the look on Brandi's face, smiled, and left the room.

After she did the same in Megan's and Christine's bedrooms, Valerie went back to her own room and brushed her hair until it shone then returned to the kitchen just as Ed entered the house.

He stood for a moment then said, "You look beautiful."

"You don't think it's too much?"

"Not at all." He set the grocery bags on the counter. "It's perfect."

"Would you like some help?"

He pulled a package of steaks from the bag and glanced back at her. "Dressed like that? Besides, this is my treat. You'll have plenty of time to get back to all the things you do for us. Let me do this."

Valerie glanced at the phone then back to Ed. He spread the groceries across the counter and began washing the lettuce. "I'm not sure what to do now," she said.

"Sit and visit with me while I work. Say whatever comes to mind." He glanced at her over his shoulder. "Did you see any interesting places?"

Valerie sat down at the table. "Not really. The inside of safehouses mostly. I was in the Baja for two days."

"That must have been interesting?"

"Not really."

He stopped chopping the celery and stood with his back to her. "I'm trying to make conversation, Val. I feel as awkward and nervous as you do, but I know we'll get through this."

His words caused a dread to seep in where her confidence had to stay. Hang on, she cautioned herself and smiled back at him.

After dinner, Ed handed her a rum and coke and sat across from her at the table. Soft candlelight illuminated the room. From the stereo in the front room, light jazz serenaded them. Their conversation consisted of nothing more than casual remarks strangers might make. Ed spoke of the thrill of driving a new truck. The suspension, the great gas mileage, and the comfort. They talked about the girls, although they never touched upon their grief. Valerie was grateful for that. As the evening progressed and

Joylene Nowell Butler

night came, she felt another wave of dread. The soft light casting shadows across the walls became an uncomfortable sight. She looked at Ed's face, anxious to turn on the overhead light so she could see his eyes. The grandfather clock in the foyer chimed eight times.

Ed set down his drink. "Before we play the video I picked out, I have to go to the office." He seemed to mistake her silence for disappointment. "I'm really sorry, Val, but I have to pick up a shipping order for tomorrow night, so I can fax it out first thing Monday morning, and it would save considerable time if I did it tonight. You don't mind do you? I won't be long."

"I can clean up while you're gone."

"Please don't," he said rising. "This is supposed to be your night. I promise I'll be back before you know it." He pushed himself away from the table.

Valerie stayed where she was and listened to the sounds of his footsteps leaving the house. She would have never admitted she was glad for the solitude. That comment would have been unnecessarily cruel. Tomorrow was soon enough to inform him the girls wouldn't be coming home until DeOlmos was arrested. Like Canaday, Ed wouldn't like her plan, but unlike Canaday, Ed didn't have a choice. Canaday had conceded Because although he did have a choice, he knew she'd leave with or without his help. For a change, her stubbornness had outmatched his.

Canaday?

Valerie tried to dismiss his image. The effort was made harder by the fact her body yearned for him. It was an exciting and unsettling feeling. He was like an unquenchable thirst and a dream that would never come true. As candlelight danced across the ceiling, she realized whether she saw him again, Canaday was in her heart and head, and that was where he would stay.

The expression on his face, while she had convinced him to let her go, was still so clear. He'd been very angry. He needed time to set up surveillance, to wire the house. "I can't wait that long," she'd told him. She supposed he knew this time she wouldn't back down. Nothing would stop her from returning to her children. Maybe in the end he had realized there was no other solution. DeOlmos knew she was alive, and he would never surface until she did.

The loud bong from the Grandfather clock made her jump. A half hour had passed since Ed left and she had wasted the whole time thinking about Canaday. If she survived this week, she knew in times of need she would

262

go to that place in her head that held only thoughts of him. Now was a bad time.

She rose from her seat and wandered to the front door. The road was quiet. She walked through to the living room and cringed at the idea of watching a video on the big screen. The room seemed so impersonal. Staring at the television, Valerie reminded herself she was the one making the rules now. She unhooked the VCR and carried it to Ed's study. She switched on the light. He had placed the old television next to the fireplace. She lay the recorder on top and connected it to the set then rearranged the two high back sofa chairs so they faced the screen. The room was much cosier than the intimidating front room.

Back in the kitchen, she retrieved a bottle of cognac from the liquor cabinet and took it back to the study. She was aware of a distant sound, like a thud. Nothing came afterwards, so she dismissed it and set the cognac on Ed's desk. From the other side of the room, she took a small table and placed it between the two chairs. She set the cognac on the table. She glanced at the fireplace. It was too warm for a fire, but burning spruce would set a nice mood. Maybe she should talk Ed into lighting it when he returned. Dressed as she was, setting it herself wasn't a wise idea.

Valerie looked down at her dress and fingered the white lace. She had to look just right when DeOlmos came. The memory of Bolina DeOlmos dressed in her long white lace gown, with her black hair pulled into a bun, with her dark kind eyes, still made the hair on Valerie's forearms dance. She was a woman Valerie would have liked. A woman she understood. A woman like her.

Would DeOlmos see that?

They didn't look anything alike. But they were. Lonely, sad women, with little control over their men. With the hope and dreams to compensate for the emptiness. Bolina DeOlmos knew what sacrifice meant. She knew without question that she would have died for her children. She also recognized that she was nothing without them. Her sons were her life just as Valerie's daughters were hers. Miguel had to see that. He had to recognize the similarities. He had to.

Bolina DeOlmos had taught Vincente how to cook. She had taught Miguel that an intelligent and gentle woman was the backbone of every family. They were ruthless murderers, but still men who cherished their mother. After seeing her photograph, Valerie knew it wasn't Because Bolina had manipulated them. It was Because she loved them beyond reason, and they felt it.

Dear God, what if I'm wrong?

Valerie shuddered. It was too late to question her decision now. She closed her eyes while another wave of doubts swam over her. Would he send someone else?

No. Not DeOlmos. He enjoyed killing too much.

Convinced she was right, Valerie settled back in one of the sofa chairs and waited. The house was quiet. More silent than she could ever remember. She glanced at the clock on Ed's desk behind her just as the lights went out.

Valerie blinked several times until her eyes adjusted to the moonlit room. The loss of power always bothered Ed, but she had gotten use to it. Tonight, especially, it was nice. She hoped this outage would last longer than the usual hour so she wouldn't have to watch a video.

A sound came from somewhere in the house. A thump. Again. But this time it sounded like the floorboards had cracked. Someone stepping across her floor?

Valerie smiled. Her house was carpeted.

Creeeeek

What was that?

A door opening?

Maybe Ed?

Valerie opened the study door and stepped out into the hallway. There was nobody. She looked at the front door. Ed was probably already heading back. How long could it take to pick up one shipping form?

A horrible sensation crawled over her skin. Not now, she pleaded. It's too soon. I'm not ready.

She squeezed her eyes shut, opened them again, while all the time convincing herself she was just spooked by the darkness, by her own imagination. No one was there. The house was settling.

After twenty years?

Shut up! You're overreacting. You're always overreacting.

Valerie took two steps forward and froze. There was a shadow at the end of the hallway, standing in front of the front door, standing still, waiting, and watching. Valerie's heart, pounding in her throat, made it difficult to swallow. It was nothing, she told herself. Nothing but her imagination freaking her out.

Only ... the shadow was now moving toward her.

CHAPTER 39

Inspector Banyan pulled at the heavy glass doors leading into the detachment, wiped his nose with his handkerchief, and nodded toward his office at the rear of the building. "He's back there?"

"Pacing like a caged animal," his staff sergeant said.

"He say what he wants?"

"Nope. Wouldn't talk to anybody but you. I told him you weren't in today." The staff sergeant shrugged his shoulders as if to ward off blame.

Banyan sympathized. He'd dealt with the FBI enough times to know they were an impatient bunch. Whatever this agent had to say would no doubt be relevant to himself but meaningless to Banyan. Still, because Banyan believed in being a courteous host, he'd hear the man out before stating the obvious: You should really talk to E-Division in Vancouver. Then, he'd recommend a good hotel for the night.

He flung opened his office door and headed straight for his chair, catching a glimpse of a man springing to his feet as if a crane was attached to his spine. Though the exasperated facial expression was hard not to notice, Banyan ignored it and sat down at his desk. "So, Special Agent ...?"

"Canaday."

"Right, Agent Canaday." Banyan blew his nose and wiped it with his hanky. "What can I do for you?"

"I need the loan of your SWAT Team and two of your best snipers."

After a brief moment, Banyan closed his mouth. He was about to spew what his subordinates considered his best retort, but something in Agent Canaday's face stopped him. "Agent Canaday, I think you already know I can't authorize anything without permission from HQ who in turn will want verification from your Justice Department."

"I'm asking for an exception, sir. There's no time, no margin for error. Aidan Roth's sister is in danger unless your men come with me now."

"Aidan's sister? How do you--" Banyan, his nose plugged again, held up his hand, ending his question; he already knew the answer. He blew his nose and put his hanky away. "Agent Canaday, you best be more specific."

"I'd like nothing better, Inspector, but I don't have time. Mrs. McCormick is at her home. I'm going to assume you are a close acquaintance of her brother and therefore aware of the family trait of bullheadedness. She wouldn't listen to reason and convinced herself the only way to save her family was to confront DeOlmos on her own. He not only knows she's alive, but he's going to find her at home unprotected unless we do something. I'm talking about a woman who is naïve enough to believe she can beat him at a game she's never played. I go through the appropriate channels and it'll be too late. She's going to die unless you and I do something. Now."

"You know all this and you still let her go?"

Agent Canaday raised his fist into the air then quickly caught himself and swept a hand through his hair. "Obviously," he said softly, "you don't know the woman. She's…." Canaday dropped his arm and stared down at Banyan. "I need your help, sir. I've got nothing to offer in return but my undying gratitude and a guarantee I'll be at your beck and call for the next twenty years if necessary."

Banyan chuckled. "Hell, I hope to be retired long before that."

A transformation spread across the agent's face. The man looked tortured, which signalled to Banyan that his first instincts were correct, there had to be more to this.

But enough to screw up a reputation that had taken years to build? Sure, Aidan Roth was a friend and the welfare of Aidan's sister was indeed important, but the SWAT Team? How could he authorize such a thing then explain it later should the situation prove embarrassing?

"You're not exactly up to speed on how things work up here, are you, Agent Canaday?"

"Inspector," Canaday said, his voice cracking.

The agent's control was gone now, and he was showing signs of shutting down. He'd just witnessed the end of hope. A dread crossed briefly over his eyes but not fast enough that Banyan didn't recognize a fear eating away at the years of training and self-discipline. The man was beyond pleading. He was desperate. Whatever had gone on between this man and Aidan's sister was none of Banyan's business. Truth be known, he didn't want to know. All he knew was that this man didn't understand what he was asking. Banyan was skating on thin ice. He'd already broken a few rules trying to help Aidan. He had a pension to consider. He couldn't just assign the SWAT Team to a situation Because of the suspicions of a FBI Agent. He'd be the laughingstock of his detachment. How do you maintain discipline when you're a joke to your people? No. He'd have to forgo the usual response. Aidan Roth had been shot and almost killed while leaving his detachment. Banyan couldn't withstand another crisis under his command.

"I'm sorry, Agent Canaday, but I can't authorize the ERT. What I can do is have an unmarked car patrol the area. If they see anything--"

"They won't see anything!" Canaday yelled. "Don't you understand who you're dealing with? DeOlmos is going to go to any length to kill her. She's his ticket to death row. You send a patrol car up there, and you might as well sign her death warrant. The only thing that'll work against DeOlmos is an arsenal. Inspector--go with your instincts! Listen to your conscience. Roth is your friend. What are you going to tell him when he asks why his sister is dead?"

Banyan, feeling a sneeze coming, pulled out his hanky.

* * *

His footsteps soundless, DeOlmos entered the foyer from the kitchen. He saw her standing at the end of the hallway and could almost feel the pounding of her heart. As he approached, she stepped back until she stood in front of an opened door. Moonlight cast her in shadows, but he saw the beautiful white gown, and as he approached closer, he saw the serenity in her face.

"I've been expecting you, please come in." Her voice floated toward him.

He mused over her words and her obvious lie. She had no way of knowing he would come for her so soon. "I'm sorry if I kept you waiting."

"Will you join me for a cognac in the study?"

Further amused, he nodded his head and continued walking toward her. At the door, he stepped aside and gestured for her to enter first.

"I was going to build a fire," she said.

He liked the sound of her voice, soft, gentle, and full of promises. She put on the gloves that lay on the wood box. He could see by her efficiency that she had done this task many times. In a matter of minutes, despite the semidarkness, the fire was set, the room illuminating into soft, flickering shadows.

"Please have a seat," she said.

He waited for her to sit down then sat in the high back chair next to her. It was comfortable.

The fire's glow reflected in her eyes. He understood now why Vincente had been captivated. She was beautiful, in a serene and delicate way. Not unlike the beauty of their mother.

She didn't smile, but she studied him. He, on the other hand, couldn't help but smile. The room was cozy and comfortably warm; and she was like a princess in that white dress; and the cognac she passed to him was at perfect room temperature.

He reached inside his jacket and waited for her to flinch. She didn't. He pulled out a cigar. "Do you mind?"

She handed him a package of matches from the table between them. "Do you mind if I ask you some questions?"

He took several deep draws from his cigar and exhaled the smoke. "Ask away, Mrs. McCormick. Or may I call you Valerie?"

Small feet peeked out from under her long, white skirt. Delicate hands, free of nail polish and jewellery, rested on her lap. Firelight revealed the strong but feminine bone structure of her face and gleamed off the smooth curves of her hair as it crested on her shoulders before falling gracefully down her back. Her lips were full, not too wide. He lingered on them before lowering his eyes. Her neck was inviting, and he could almost taste the skin of her shoulders. Smooth, soft, touchable skin. Breasts not too large, but round and firm without the support of an undergarment.

"Mr. DeOlmos." Her melodious voice broke his trance. He liked her clear dialect, her soft tone. A voice pleasing to his ears. "Did you know those two men in Seattle were FBI agents?" she asked, and he liked that her voice wasn't confident.

"Not at first."

"What were you thinking when you shot them?"

DeOlmos smiled. These were not the questions he expected. "They were corrupt and greedy and deserved to die."

"That was what you were thinking?" Her voice sounded doubtful.

He laughed quietly. "Apart from that I felt immense power over an obvious enemy."

"When you discovered they were federal agents, what did you think?"

"It was an unfortunate situation, which could not be reversed. We are not speaking of bus drivers, Valerie. It is the risk they took when they chose their career."

"Did you experience regrets, Mr. DeOlmos? Since the day I first heard your name, many people have died. I was wondering how you found the house in Santa Cruz and why those agents had to die."

"I take no pleasure in issuing certain orders, Valerie. History proves killing and dying are essential to survival. Haven't you learned that?"

"Yes. But you still haven't answered my question. How did you find the house in Santa Cruz?"

"An informer, Valerie. Nothing personal. Debts. Many things in this world take place only Because of debts."

"I'm not entirely sure why I need to know, but could you please tell me his name?"

"Rostov."

"The prosecutor?" Her eyes glowed.

"Yes."

"I don't understand. If he was the one helping you, why didn't you have me killed long before the trial. You had a month."

"It took time to ascertain he was the right man for the job. I learned much later that his wife was a compulsive gambler. Her debt of eighty thousand dollars was not a large amount, but enough to ruin a promising career. Rostov is a very ambitious man. A man, as you can appreciate, who I fully understand."

"He's responsible for those agents dying in Santa Cruz. People he had worked with."

"Yes, he is. Of course, I must give Sergeant Jackson of the Olympia Police Force some credit as well. He convinced Mr. Rostov to help."

"Sergeant Jackson? I know the name."

"He's the police sergeant you met in the Seattle precinct the day the agents died. He wouldn't take you seriously. Remember?" Miguel puffed on his cigar and enjoyed her sudden silence. She knew when to speak and when not to. "Are you happy to be home?"

Her body stayed perfectly still, but her thick eyelashes closed. It was a moment before she looked up. He saw an incredible sadness in her face.

"It doesn't feel like my home anymore. Time has changed me."

"Or maybe you weren't really expecting me?"

"I was expecting you, but that's not why I feel like a stranger in my own home."

"You were happier in America?"

"In Baja."

He was surprised by her answer. He too felt at home there. "It's a beautiful place."

"Very beautiful."

"But this is a lovely home. What I have seen of it." He stood. "Show me the rest?"

"If the lights come back on."

He laughed. "You don't have a backup system? A generator?"
"We did, but the noise irritated my husband, and we sold it."
"Do you have a flashlight?"
"There's one in the desk behind you."
"Get it for me, then show me this house that feels so strange to you."
Valerie retrieved the flashlight from the drawer, and DeOlmos followed her from the room. She led him to the stairs. He nudged her arm gently, took the flashlight from her hand, and gestured for her to continue. They reached the top landing and turned left. DeOlmos searched each room carefully before finally reaching the master bedroom. Valerie sat on the edge of the bed, smoothed a hand over the pillowcase, and watched him look through the closet, the bathroom, and under the bed.

He walked to the other side of the room, checked the window locks. Her back was to him. "Valerie?" He waited until she glanced over her shoulder. He shone the light across her face. "Where is my brother?" He had hoped the question would upset her, but she seemed neither shocked nor afraid.

"I'm not sure."

"Please. Don't insult me."

"It's the truth."

He lowered the light. "Did he harm you in any way?"

"Of course not."

"Really? My brother isn't known for keeping his hands to himself."

"He was kind and sweet."

"Did he make love to you?"

"No. It wasn't like that. I told you, Vincente was kind and sweet."

"You expect me to believe that? Vincente is an animal when it comes to women."

Valerie looked shocked. "How can you say such a thing about your own brother? He adores you."

"What did he speak of?"

"He talked about God's gifts: art, music. Your mother's wonderful cooking. The importance of family. He told me you took care of family and employees alike. That you were a just man, but if provoked, your fury was unrelenting."

"He said a great deal in such a short time."

"We spent an entire day and two evenings together. He didn't tell me who he was until the day after you called."

"And then?"

"He confessed. He offered to take me away."

"Really? Where?"

"I don't know. We were near the Baja and American border when he spotted the roadblock. He told me to go on alone, and he would contact me when he could. He said he had a friend. He said he couldn't trust any of your people."

"Valerie, are you lying to me?"

"No."

"You expect me to believe my own brother helped you to escape?"

"He knows I won't testify, but he said you wouldn't believe me."

"What were his last words?"

"He said, Because you loved him very much, one day you would forgive him. He handed me a piece of paper with the address of a woman in Seattle and said I should stay with her until he contacted me. He promised to take me and my children far away."

"Yet, you disobeyed."

"I had no choice. The Americans were very angry. At the border, they took Vincente's car and his note, flew me back here, and told the RCMP I was their problem now."

"Where are the police?"

"At the airport they put me in a cab. I haven't seen them since."

Her face was sombre, unflinching. He didn't want to believe her. "Why do you think Vincente trusted you?"

"I don't know."

"Did you love my brother?" he asked, deliberately referring to him in the past tense.

"I care for him."

"But do you love him?"

"No."

"Why?"

"I don't know."

"Because he is a simpleton?"

"I don't understand how you can speak of him in such a manner; you loves you so much." She brushed a strand of hair off her face. "Maybe I couldn't love him Because he sees me as someone better than I am."

DeOlmos shone the light across her face. She looked at him squarely then squinted against the bright glare and covered her eyes. He moved the light back to the floor. Time was running out. He should kill her now. He should squeeze his hands around her neck until her breathing stopped. She had bewitched Vincente, and if he wasn't careful, she would do the same to him. He shone the light across her smooth shoulders. Was it already too late?

* * *

Canaday sat in the backseat of the SWAT van and adjusted the vest over his suit jacket. When the vehicle jerked to the left, he gripped the door rest and fought to stay out of the lap of the ERT member beside him. Nobody spoke. The Team Leader held a handset to his ear and conveniently avoided looking at Canaday. This irritated Canaday to no end. Though he was grateful, he needed answers. Worse yet, he needed a gun.

Seven minutes passed and he was about to ask when the hell they would get there when a thundering blast exploded outside the left side of the van. Another loud bang and shrieking tires and Canaday was thrown against the guy beside him. More screeching of tires and the van came to a sudden and violent stop.

Canaday flew forward, his head connecting with the side door, which flew open. He was glad to see it wasn't from the force of his head. The driver stood outside and yelled something. But the firefight erupting behind the man drowned out his words; though it left their meaning clear.

Canaday jumped to the ground and with his head low, followed the rest. Bullets skimmed past his left temple. He spotted the source before diving for the ditch. A black sedan was parked at the vacant lot across the road. A M-60 lay across the roof of the car, empty cartages spilling across the hood.

He yelled for a gun, but everyone was too occupied to hear him. An ERT member made his way around to the front of the van. The man next to Canaday yelled then flew back, blood gushing from his neck just above the vest. Canaday grabbed the man's rifle before it hit the ground, swung it in to play, and fired rapidly.

* * *

"How did you know I would come for you tonight?" DeOlmos asked, while at the same time wondering if the distant noise was something to be concerned about.

"I just knew."

"*¿Un instinto?* An instinct?"
"I suppose."
"Any more questions, Valerie?"
"Why did you try to kill my brother?"
"Your brother is inconsequential. I had no need to dispose of him."
"You're not responsible?"
"No."
"Do you know who is?"
"Yes."
"Who?"

Spotting the brass candlestick and tall white candle on the headboard, he tossed her the matches. "Light the candle behind you."

She lighted them while her hands shook.

He walked away from the window to the other side of the bed and sat down at the bedside table beside her. The candlelight reflected across her features. Large, blue eyes looked up at him. His eyes wandered to the smooth skin on her neck, and it occurred to him that he could do anything he wanted, and she could do nothing to stop him.

After a long moment he asked, "Are you afraid to die?"
"Dying, yes, but not death."
"Do you believe in God?"
"Yes."
"And you understand I have come here to kill you?"
"Yes."
"If I kill you ... will Vincente return?"
"I don't understand."
"Is my brother so intrigued with you that you mean more to him than I do?"
"No ... no, I'm sure that's not true. He loves you very much. In time he'll forget me."
"He risked everything for you."
"I don't know what you want me to say."
"Say whatever is in your heart, Valerie. Tell me 'your' truth."
"I'd like you to do whatever you have to do then leave before Ed returns. My children will need their father, and I don't want anything happening to him."
"Ed won't return for another hour."

For the first time since he had laid eyes on her, he saw the subtle change in her manner. Although, she sat perfectly still, her expression blank, for a brief second, he sensed that his words had left much pain.

"He called me from his office," Miguel spoke softly.

She remained silent, but he was certain he saw the glimmer of a tear at the corner of her eye.

"I'm sorry. This news must be a terrible shock. He said he was doing it for the children. If you returned, they would lose everything. The house. The vehicles. That is why he shot your brother. He said he shot Mr. Roth to please me. I can assure you, Valerie, I had no idea he would do such a thing."

Her lips parted. A single tear glistened in the corner of her eye.

Ed McCormick was a fool.

Her chest rose and sank quickly as she struggled to maintain her dignity. He knew she wanted to cry but would not in his presence. Suddenly, he felt compelled to look away; witnessing her suffering had become difficult. He heard a quick intake of breath. What he was about to say surprised him as much as he was certain it would surprise her. "We must leave this place, Valerie."

"What?"

"I will take you with me. You are right, this is no longer your home."

"I'm not going anywhere with you."

"You misunderstand, Valerie. I'm not asking. You will come with me Because I have decided to let you live."

"Why?"

"Because I know my brother, and I acknowledge his weakness. For his sake, I shall not kill you. As long as you understand, Because I give you back your life, it belongs to me now."

"What are you saying? I've spent the last four months hiding from you and now you're...."

"In time you will understand."

"And my children?"

"They are inconsequential." He saw the fire in her eyes

"I don't understand you."

He smiled. He didn't blame her. How could he explain that no amount of money or power had ever given him what he knew she would. He rose from his chair. "Where is your coat?"

She remained where she was, her eyes widening, her gazed fixed on him. "You said Ed called you? How did he know your number?"

He wanted to touch her but knew it was too soon. The only women he had ever laid with were women he paid for. This time was different; this woman was different.

"It doesn't matter, Valerie. We will leave this place. Come with me now. You will have a comfortable life. Though you'll never see your family again, I will secure pictures and reports of your children's progress often. Now come. Refuse and you die."

"This isn't the way it was supposed to happen. You're changing the rules. I don't know what to do now. What if you kill someone else, will you expect me to sit by and do nothing?"

He gripped her shoulders and lifted her from the bed; her arms pressed to her sides. "I am who I am, but I swear I will not harm you in any way, if you come with me now. If you don't ... I will kill you, Ed, your three daughters, and then you brother and his family."

"Please!"

"You know I can, Valerie. You know my power exceeds all others."

She tried to free her hand from his grasp while her other arm remained locked at her side. "This is too fast. I can't think."

He grabbed her shoulder and gave her a light squeeze. "Don't think."

He squeezed her hand again, shone the flashlight in front of him, and pulled her down the hallway. His men would be waiting down the road as instructed. They would be surprised he wasn't alone, but they would know not to question him. He continued down the stairs, pulling her, knowing explicitly that he was doing the only thing he could. He would give her everything a man could give a woman. He envisioned her moving like an angel through the palace that he would build her. Surrounded by beauty unimaginable, she would soon soften her heart toward him.

At the bottom of the stairs, Valerie pulled her hand away. "The FBI are probably out there right now. You can't escape. They'll kill you before they let that happen."

"We will go through the back." He'd earlier outlined his path to his men and the shortest route to his jet.

She stood frozen in the semidarkness.

"We haven't time to discuss this, Valerie. We must go now."

She backed away from him. He moved toward her and saw the glitter of steel. She held a gun in both hands, aiming it at his chest.

He wanted to laugh. He flashed back to the last few moments and could not comprehend where she had picked up the weapon. In the master bedroom, he surmised and realized, if that was so, she'd had plenty of time to shoot him. But she hadn't, and he knew why. She couldn't.

His silencer was loaded and safely snug in his holster. He had planned to shoot her twice in the head, after he strangled her first. He looked at the gun in her hands. For the first time in his life, Miguel didn't wish to kill. "Valerie?"

"No, don't say anything else. I don't want to shoot you, but I will. Please don't move. We'll wait for them together. You're Canadian, and yes you will go to prison, but you don't have to die."

"We must go now while we can."

Her tears flowed heavily. "You'll continue to kill. You're incapable of changing. You think you want me, but you don't know who I am. I'll never be what you want. I'll only grow to hate you for destroying my life. If I let you go, you'll kill again. Please don't make me do this."

DeOlmos slowly inched his hand toward the gun inside his coat. She was right, he would kill anyone who tried to stop him. Including her.

"Please," she whispered.

Miguel pulled his gun out of his chest holster and heard a loud bang. He associated the fire burning in his chest with an unrecognizable phenomenon. But even in his daze, he knew Valerie had shot him. His body no longer cooperated; he fell while his eyes stayed focused on her face.

Éste es tan el dolor de ser tirado. So this is the pain of being shot.

DeOlmos opened his eyes and saw an angel standing over him. Tears filled her beautiful blue eyes and streamed down her cheekbones. He heard gunshots in the distance; yet their relevance no longer matter. He couldn't take his eyes off this apparition. The light around her was the most brilliant light he'd ever seen. But it was fading now, drifting into blackness.

"Valerie ...? Mama ...?"

* * *

Valerie felt the gun taken from her hand. She couldn't remember how long she'd stood there. Minutes? An hour? She looked into Canaday's face. He handed the .38 to a RCMP officer then shone his flashlight across DeOlmos. She watched and waited, unsure what to do now. Canaday reached for her elbow and guided her to the living room. He sat with her on the tan leather sectional. He took a handkerchief from his breast pocket and wiped at her face. "I'm sorry. I should have been here. We ran into a problem down the road."

"Police Sergeant Jackson of the Seattle Police Force told DeOlmos who I was. Mr. Rostov gave him the location of the safe house in Santa Cruz."

Canaday didn't move. Valerie didn't have the strength to look at his face. She wished she hadn't blurted it out like that.

The house filled with strong lights while officers continued to file through the doorway. She heard muffled voices and watched as each man seemed to know instinctively what was expected of him. Someone brought her a Styrofoam cup filled with hot coffee. Someone else set a bright lantern on the coffee table in front of her. She sipped the bitter coffee and set the cup next to the lantern. The light was blinding.

"Mrs. McCormick, we need to ask you a few questions."

Valerie could sense Canaday's stiff body next to her. She looked up and saw two men standing before her. They were dressed in suits, not unlike those of the many FBI agents she had met over the past nine months. Only these men, she couldn't avoid.

CHAPTER 40

After a restless night, Valerie and Christine lifted one mattress off the floor in Aidan's rec-room, while Megan and Brandi lifted the other. They carried them to the spare room down the hall and placed them back on the two twin box springs.

They had spent most of the night crying, sharing, and talking. At midnight Canaday had called to say her appearance before an investigative team wasn't required. After pleading guilty to fraud and attempted murder, Ed had been booked and would appear before a judge first thing in the morning. Canaday had no idea how much time Ed would serve; that would depend upon the judge.

Did he show remorse?

"Yes," Canaday said.

He also told her that General Emilio Sanchez, and the man who had planted the bomb under her van, David Philips, plus four other members of the DeOlmos Cartel were killed in a shootout with police down the road from her home. They'd been expecting police and had set up a barricade at both ends of the road. They found a detour barricade set up to divert traffic from entering off the highway. Canaday told her not to turn on the television but to sleep in peace.

When she asked about Attorney Rostov, Canaday spoke in a soft and controlled manner. "He's being taken care of."

"Mummy, do I have to go to school tomorrow?" Brandi asked.

"You're worried about tomorrow already?" Valerie followed Brandi back to the rec room, smoothed a hand over her tangled hair then pulled her close and kissed the top of her head. "No," she said, standing straight. "I think maybe not the day after that, either. But I want you to do me a big favour. Stay with your sisters while I visit Uncle Aidan."

"Can't I come?" Brandi asked.

"As soon as Uncle Aidan's transferred out of ICU."

Megan stepped forward and put an arm around her little sister. "We understand, Mum. Don't worry. We'll be fine. Please give Uncle Aidan our love."

"I will." She stood for a moment, looked at her three daughters, and felt a great joy flowing through her veins. "I love you all more than I can ever say."

Christine grinned. "Mother, please! If you keep it up we'll end up crying again, and already my eyes ache."

Valerie reached out, embraced her daughters, and whispered, "Thank you, God."

* * *

Sensing something, Aidan opened his eyes. A stranger was scanning the many tubes and hoses connected to Aidan's body. His eyes were hard and intense and fixated on the heart monitor. Aidan tried to speak but groaned instead. Their eyes locked. The man said nothing, but his steel blue eyes showed an expression Aidan recognized. For a moment, he couldn't place it ... until he remembered. It was the look of being there. It was the look from a brother-in-arms.

The man wet his lips and stepped closer. He pulled the chair to the side of the bed. He sat down. "Mr. Roth ...? My name's Mike Canaday. I ... I'm the one who took your sister away."

Although his thoughts were still groggy from the drugs, Aidan remembered ... FBI.

"I, uh, I thought you might want to know ... DeOlmos is dead."

The machine on the wall gave Aidan away. The FBI Agent jerked his head toward the monitor then back. "Are you okay? Should I call someone?"

The machine slowed.

"Your sister's fine. When you're well enough, I'm sure she'll explain what happened. But I guess that's one reason why I'm here. You have to get well. She's going to need you. Mr. McCormick is in jail. Last night he confessed to shooting you. I'm telling you this Because I didn't want Valerie--I mean...."

It's too late, buddy. I can see it in your eyes.

"I didn't want Mrs. McCormick to have to tell you. It was hard enough when she found out."

Aidan wondered what this man had risked for Valerie. What had it cost him to fall in love? Because he was definitely in love with her. It was as clear as the pain in his face.

"But that's not the only reason you have to get better." FBI Agent Mike Canaday dropped his head, swept a hand through his hair, rubbed at his forehead, the back of his neck; his eyes squeezed shut.

Aidan wished he could yank the tubes from his throat. If he could, he'd tell this man it was all right. He understood. It was over now. Whatever happened, it'd be okay.

Mike Canaday looked at him. "Man, your sister is stubborn. When she makes up her mind ...." His head bowed. "I didn't get there in time. I let her down. I should've been there. She shot DeOlmos. He was going to kill her. But she shot him. He died at the front entrance of their home. I tried to get to her. I ...." Canaday glanced over his shoulder at the door.

Aidan willed himself to speak. "It's okay."

"I should have been there."

"It's okay."

Mike shook his head, his eyes moistened. He stood up. "Anyway, that's why I'm here. She's going to need you, so get better."

Aidan blinked slowly.

* * *

Valerie walked out of the elevator, passed the waiting room, and headed toward the west wing. Her legs felt light, her head clear. She glanced at every face and smiled. Strangers, surprised at first, smiled back before disappearing behind her.

"Good morning," she said to an old man inching down the hallway.

He lifted his stooped shoulders and gave her an equally warm smile.

Valerie turned at the entrance to the south wing and picked up her pace. She swung her arms and hummed Jann Arden's song, 'Could I be Your Girl.'

"Val?"

Valerie turned, spotted Susan, who looked more worn out than usual. Valerie rushed toward her.

Joy rushed from Valerie's body and left her cold. "Is Aidan okay?"

"He's fine. He's got company, and I thought give them some space."

"Who?"

"We didn't introduce ourselves, but that's him." She nodded toward the other end of the hallway.

Valerie turned around and saw Canaday coming toward her.

"Who is he?"

She laid a hand on Susan's arm. "I'll explain later." She walked toward him.

When the distance between them disappeared, Canaday grabbed her arm, turning her back to the door. "I have to show you something."

Valerie looked back down the hallway toward Aidan's room. "I'm on my way to see--"

"This won't take long."

Inside a matter of seconds, they were in an elevator, and headed for the top floor. Canaday never let go of her arm. She kept glancing at his face, torn between a sheer delight at seeing him, and confusion as to what he was up to. They left the elevator and headed toward the exit. Where could they possibly be going? But they stepped out into the brilliant sunshine, and Valerie saw the reason. A helicopter was parked on the pad fifty feet away. As soon as the pilot saw them, the rotors started to move.

Valerie laughed then turned and looked up at him. His blue eyes searched through hers, sending quivers down her spine. "Whose idea was this?"

"I think Inspector Banyan likes me. I happen to mention you needed to go for a ride."

"How did you know?"

"Just a guess."

"Will you come with me?"

He shook his head. "This is something else you have to do on your own, Valerie."

She nodded, captivated by his eyes. "Will you be here when I get back?"

He lowered his eyes.

"But I thought--"

"I have to go back, Valerie."

She glanced at the helicopter waiting. He had given her a gift of a lifetime, and suddenly its relevance seemed unimportant. He was walking away. Just like that. Present her with a gift, which would finally tie the loose ends of her life, then walk away without looking back. Her heart thumped in time with the whipping blades. She felt like crying, laughing. Her body ached at the thought of losing him. The blades whipped faster while her pulse kept time. "Mike." She had to yell to be heard over the rotors. "I ...."

He looked at her, his face breaking into a smile. Then a grin. Then the biggest smile she'd ever seen.

"What?" she yelled.

"You just called me by my first name."

"Did not."

He nodded. Then laughed. She couldn't hear his laughter, but she knew it was a wonderful, beautiful sound.

"Geez, Canaday, what d'ya suppose that means?"

He laughed again and gripped her hand. Heads low, they ran together toward the helicopter.

Made in the USA